William John Locke

At the Gate of Samaria

A Novel

William John Locke

At the Gate of Samaria
A Novel

ISBN/EAN: 9783337032074

Printed in Europe, USA, Canada, Australia, Japan

Cover: Foto ©Andreas Hilbeck / pixelio.de

More available books at **www.hansebooks.com**

AT THE GATE OF SAMARIA

𝔄 𝔑𝔬𝔳𝔢𝔩

BY

W. J. LOCKE

LONDON
WILLIAM HEINEMANN
1895

Dedication.

TO ONE WHOSE WORK IT IS AS MUCH AS MINE
I INSCRIBE THIS BOOK.

AT THE GATE OF SAMARIA.

CHAPTER I.

It was a severe room, scrupulously neat. Along one side ran a bookcase, with beaded glass doors, containing, as one might see by peering through the spaces, the collected, unread literature of two stern generations. A few old prints, placed in bad lights, hung on the walls. In the centre of the room was a leather-covered library table, with writing materials arranged in painful precision. A couch was lined along one wall, in the draught of the door. On either side of the fireplace were ranged two stiff leather armchairs.

In one of these chairs sat an old man, in the other a faded woman just verging upon middle age. The old man was looking at a picture which he supported on his knees—a narrow, oblong strip of canvas nailed on to a rough wooden frame. The woman eyed him with some interest, as if awaiting a decision.

They were father and daughter, and bore a strange family resemblance to each other. Both faces were pale, their foreheads high and narrow, marked by faint horizontal lines, their eyes gray and cold, their upper lips long and thin, setting tightly, without mobility, upon the lower. The only essential point of difference was that the father's chin was weakly pointed, the daughter's squarer and harder. Both faces gave one the impression of negativeness, joylessness, seeming to lack the power of strong emotive expression. One can see such, minus the refinement of gentle birth and social amenities, in the pews of obscure dissenting chapels, testifying that they have been led thither not by strong convictions, but by the force of mild circumstance.

Indeed, as is the case with hundreds of our upper

middle-class families, the Davenants had descended from a fierce old Puritan stock, and though the reality of their Puritanism had gradually lost itself in the current of more respectable orthodoxy, its shadow hung over them still. The vigorous enthusiasm that spurred the Puritan on to lofty action was gone ; the vague dread of sin that kept him in moral and mental inactivity alone remained. Perhaps it is this survival amongst us of the negative element of Puritanism that produces in England the curious anomaly of education without enlightenment. It has dulled our perception of life as an art, whose "great incidents," as Fielding finely says, "are no more to be considered as mere accidents than the several members of a fine statue or a noble poem." It has caused us to live in a perpetual twilight in which the possibilities of existence loom fantastic and indistinct. The Davenants were gentlefolk, holding a good position in the small country town of Durdleham ; they visited among the county families, and, on ordinary, conventional grounds, considered themselves to belong to the cultured classes. They were the curious yet familiar product of the old-fashioned, high-church Toryism impregnated with the Puritan taint.

The light was fading through the French window behind the old man's chair. He laid down the canvas on his lap and looked in a puzzled way at the fire. Then he raised it nearer to his eyes for further examination.

"This is really very dreadful," he said at last, looking at his daughter.

"Something will have to be done soon," replied the latter.

"It is so horribly vulgar, Grace," said the old man ; "look at that boy's nose—and that drunken man—his face is a nightmare of evil. I really must begin to talk seriously to Clytie."

Mrs. Blather smiled somewhat pityingly. Since the earliest days of her long widowhood she had undertaken the charge of her father's house and the care of her two younger sisters, Janet and Clytie. Her familiarity, therefore, with the seamy side of Clytie's nature had been of long duration.

"You might as well talk to that fender, papa," she said. "Clytie has got it into her head that she is going to be an artist, and no amount of talking will get it out."

"It's all through her visiting those friends of hers, the Farquharsons. They are not nice people for her to know. I shall not let her go there again."

"If she goes on like this there is no knowing what will happen."

"Where did the child get these repulsive and ungirlish notions from?" the old man asked querulously.

The conception of the picture was not that of a young girl, and though the execution was crude and untrained, there was a bold cruelty of touch that saved it from being amateurish. The canvas was divided into two panels. On the one was painted a tiny bully of a boy with his arm rounded across his throat, about to strike a weakly, poverty-stricken little girl. They were children of the poorest classes, the boy realistically, offensively dirty— the *petit morveux* in its absolute sense. Behind them was the open doorway of a red-brick, jerry-built cottage, showing a strip of torn and dirty matting along the passage that lost itself in the gloom beyond. On the other panel was the corner of a public house in a low slum, the window lights and a gas-lamp throwing a lurid glare upon wet pavement and the figures of a woman and a drunken man. The faces were those of the children in the first picture, and the eternal tragedy was repeating itself. The man's face was loathsome in its sodden ferocity ; the woman, with a child in her arms, was reeling from the blow. The evident haste in which the panels had been painted, the glaring, unsoftened colouring, heightened as if by impressionist design the coarse realism of the effect. Above was written the legend, "*La joie de vivre*," and in the left-hand bottom corner, "*Clytie Davenant pinxit.*"

"She has certainly grown much worse of late," sighed Mrs. Blather, holding out her thin, short hand to shield her face from the fire.

There was a pause of some moments. Mr. Davenant ceased nursing the picture and stood it on the floor.

"Have you quite made up your mind, papa," said Mrs.

Blather at length, " not to let Clytie go to the Slade School in London ? "

" It is out of the question," replied the old man.

" I don't think so, papa. It would perhaps do her good. A year or so's hard work would take all these silly ideas out of her."

" I question it," said Mr. Davenant. " They are not silly ideas. They are debased, degraded ideas."

" My dear papa, they are only fads. All young girls have them. Look how crazy Janet was to join the cookery classes. We let her join, and now she hates the sight of a pie-dish. With Clytie it is quite the same, only she wants to daub."

" Well, let her daub in a decent way at home," replied the old man testily.

Mrs. Blather shrugged her lean shoulders.

" We have tried that and it hasn't succeeded, apparently," she said drily. " You seldom come in her way ; you don't know how unpleasant things are for Janet and myself. What do you think she had the impertinence to tell me this morning ? She said that we were not real people. We were machines or abstractions based, I think she said, on a formula, or something of that sort. She was pining to live amongst living human beings. And then she is so rude to visitors. What do you think she said to the vicar, who came, at Janet's request, to talk to her about her shameful neglect of her religious duties ? She said, if he was a pillar of the Church, she saw no reason why she should be a seat-cushion."

" Tut, tut," said the old man angrily. He was vicar's churchwarden, and a power in the parish.

" And then," continued Mrs. Blather, " when I scolded her for her rudeness, she said that if she had been a man she would have sworn at him for his impertinence. Really people will soon be afraid of coming to the house."

" They will indeed," said Mr. Davenant.

Like a wise woman, Mrs. Blather did not press her point. She knew she had thoroughly alarmed her father and had shown him but one way out of the difficulty. His taking it, if left to himself, was only a question of time. She rang the bell for the servant to come and light

Mr. Davenant's gas, and then she left him to his reflections.

Mr. Davenant possessed some landed property, which he had occupied his life in mismanaging. Fortunately for him, his wife had brought him a small fortune which sufficed to keep up a position, modest when compared with that of the Davenants of former days, but still high enough to satisfy the social aspirations of his family. He had lived a colourless life, severe and respectable. Even his university days had passed in a dull uniformity, leaving no glamour behind them. He had walked honourably and blindly in the paths his parents had indicated, and, now that he was nearing the end of the journey, thanked God for having given him the grace not to err from them. He had married when still fairly young, and he had loved his wife in a gentlemanly, passionless way. She, poor thing, had filled up so small a space in life that she had faded out of it almost unnoticed—even by himself. He had no storms of joy or sorrow to look back upon. His thoughts, as he brooded over the fireside, generally wandered back to trifling incidents : ancient municipal interests, the mortgages on his estate, the boundary quarrels with the old earl, his neighbour.

But lately he had been thinking anxiously over his daughter Clytie. She had suddenly developed out of a naughty, rebellious child into a problem. He assumed as a matter of course that he bore her the ordinary well-regulated parental affection, but in his heart of hearts he never really loved her. Until lately it had not occurred to him to think of her as anything but a child of his with a singularly unfortunate disposition which time would modify. But time, on the contrary, was accentuating it, and he realised at last that Clytie had a distinct individuality. His philosophy had left many things in heaven and earth undreamed of. He was mystified, puzzled. How could he and his delicate wife have brought this bright-haired, full-blooded, impulsive creature into existence? Her sisters were gentle, quiet women, possessing the virtues inculcated in his conception of life. Clytie seemed to possess none of them. The peasant woman in the legend could not have wondered more over her changeling. How could a daughter of his and a sister of Janet's scoff at sacred things, defy social rules, and have an imagination that ran riot in scenes of drunkenness and outcast life?

Physiology might grant a solution to the old man's problem in the law of the alternation of heredity. His father's youngest brother had been a family black sheep, and being the only one of the generation who had led an eventful career, was naturally never mentioned by his relations, and the record of his life perished with him. But it is possible that the positive enthusiastic principle of Clytie's Puritan descent, reasserting itself once in every other generation, to the horror of the negative principle that otherwise ran through the race continuously, came out in her with all its strength and vigour. It brought her eager, panting up to the brink of our surging nineteenth century life, imperiously bidding her plunge in and take her part in the tumult.

She was now nineteen, an age when girls try to realise themselves. She discovered that she was a greater problem to herself than to her sisters. They simply looked upon her as odd, eccentric, unpleasant to live with, and if she had not been their sister would have almost gathered up their skirts around them as they passed her by. But she was conscious of a craving within her that did not proceed from mere wilful caprice. In her earlier girlhood she had thought long and humbly over her shortcomings. Why could she not be as contented and dutiful as Janet? Why could not the interests that satisfied her sisters' life satisfy hers? Often and often an impulse of scorn and ridicule at the littleness of Durdleham would overmaster her, and then would follow a passionate fit of remorse and repentance, received with coldness and ruffled dignity on her sisters' part, that would send her back humiliated and rebellious to her room. From what springs of desire did all this proceed? Whither were these impulses tending?

Ever since she could hold a pencil she had been able to draw. She had received lessons in painting later on, and had covered canvas after canvas with the graceful futilities the Durdleham art teacher suggested. He was a landscape painter, and Clytie had little or no feeling for landscape. Bright colour, vivid contrast, sharp tone, attracted her, but the quiet grays and faint blues of our English scenery came out dull and mechanical when she tried to paint them. At last she gave up her lessons in despair, much to the wonderment of Janet, who improved greatly under instruction, and turned out neat, compla-cent little water-colours which she sold at bazaars or distributed among her friends. For months Clytie never touched a brush. Art of this sort revolted her. It was soulless, futile. But by degrees, as the breach between herself and her sisters widened, her power of painting became a source of ineffable consolation—a means of self-commune. She could give external expression to the voices that haunted her. She read books with the eagerness only-exhibited by the young girl craving for self-development ; and the pictures they vividly im-pressed on her young imaginative brain she transferred to paper or canvas—not lovingly, tenderly, with the pure artistic delight of gradual creation, but hurriedly, fever-ishly, longing to see the thing done, the impression realised in a way in which she could understand it. When finished, or rather as soon as it had reached an impressionist stage of artistic completeness, she would feast her heart upon it for a day or two, and then throw it away, or let it lie about in a corner disregarded and forgotten.

Until she was nearly eighteen Mrs. Blather had scru-pulously supervised her reading, and Clytie, chafing with irritation, had been compelled either to submit or to smuggle condemned books into the house and read them surreptitiously. But at last her angry impatience at the impeccable literature that satisfied her sisters' needs burst its restraints, and resisted vehemently and finally all censorship on the part of Mrs. Blather.

It was not wholesome, this solitary, emotional, imagina-tive life. Her health showed signs of giving way. They called in a doctor, who prescribed rest and a change of air. One of her aunts, who lived in London, happened to want a companion for a tour on the Continent, and with many misgivings undertook to take Clytie with her. To the girl the trip was an endless succession of delight. Impressions followed each other too fast for her to realise them. The superficial features of continental life, familiar and commonplace enough to the ordinary traveller, were new to her. Groups at street corners, strangely attired soldiers, odd un-English-looking shops, the very waiters hurrying along through the intricacies of café tables with their fantastically laden trays, all excited her, filled her with the exhilaration of life and movement. Her aunt, who had hitherto shared the family opinion of Clytie, wondered greatly at the transformation. It never occurred to her that this was the natural Clytie filling her heart at last with the emotions it had hungered for.

It was during this time, at a pension in Dresden, that she formed the acquaintance of the Farquharsons. Miss Davenant discovered that they and herself had common acquaintances in London, and that she had heard of Mr. Farquharson as an archæologist of some repute.

The acquaintance thus formed developed quickly into a pleasant intimacy of travel. Mrs. Farquharson, a bright, clever woman of forty, was attracted toward Clytie, who, for her part, found in her new friend a natural sympathy that touched her heart. So far did their sudden friendship go, that before they parted Clytie had conditionally accepted an invitation to visit the archæologist and his wife in Harley Street.

When Mr. Davenant's permission was asked he at first demurred. He had the country-bred man's distrust of strangers; but when his sister vouched for the social position of the Farquharsons he reluctantly consented. Clytie paid her promised visit the following winter. This was one of the turning points of her life. For the first time she found herself in an intellectual, artistic society. It was a glimpse of another world. At Durdleham young men seldom came to the house. When they did, they avoided her and talked platitudes to her sisters. At dinner parties the men remained in the dining-room long after the ladies had left. They seemed to regard them as somewhat picturesque but wearisome household adjuncts, whose absence their masculine intellects unreservedly welcomed; conversation with their partner was a dinner incident to be got through, like shaving or putting on their white ties beforehand. And the Durdleham ladies seemed to take this as a matter of course, and were equally happy to get by themselves and gossip mildly.

But in Harley Street Clytie found a different order of things. Men and women seemed to have interests in common and to discuss them on a basis of perfect equality. She found, too, women speaking authoritatively on certain subjects and listened to with deference by men. All, young and old, talked to her as if she were as much absorbed in life as themselves. No one made her rage with humiliation by tolerating her with an air of languid or pompous condescension. Even the frivolities and platitudes of everyday conversation were treated in a way new to her experience. The talk was keen, incisive, exaggerated. Everyone could say what he wished without fear of springing some mine of prejudice or prudery. The atmosphere of the house breathed freedom of thought and action. She beheld others putting into form her own vague aspirations. She saw people who wrote, painted, acted, living fully and intensely every day. Even the professed idlers whom she met seemed to hold their fingers on the throb of life around them.

In the streets—she had been but little in London before—she saw things strange and fascinating—things she had read about, dreamed of, painted, and yet not understood. She was appalled by her ignorance, the narrow gauge of her sympathies. What did all this restless life in the great city mean, its wild cries and passions that struck upon her tightly strung nerves with a deep, mysterious resonance?

She filled a sketch-book with the vivid impressions each day brought her, seeking, as her way was, to realise them by tearing them out of herself, and giving them objectivity. A royal academician picked up the book from the corner of a table in the drawing-room, where Clytie, falling easily into the careless ways of the household, had thrown it. He was turning over the pages when Clytie perceived him, and rushed impulsively to him across the room.

"Oh! you mustn't look at that, Mr. Redgrave. Please don't!"

He looked up at her amusedly.

"Why not? It is rather interesting. Why don't you learn to draw?"

"What would be the good?" she said. "This suits my purpose."

The other shrugged his shoulders good-humouredly.

"That all depends upon what your purpose is," he replied. "If you want to become an artist you must train properly for it."

Become an artist! The words haunted her all that night. They opened up before her infinite vistas of possibilities, life in the midst of the world, the knowledge of its greatnesses and its mysteries.

In the morning she wrote to him. He invited her to come to his studio and talk over the matter. She asked Mrs. Farquharson to accompany her, but her hostess was engaged at the hour in question. Clytie looked disappointed. The home traditions asserted themselves and prevented her from thinking it possible to go unchaperoned. Mrs. Farquharson divined this and laughed in her bright way.

"Goodness gracious, my dear," she said, "the man isn't going to eat you!"

So Clytie went alone to the studio to learn her destiny.

"You have great talent," said the artist, "but it needs cultivation. After two or three years' severe training you may do something."

Then Clytie asked him the question that had been burning her heart for two days.

"Do you think I shall ever be able to earn my own living?"

"You might do that now, if you chose, and had patience," he replied.

"How?"

"By book illustrating."

"But I want to become a great artist."

"Doubtless. Most of us do. You may if you try hard, and love art for art's sake. But," he added, looking at her keenly—"there always is a 'but,' Miss Davenant."

"Why do you say that?" she asked quickly.

"*Parce que*, as the French say—begging your pardon."
And that was practically the end of the conversation.

All this had happened to Clytie three months before Mrs. Blather had discovered the offending picture in Clytie's attic studio and had carried it to her father. After this foretaste of life the girl wearied more than ever of Durdleham with its soullessness, its stagnation, its prim formulas. A dangerous reaction of spirit set in, leading her to long spells of hopeless melancholy, alternating with outbursts of passionate rebellion. She would stand for hours in the recess of her window gazing over the flat stretch of country, and dreaming strange dreams of the world that lay beyond the dreary horizon—dreams in which sharp reminiscence mingled with fancy in vague, weird shapes. But still she was beginning to realise herself, her needs, her vague cravings. Her passionate desires now flowed into some definite channel—to escape at all costs from Durdleham, and consequently to enter that free world of art the glimpse of which had enchanted her.

The scenes between her sisters and herself were of daily occurrence. The narrower, gentler women were shocked at her wilfulnesses, her unladylike behaviour ; she was revolted to her soul at the pettiness and sordidness of the disputes. Existence at Durdleham had become impossible.

"For God's sake, Gracie, let me go away from here," she cried one day, " or I shall hate you—and I want to love you if I can. Let me go to London. Auntie will take me in. Oh, my God ! I shall go mad in this place among you."

And Mrs. Blather, for the sake of her own tranquillity and the reputation of the family, made up her mind that Clytie should have her desire and that Durdleham should know her no more. And in the end Mrs. Blather gained her father's consent to the arrangement ; but the old man looked upon Clytie almost as a lost soul.

CHAPTER II.

When the eager young soul starts out unaided to solve the riddle of life, it meets with many paradoxes that admit of no solution, and many sordid simplicities that only unfamiliarity made it regard as enigmas. Despair in the one instance and disgust in the other not unfrequently drive it into a hopeless pessimism, in which inaction seems to be the least pain. Or else the soul bruises itself in vain against the mocking bars, shrinks in loathing from the disveiled corruption, and flies back to the unavailing aids that it spurned afore-time. It is cast in the valley of the shadow of death which only the stout-hearted can pass through unshaken.

The multitude stands by the formulas that profess to solve the eternal problem. It follows them blindly, like the schoolboy who cares not whether they are right or wrong, or whether the answer is conclusive. So long as there is an answer of some sort its mind is easy. But there are earnester inquirers whom these formulas do not satisfy—who see that they are followed for their own sake, that they never can lead to any conclusions. The soul, now of a people, now of an individual, rebels; it rejects the formulas; it starts from the first principles of being, asserting fiercely its individuality, its inalienable right to seek after truth according to its own methods. These are prejudiced. All great action must be. Because a system is rotten and incomplete the perfervid spirit judges that every factor must be false. It misses the fact that every great human system contains elemental truths of vital importance, without which it must fail in its struggle. And at last, when the forces of endeavour are well nigh spent, it finds the key of the great enigma inwrapped in a greater one still, in the eternal tragedy of things.

It was with this burning protest against formulas that

Clytie entered into the world. They had been presented to her in their smug complacency as solving all mysteries human and divine. She had seen them worshipped as fetiches, and her soul revolted against the futile idolatry. She was too young to examine them carefully, to see that the sacrosanctity of some was miserably justified by human experience. She spurned them all, and she plunged into the waters of Life, a rudderless bark in search of the unknown.

She spent two years in study at the Slade School in University College, living under the protection of her aunt, who had a house in Russell Square. The training was severe and at times irksome. But she learned strict academical rules of drawing, in spite of her repugnance to the stern coldness of the antique. After her term of hard training was over she went for a year into a painter's studio and learned colour and painting from the live model.

They were years of probation, as Clytie well knew, and they brought her lessons in self-restraint, both in art and in the conduct of life. Her aunt, Miss Davenant, was shrewder and broader-minded than her brother, having lived more in the whirl of humanity, but the formulas of Durdleham were ranged as household gods upon her hearthstone, and Clytie, out of pure self-interest, was bound to show them outward respect. To compensate, however, for this, Clytie found in her student life many experiences, as she had found during her continental trip, with which she could fill her heart without violating her aunt's Lares and Penates.

She seldom went to Durdleham. She had an odd feeling that she was in disgrace there for having wished to leave it. Besides, both Mrs. Blather and Janet, as is the inconsequent way of such women, spoke tauntingly of her gay life in town, and contrasted it enviously with their country dulness. And then, too, her father was always querulous, complaining, not of her absence from home, but of her dissimilarity to her sisters.

" My dear papa," she said one day, " I could no more be like them than they could be like me."

" You might if you had tried," said the old man.

Clytie looked hopelessly out of window. What possible reply could be made?

The happiest, most expansive hours that Clytie spent during these three years were in Harley Street with the Farquharsons. At first her aunt was rather averse to a continuance of the intimacy. Although she had kept up a visiting acquaintance with the Farquharsons since their return from Switzerland, and liked them both personally, she was conscious of an unfamiliar atmosphere in their house. The instinctive shrinking from the unknown made her seek to draw Clytie back with her towards the security of her own accustomed circle. But eventually, when she saw that the girl, to whom she had grown sincerely attached, found real happiness in going to Harley Street, she withdrew her tentative restrictions altogether. Perhaps she read deeper into the girl's heart than either was conscious of, and realised that in the Farquharsons' society Clytie found a relief from the strain of everyday life with her, which otherwise might have been unbearable.

The conditions of the household in Harley Street were favourable to the development of unceremonious intimacy. Mrs. Farquharson herself was bred in that strange London world we call Bohemia. Her father, long since dead, had been a journalist, a hack story-writer, a maker of plays, sometimes editor of a smart weekly, at others acting manager of a provincial company. Like most men of his type he spent his money as fast as he earned it, and when work came to a temporary standstill drew upon the prospects of his next success. His daughter Caroline had grown up in cheerful familiarity with this hand to mouth, makeshift existence. She had been called upon so often from her earliest childhood to condone the faults of her father and those of his intimates, who were men of much the same mould as himself, that a general habit of indulgence became natural to her. Folly seemed so inherent a quality in humanity that not to smile tolerantly, even though reprovingly, upon it was with her an impossibility. The lowering of moral tone that might have resulted from this mental attitude, and from a continuance of the same conditions of life, was prevented by her early marriage with a man of assured income and position. Her father died shortly afterwards and her connection with the seamy side of Bohemianism was thoroughly broken off. But the ingrained habits of freedom and carelessness still remained. She could never learn to be methodical, systematic. She had an inherited dread of account-books, household rules, fixed hours for meals, and appointed places for every domestic article. It was fortunate for her that she had married a man who worshipped her, and himself shared her distaste for rigidly organised life. His means had placed him beyond the necessity of working for his livelihood, and so the free life in a home where he could work, idle, eat, and receive his friends at any hour of the day or night was as much to his own taste as to that of his wife.

It was impossible that such a house should not possess a charm for those to whom the Farquharsons gave their friendship. The absence of formality encouraged expansiveness and individuality. There was a tacit understanding that one had a right not only to oneself, but to the appreciation of oneself by the host and hostess. It was this that Clytie had felt during her first visit, and it attracted her more and more to them as time went on. Gradually the house became a second home to her, and Mrs. Farquharson a friend such as she had never known before. She could go to her for strength and comfort during her fits of depression when the time seemed out of joint, and she did not in the least seem called upon to set it right. The restraints of strict draughtsmanship, academic modelling and grouping, chafed her as her simple arithmetic had done at school. She longed to throw them off and to plunge back into her old artistic wilfulnesses. But these occasions generally coincided with fresh sensations of restraint in her home life, and she was wise enough to appreciate the fact.

During this period an incident occurred in her life, giving it fresh colour and helping her to realise herself more fully. Her girlhood had been far removed from the lax sphere of idle flirtation in which many girls are brought up. The young men of Durdleham, who might have been attracted towards her by her beauty, were frozen by her scarcely veiled impatience at their society.

The dominant impulse towards active search after life had swayed her to the exclusion of any less powerful motive, and it had scarcely yet occurred to her that her personality might interest and possibly influence others. She was too absorbed in her work, in her dimly shadowed yet ever-haunting plans for the future, in the individualities round her, in the foretaste of that full sense of living, in the stirring objectivity of London life, to dwell at all earnestly on subjective matters and to devote much attention to self-analysis. It is only when the question, "How do others affect me?" ceases to interest that the other question, "How does my personality affect others?" begins to assume a paramount importance. The possibility of a man falling in love with her was a factor as yet absent from her scheme of practical life.

She learned that such an event had occurred from Mrs. Farquharson. She had gone to her one Monday morning, depressed, out of tune, to seek consolation.

"Oh, why am I not a man?" she exclaimed petulantly. "Why can't I live by myself, go where I like, and see what I want to see?"

Her friend laughed good-humouredly.

"You want to do too much at once, my dear. The world's your oyster, as ancient Pistol said, and you would force it open with one wrench. As for wishing to be a man, you are by no means original. Lots of girls say that, but when they grow older they think it's just as well for them that they are women."

"What on earth's the good of being a *woman?*" asked Clytie, with rather unnecessary emphasis.

One of her studio companions had asked her to join a party at a theatre, and her aunt had demurred on the ground that ladies ought not to go to that particular house. It showed a certain knowledge of the world on the old lady's part, but Clytie did not realise it, and although she accepted the decision with good grace, it fretted her. These trivial things fret even the wisest amongst us quite as much as the important ones do.

Mrs. Farquharson did not reply, but continued placidly her usual Monday morning's occupation of putting her music in order, while Clytie watched her from the long rocking-chair where she was sitting, her hands clasped behind her head.

"What's the good of being a woman when one has to pass half one's life shut up in darkness? It's bad enough being a human being as it is, and having to sleep the other half."

"How old are you, my dear?" asked Mrs. Farquharson, looking at a song.

"You know," replied Clytie. "Twenty."

"Then how would you like to be a young man of twenty—or even two-and-twenty? How would you like to be young Beaumont, for instance? Do you think he knows so very much more than you do?"

"He's such a boy," said Clytie.

"And you, my dear, are such a girl," said Mrs. Farquharson, coming up behind her chair and smoothing her cheeks. "But you are many years older than he is—and likely to remain so. Do you know why we women like to be women? Because we see so many things that men would give the eyes of their heads to know. Hasn't it ever struck you that we are familiar with a side of life that is almost forever hidden from men? And as for that particular side that men have exclusively to themselves, it is neither very pretty nor comfortful."

"I suppose that is why men stop talking when one goes into the smoking-room," said Clytie. "You hear shouts of laughter outside the door, and you think they must be having an awfully good time, and when you appear in the doorway they seem to pull themselves together, and one or two always look red and sheepish."

"I should advise you to read the story of Bluebeard," said Mrs. Farquharson.

"You are just as bad as the rest," cried Clytie, half laughing and half vexed. "I never thought it of you. That's what I have always been told: Never try to find out what you don't know. Always remain in a state of blissful ignorance. Men are superior beings, and a good little girl ought to accept her position with meekness."

"I could a tale unfold," said her friend, "but I won't. It is too early for you. If you want to make experiments on your own account there is young Beaumont for you. He will tell you the sum total of his knowledge in ten minutes."

"Do you know, I like him," said Clytie, leaving the main track of the conversation. "He always looks so clean, and his clothes fit him so well, and he is so serviceable. He always seems to be trying to make the best of himself, since God has done so little for him. And it's very plucky of him to try to improve on the Almighty."

"I would not like him too much."

"Why?"

"My poor Clytie! You haven't even got the elements of woman's knowledge yet. Can't you see why Beaumont wears those very chaste ties and those wonderfully shiny boots, and does errands all over London for you? Oh, dear!"

"Do you mean that he——?"

Mrs. Farquharson looked at her quizzically and nodded.

"Therefore I would not like him too much."

Obeying a first impulse, Clytie burst out laughing. It seemed so ridiculous. Beaumont was a good-looking, fresh-faced young fellow of two-and-twenty, a distant relation of the Farquharsons, and a habitué of the house. She had met him there many times and had begun to feel quite friendly towards him. Besides, he had fetched and carried for her in the most useful way. She had never thought of his falling in love with her. As he was the last man she herself would have thought of falling in love with, she found the event ludicrous.

She stopped laughing suddenly, and crimsoned to her hair; then rushed impulsively up to Mrs. Farquharson, and put her arm round her waist.

"I am sorry; forgive me. What must you think of me! I could not help it, indeed I couldn't. You put me in such a new light before myself. And, dear Mrs. Farquharson, I do so want you to see the best side of me."

"My dear girl," said her friend, "you don't suppose that with your face and your nature you are going to pass through life without having men falling in love with you! You see what a lot you have to learn. You want to have a man's experiences before you have passed through the elementary ones of a woman."

"And Mr. Beaumont—what shall I do?"

"Oh! don't fret yourself about him. He will get over it. He has no end of this sort of thing to go through before his life is up. It will do him good."

Clytie had not much time to map out any fixed plan of treatment of her would-be lover, for he met her an afternoon or two afterwards outside University College, where he had been waiting for her, and pleaded that she would walk a little way up towards the Regent's Park, as the afternoon was fine.

Clytie looked at him and hesitated.

"Only just a little way. I have something I must tell you."

"Perhaps you had best never tell it," said Clytie.

The red-waistcoated gate porter behind them beamed on them smilingly. He had seen something of youthful love in his professional career.

"I must, whatever happens," replied the young fellow. "I know it's wrong to ask you to walk in the street with me, but I don't know when I shall get another chance."

"I don't see anything wrong about it," said Clytie. "I will go with you wherever you wish."

So they wandered up Gower Street and the Euston Road into the park, and there, for the first time in her life, Clytie heard a man confess his love for her and ask her to marry him. He was only a boy after all, but he was in great earnest. Clytie felt humbled, almost guilty, and yet a great, unknown pleasure thrilled through her. Although she knew that the sooner and more summarily the interview was brought to an end the better for both herself and him, she could scarcely resist the temptation of allowing him to pour out the fulness of his boyish love for her.

She suddenly found herself listening to the sound but not the meaning of his words, her senses filled with the sweetness of the new sensations and the pure May sunlight that flooded the trees and the gay flower-bed opposite the bench where they were sitting. Then she realised her situation, and in a few kind words, harder to speak than she would have expected, dismissed him.

And that was the end of the matter. He went off whither young men in his predicament generally betake themselves, and Clytie returned slowly home to Russell Square.

When she had reached her own room she went deliberately up to the glass and scanned her features. Then she laughed a strange, contented little laugh, and taking off her hat and gloves, went downstairs to tea. She had advanced several steps along the road to knowledge.

Three years! How quickly they passed! How sure yet dimly working were their influences! If they were years of probation and self-restraint for Clytie, they also brought with them softening influences. Hitherto her life had been one of revolt and harsh, crude judgments that had turned away friendship and had left her solitary. Mutual misconception and misunderstanding had crushed sisterly love. Her heart had never been touched by real affection. Now she had friends, real ones, in the Farquharsons whom she could love for their own sakes, and pleasant, sympathetic ones in her companions at the Slade School and at the studio. She learned, too, the sweetness of active protection and helpfulness. Her aunt, though somewhat stronger-fibred than the rest of the Davenants, possessed their essential physical characteristics. Her health, which had been failing for some years, gradually gave way altogether. During the few months of her last illness she depended entirely upon Clytie for care and tenderness. It was a new, strange experience for the girl. She learned to love the faded elderly lady who bore her sufferings so calmly, so cheerfully. Both Mrs. Blather and Janet offered to come and nurse her, but Miss Davenant would have none but Clytie. If this period of selflessness and sacrifice had lasted, who knows what sweet effacement of individuality might have resulted? Who knows into what channels of pity and sublime endeavours of mercy the girl's full, ardent nature might have been directed? But the high gods had ordained otherwise. Miss Davenant died, and Clytie again found herself with the unknown destiny before her that had to be worked out unaided.

It was only after the first outburst of grief that she realised this fully. She had gone back to Durdleham, with a new range of feelings freshly revealed. Her sisters she found were gentle, quiet women like her aunt, narrower perhaps, with thin currents of old prejudice still running through them, but still lovable and sympathetic in her sorrow. They welcomed her back like a lost sheep to the fold. Never had her home life seemed so peaceful, comfortful; London was scarcely mentioned, and her sisters agreed between themselves that Clytie's absence from home was an episode of the past, never to recur.

But time wears and effaces the deepest intaglio of impression, even that of a young girl's first knowledge of death and eternal loss. Gradually the quietude of eventless life, as the need for it wore away, grew wearisome, oppressive, and the old restless cravings began to gnaw at her heart. The breach that death had closed slowly widened again, so gradually that not till it was fully appreciable did the sisters recognise it. The formulas seemed narrower, more lifeless than ever. She had viewed dimly the potentialities of life, and her soul burned within her with a fiercer hunger. Almost against her will she revolted finally.

"What is this that Janet has been telling me," said Mrs. Blather one morning, "about your wanting to go back to London? You cannot be in earnest, Clytie?"

Clytie looked at her sister rather sadly, tears springing into her eyes.

"You have been very good to me since I have come back, Gracie, and I have learned to love you more than I did before—much more. But can't you understand, dear, that if I am to go on loving you I must go away?"

"I can't see it at all," replied Mrs. Blather. "If we have got on so nicely together these last few months, why can't we continue? Janet and I are willing to give you all in our power to make you happy."

"Ah! but don't you see that what I want is out of your power to give?" said Clytie. "Don't think I am wicked and ungrateful. If a man wants five pounds, he is grateful to anyone who gives him one; but that does not lessen his need of the other four. Now the other four pounds are not to be got in Durdleham, Gracie, and I must have them."

"You should learn content, Clytie," said her sister. "We have all to put up with our lot in life."

Clytie checked an impulse of impatience at the platitude, and answered with great gentleness of voice and manner:

"This is not my lot in life, dear. It is quite different. You and Janet can bear it, because your natures crave this tranquillity. Mine craves movement, excitement, strange faces. Oh, Gracie, it is no use talking—I must go away, or I shall begin to hate Durdleham as I used to do. There is nothing for me to do here. I am too bad for it, perhaps. I don't know. I can't explain it to you; you have never felt it."

"My dear Clytie, that is all nonsense," said Mrs. Blather, who prided herself, above all things, on being a woman of common sense. "As a matter of fact, you can't go to London, because you would have no one to live with, and you would only have your hundred a year to support you, as papa has lost a great deal of money lately and can hardly afford to give you an allowance. When your aunt was alive it was a different thing. The whole idea of going to live alone in London is silly. So there's an end of it."

Mrs. Blather went on with her sewing, with mingled feelings of content at having done her duty and disappointment in the failure of promise of reform in Clytie. She would have judged her sister mercifully had she been able. She was naturally a gentle woman, full of kindness. But her canons of duty would not allow her to encourage or condone wilfulness, caprice, and a tendency to wrong-doing. She earnestly believed it was for Clytie's good to stay in Durdleham. The girl's wider needs she could not understand.

Clytie turned from the hearthrug, where she had been standing, to the drawing-room window, and looked out blankly at the rain. Her young face was set rather hard; her lips quivered a little; her heart beat quicker than usual. A struggle was taking place within her—the struggle between the girl and the woman. She felt that the great moment of her life had come. She must choose. Which should it be : the dazzling light with its weird shadows of things unseen, or the gray, easeful glimmer in which the familiar realities cast no shadow ? Which should it be : daughterly duty and maidenly retirement, or the sundering of home ties forever and going out, one woman, to battle with the world ?

She turned away from the window at last and called to her sister. The latter looked up and was filled with foreboding as she saw the girl's pale face.

" Yes. What is the matter, Clytie ? "

" I have made up my mind, Gracie," she said a little huskily. " I am going to London to live by myself. I can share lodgings with one of the girls I know at the Slade School. There will be no difficulty. I can earn money ; I have already earned a little. As for mamma's money, I am of age now, and it is my own to do what I like with it—as you and Janet do. Let this be an end of the discussion, Gracie. I am going."

CHAPTER III.

Few people, in an outburst of enthusiasm, would select the King's Road, Chelsea, as an ideal locality to reside in. It is an important thoroughfare, no doubt, but it lacks nobility and distinction. There are isolated, quiet spots in it, with houses lying back from the road; and from the upper windows of favoured residences one can obtain a view over Veitch's or Bull's extensive hot-houses, and catch dim shadows of great tropical palms and a mellowed dash of brilliant red and yellow. There are others which look over Portman Square or St. Luke's Churchyard. But on the other hand, there are long stretches of dreary shops and factories, grit and general uncomeliness. Without being squalid, it has a careworn, untidy appearance, as if it was far too much harassed with the petty worries and strain of workaday life to think of cheerful adornment. Few people, except errand boys whose sense either of æsthetics or duty is usually undeveloped, saunter casually along the King's Road. A stranger tries to get out of it as fast as he can; a frequenter has his business to attend to. Fashion does not pass along it, except on tearing drags bound for Hurlingham. It is essentially a small bourgeois part of London, with all the small bourgeois unpretence and honest, if somewhat dismal, solidity.

It was in the middle of such a dreary stretch of the road, some half mile west of Sloane Square, that Clytie found a lodging. The fact that a green-grocer's shop, owned by the landlord of the house, occupied the ground floor was compensated, in a measure, by the existence of a small studio at the back, on the first floor, originally constructed by a struggling photographer, who had since worked his way upwards into a more fashionably perfumed atmosphere. One of Clytie's favourite fellow-students, Winifred Marchpane, who lived in Lower Sloane Street, and whose family obtained their potatoes and salads from Mr. Gurkins, had recommended the establishment, and offered to share with her the expenses of the studio. The cheapness of the rooms suited Clytie's modest purse, and the prospect of pleasant companionship in the studio was an additional attraction. It is true that the acrid smell of the potatoes, when the side door from the shop on to the private entrance lobby was left open, ascended the stairs, together with a vague odour of cooking, bearing upwards, as it were, on savoury breath the disputes of Mrs. Gurkins with the shopboy and the cries of her apparently ever-youthful progeny. The incessant rumble, too, of omnibuses, drays, and furniture vans, and the peculiarly aggressive rattle of tradesmen's carts, shook the floor and the windows and shivered the lustres of the chandelier. There were many drawbacks to elegant life, but Clytie, borrowing some philosophy from a talk with Mrs. Farquharson, proceeded to disregard those she could not eliminate. The sitting-room, when the door was shut and the curtains drawn of an evening, was cosy enough. The pictures, nicknacks, hangings, and other minor accessories of furnished apartments Clytie had returned to Mrs. Gurkins' keeping, on the plea that she scarcely had room for her own—which was true ; and, by some miraculous art of persuasion, she had induced Mr. Gurkins to remove the nerve-shattering chandelier, on the ground that she could not work by gaslight— which was not true. She hung thick curtains over the door to keep out noise and odour, broke up the rigidity of the furniture by screens, small tables, and plants, and painted a long panel for the old cottage piano that made it look fresh and companionable. When all the arrangements were completed the room appeared dainty and homelike, bearing, however, here and there, in bold notes of colour, folds of drapery, and odd bits of semi-impressionist painting, a peculiar impress of its tenant's personality.

She was living at last the life she had so passionately longed for. There was not a human being to control her actions, not a conventionality to check the utterance of her thoughts. During her early days here she almost felt tempted to hang up her latchkey over the mantelpiece as a glorious symbol of liberty. It seemed not only to serve to give her entrance to her own modest home, but to be the power that would unlock the heart of the great London that lay before her.

From the first she had little difficulty in finding work. Dealers bought small pictures and gave her orders. She also pleased a firm of publishers to whom she had gone with letters of introduction and specimens of her draughtsmanship, and obtained work in the way of book and magazine illustrating. Her earnings were not large, but there was the promise of success to come. At the end of two years her income was large enough to have enabled her to move from the King's Road into a more refined locality; but she had grown accustomed to its noise and rattle, and to the hurried, joyless stream of life that flowed along it day by day. And Mrs. Gurkins understood her tastes and habits, a quality in a landlady appreciated by women as well as men. So she stayed on.

She read widely during these years, learned much. Between the ages of twenty-two and twenty-four a woman is capable of vast assimilation of ideas. They can flow into the freshly opened, unpolluted channels of her being, as yet unclogged by the refuse of sorrows and wearinesses. Her rejection of the old formulas, and the paramount necessity of gaining knowledge wherewith to provide herself substitutes, checked in her any impulse towards moral or artistic idealism. She read deeply, instinctively seeking after the roots of life, the elemental passions that shake our nature, be its superstructure never so delicately complex. The dawning knowledge half frightened, half attracted her. The barbaric feminine in her struggled to escape into solitude. With fluttering eyelids downcast it recoiled from the idea of passion as yet unawakened responsively within her. But the higher needs of modernity constrained her to a just, resolute system of inquiry. She learned that there are deeper laws regulating our being than those which could be enunciated at Durdleham tea-tables, where the ingrained habit of non-recognition of them restricted life within narrowest limits, and put, as it were, a prohibition tax upon exoteric sympathy.

At four-and-twenty Clytie was a woman—emotional,

impulsive, eager to taste of any new experience. The old rebellious habit of mind had developed into a frank independence. Her step was elastic, her bearing confident. Her life was full and happy.

"I am glad I am a woman now," she said to Mrs. Farquharson. "I seem to have all the advantages of both sexes."

"Wait till you're married, my dear," replied her friend.

Mrs. Farquharson was fond of the use of affectionate irritants. They are often valuable preservatives of friendship.

Clytie laughed.

"I suppose I shall marry some day. I don't want to end up by leading half a life ; but I want to have two or three years more of this. I must play at being a man a little longer."

"A pretty sort of man !" said Mrs. Farquharson, resting her chin on her hand and looking at Clytie with amused eyes. "You are the most deliciously feminine young woman I know. Look at your frock and your hair."

Judging by outward appearances Mrs. Farquharson's criticism was correct. Clytie had the artistic sense in dress. It was like most of her other artistic impulses, with the personal note dominant—soft textures, falling easily into folds, quiet in tone, dark grays, subdued half shades of yellows, suddenly brightened by a small, daring flash of colour at throat or bosom. Lace, with its creamy, clinging softness delighted her, and she wore it defiantly, with a certain sense of triumph that she was perhaps the only girl in England who could wear it with faultless taste.

She was of medium height, but her slender, fully formed figure and its erect carriage gave her an air of tallness. Her head set well on her shoulders, and a habit of holding it back, with the chin pointing upwards, free of the throat, added to the impression of young, fearless womanhood. Her eyes were dark blue, wide apart, yet sunk in finely moulded orbits. A light of humour playing in their depths, together with a soft modelling of the nose contours beneath them, atoned for an impression of hardness and sensuousness that would have been given by the ripe, full lips with their little curl of disdain. Her face was rounded delicately —that much she inherited from the Davenants—but a faint flush of colour showed the buoyant young blood within, just as her deep red hair, with a thousand lights dancing in it, attested the rich, vigorous strain that had asserted itself in her. She was proud, womanlike, of this hair, and had a way of dressing it in bewildering confusion.

Her Slade School friend, Winifred Marchpane, continued to share the studio with her. At first she had been a little afraid of Clytie, whose bold judgments and fearless expression of opinion were not qualified always to attract a timorous, shrinking nature. But gradually the stronger personality had overpowered the weaker and bound it to itself by unbreakable bonds. A great friendship had thus arisen between the girls, based on Winifred's side on enthusiastic admiration, almost worship, and on Clytie's on a tender feeling of love and protection.

Winifred was one of a large family, her father, a retired officer in the army with limited income. Two of her sisters were governesses, earning their livelihood miles away from home. Another one took charge of the smaller members of the household. Winifred, who had a dainty talent for the painting of still life, supported herself, living at home and paying her share of the household expenses. She was a little, gentle creature, with dark hair, and with a rich colour showing beneath a brown cheek. Her deep brown eyes had a doglike trustfulness in them, and a steadfastness withal such as makes the heroine. A girl of few moods, few caprices. Her work was always beautifully, conscientiously finished. She always loved it, always found in it the same quiet charm. There was no element of passion in it to set jarring the strings of futile endeavour. A fine sense of colour and gradation and subtle curve, a supreme delicacy of touch—that was her sole artistic stock in trade, and she never sought to stray beyond the limits imposed. She had had a little picture accepted at the Academy, hung in a far, far corner—a bunch of Maréchal Niel roses, full-blown, in a Venetian glass vase of exquisitely veined transparencies—a perfect little picture, sweet and pure, like herself.

It was a cold March day. The sun shone cheerfully through the drawn white blinds of the studio skylight, but an east wind blowing outside came in through the cracks and defied the blaze of the fire in the stove.

"You are quite blue with cold," said Winifred, laying down mahl-stick and palette. "Here, put on this wrap. Why don't you take more care of yourself?"

"I never thought of it," said Clytie, shivering a little and accepting contentedly the wrap and a caress. "I was sketching out quite a history of that boy who has just left."

Winifred drew a stool to Clytie's chair near the fire and took up her position upon it—a favourite one with her, as she could have both the moral solace of sitting at Clytie's feet, and the physical comfort of resting her head in Clytie's lap.

"I hope he won't bring all kinds of horrible people into the house—burglars, you know, like Oliver Twist," she added vaguely.

"I suppose it is rather rash picking up a model out of the streets. But he is just the boy I wanted to give character to the group. I was going to paint in one out of my own head."

"I don't know how you get all those street types out of your head, Clytie. I wish I could do it."

"I would like to see you try, you silly child," said Clytie, laughing. "Your street arabs would look like stray Cupids hastily huddled up in old clothes by a shocked and modest policeman!"

"I did not mean that; you know I didn't. What I meant was—I wish I could paint without models. I don't think I could paint a common flat leaf without having it before me. As for painting that "—and she pointed to a basket standing by her easel, overflowing with anemones, snowdrops, and violets obtained that morning by Mr. Gurkins from Covent Garden—"without a copy, I might just as soon think of flying."

"You are an artist, Winnie, and love your art for its own sake. I am not quite so sure that I do, now. To have to finish all the thousand little convolutions of those bells would drive me raving mad. I should like to have a ghost as sculptors do, only mine would do the finishing and put in all the nuisance of detail. That's why I can get on without models. It saves time. I can bring home a face with me from the streets, and I can paint it in rapidly, and then I am done. I suppose I oughtn't to be, but Burrowes seems satisfied. He says he has got quite a 'line' in my pictures—the correct ones—and is thinking of raising the price. I am sure that man has been a linen-draper."

"If you could remember the boy's face why do you bring him here?" asked Winifred. "I only want to know why you want him so particularly, dear," she added, raising her chin and looking upwards at Clytie.

The boy had been ragged and uncared-for, not exactly a street urchin, but on a vague borderland of respectability, between the newspaper arab and the errand boy. —a hybrid with the vices of many strains.

"Do you really want to know, Winnie?" said Clytie. "Perhaps you'll be shocked. However, you'll have to know sooner or later : I am going to make a picture of him on my own account, just a little bit more fantastic than he is, and call him a—an—oh, dear! what shall I call him?"

"An elf?"

"Good gracious, no. What have I to do with elves and fairies and that sort of thing? He is the son of Cophetua—supposing the king had not married the beggar maid."

"Then why not the son of any other king?"

"Why not, indeed?" said Clytie drily. "Or of any other beggar maid?"

"Oh!" said Winifred, looking into the fire.

And then after a pause :

"What makes you think that?"

"Did you see his mother? I did. Such a stupid-looking, red-faced woman. I think she said she was a charwoman by profession. There are generations of drudgery in her face, whereas in Jack's there is vigour and intelligence—something so different ; he must have some better strain of blood in him than she and a husband of her class can have given him. Don't you think so, dear ?"

"He's a very pretty boy," replied Winifred, "but, oh, he is so dirty and "—with a shudder—"so animal."

"Well, he fascinates me," said Clytie meditatively. "I am going to paint one of my wildest pictures—all for my own self—and a bit for you if you like, Winnie."

Winnie accepted this tribute of affection with a little flush of pleasure, although Clytie's "own" pictures seldom gave her unqualified æsthetic delight, and turned her face towards Clytie, who laughed in her frank way.

"Don't look at me with those great eyes of yours, child ! You make me angry for you. They are just the sort of eyes that make women miserable. You must not trust in people like that, believe me."

"I trust them when they are good like you, dear."

"Oh, but you mustn't. Don't you know I am the wickedest girl going—always thinking of the most dreadful things ? Look at the wall. How can you love anybody that can do these silly things?"

She pointed to a series of grotesque charcoal caricatures on the studio wall. She had been dissatisfied a day or two back with a picture she had been engaged on for a month, and in a fit of wilfulness had daubed it out and then proceeded to make a cruel, fantastic travesty of it on the wall.

"You wanted your tea, dear, just as you do now," replied Winifred.

This tea hour was Winifred's great delight. At home, on account of the children, they had to sit round the dining table and butter their own thick slices of bread and drink out of substantial breakfast cups. In the studio the girls had provided a dainty little afternoon tea equipage, and Mrs. Gurkins always cut thin bread and butter from a fancy loaf. Generally it was Winifred who poured out the tea, but to-day Clytie busied herself with the cups, thus making some slight amends, perhaps, for having shocked Winifred. Women are full of these odd feminine impulses, and other women understand them. Men don't.

They sat talking, as they usually did, over their tea,

and long afterwards, until it was time for Winifred to go home. As they were taking leave of each other on the landing a man sprang up the stairs, checked himself, and raised a slouch hat as he passed them and vanished up the next flight. He was a fresh-faced man, with a brown and tawny beard ; tawny ends, too, to his moustaches ; bright gray eyes flashing humourously as he passed the girls. His dress was careless, loose and unfashionable, yet it was marked with a certain individuality.

"Who is that ?" Winifred whispered when the last foot of the ascending figure had disappeared.

" That's another protest," said Clytie—"a better one. He has the courage of his convictions."

" What do you mean, Clytie ? "

" Well, can't you recognise a protest when you see one ? "

" Oh, Clytie, don't tease and puzzle me," cried Winifred, giving her friend's arm a little shake. " Do you know him ? "

" Of course not. How should I ? But Mrs. Gurkins was telling me about him only this morning. His name is Kent. He seems to frighten the life out of her, and therefore I say he is a protest. Now you know, so run away home."

When Winifred had reached the street door Clytie leaned over the banisters and called after her.

"Winnie ! I must have been in a sweet temper this afternoon."

" Of course, dear. Why do you say so ? "

" Because you have left your basket of anemones for me to take care of ! "

CHAPTER IV.

When Winifred had gone Clytie took an omnibus to
Cheyne Walk, where some friends of hers lived, and
after her visit returned to her solitary dinner. It argued
some strength of mind in Clytie that she did not give
way, as many lonely women do, to a distaste for ordinary food, and a corresponding craving for the miscellaneous and not over wholesome meal denominated
high tea. She had not reached the stage of feminine depression and sense of helplessness when inchoate banquet-
ing on bread and butter and penny buns seems to bring
cheerless solace. Her temperament seemed almost virile
in its vigour, and although she had her sex's antipathy
to gastronomy, she nevertheless found it reasonable that
she should be provided with a decently served dinner.
Besides, Mrs. Gurkins, who was professionally interested
in food stuffs, held solid views on the subject. She
herself had a good appetite, and her little girl children
ate everything they could lay their little white teeth to ;
she did not believe in not being hungry. It was one
of her grievances that her other lodger, Mr. Kent upstairs, cooked his own victuals scramblingly, and would
not allow her to see that his wants were duly satisfied.
Accordingly she bestowed extra care upon Clytie.

After the cloth was removed Clytie continued the
book she had been reading during the meal, and at last
flung it aside. She rose and walked about the room,
somewhat restless. She felt lonely—vaguely desirous of
action, and yet idle. Was it a dumb premonition of
fate, this restlessness ? At any rate it led her to perform a trivial action which set in motion the currents of
her future life.

She sat down at her writing table that stood in the
recess between the fireplace and the light-curtained
window and lit a couple of candles, whose pretty red

paper shades threw a rosy glow around the corner of the room. It was only a simple note that she scribbled, hastily, boldly, as was her wont. Then she left the candles burning, and returned to her armchair by the fire and gave herself up to meditation.

The boy model she had engaged that morning interested' her powerfully. She shrank from an insistence upon the solution of the little problem she had offered to Winifred during the afternoon, hovering over and away from it. Her sense of type and personality was too acute not to be profoundly struck by the difference between his mother and himself. On the one hand was dulness, commonness, a coarse-fibred nature responsive to the stirrings of neither hope nor despair, a dull, uncomplaining drudge ; on the other hand a quick, fiery temperament, showing itself in flashing black eyes, delicate nostrils, wiry, curly brown hair—all made picturesque by unqualified dirt. And yet, despite this refinement of feature, there was cruelty, brutality even, written on the childish face. That might be the fault of his upbringing, thought Clytie. But his beauty—where did it come from ? She smiled as she thought of King Cophetua. It was the beggar maiden's grace that had won the king's heart, and grace was a quality that Jack's mother most distinctly lacked. Clytie felt dimly conscious of being on the verge of an appalling discovery. Her reading had been catholic enough, and her independent acquaintance with life sufficiently broad, to render the fact familiar to her that kings and beggar maidens if they fall in love with each other usually dispense with the ceremony of marriage. But then love pardons all—a formula in Clytie's new theory of social statics, perhaps wisely not accepted in Durdleham—and all the sorrow in lawlessness that had come within Clytie's small experience had been in her eyes sanctified by love. Yet who could have loved this woman ? She was not more than three-and-thirty now—young enough to show that she had never possessed the mere attraction of comeliness. The boy remained, however, a living proof.

She thought of Winifred, and sighed a little. Why should she be forever craving after this strange hidden knowledge, after the taste of things bitter, when there

was so much sweetness in life ? The thought of Winifred's pure, gentle touch in flowers and delicate bloom of
fruit and calm, transparent glass came over her like a
rebuke. And then she smiled again, remembering how
Winifred had coaxed her once to try and paint a bunch
of roses, and how dismayed she had been at the egregious
failure. No ; the cobbler must not go beyond his last.

"I don't suppose I am very wicked after all," she said
to herself.

She rested her chin upon her hand and let her thoughts
wander idly, building up a romance for Jack. He was a
foundling, of noble parents, and Mrs. Burmester was only
his foster mother. Then she roused herself with a little
exclamation of disgust :

"What a perfectly Durdleham solution !"

The next moment, with an instinct common to folks
whether at Durdleham or London, she sprang from her
chair and cried :

"There's something burning ! "

The room in fact was full of thin smoke, and, as Clytie
rose, a snake of red flame ran up the curtains by the
writing-desk. She rushed to them, but as soon as she
had touched them, the folds being shaken out, the whole
burst into a blaze. She fled to the door about to scream
" Fire ! " at the top of her voice.

What happened next neither she nor John Kent could
afterwards exactly explain. He was on his way downstairs when the door was suddenly thrown open and a
stream of light burst on to the gloomy landing. Clytie
ran almost into his arms crying, " My room is on fire ! "
and then he was tearing down blazing, fiery curtains,
smothering them with rugs, and stamping out glowing
masses of drapery amid much smoke and confusion. It
did not take very long to extinguish the flames, but the
struggle while it lasted was fierce and exciting. Clytie
stood by watching him, her hand at her throat. It was
a new sensation to her to have a man acting for her in
an emergency. She had failed. She saw by the man's
energy, his fearless dealing with the blazing mass, his
strength, his violence, that she never could have succeeded. She admired him, was angry at it ; felt herself
a helpless woman, was angry at that too ; wished that

the danger had been a little greater, at which she was more angry than ever.

However, when the last traces of the fire were extinguished, and the man stood before her, somewhat out of breath, wiping his forehead, this little train of emotions came to an end. She gazed piteously at her curtainless windows and scorched wainscoting. He turned and opened the window, whence the damp, gusty wind whirled the smoke in billowing drifts about the room.

"There !" he said, with a breath of relief.

"Oh, how can I thank you ?" said Clytie.

"Don't," he replied with cheerful laconism. "I am glad I was handy—for your sake as well as my own. I live upstairs."

"I know; I have seen you come in and out. In fact, you passed us to-day. But still you have saved the whole house, and I thank you very, very much !"

"How did it all happen ?" he asked, removing for the first time his white slouch hat and disclosing a shock of brown curly hair.

"The candle-shade on the desk; do you see? It must have caught fire and toppled over on to the curtains. I was sitting here and forgot I had left the candles alight; and then I smelled something burning and saw the curtains in a blaze. Then I ran out to call somebody."

"That was very stupid," said Kent, pushing back the desk from the middle of the room, where he had wheeled it ; "by opening the door you made the things burn quicker. All you had to do was to drag down the curtains and cover them with the hearthrug. And then it is very silly to use paper candle-shades. They are no good, and they are always causing accidents. I hope you are not going to get any more."

The assured paternal air with which Kent delivered himself of this little speech did away with its apparent rudeness. Clytie, who at first looked rather resentfully at her rebuker, laughed.

They bent down together to restore order among the singed rugs. Beneath them was Kent's waterproof, on to which he had thrown the blazing curtains. It was very badly burned and of course rendered useless.

" It is utterly ruined ! " exclaimed Clytie, examining the holes with a helpless expression of regret on her face.

And then her eyes suddenly fell upon a great ugly red splash upon his hand. He withdrew it hastily, but she caught the sleeve of his coat. The stuff came away between her fingers.

" You have burned yourself horribly. Oh, what can I do ? "

" It's nothing," said Kent. " It doesn't hurt. I'll go and put something on it. Please don't trouble. Good-night."

He moved towards the door, with his hat and burned waterproof in his hand. But Clytie could not let him leave in this way. The woman in her was moved.

" Oh, please don't go until I have seen what harm you have got. I should feel so unhappy about it. I may be able to dress it for you—until you can see a doctor."

She spoke so sincerely, so frankly, and looked at him with such genuine concern, that he surrendered with a good grace. He came forward to the table where the big lamp was burning and put out his arm for her inspection. It was really injured, and was beginning to be exceedingly painful.

" What can I do for it ? " she asked rather helplessly.

" Oh, some olive oil and a bit of rag will be the best."

Clytie produced some cotton wool and some oil from a cruet in the sideboard and then sought after some linen to bandage with. Kent noticed that she did not ask him for his handkerchief, nor did she use her own, but went rather impulsively to a workbasket and tore off a strip of soft material that was lying on the top. It was very expensive stuff, and the whole piece of work of which it was to form a part was spoiled. It was characteristic of her. Another woman would have remembered where she had stored some odds and ends of old linen.

Kent watched her curiously as she was bending over his hand. He had often seen her before, but his life went on so far outside the sphere of women that he had scarcely given her a thought as he had passed her by. He had never even inquired her name. From the mere fact of her renting the studio it had come involuntarily to his knowledge that she followed pursuits more or less artistic ; but his curiosity had never been aroused. Now that he had been suddenly thrown into close contact with her he was interested. He smiled at himself for the unwonted pleasure he found in watching the lights dancing through her hair, the brows contracted ever so little in the absorption of her occupation, the long nervous fingers, set on the broad palm, deftly arranging the cotton wool, the scrap of old lace at her throat and wrists. She was pretty, striking, to look upon, but he had not formed a very high impression of her otherwise. It was just the sort of thing a woman would do, to run out of the room when it was on fire, to give up thinking for herself in any emergency and trust blindly in Providence— or a man. It is a strange thing that those men who see least of women know most concerning them.

As she raised her head after pinning the bandage she caught the expression of amusement on his face. He was quick to note the little shadow of resentment that passed over hers.

"I was thinking what a mess I should have made of it by myself," he said with a tact that surprised him. "Thank you very much."

"It was the least I could do," replied Clytie. "I feel so guilty about it all—and your poor waterproof too."

"It's a very old one," he replied good-humouredly, holding the garment out for inspection. "My friends will be delighted. They have threatened to cut me in the streets if they saw me in it again. So you see you have secured my friendship for me. And I shall get on much better with an umbrella to-night."

"But you're surely not going out to-night !" cried Clytie, moving to the window and shutting it, as if he were intending to escape through it. "It is pouring wet, and you would catch cold in your hand—it would get inflamed, or something dreadful. It is stupid of people not to take care of themselves. It's hurting fearfully, isn't it ? Tell me."

She looked at him so frankly, her head thrown back a little, and spoke with such a faint touch of imperiousness in her voice, that Kent checked his impulse of retreat.

"Of course it hurts. But I don't mind. If one

minded all the little pains of this life, one would have no
time for anything else.   Besides, I am used to rough it a
bit.   It is my own choice, more or less, and I like it."
. Clytie remembered the strange stories Mrs. Gurkins
had told her about Kent's way of life.   She had listened
to them with idle interest, never imagining that Kent and
herself would ever become acquainted.   Now that he
alluded to his habits she felt bound to confess her share
in the gossip, which she did somewhat rebelliously, checking certain more timorous promptings of silence.

"So you see I know all about you," she said in conclusion.   "When people are eccentric they become, as it
were, public characters.   Now if you were to talk to
Mrs. Gurkins——"

"Heavens forbid!" cried Kent with much warmth.
"I was fleeing from her this afternoon when I nearly
knocked you down."

"Why?" asked Clytie, laughing.

"I don't know—instinct, I suppose.   Perhaps I have
been wrong.   Otherwise I might have known something
more of you.   It's a bad compliment, I am aware, but I
have been here a whole year and I have never seen or
heard your name.   Might I know whom I have had the
pleasure of assisting?   I did not in the least care before,
but now it is different."

There was an honesty and directness in his voice that
pleased Clytie.   She felt glad he had asked her.   There
is a touch of susceptible vanity even in the most emancipated of women.

"My name is Davenant, and I am by way of being an
artist—that is to say, I gain my living by it."

Her eyes wandered unconsciously round the room
hung with many of her half-finished sketches.   Kent
followed her glance, and then crossed to the wall and
examined one or two of the pictures.

"Are these yours?" he asked, turning round quickly.

They were charcoal sketches of street scenes, direct
and daring.   Kent received Clytie's nod of assent, and
glanced at the pictures and then at her again, as if trying
to reconcile the two.

"Is all your work of this kind?"

"Mostly.   Sometimes I draw it milder," she added,

with a smile, "when definite orders come in ; but I feel more at home with this sort of thing."

Kent returned to the centre of the room, where he had been standing before.

"I am not an artist myself," he said, "but I have been brought up in an atmosphere of art and I love it. My father was Rupert Kent, painter-etcher ; he did that little thing over your mantelpiece."

"Isn't it a perfect little piece of work?" said Clytie, looking round at it. "I am very fond of it."

"So was my father. Well, you see, I am not a Philistine in art matters, and when I say your work interests me I mean it. I should like to look at some more of it. Where is it to be found?"

"You can come any time to my studio if you like. It is my place of business, you know, and perhaps you may get me some orders. Art is terribly mercenary in these days."

"I want to see the things you do for yourself," said Kent bluntly, ignoring the little hedge wherewith she had fenced her invitation. "It will be very kind of you to let me come."

Clytie held out her hand to him as he bade her good-night and thanked him for his help.

"And now that we know each other," she said, "I hope—I hope you won't cut me on the stairs."

When he had gone Clytie looked ruefully at the damage that had been done. Her pretty inside curtains were destroyed ; the heavy outer ones burned into great charred holes. The carpet and hearthrug were badly scorched, and the side of her writing-table warped and blistered. As she gazed at the wreck she went over the little scene in her mind. Why had she stood still, leaving the whole of the work to Kent? What must he have thought of her?

If he had been any ordinary man of her acquaintance she would have been still angry with herself for her helplessness, and her anger would have reflected itself on him. But now she put the question to herself more through curiosity than irritation. There was a simplicity about the man that attracted her. His words had been blunt, almost rude sometimes, but his voice had been kind, his manner protective, straightforward. She had signally marked her approbation for him by asking him to visit her studio, a privilege she only accorded to a few tried and very sympathetic men friends. Kent interested her, and yet she had not the slightest desire to transfer her impression of him to canvas.

The next morning she gave Winifred an account of the last evening's incidents, confessing her own impressions in her wilful, half-cynical way. Her friend listened meekly, wondering at her earnestness. The curtains had caught fire, a gentleman had come opportunely to her aid, had burned his hand, which she had tended in common courtesy. It was all so very natural. As for feeling humiliated at being helped by a man, what are women put in the world for except to yield and give way before men ?

But Winifred did not say this to Clytie.

CHAPTER V

John Kent, antiquarian, scientist, Bohemian, and assistant curator in the British Museum, dwelt in the attics, far above the limit of the stair carpet. By the time you had reached them you had lost all sound of the thoroughfare below, and even when you looked out of the windows all sense of locality was lost. Nothing could be seen but roofs and chimney-pots, except on very clear days, when, through an accidental vista of streets, the tops of the trees in Chelsea Hospital were dimly visible. But in Kent's rooms no one cared to look out of window. In the first place, it was difficult of access, and in the second, the extraordinary appearance of the apartment riveted one's attention entirely to things within.

On the floor was neither carpet nor rug. The place of a fender was supplied by three large iron tripods, waifs from some dismantled chemical laboratory, which, when they were not otherwise engaged as footstools, served to support a kettle, a saucepan, and a glue-pot. All around the walls, with just one space for the door, ran a broad deal dresser that did duty for several tables, and below it, here and there, were cunningly contrived cupboards. Above, every inch of wall was covered : one side completely with books, the others with pictures, mostly old engravings, little masters such as Cranach and Behm, a frame of perfect little Aldegravers, a Prince Rupert mezzo, two Woolmers with their exquisite wavy lines, Bewicks, and a magnificent modern Jacquemart etching of a Sèvres vase. The intermediate spaces were filled up with a heterogeneous assortment of curios. The dresser-table was likewise laden with books, coin cases, scientific specimens, strange weapons, old axe-heads, Japanese sword hilts cunningly carved, newspapers, journals, pamphlets, and papers innumerable. There were only two fairly clear spaces around the whole extent : one where Kent worked, and another where he took such meals as he had in his lodgings. Save for one solitary leather writing-chair, the centre of the large room was absolutely empty ; but in a corner, on the floor, were piled up a set of canvas deck-chairs which Kent brought out and opened whenever he had visitors.

All the fixtures in the room he had made with his own hands. Manual labour was a delight to him. He also cooked his own food and cleaned out the room. The latter operation consisted in raking out the ashes from his grate and laying the fire afresh. No peace-destroying woman disturbed the precincts with broom and duster. When the dust grew so thick that it interfered with his breathing and clouded the lens of his microscope he went round with an old towel flicking and flapping with great energy, and then he watered the floor out of an old bronchitis-kettle.

Kent was a happy man. He had convictions, enthusiasms ; manifold interests in life for his lighter moments, one great absorbing work for his serious hours. His slender income sufficed amply for all his wants, and there was always a margin over for the purchase of an occasional rare edition or print or curio. Whenever his salary was increased that margin was greater. His mode of life never changed, for the simple reason that he considered it to be the most delightful one possible. Purple, fine linen, and sumptuous fare had no charms for him. It was always with much groaning of spirit that he put on dress clothes when he went out into the world. He cared not for the high places in the synagogues. Provided he had not to wait outside the doors, the pit of a theatre was a place as desirable as the stalls.

In his friends too he was happy—a few men different from himself and from each other—and to these he clung loyally. But the conditions of his life removed him from feminine influences. Beyond those girls in his immediate family circle, whom he called by their Christian names and treated with an old-fashioned, brotherly protection, scolding them when they did foolish things, such as wearing light shoes in wet weather, performing little services for them when they behaved themselves nicely, he never troubled his head about womankind.

On the night when Clytie's curtains caught fire he had been on his way to visit a coterie of three bachelor friends who shared a house in South Kensington. They were accustomed to his nocturnal appearances, and the worse the night and the later it grew the more likely was Kent to present himself at the sitting-room door, a dripping, ruddy apparition, his cheeks and beard glistening with raindrops. And then he would throw off his mackintosh, call for slippers, and join the circle round the fire. The thoughts of the dreary tramp home between two and three never seemed to dismay him. Cheerlessness of environment in no way affected his happiness.

They formed the chief part of his social life, these three friends, tried by the changes in fibre, tastes, affinities, that over half a score of years effect. There was Fairfax, the doctor, ruddy, full-blooded, magnetic with health and vitality, whose brass plate shone huge on the front door, inviting confidence ; Greene, the solicitor, shrewd, hard-headed, a speaker of few words ; and Wither, the civil servant, the little gnomelike man, full of strange sayings, whimsical, non-moral, a man of boyish, elfin beauty, trusted by men, petted by women. Of the three Kent loved Wither best. Wither saw deeper into the world's mysteries than he, but his own sturdy honest sense had kept the other from many an abyss.

After bidding Clytie good-night, Kent stood irresolute on the landing. Should he wrap the remains of his waterproof around him, and still go whither his truest happiness had hitherto always led him ? Considerations of the chill, sleeting night and the throbbing pain in his hand went for nothing in his decision. The girl who had tended the burn had almost besought him not to go out. To disregard her would be an act of discourtesy. Thus thought honest Kent as he turned on his heel and slowly mounted the stair. But his evening had been spoiled, he told his briarwood pipe, with a consoling sense of martyrdom, and the cause thereof was feminine.

"It is just the silly sort of thing that Agatha would do," he said to himself.

Agatha was his sister, whom he pitied intensely for

being a woman. He thought of Clytie's pictures, the signs of virility in them, and he began to pity Clytie too. Yet there was a difference of kind in his sentiments. He pitied his sister for being constrained to ambitionlessness and futility ; he was sorry for the handicap of sex to Clytie's ambitions.

In some such attitude of mind towards her he knocked at the studio door the following afternoon. It is true that a warning throb of the bourgeois in him, that still sometimes mutely guided the Bohemian along certain tracks, had made him consider for a vague moment the correctness of calling so immediately upon Clytie ; but the directness and simplicity of his nature disregarded it. It was only natural that Clytie should like to know how his burned hand was faring.

He found the girls busily painting, Winifred at the side, with her basket of flowers near her, Clytie standing at her easel, in the middle of the room, her back to the door, her face turned half round to see who would enter in response to her call.

On the floor by the fireside sprawled Jack, the model, eating an orange. His face was still dirty, his curly hair matted. Winifred had pathetically besought Clytie to have him washed. Why should his poor little face be all over dirt ?

"Because it could not exist without it," Clytie had answered. "It was so before he was born."

Winifred had given her one of her appealing looks from swimming brown eyes, and Clytie, remorseful, had run impulsively up and caressed and kissed her. But she had not washed Jack's face. He scrambled to his feet and looked defiantly, like a young animal, at Kent when he entered.

The ground-glass roof, the white walls scored over with Clytie's fantasies, and the bright red curtain at the back behind the stove gave a singular setting to the picture.

Clytie's eyes brightened. She threw a cloth over the picture she was engaged on.

"How good of you to come—and the hand ?"

"A trifle. It will be quite well in a few days; I thought you would not mind my coming to tell you how your doctoring had succeeded. I am keeping it in a sling—so ; otherwise I should be always trying to use it. You are none the worse, Miss Davenant ? "

" I ? Why should I ? "

" Oh, nerves, shock, headache—and all that. My mother, I know, would have been upset for a week."

Clytie laughed ; a gay little laugh. She pierced through the words to the simplicity that lay behind them.

" I have never cultivated nerves, Mr. Kent. They sadly interfere with practical life. How do you think Miss Marchpane and I would get on with this sort of thing "—and she nodded towards Jack—" if we had nerves ? Winifred, this is Mr. Kent, who put out my fire last night. Miss Marchpane and I share the studio together, you know."

" You work on very different lines," said Kent after a while, leaning back in his chair so as to catch a glimpse of Winifred's tiny canvas. " What a strange thing temperament is ! I suppose neither of you does land-scape."

" Oh, yes, Winifred. Dainty little bits of meadow and stream. I can't; I always want to put legs and arms to my trees, and make the branches twist and writhe about, like Gustave Doré in the ' Wandering Jew.' "

" You scarcely look like a painter of the weird," said Kent.

" You think I have not enough strength of imagina-tion ? "

" You have too much strength of mind," returned Kent judiciously. " You hanker too much after the real. I can only judge," he hastily added by way of explana-tion, " by what I can see of your work around me."

" You will get into difficulties," said Clytie, laughing. " One moment you accuse me of nerves, and the next of strong-mindedness. Which is right, Winnie ? "

" I should be telling too much or too little if I were to say," replied Winifred. " Mr. Kent will have to judge for himself. We had better show him something to go by."

They turned to an exhibition of Clytie's paintings ; small stacks of canvases were ranged on the floor, along the walls ; here and there one hanging or standing on a table or on an easel. Clytie stood by in her nonchalant, professional way, giving a word or two of necessary explanation as Winifred placed them one by one upon an easel for Kent's inspection. Painters, sculptors, musicians and actors have a moral advantage over poets and novelists, in that they are not ashamed of their work. An artist shows you his picture frankly and hopes you will like it ; if a poet reads you a sonnet, he has an all-devouring dread lest you may deem him a prig. And the strange part of it is that you do ; whereas you think the painter rather a good fellow. A little problem in sociological æsthetics.

As Kent looked at the pictures he lost his sense of Clytie's Agatha-like behaviour of the previous evening. He forgot even to pity her. He expressed genuine admiration for her work, interspersing his remarks with outspoken criticism which Clytie recognised as deeper than that of the mere virtuoso. It was qualified, too, by the supreme attribute of simple common sense. He judged the pictures on their merits ; he judged Clytie as a woman of genius, strong mind, out of the ordinary run of women. The inner promptings and cravings that had thus found artistic expression it was beyond his philosophy to suspect. Nor did Clytie think of enlightening him.

"I like your realism," he said. "It is straightforward. There's always a great danger of this sort of thing degenerating into morbidness. But if you can keep it true, it's healthy ; it means sober, honest work, and not an intermittent fever. I see you work off your superfluous energy on the walls."

"Oh, I forgot them," cried Clytie somewhat shamefacedly. "You must not look at them, please. They are not part of the show. Miss Marchpane gets tired of flowers and peach-bloom, and sometimes——"

"Clytie !" cried Winifred reproachfully.

Clytie laughed ; and Kent with her. The light jest brought them nearer together.

"No ; I do that when I feel wicked," said Clytie. "I paint a nice, correct little picture for the nice, correct people who are going to buy it, and then I grow angry with them and feel I should like to shock them, take the stiffening out of them, reduce them to elemental bits of humanity. Look at this group of street urchins. I am doing that on order for my dealer. Here is Jack—look at him now staring into the stove with the unreasoning content of a young dog. Doesn't he seem nice and conventional in the picture? You can hear the young lady of the house saying to the curate, 'Aren't these little street children too delightful?' Now if they were shown the real Jack, it would give them to think, as the French say—and they hate doing that. This is *my* idea of the real Jack."

She whisked the cloth off the easel and showed Kent the charcoal *ébauche* of her own particular study of the urchin.

She had worked rapidly that day, with the feverishness that Kent deprecated. Whether she would convert the sketch into a finished picture she did not know. She had desired to fix the haunting impression of Jack's possible history.

Kent was somewhat startled by the suddenness of the presentation. There was the boy, refined, delicate in feature, great-eyed, curly-haired, but repulsive with cruelty and animalism ; in a degraded attitude, head bent forward, knees bent, lips parted in a sneer.

"He does not look like that now," said Kent, comparing the original with the copy.

"Wait," said Clytie. Then imperiously to the urchin : "Jack, what are you thinking of ? "

He turned, looked up at her shiftingly.

"Dunno."

"Weren't you thinking of the nice little story of the cat you told me this morning ? "

No answer.

"It's about a stray cat that came into his mother's house half dead, you know, and this boy was so kind to it—like a dear little girl——"

"Yer lie ! " cried the boy, starting to his feet. "Oi told yer Oi killed 'er. I lammed her bloomin' 'ed open with a chopper. I 'ates cats ! "

"*Voilà !* " said Clytie. "That's the real Jack. That's the Jack I'd like to startle Peckham Rye with."

And then turning to the boy :

"That will do for to-day, Jack. Here's your shilling ; give it to your mother."

"Shan't," said Jack.

"Oh, but you must," said Winifred ; "look how hard your poor mother has to work to keep you, Jack."

"She's bloomin' well got ter," said Jack. "I aint going to give 'er no money. She never gives me none."

"But your mother will beat you," said Clytie.

"Wot do I care ?"

"And your father, you sweet boy ?" asked Kent.

"Aint got none."

"Never had one ?" continued Kent.

"No ; mother aint that sort. Blamed glad."

"Here, you'd better run away," said Clytie hurriedly. "Keep your shilling and make yourself as ill as you like with it. Come the day after to-morrow—Friday. Can you remember ? It's unnecessary to request you not to wash between then and now. Go on. Good-bye. Out you get."

The boy took up the remains of his cap and went, with an air of relief, out of the room.

"What a little brute !" said Kent. "Why don't you try to reform him—make him human ?"

"He is human," cried Clytie with some warmth. "That's why I cultivate him. Delightfully human ! Refreshing ! As for reforming him "—with a shrug of her shoulders—"I am not a Sunday-school teacher. I have nothing to do with the submerged tenth ; let the good respectable folks who have submerged them raise them with their polite and respectable hands. I am an artist—a student of life—what you will. Each one to his trade. Perhaps when I have got what I want out of Jack it may amuse me to show him the desirability of not 'lamming cats' bloomin' 'eds open with a chopper.' I don't know—I'm not altogether devoid of moral sense. Winifred's tender heart may be touched, and between the two of us we may turn him out a mild-eyed journey-man carpenter, a member of the Y. M. C. A., a model of all the virtues. But I very much doubt it. He has vice in his blood. But perhaps I am wounding some of your susceptibilities, Mr. Kent ? You may be a social reformer, and keener than I on these matters. If so, pardon me. We artists are privileged, you know, to view life from our own standpoint."

Kent threw up his hand and dropped it—a little gesture of deprecation. He, too, had large views on humanity and its needs. He was even then sacrificing comfort, fame, ease, such as other men understand them, so as to serve it. But it was according to his own capabilities. It was a darling scientific work, that on the most modest computation would take him twenty years to complete—an unthankful task ; his name to be remembered with reverential gratitude by some half dozen workers, to perish unheard of by the remaining millions of mankind. But these half dozen would use the result of his life's energies to the advancement of human prosperity, and that thought glowed within Kent's heart. Still a man has not time for all things. He honestly disclaimed pretensions to being a social reformer. He was also artistically sympathetic enough to appreciate Clytie's attitude as regards Jack. He was nearer to her in spirit than Winifred, who was pained at Clytie's speech. She would have cried out with the sharpness of the pain had it not been for Kent's presence. And she would have been revolted at the cynical callousness had it not been for the blind adoration with which she bowed before Clytie. Whatever Clytie did was right, she told herself, and she was a poor little body who could not understand these things. But her heart bled for Jack, and she wondered why Clytie's did not bleed also.

"I spoke idly," said Kent. "I am sorry. If all artists set about reforming their models, their hands would be too full for art. But he is a little brute all the same, and, as you say, Peckham Rye would be startled by him. But why do you want to shock Philistia ? "

" Would *you* like to live in it, be of it, and worship at comfortably timed intervals in its correctly appointed temple of Dagon ?"

" No," laughed Kent. " They wouldn't have me in it. I think they could stand less of me than I of them. They are God's creatures after all, you know. If you prick them, they bleed—and so forth. If they admire your little pictures, which I too admire vastly, there must be some saving grace in the Philistines."

Clytie shrugged her shoulders.

"But why should I be obliged to paint in their way, and not in my way? That is what irritates me."

"Have you tried them with your way, as you call it?"

Even Winifred could scarcely forbear flashing at Clytie a little smile of tender malice.

"God bless my soul!" she whispered softly, and the two broke into unconstrained laughter.

"Winifred is quoting, Mr. Kent. It was an elderly gentleman, stout, florid, lots of watch-chain—one of my patrons. He had bought one of my pictures at the dealer's, and came for another. Burrowes showed him one of my own own things. Winifred and I happened to be at the back of the shop at the time. The old gentleman put on his spectacles, looked at the picture, gave such a jump, held it in the light, and then gasped out : 'God bless my soul, Burrowes, has the young woman taken to drink?'"

"What did you do?"

"I don't know what I should have done if Winnie had not held me back. As it was, Burrowes whispered to him that the artist was overhearing the conversation. 'Well, it will do her good,' says the old gentleman, and he went out storming. Then Burrowes came to me and complained that I had lost him a customer. He has the soul of a pork-butcher, that man!"

Then turning to Kent, her cheeks still flushed with anecdotal animation:

"That's how it is, you see!"

"Well," said Kent, "perhaps you have reason to owe Philistia a grudge. I haven't. If it shuts its respectable doors on me, I shrug my shoulders and set up my wigwam outside, where I can smoke my pipe in peace. It is better not to care for the world—or anything, for that matter, if one has work to do. One's keenness on life ought to leave one no time for hating one's fellow-creatures."

Winifred looked at Clytie, expecting to see her resent the implied rebuke. But Clytie only laughed softly to herself, leaning back in her chair, looking at her finger tips.

"You are by way of being a tonic, Mr. Kent," she said, without looking at him.

Kent was disconcerted, could not find a reply. He stroked his tawny beard and moustache with his free hand, and looked at her somewhat puzzled. He had uttered his own robust faith, and she had seized a personal reference with which she appeared not displeased.

At last he said :

"I don't mean to imply that you are cynical, Miss Davenant. But you are a little vindictive. I, too, often think of that passage in 'Sartor Resartus' where Carlyle strips the clothes off the courtiers at St. James's and leaves them bare, with their bowings and scrapings —do you remember? Well, it would be a very good thing for them. You would come down to pure humanity and find it really a very lovable, great-hearted thing after all."

"Then, for goodness' sake, let us begin to strip the clothes off them at once !" cried Clytie, changing her attitude, with her usual suddenness. "That's what I want to do. I want real men, real women ; that's why I take human nature in the rough "—making a comprehensive sweep with her hand round the studio. "The clothes these things wear don't matter ; you can see the passions working through the rents and tears."

"Umph !" said Kent. "You may see something that will frighten you one of these days. There's plenty of good in humanity, but there's plenty of bad. You had better get hold of what is good first. It will give you a foundation."

Shortly afterwards Kent took his leave. He had paid a longer visit than he had anticipated. He found himself pitying Clytie again upon new, less definable grounds. He was much struck by her work, her frankness, her independence. She was a novelty to him, different from the few other women he knew. She seemed to have everything calculated to make a woman happy and her life full, and yet he was sorry for her. Why, he could not tell.

He went up to his attics, and prepared to spend his usual working evening. Afterwards, towards half-past eleven, he might walk across to South Kensington. He took from one of the cupboards beneath the dresser-table plates, knife and fork, a half-finished tin of sardines, bread and butter. This, together with a bottle of beer, formed his frugal evening meal. His midday dinner he took at an Italian restaurant near the Museum. He ate standing, walking about his room between the mouthfuls, selecting the books he would require for his work, and pausing now and then over an idly opened volume. His meal finished, he collected the soiled utensils and stacked them on the landing outside his door for Mrs. Gurkins to remove, wash, and return to the same place in the morning. Then he lit his pipe, and settled down to his long evening's work.

Thoughts of burned hand, new-found friends, occupied him not. The crisp whisk of the leaves of his reference-books, the rapid whirr of his quill pen, the occasional bubble of his green-shaded reading-lamp, were the only signs of external life of which he was conscious. The rest of the bare-floored room, with its oddly covered walls, was deep in shadow. But the light shone in a circle upon the pile of books and papers on which he was engaged, and lit up strongly his honest, resolute face, with its intent gray eyes and its kindly mouth half hidden in the moustache and beard. Kent was happy. The darling work, that served him as mistress, religion, ambition—over which he had never known a heartache—held him in its enchantment. And the wet slips grew in number around him.

CHAPTER VI

"You are going to spend a dismal evening, my dear," said Mrs. Farquharson, with a sigh.

They were sitting on either side of the drawing-room fire, awaiting dinner guests.

"Why?" asked Clytie.

"Oh, the crowd that's coming—fossilised London, with figures like amphoras and faces like old coins. It's the principle of assimilation, I suppose. And they'll talk as if there were nothing new under the sun."

"There isn't much."

"Isn't there? Wait till you have lived a little longer. At any rate there are murders and divorces and new pictures and the latter end of the nineteenth century. Why people choose to live a couple of thousand years before their time I can't make out. You'll see. They'll all look as if they had been excavated—except George, and he looks as if they had never taken the trouble to bury him. Thank goodness, they have all got weak digestions and don't dine out much, or else we should have them here every week."

"But the wives are coming too," said Clytie by way of consolation.

"Poor things! They all look weary with many proof-sheets crammed with circumflexes over impossible letters, and wrong-headed pictures of birds and beasts. All archæologists are not like George, you know."

"But then no one is like George."

"That's a mercy," said Mrs. Farquharson settling herself with much comfort among the cushions of her chair. "Don't you get married, my dear; stay independent. Do you know, one of the beings is going to read a paper. Pity me."

"It seems as if I am to be pitied too," remarked Clytie.

"Ah! but you are young and can make fun out of them. I can't."

The occasion was a meeting of Mr. Farquharson's archæological set. The inner circle dined at each other's houses in turn once a month, and the outer circle came in later, for the "conversazione,"as Mrs. Farquharson called it, with a little shudder. A paper was usually read, followed by a discussion, from which the more flippant seceded and gossipped casually in odd corners. Clytie had never been to one of these strangely homogeneous reunions. The people she generally met at her friends' house were miscellaneous, and the talk danced about upon all subjects under heaven, wreathed in blue curls of cigarette smoke. Mrs. Farquharson had begged her to come and support her—"to strike a note of colour among the gray ruins." Clytie looked forward to the incongruous formalism of the evening with an anticipation of amusement.

She hinted as much to Mr. Farquharson when he came into the drawing-room. He laughed, bowed his long, ungainly figure, hoped that Miss Davenant had come to be instructed. Professor Petherick was to read a paper on an aureus of Geta of the type Cohen No. 11,—Clytie and her hostess communed with each other dumbly,—and many rare coins were to be exhibited. He trusted that Miss Davenant would be appreciative and on her best behaviour. Numismatics was not a subject that lent itself to flippancy.

"My wife can turn the house into a bear-garden every Sunday evening, 'more shame to her, though she does sit and smile in her superior way. But twice a year I assert my individuality and this house becomes sober and respectable. So no cigarettes to-night, Miss Davenant. When I put on these dress-clothes I am rigid."

"You look very nice," said Clytie.

He looked down at himself complacently, accepting the flattery; such is man. He always insisted upon wearing very square-toed kid boots, a high buttoned waistcoat with a chain made of old coins banded across it, a deep velvet collar to his dress-coat, and a shirt-collar, with two long ends that served as a tie, beneath his beard.

"I like him better in his velvet jacket," said Mrs. Farquharson. "Go and put it on, George."

But George shook his head sadly. He must be properly attired to discuss an aureus of Geta.

The guests arrived, seven in number, and they went down to the dining-room. Clytie sat between Professor Petherick, a little rosy man with a bald head and gastronomic appreciation, and a young clergyman who had taken her in to dinner. She had been for so long a time outside Church influences that a strange little Durdleham qualm come over her. He looked stern, overworked, dreadfully in earnest, she thought, not likely to sympathise with the Thelemite joyousness of life of the house whose motto was, "*Fays ce que vouldras.*" He was the only bachelor among the guests. The six others, including the professor, consisted of three married couples, middle-aged, respectable. Mr. Vansittart was a great Egyptologist. It was of his wife, a faded, weary-looking woman, that Mrs. Farquharson had so pathetically spoken with reference to the correction of proof-sheets. Mrs. Petherick was literary, fond of lions. Her talk was a *catalogue raisonné* of her menagerie. Mr. Farquharson listened politely and went on with his dinner. The remaining couple were the Chowders, retired Anglo-Indians, who found only late in life an opportunity of gratifying their ruling passions—on her part an undisturbed warm bath of domesticity ; on his, archæological dilettanteism. She was florid and buxom ; he bronzed and shrivelled. Both talked on their pet subjects. The Rev. Victor Treherne was a keen numismatist. "A recognised authority," Farquharson had whispered to Clytie. "Will give Petherick beans if he goes wrong."

Clytie knew nothing of numismatics. She did not know the difference between a moidur and a bezant, nor did she seek enlightenment from her neighbour. She questioned him as to his environment—North London, a large parish, chiefly poor. The conversation languished, then it brightened up through common effort. Each had a King Charles the First's head to keep in the background, feeling it to be distasteful to the other. Treherne had left his parish behind, and had brought no other interests with him save those circling round the famous aureus, a matter of supreme indifference to Clytie, who, for her part, had been cautioned to act as the superior Ki-Pi-Yu, friend of Confucius, did on certain occasions—roll her principles up and keep them in her breast. Each, too, divined dimly the other's personality, and they talked eagerly, seeking to like and interest one another through a current of mutual antipathy.

The professor and Mrs. Farquharson were talking less unreservedly on the question of female disabilities. He had theories on the sacredness of woman's mission. Mrs. Farquharson's views were more materialistic. Her early training had disabused her of the oak and ivy illusion, which the professor still entertained.

"No, it's no use, professor," she said. "A man has got to go his way and a woman hers. If their ways lie together, so much the better—they can help each other ; if they lie apart, so much the worse. Besides, I cannot conceive anything more irritating to a man than to be followed all about by his wife—like a dog. No wonder some men beat their wives."

Treherne had caught the speech. He turned to Clytie.

"Do you believe that ?"

"Of course. Mrs. Farquharson and I are sworn sisters. We hold advanced views concerning ourselves. I hope you don't think we have a mission ! Have you ever thought how distressing it is to try to live up to a false ideal, and somebody else's into the bargain ?"

"We all have to live up to an ideal. This one may be false ; I don't know. At any rate it is a high one, and worth aiming at."

"That is Jesuitical. What is to become of a woman's self-respect when she knows all the time she is a humbug, although a sublime one ?"

"By seeking to inspire others with faith in her she will at length acquire faith in herself."

"Don't you think that's rather vicious ?"

"I don't know. The same principle obtains in my own calling. Many a man enters the Church who is not really fit for it. But the professional effort he has to make to raise others in most cases raises himself."

"That may be quite true," said Clytie, "but it does

not prove the principle to be right.   Besides, the cases are different.   You undertake, when you enter the Church, to do certain things.   Now when a woman enters the world she does not undertake to do anything, any more than a man does.   They both clamour to assert themselves as human beings.   They may go about it in different ways,—it is merely the difference of sex,— but their ultimate end is the same."

"And what is this?"

"To get as much out of life as possible."

"That's scarcely orthodox."

The accompanying smile was a touch of the curb on Clytie.   She paused.   There was an interval of dining. Then she turned to reply to a remark of the professor. Mrs. Farquharson, who hitherto had steered skilfully through the shoals of antiquity, was run aground by Colonel Chowder.   Clytie was astonished to hear her friend talking learnedly of coins and Latin inscriptions. She ran discursively over the points of George's collection, toning her speech with a light counterpoint of mockery, so that its echo should reach Clytie's ears. Mrs. Chowder bubbled domesticity over the Egyptologist; spoke of her sons, the difficulty of army examinations.   She was bent upon their getting into the service, also upon their marrying young.   The reconciliation of these incongruities was the problem offered for Mr. Vansittart's solution.

Clytie again turned to Mr. Treherne.

"Do you often come here?   I am almost of the house and I have never met you."

"Once before, on a similar occasion—almost the same circle.   A common hobby brings the most divergent people together."

"It is a pity you and I have not got one," said Clytie, flashing a malicious glance at him.

"Perhaps we have.   What do you mostly do?"

"Paint—for my living."

"An artist!   What is your line?"

"Anything human—they call it *genre*—street life— the very poor."

"The poor?   Then we have a common hobby after all!"

"Perhaps," replied Clytie. "But I am afraid we ride it in opposite directions."

"Do you know much of their lives—go among them?"

"Not much; I see them only externally, from an artist's point of view. I should like to see deeper."

A light burned for a moment in the young clergyman's gray eyes.

"Would you care for work among them?"

"As a student, perhaps; as a reformer, no!"

"One generally leads to the other."

"In that case I'll not run the risk," she replied laughing.

An hour later the drawing-room was filled with the evening guests, mostly men. Women archæologists are scarce. The sentiment with which they inwrap relics of the past harms the pure scientific spirit of inquiry. Thus Mr. Farquharson to Clytie, briefly explanative. She laughed, reminded him how lately in a sentimental mood he had accused women of lack of imagination; she reproached him for inconsistency.

"Inconsistency is a principle of the art of living," he replied epigrammatically, moving away.

The men stood in groups about the room chatting on personalities, examining the display of coin-cases arranged here and there upon the tables, each under the soothing light of a shaded lamp. The professor stood by himself on the hearthrug, hemming irritably, anxious to read his paper. The talk was subdued, attitudes formal, a contrast to the ordinary easy abandonment of that drawing-room. The men were of a different type, mostly elderly, sedate. Mrs. Farquharson rested for a moment from her exertions as hostess by Clytie's side.

"Now for a minute's peace. I wish the men would smoke, they all look so woebegone; but George says they mustn't. Now, then, my dear, I haven't seen you for ages, except for those five minutes before dinner; what have you been doing lately?"

"Nothing much—working. Oh! yes, I have, though. I have found a new chum."

"What is she like?"

"It isn't a she, it's a he."

" Where does he come from ? " asked Mrs. Farquhar-son, arching her eyebrows.

" From the skies, apparently : in the first case to put out a fire in my room—he lives over me in the attics——"

"Clytie ! You must be careful. Who is he ? What's his name ? "

" Caroline," said her husband's deep voice behind her chair, " I don't think you know Mr. Kent."

Clytie started round violently at the shock of the coincidence. Kent was standing by her side, looking odd, changed, a bit Philistine in his evening dress. He wore a glove over his burned hand.

They talked, explained their meeting. He had had a numismatic acquaintance with Mr. Farquharson for a long time past. Had received his invitation at the Museum, his private address not being known to his host. Clytie described her own privileged position in the house-hold, speaking frankly, vivaciously. She felt a little thrill of pleasure at seeing him there. He seemed, more than the other guests, in harmony with the traditions of the house. They had not time for much conversation, social exigencies separating them. Besides, a general buzz and a subsiding into chairs or restful attitudes sounded the warning that Professor Petherick was about to read his paper.

He described the coin that had come into his posses-sion,—previously it had been passed round for the inspection of the guests,—claiming it to be a finer speci-men than the one in the Caylus collection. The figure of Castor beside his horse, without the pileus, on the reverse, he argued was a portrait of the unfortunate young co-emperor. The legend on the obverse pro-claimed that it was a coin of Geta. He took this as the text for a learned disquisition upon the aureus, tracing its origin, the variations in its weight, to the time of Justinian, who fixed it as a limit stake for a throw of the dice. He quoted Pitiscus, Eckhel, many learned author-ities. He read in a bland, easy tone, confident of his facts and his deductions.

Clytie felt relieved when he had finished. Across the room she had now and then caught Kent's eye, which had a humourous twinkle in it. She, who an hour before had been scoffing at the dry-as-dust nature of numismatics as a pursuit, now felt a consciousness of inferiority, of being relegated to the tribe feminine, who are not expected to care for intellectual matters. She nourished a seed of resentment against Kent and all archæologists. But when the usual discussion on the paper began she set an example of interest in it to Mr. Vansittart, who had come over and sat down by her side. Really, she was curious to see what part Kent would take in the discussion. He seemed to find many acquaintances in the room, and an appreciative welcome from each. She experienced a strange sense of satisfaction at the dispelling of an unformulated apprehension lest he might be unknown, insignificant. She had seen him several times since his visit to the studio ; once they had met at Sloane Square station and had walked home together. The acquaintance was ripening into friendliness. Now she was interested at seeing him in a new environment. Our conception of people changes very much according to the conditions with which we associate them. But Kent in the drawing-room, despite his unfamiliar attire, seemed much the same as Kent in the studio, his manner towards the men she saw him talking with much the same as his manner towards her. Presently he rose, broke into the discussion. The principal participators listened with apparent respect to his remarks, few in number, but apt.

"Well, Mr. Kent is an authority," said the professor, surrendering a particular point with a certain grace.

The little tribute fell gratefully on Clytie's ears. Suddenly she became conscious that her pleasure was greater than the occasion warranted. She turned round quickly to Mr. Vansittart, who was taking but mild interest in the affair, and somewhat abruptly opened a conversation. The Rev. Mr. Treherne joined them soon afterwards, asking permission to introduce a friend. Thus it came about that Clytie had a small group around her, and her interest in Kent's proceedings was checked for a time.

Meanwhile Mrs. Farquharson had threaded her way through the crowd of black coats, and taken Kent off with her to an undisturbed corner. She was curious to examine Clytie's new "chum."

"So you live in the same house as Clytie Davenant,

You rescued her from the flames, didn't you ? She told me something about it. What happened, exactly ? "

Kent sketched briefly the little scene with the blazing curtains, and mentioned his visit next day and his subsequent meetings with Clytie. He politely expressed his agreeable surprise at meeting her to-night.

" And what do you think of her ? " asked Mrs. Farquharson confidentially. " I dare say it's an odd question, but if you will come and see us again, you will find we are given to saying odd things."

" Like Miss Davenant ? "

" You have found that out already ? Well, come, what do you think of her ? "

" Honestly, or conventionally ? "

" If I meant conventionally, I should not ask you the question."

Kent waited for a moment, stroking his beard. He was scarcely prepared with an answer even to satisfy himself.

" I don't know. She is a bit too complicated to be defined in a phrase like a term in Euclid. She is nearer to a man than any woman I know."

Mrs. Farquharson smiled inwardly, noting the phrase, yet liking him for it. It was so deliciously wrong, so absurdly off the track. She contemplated him from the empyrean of feminine wisdom, and from that moment took him under her protection. To blunder honestly in things feminine is one of the ways to a woman's pity, thence often to her heart. She encouraged him, however, instead of correcting him.

" Why do you say that ? "

" For one reason, because I can talk to her as I would to a man. She has ideas and is not afraid of expressing them. In fact, she is different from the ordinary women one meets."

" Oh, yes ! she is that," Mrs. Farquharson granted. " She is all for *le nouveau jeu*. When I want to tease her I tell her she will find it *le vieux jeu* all the time, but she won't believe it." Then suddenly, " Don't you think she is very pretty ? "

" Pretty ? " echoed Kent in some confusion. " Really, yes, I suppose she is. I hardly thought about it," and leaning his body aside, so as to catch a distant glimpse of Clytie between the forms of the little circle of men round her, he added, "she is very pretty."

And truly it was a fair picture that his eye fell upon. She was wearing a simple dress of ivory-coloured silk, falling in soft, straight folds to her feet. Her low-cut bodice was relieved only by a ruffle of old lace along the top, and the sole ornament she wore, a necklet of antique silver, brought out the delicate modelling of her shapely neck, as she sat talking animatedly, her chin pointing upwards. Her rich, vivid colouring compensated for any lack of relief in her costume. The intense blue of her eyes, the many glints in her auburn hair, twisted in a careless knot at the back of her small, shapely head, and kept in place by a broad silver arrow, would of themselves have supplied the place of any ornament.

"She is very pretty indeed — striking!" repeated Kent.

Mrs. Farquharson looked at him amusedly.

"You must be an original, Mr. Kent. Fancy knowing Clytie Davenant without thinking of her looks!"

"I am a great bear," replied Kent. "My sister says so, and brothers and sisters generally speak the truth to each other. Of course I have thought of Miss Davenant's looks, in a way—admired her artistically ; but I have never realised in her society that I have been talking to a pretty girl—one consciously so. She does not seem to expect you to be impressed with her looks. That's one thing that I like about her."

Mrs. Farquharson carried on the conversation a little further and then directed it into other channels. She was pleased with Kent, and made a mental note to see more of him. A man who could like Clytie and yet not reflect upon her personal attractiveness was, as she had said, an oddity, and Mrs. Farquharson made oddities rather a speciality.

It was growing late and there was a perceptible thinning in the numbers of the guests. A few enthusiasts lingered fondly over the showcases, comparing their contents with specimens in their own or other collections. Among these was Treherne, by himself, deeply cogitative. He arrested Kent, who was passing by to speak to Clytie, whom he had scarcely seen during the evening, as he had felt bound to take an honest and practical interest in the proceedings. The question that Treherne desired Kent's help in solving was a knotty one, and the two men bent over the table absorbed in deciphering an obliterated obverse. When the matter was settled Kent looked around for Clytie, but she had already disappeared. There was nothing left for him to do but to take his leave.

"If you care for a Bohemian Sunday evening scramble, when everyone talks inconsequent nonsense—quite a different thing from to-night," said Mrs. Farquharson, shaking hands—"we shall be very glad to see you."

In the hall he was pleased to see Clytie, fur cloaked, waiting for a cab. She gave him a frank smile of recognition. With his white slouch hat and waterproof—a new one—his figure seemed to her very familiar. He talked to her for a moment or two, until the cab was announced.

"How are you going home?" she said when they were on the pavement.

"Walk," he replied briefly.

"But it's raining hard—would you accept a lift?"

He opened the swing doors for her, shielding her dress from the muddy wheels as she entered, and then hesitated a moment. He had in fact been intending to pay one of his midnight visits to his South Kensington friends, but Clytie thought his hesitation was due to considerations of propriety. She laughed with a little thrill of defiance as she settled herself comfortably in a corner. The touch of rebelliousness let loose an unwonted shaft of coquetry.

"Of course if you think it would do you more good to walk in the rain than drive dry with me——"

The interval between her two remarks had been very short, taken up entirely with the process of Clytie's seating herself in the cab, but still Kent felt he had been somewhat unchivalrous.

"If you really don't mind, I shall be very grateful," he said by way of making amends as he took his seat by her side.

After all, driving with Clytie was not unpleasant,

he reflected, and he could see Wither and Fairfax any day. That Clytie should have made her offer did not seem unnatural. He frankly informed her of the cause of his hesitation.

"I paid you the compliment of being mistaken," said Clytie.

"What do you mean?" he asked, catching a glimpse of her face in the swift gleam of a gas-lamp. She was smiling, in good humour.

"Oh! if you are mystified, so much the better," she exclaimed, "It will be my little revenge."

And that was all the explanation she vouchsafed him.

However, that drive spun a thread of intimacy between them. There are few conditions of companionship so favourable as those in a hansom cab. The driver is practically non-existent; the three sides and roof of the vehicle form a temporary home, a *chez soi.* The outside world lies in front of one, very near, and yet one is out of it. Even the desolate squares, with their occasional lamps blinking through the mist, and their wet, sooty trees rustling reluctantly as the wind passes through them, and their gaunt houses, each grimly and jealously guarding its household, giving the sense of the awful isolation of souls, fail to depress as they invariably depress the sensitive pedestrian. There is again the cheerful rattle which precludes sustained conversation, but encourages disjointed, intimate talk. The rush of the air, the whirling past of figures and objects, is exhilarating even in the vilest of weather and in the dreariest of neighbourhoods. The rapid night glimpses, too, of coffee-stalls, their lamps glaring upon the surrounding idlers; public houses, with the sudden babel of voices issuing from an opened door; walkers of the pavement forlornly standing with white, indistinguishable faces, 'buses steaming and labouring with their somnolent fares; every 'bus-load the counterpart of the last; swifter still, the glimpses of the occupants of other cabs that pass, stimulating the imagination; a phantasmagoria of life, almost unreal, yet bringing into play some of the lighter elemental forces of nature.

Clytie was almost sorry when the cab stopped at the familiar side-door next to the shop where the legend of

"Gurkins, green-grocer," was dimly visible through the gloom. Much of the mere woman in her had risen to the surface, obscuring the artist, the hater of formulas, the restless seeker after the mysteries of life. She had felt childish, frivolous, thus appearing in a new light to Kent, not without a certain charm, although he wondered to himself whether she, after all, was not like the rest of womankind—"fundamentally silly." This was a famous dictum of his.

But when the door closed behind them, and the narrow, ill-lighted, close-smelling passage leading to the gloomy staircase struck upon her senses, the realities of life came sharply before her, and her usual independence of thought and action reasserted itself. Otherwise, when she had said good-night to Kent on the landing and had found her room in darkness, she would not have called him back to light her lamp for her, and, that done, have asked him to remain for a short chat. He was struck by the change to her usual frank tones, and seeking half unconsciously for a reason, attributed his late impression to an illusion on his part caused by the darkness and dispelled by the light, by which he could see her face.

"You smoke, I know," she said, throwing her wraps on to the sofa. "You must be dying for some tobacco. What do you smoke?"

"Oh! a pipe," he replied with much fervour, instantly seeking for it in his pocket.

Clytie turned to poke the fire. It was black and sulky, and her efforts were of not much avail.

"Let me try," said Kent, bending down with her on the hearthrug; "this is a thing not generally known."

He threw a lighted match on to the fire, the escaping gases burst into flame, and cheerfulness was established in the grate.

A trivial incident, but it was recognised by them both in after years as having served to cement their comradeship.

CHAPTER VII.

THE friendship between them ripened imperceptibly.
Each day brought its tiny thread linking them together,
so gradually, so subtly, that it was not until long afterwards that they realised the immense strength of the
bond. At first it was mere honest liking on both sides,
a pleasant consciousness of discovery, an ordinary attraction between two natures, distinct, yet more or less
complementary. Clytie found it written in her Book of
New Formulas that the loyal friendship between a man
and a woman was a strengthening element of existence.
In her fierce pride and young vigour she would not
allow that each supplied what the other lacked, according
to the popular theory—the man strength, the woman
grace—but asserted strenuously the truth that each could
lend the other elements of strength the same in degree,
but different in kind, owing to the difference of sex. If
it had been suggested to her that her weaker woman's
nature instinctively, in spite of perfect emancipation and
proud independence, sought the man's protecting fibre,
the whole amazon within her would have been up in
arms. She found in Kent a man whom she could meet
upon a ground of perfect equality—perfectly even,
neither blocked by prejudices and social barriers nor
haunted by sexual spectres. She was woman enough,
however, to perceive intuitively certain shynesses in Kent,
resulting from a half knowledge of her, that would have
kept him aloof in spite of a very sensible attraction
towards her ; and in showing him, therefore, that this
attraction was mutual she felt no compunction,—rather
pride, on the contrary, in reaching a superior plane in
which conduct was measured by superior standards.

And thus it came about that the eternal feminine once
more deceived itself, mistaking nature for what it called
the Fine Art of Life.

Kent, for his part, did not attempt to realise the charm that made his fingers close daily on the handle of the studio door. He accepted the offered friendship, and returned it as frankly as it was given. It became as natural to stop at the studio, before mounting to his attics on his return home from the Museum, as to burst into the South Kensington "monastery" for a midnight rubber. Variety, fresh interests, were brought into his life, vivid as it was with darling hopes and full working energies. It was refreshing to come once again into the sphere, familiar and dear to him during his father's lifetime, of practical art. It was something for him to look forward to, during his tramp home—the stage nearer completeness effected during a day's work in an artistic creation. Gradually, in his blunt, paternal way, he constituted himself the censor of Clytie's work, criticising irregularities, suggesting treatment. There grew within him, too, a brotherly kindness towards Winifred, who looked forward also to his afternoon visit, when she would shyly uncover the small canvas and receive with a gratified flush his meed of appreciation.

He arrived after the tea-things had been cleared away, when the day's work was over, in the twilight hour, outstaying Winifred a short while, whose evening family meal was half an hour before Clytie's dinner. It was in these short periods of companionship, when they were alone together, that, unconsciously to themselves, the finer touches were added to the broader intimacy that the previous half hour had brought one step further in development. Piece by piece, by means of a reference here, a petulant outburst there, he grew familiar with the ambitions and struggles of her past life. He was quick to catch a certain note of disappointment. She had not yet become a great artist, was defiantly certain that she could never be one.

"Of course you won't if you use your art as a stepping-stone to life," he said one day.

She marked the saying, resolving, however, half rebelliously to make him belie his words in the days to come. She, too, gathered from him the nature of his hope and aspirations, wondered at the cheerful selflessness with which he contemplated the work that would bring him neither name nor fame, nor the things that many men desire.

One day he took Clytie and Winifred up to his attic museum, pleased as a boy to show them his treasures. Winifred praised the bright neatness of his arrangements. He confessed guiltily that he had been "tidying up"—a process that had cost him the whole of the previous Sunday. Many of his pictures had been left him by his father, particularly his collection of Aldegravers, over which he fondly lingered, lamenting that the old days of pure design were over, and railing at the mercenary spirit of modern art. He counselled Clytie to study the little masters for her book illustrating. She would learn restraint, abstraction.

"But it's no good preaching Dürer and Behm in these days," he added pathetically, with the resignation of the collector who does not expect his hobby to be understood.

Clytie laughed softly, sympathetic with his enthusiasms. No real artist can help loving the little masters. But Clytie's artistic impulses warred with each other, with circumstance, and with herself. So she refused to sit, for practical purposes, at the foot of Aldegraver. She ran over the titles of books, borrowed a couple, which he recommended, from the general literature section, stood in some dismay before the scientific specialist's library, and asked to see what was visible of the great work. He gave her some bundles of manuscript, which she turned over helplessly and handed back without a word. They were evidences of a world of infinite toil and devotion not yet intelligible to her. She gazed around the picturesque walls of the room that contrasted strangely with the carpetless floor and the fenderless grate. The absence of the minor softnesses of material life struck her vividly. There were evidences of a high love for art, but art in a too rarefied atmosphere for her nature. She would have liked to curtain the windows,—they were even destitute of blinds,—to put rugs about the floor, to soften the room with drapery, plants, flowers; even an armchair beside the fire would have been æsthetically as well as physically reposeful. Winifred's simpler feminine impulses struck the true chord.

"Why doesn't your sister make you some pretty things for your room?"

"She does—heaps of things."

"Where are they, then?"

Kent looked at her with humorous shamefacedness.

"I am afraid I have a drawer full of them somewhere," he replied.

"Well, your room is very much like yourself," she said in a low voice, and hesitating a little. "You both lack the same thing."

And blundering John Kent misread the oracle, accepting it as a reproach for brotherly unkindness.

Meanwhile Clytie's "own" picture of the model Jack was developing into a more finished and more ambitious work than she had originally intended. On Kent's suggestion she had toned down some of its brutality without rendering less vivid the presentation of the problem. She thought of trying to exhibit the picture when it was completed; Jack therefore continued to appear in the studio at irregular intervals. Winifred encouraged him now, trying to humanise him with picture-books, stories, and simple talk, but Clytie shook her head at her gentle friend's efforts, conceiving them, with her fuller and more materialistic knowledge, to be entirely futile. Still Winifred obtained from him more details of what Clytie called his private life than she herself could do. With both of them he was fierce and sullen, but with Winifred he was more cynically expansive. These details only supplemented the data afforded by his own personality. Sometimes he went to the board school, where he was in the third standard; oftener he stayed away. He slept in his mother's room, ate his desultory food there with the fierceness of a young wolf; but his real home was in the street. Once he had been given a situation as satellite to a thriving costermonger, but the restraints of regular employment had chafed him into resignation of his post. Besides, his employer had thrashed him unmercifully. As for his parentage, he was entirely ignorant; he did not care. To his mind it was a merciful dispensation of Providence that he only had one parent to irritate and annoy him. He liked to come to the studio because it was warm and comfortable, besides which he obtained a shilling at the end of the day to be expended on inferior tobacco when together with his playmates.

One morning, earlier than usual, he slouched up the stairs and, contrary to custom, found the studio door open and the apartment empty. He entered, swinging the door with him, which, being caught by the draught from an open skylight, slammed with sudden violence. If he had heard the quick rattle of a falling door-knob, his subsequent conduct would doubtless have been modified. He was alone in the studio ; he waited idly, lying in front of the stove ; but as no one came, he began to feel restless. He rose to his feet, wandered about, shut the skylight, examined the contents of the studio. He found a packet of cigarettes lying about, which he pocketed ; an investigation of the cupboard in the wall rewarded him with some lumps of sugar and some sweet biscuits. Still no one came, which was not extraordinary, as his employer had not yet thought of breakfasting. No further resources being offered to his predatory instincts, he proceeded to look at the pictures, with which he had already a contemptuous familiarity. The only one for which he had a genuine admiration, or rather the barbarian's feeling of awe at any counterfeit presentment of himself, was his own portrait. At this he seldom tired of looking.

He took down from the wall a little painted mirror, and, sitting on the stool in front of the picture, proceeded to compare the original and the portrait. He saw that the resemblance was not quite perfect, and like a monkey he grimaced into the looking-glass until he had reproduced the expression that Clytie had fixed upon the canvas. Then he laughed in great glee, scratched his black curly head, and went in quest of further occupation. He crossed over to Winifred's easel and took off the cloth. He had no great idea of "the other one's" picture. It did not interest him. But, unfortunately, in his simian mood, an idea shot through his mind. Why should he not try to paint too ?

He mounted upon Winifred's seat, took her palette in his hand as he had seen her hold it, with his small, dirty thumb through the hole in the white porcelain, gathered the little sheaf of brushes, arranged the mahl-stick imitatively, and, dipping a brush into the remains of some Chinese white, tried to fill in some anemones. They were only splotches of white paint, but the occupation absorbed him. In a very few moments the whole canvas was starred with Jack's white dabs. Then, growing tired of the monotony of white,—the colours on the palette did not attract him,—he fetched Clytie's, which was more richly prepared, and painted in strokes of crimson and yellow. The delight of colour fascinated him. He obliterated all the white, daubed the canvas over and over with heavy streaks, laughing aloud with the spirit of diabolical mischief. Then, with a fox terrier's or a monkey's instinct of destruction, he took up the palette-knife and stabbed holes through the canvas.

He contemplated his work for a moment, and then, the very human anticipation of consequences occurring to his mind, he bethought himself of flight. But, to his dismay, he found the door-handle had fallen off when the door had slammed, and that he was a prisoner until someone should open it from outside. He paused for a moment in the middle of the room, reflecting. Then he covered up his handiwork carefully with a cloth, scrupulously replaced the palettes and brushes, and curled himself up in his usual doglike attitude by the stove, there to await events.

After a time there came a rattle of the knob-screw being fitted into the vacant hole in the lock, which made his heart beat, and Clytie entered the room humming a song. She was surprised to find him there, and elicited a monosyllabic explanation of his presence. She was in a good humour and talked lightly to him as she moved about the studio, changing the water of some flowers. The errand-boy from the shop below came up with Winnie's anemones that had been put in a cool place over night to keep them fresh one day longer. Clytie set them on the stand beside Winifred's easel. Jack watched her, looked at the door, measuring the distance.

"Where are you going?" Clytie asked sharply as she turned round and caught him stealing across the room.

He was terribly afraid of her. Those great dark blue
eyes seemed to command him. He never could meet
them with his own. He relapsed doggedly into his
position by the stove. Clytie touched the anemones
daintily, picking some faded leaves, still humming her
song. In lightness of heart she took off the cloth to
look at Winnie's work, and then fell back with a cry of
horror and anger. A swift glance at Jack brought her
knowledge.

"You little fiend!" she cried with eyes aflame, and
catching the cowering, sullen urchin by the collar of shirt
and jacket, she dragged him out of the studio, on to the
landing.

Kent happened to have just gone down the stairs on
his way out. The noise of the scuffle reached him in the
entrance passage and brought him up to the studio door.

"What is the matter?" he asked, taking the boy from
Clytie's grasp into his own.

"The matter? Go inside. I must call Winnie.
Winnie!"

She opened the sitting-room door. Winifred ran out,
holding her gloves, which she had just taken off, in her
hand.

"That boy—that little devil!" cried Clytie, and they
both ran into the studio.

Kent had just entered, and was standing before the
mutilated picture holding the boy, who in Kent's hands
was struggling violently. Winifred looked at it for a
moment blankly, scarcely understanding. Then the sickening truth rose to her brain, and she leaned, very white,
against the wall, looking at the others.

"For God's sake take the little brute out and kill him,
Mr. Kent!" Clytie broke out fiercely. "Murder him!
break every bone in his body! To have done such a
thing as that! It is not human."

"I'll give him a thundering hiding," said Kent wrath-
fully, dragging him towards the door.

But Winifred rose quickly, moved her neck, cleared
her throat, and laid her hand on Kent's arm.

"Don't beat him—I couldn't bear it."

"Nonsense, Winnie! sit down," cried Clytie. "Take
him away, Mr. Kent, or I'll do him some mischief myself!"

Kent shook the urchin till his teeth chattered and his evil little face grew red. Winifred still clung to his arm.

"Don't! you shan't do it! He is no better than an animal! He did not know what he was doing. Nothing you could do to him would give me back my picture. It would be simple vengeance. Oh, send him away! Send him away!" and turning from Kent, she burst into tears and clung to Clytie, sobbing.

"Miss Marchpane is right," said Kent slowly and looking at Clytie. "Let the little brute go. Here, you, go! If ever I see you near the place, I will give you to a policeman!"

Visions of the lowering blue storm-cloud, ever seeming to the children of the streets ready to burst upon their heads, loomed before the little outcast's imagination. He shivered, shrunk away from Kent's relaxed grasp, darted a keen, swift look of malignity at Clytie, and disappeared like a flash through the open door.

Clytie held Winifred protectingly with one arm, soothing her, mingling words of comfort with outbursts of self-reproach and unrighteous indignation. As Jack slipped away she made an impulsive movement forward, but Winifred restrained her.

"How dare you let him go?" she exclaimed, turning her anger upon Kent. "If it had not been for you I would have given him a lesson he'd have remembered all his life. To do a work of devilry like that and not be punished! I'll set the police upon him!"

"No, no!" murmured Winifred.

"I will. What are reformatories for? Go and call a policeman, Mr. Kent. It is the least you can do!"

"I shall leave him alone," replied Kent. "It would not do him any good and it would not do Miss Marchpane any good. He'll never come here again, and I should advise you not to introduce any more of his sort into your studio. When a child of the flesh and the devil gets hold of a thing of the spirit, the spiritual suffers."

"I do not wish to be lectured," said Clytie stonily.

"I am sorry if I have offended you, Miss Davenant," replied Kent. "I have the sincerest sympathy with

Miss Marchpane for her loss, and I would do anything in the world to help her or you ; and so—good-morning."

Kent worked hard that day at the Museum. He was troubled over the morning's occurrence. He was conscious that he had acted rightly in acquiescing in Winifred's counsel of mercy, but he had a vague, inarticulate regret that he had not pleased Clytie. He resolutely set himself to forget everything in his work and finished earlier than usual. On his way out he met his friend Wither in the great hall.

" I have come to carry you off to the club to dine and there to reason with you," said the small, gnomelike man. " They are spring-cleaning at home and the place reeks of freshness and innocence. Greene and Fairfax like it ; they say it's healthy. I prefer the accumulated and mellowed deposit of winter. It's as bad as washing a meerschaum. Anyhow, it's got to get coloured a bit, and until it does I clear out and you are coming to clear with me."

" Very well," replied Kent ; " I will waste part of an evening upon you—to prevent you wasting it yourself more sinfully. You were lucky to catch me ; I was just going."

The policeman at the door saluted Kent as he passed out.

" That ought to have been for me," said Wither. " I am far the more reputable-looking of the two."

Kent laughed good-humouredly and grasped his ash stick sturdily in his gloveless hands. The contrast between the dandified elegance of Wither's dress and his own careless, loose attire appealed to his sense of the humorous.

" I'll walk a few yards behind you if you like," he said, repeating a familiar and time-honoured jest between them.

They walked down the great flight of steps and across the courtyard, where the pigeons were fluttering joyfully in the afternoon sunshine. When they had arrived at the railings, whose gilt spear-points caught the sun, Wither turned and looked for a moment at the frowning mass of the edifice.

" This always suggests the brain of London, immeasurable in this ugly poll of a Bloomsbury, with its watery eyes and dejected face, that seems to be perpetually meditating on death and influenza. I am going to work up the idea one of these days and turn it into copy."

"It certainly does not look promising in the crude state," observed Kent by way of encouragement.

They walked along Oxford Street and down Shaftesbury Avenue. Here, while passing in front of a photographer's window, their eyes were caught by a group of complacent people of both sexes—" with superior smiles and inferior clothes," as Wither said—described by a legend printed on the mount as the " Parnassus House Mutual Improvement Society." Wither entered the shop and purchased a copy, as a " monument of the stupendous fatuity of man." In the comfortable smoking-room of the Junior Cosmopolitan, St. James's Square, Wither held the photograph out on his knees before him and discoursed upon it.

"Look at them," he said, half hidden in the great armchair. " Dear old Philistia ! When is the Almighty going to redeem his promise and triumph over it? Mutual improvement !—on the principle of Mark Twain's islanders, who eked out a precarious livelihood by taking in each other's washing ! This pathetic kind of person belongs to home reading societies. Do you know what they are ? I was staying with the Brownes last summer ; asked the youngest to come and play tennis. She replied with awful solemnity that she was going to read her ' half hour.' I was impressed ; good girl, I said, and pictured her to myself conducting her devotional exercises over St. Thomas à Kempis or St. Augustine's ' Confessions ' in the sanctity of her maiden chamber. Next day I found her reading the report of an agricultural commission for the year 1831. Asked her what the deuce she was reading that for. She replied she was reading her ' half hour ' ; it was the only ' solid ' book she could find downstairs ! Novels and poetry and magazines were tabooed. I asked her whether she thought George Meredith or Dante flippant. She could not exactly say—but they were not solid. God help us ! "

" You are as bad as my friend Miss Davenant," said Kent, laughing. "She is always railing at Philistia. You might lend me the photograph to show her ; it would amuse her—perhaps it might teach her something."

Wither gave him the photograph, but after a short pause Kent returned it.

" I'll take it some other time. I don't quite know at present how we are going to stand to one another ; we had a bit of a scene this morning."

Wither raised his eyebrows and turned his head lazily, looking at Kent.

" You interest me, friend John. Is Saul also among the prophets ? Expound."

Kent roughly sketched the morning's episode in the studio.

" So, you see, there's something in the nature of a split," he added.

" She will come round all right," said Wither, "if she cares about you. If she doesn't, she is not worth caring about. Never you mind. There is nothing does women so much good as a little wholesome neglect. *Crede experto.* As for the matter in question, of course you were wrong. You should have thrashed the little devil's life out. But with a woman, having right or wrong on her side has nothing to do with it."

" That may be true in the case of the woman you like to philander with, Teddy, but Clytie Davenant's different."

" Bah, my dear old boy, they are all the same, every one of them."

" You have never met one of them whom you could treat in the ordinary straightforward way—make a friend of as if she were a man."

" No, old chap, nor do I want to. If you've got to treat a woman as if she were a man, what the devil's the good of her being a woman?"

" You are talking for the sake of talking, Teddy," said Kent with some earnestness. " You know it's all nonsense. Women generally are foolish enough, God knows, but the sole end of their being is not to be fooled about with in flirtations and love-makings and such sickening nonsense. And when one does come across a girl with an intelligence above the ordinary and instincts above bazaars and the river, one likes her and is exceedingly sorry to have any row with her."

"Ah me!" murmured the little man, examining his trim finger nails with intent brow, "whether we cultivate the 'languor and lilies of virtue,' or the 'roses and raptures of vice,' it doesn't matter—the trail of the petticoat's over us all. Come and have a 'hundred up' before dinner."

Kent did not carry home the ridiculous portrait, and Wither, to avoid the trouble of taking with him the awkwardly sized parcel that would not fit into his pocket, very characteristically posted it to himself. As Kent passed Clytie's door he noticed that it was ajar and that the room was dark. Evidently she had gone out. If she had retired early to bed, she would have shut the door, as her bedroom opened into the sitting-room. He felt a certain sense of loss, he did not know why, for even if the little streak of light beneath the door had announced her presence within, he certainly would not have sought admittance. He went upstairs more slowly than usual, thinking of her and of the morning's scene. By the dim gas on his landing he perceived an unframed picture leaning, face-hidden, against his door, and on the ground a letter. This was addressed to him in the bold, rounded handwriting which he recognised as Clytie's. He opened it and read:

You were right. I am sorry. Keep the picture as a token.

C. D.

Kent turned the canvas round. It was the exhibition picture of Jack.

He took it in with him, and placed it on his dresser-table. It formed a strange contrast to the calm-faced Woolmer cavalier that was hanging above; a strange contrast, too, with its colour, its modernity, its realism, to the cold classicism of the pale, pure relics of the past that lined the walls. Troubled by the discord, he turned its face to the wall, but immediately, ashamed of the impulse and calling himself a fool, he turned it again. Then, after lighting his reading-lamp and turning out the gas, he sat down at the writing space on his dresser-table.

The room door was open. The house was perfectly still, save for the occasional creak of the stairs and banisters near the attics. From the street outside, far beneath, came the faint, ghostlike rumble of passing vehicles. Kent had never realised what absolute silence reigned at night in that quiet household. A cuckoo-clock in the bedroom below struck with a suddenness and clearness that startled him. It was only twelve o'clock. Clytie would be back soon if she had gone out to spend the evening with friends or at a theatre. He proceeded with some mechanical work, docketing papers, his ear expectant of the sudden drag of a hansom at the street door. Several times he was deceived and went out on the landing to listen for the sounds announcing Clytie's arrival. Then he resumed his occupation. Perhaps she was indoors and asleep all the time, he thought; but the open door surely betokened her absence. He persuaded himself into this belief, desiring intensely to see her. The immediate fulfilment of Wither's prognostications troubled him. Had it not been for his friend's bantering remarks he would have judged Clytie's frank confession by the touchstone of his own simplicity, and found it natural, prompted by no other motives than kindliness and common sense. But what if it proceeded from the " fundamental silliness " of woman, that he himself pitied and Wither professed to hold in contempt ?

At last an unmistakable pause in the dimly heard rattle of a hansom made him rise again and go on to the landing. Someone entered the house. He heard the far distant creak of the stairs and the vague rustle of skirts. It was Clytie. In the deathlike stillness of the house he heard the sharp striking of a match. He waited for a moment or two and then went down.

Clytie, in her hat and cloak, was reading, by the light of her bedroom candle, a letter that had arrived by the last post.

" May I come in for one minute ? "

" Of course—for two if you like. Do you know, I had an idle fancy that I should see you when I got home ? "

"Did you? I am very glad; it assures me that you don't think me—what shall I say?—presumptuous in waiting for you to come in and then intruding."

"Did you listen for me? You are good. I am scarcely worth it."

"I felt I must thank you for your little note—and the picture."

"Well? And are we going to make friends again, Mr. Kent?"

She looked him in the face proudly, yet laughingly, and held out her ungloved hand.

"There!" she added. "I behaved very badly to you this morning, and you must thank Winifred for bringing me to a sense of decency; but really when I saw the dear child's work done to death by my own fault I was not mistress of myself. I suppose it is best when one is in the wrong to own it—to one's friends."

"It is sensible," said Kent, "and I am very proud of your reckoning me among your friends."

She looked at him, a strange little smile playing round the corner of her lips as she put up both hands to withdraw her hat-pin—a graceful attitude, instinct with femininity. The look and the attitude disconcerted Kent for a moment. However, her next words reassured him.

"I judged you by myself, you know. I had found our friendship a pleasant thing, and felt that you did so, too, and I was sorry lest anything should break it; otherwise I should not have taken the trouble to 'climb down,' as they say."

"Let us say no more about it," replied Kent magnanimously. "If we pride ourselves on being superior to certain conventionalities of habit, we ought to extend our conventionalities of sentiment. I have been very troubled all day, Miss Davenant, I must confess, and I can't tell you how touched I was by your message. It's not every woman by a long way that would have sent it."

"And I would not have written it to every man," returned Clytie; "of that you may be quite certain."

And so they parted for the night.

Thus the breach between them was quite covered over

and their relations strengthened by a newer impression of mutual dependence, a more active sense of comrade-ship. They laughed frankly at the Great Convention-alities, and went about together to theatres, concerts, picture-shows. Kent accompanied her to Mrs. Farquhar-son's Sunday evenings, where he found a ready welcome from the artistic and literary circle, to whom his father had been well known. Mrs. Farquharson called them " Ores-tia and Pylades," by this time recognising their compan-ionship as a social fact. They always went back together, generally for a great part of the way on foot when the weather grew warm and the nights were dry and clear. On the weekday evenings, when Clytie was at home, Kent would bring down his work and his reference-books to Clytie's room, and write there, while she drew or read or busied herself with odds and ends of needlework. It had all the outward seeming of friendship—nothing more. For hours they would sit together without ex-changing a word—a real test. But Clytie grew interested in the progress of Kent's work, gradually obtained a clear idea of its scope and proportion, and could speak intimately to him concerning it, although its matter was as incomprehensible to her as to any other non-specialist. It gave the girl, too, a sense of rest and strength to see him sitting there, patiently, serenely working. She be-gan to have doubts as to the completeness of her own scheme of life, its worthiness, satisfaction. Hitherto the sense of independence, freedom, accumulating know-ledge of that whose foreshadowings had filled her girl-ish heart with unrest, had almost satisfied her. Now she began to look beyond. With her young being as yet untouched by passion, she did not realise the fulness that love must bring into life. She vaguely speculated upon it, faint, elusive gleams of perception passing rapidly through her into the darkness, but that was all. The secret of life, she thought, could only be wrested from the tangle of the labyrinth by single-minded en-deavour, sacrifice, devotion. Was not Kent right when he accused her of making her art a stepping-stone in-stead of an end ?

Kent, manlike, and honester, too, than most men, was unconscious of this self-abasement. Since the day of that fierce struggle with herself which had resulted in her sending him the missive of submission he had vaguely felt that she was dependent on him for many things ; but he had helped her in his frank, unquestioning way, feeling pleased, warmed by the flame of a newly kindled spark of vanity. He preached to her his simple doctrine.

"Work while work pleases you. Love it for its own sake. Set a great end before you ; but the attaining it is the delight, not the ultimate attainment. If you think of nothing but the end, the reaching it is all feverish unrest and toil."

She listened, rebelled, submitted, without loss of her proud fearlessness. Yes ; it was common sense, she agreed. No one can be humiliated by giving in to common sense and acting in accordance with it. Kent persuaded her to finish the picture of Jack.

" It is the best thing you have done. There is more work in it—real work. It will not take long to finish. Then send it for exhibition."

He appealed to Winifred, who added her soft note of encouragement. The picture was painted. Kent stonily refused to keep it as his possession. There was a heated argument. He valued her gift and her friendship ; he valued her fame and life-interest more. He would not refuse a replica. In the end she acquiesced. The picture was accepted by the hanging committee of the exhibition, made a stir, was sold for £120. Clytie was launched.

CHAPTER VIII.

The summer came. Clytie went abroad with the Farquharsons, through the old towns of Normandy and Brittany. Kent joined them at St. Malo, and spent his month's holiday with them. This was such a departure from his usual habit of solitary pedestrian travel in the rough wilds of Norway, whither he went every year, with little else than a stick and a knapsack, that Wither had been quite alarmed.

"You'll be taking a holiday with me next," he had said.

But knowing the terms of intimacy between his friend and Clytie, and knowing Clytie herself,—he had accompanied Kent to the studio, at first out of curiosity to see what kind of " being feminine " Kent had made a friend of, and afterwards because he liked to go there,—whatever sceptical imaginings might have exercised him, he forbore to give them expression. He had only looked at Kent, on saying good-bye, in his odd, half-mocking way, and had chuckled noiselessly to himself when the door had closed upon Kent's broad shoulders.

Kent did not regret Norway. A charm, unknown to him before, filled all the days. The Farquharsons were perfect travelling companions : Caroline bright, satirical, helpful, learned in the ways of men ; George easy-going, happy either to lounge in the sun with a pipe and bandy chaff with his wife, whilst Kent and Clytie went their own ways, or to spend an antiquarian afternoon with Kent in some old Keltic village. Clytie seemed also to him to expand under the sunny cheerful influences, to grow more feminine, without falling in his estimation. No ; he did not regret Norway. He half formulated an intention of abandoning it permanently and substituting Brittany as his habitual tramping-ground. From the first morning, when his boat steamed slowly through the narrow St. Malo docks, and he saw Clytie waiting there to meet him, he felt friendly towards it. The high ramparted wall, with just the top-story row of green shutters and roofs peeping above it, and beyond them the spire of the cathedral; the glimpse through the sentry-guarded gate up the narrow cobble-paved street, gaudy with blue blouses, red handkerchiefs, and yellow oilskins exposed all along at shop doors; on the quay itself the stalls of the hucksters under the lee of the wall, and the busy crowd of swarthy Breton sailors, porters, and green uniformed *douaniers;* and Clytie standing, fresh in her pure colouring heightened by the light summer dress, in the midst of this mellow setting—all the picture fixed itself as a whole indelibly upon his mind, and caused a strange little thrill of pleasure to run through him.

They sat on the sands—the finest in the world, perhaps, when the tide is low—that run in a broad, golden sweep from crag-bastioned, grim old St. Malo to the white houses of Parame, amid the babel of bathers and visitors, watching the types Parisian and English, Kent smoking contentedly, while Clytie filled her sketch-book with oddities of personality and costume. Three days slipped away there very pleasantly.

In spite of its banality as a pleasure resort there is a grim charm about St. Malo that is never quite forgotten by those who have once known it. It has an air of stability, of defiance. It is out of the reach of the improver, extender, and suburb-maker. Its great walls guard it as jealously on three sides as the sea does on the other. Almost alone of populous cities, it can never grow. As he left with the party to continue the tour Kent felt this charm, although his associations with the city had been of the lighter kind. They idled through the old towns: Dol, with its dark granite cathedral, looking rather hewn out of the rock than built; Dinan on its granite steep above the Rance, where the heart of du Guesclin is enshrined; Brieux, Paimpol, over which Pierre Loti has thrown the glamour of his sentiment; Morlaix, and so to Brest, with its great harbour and strong sea breeze from the Atlantic. For Kent this journey was an uninterrupted pleasure. No country is richer in things old, worn by weather and time, than Brittany : here an old chapel built of rough unhewn granite; here a shapeless wayside cross erected by some pious crusader on the ragged hill slope, railed round to prevent the encroachments of the broom and heather; here a Druidic mass of boulders ; in the cottages curious smoke-dried strips of old Breton work, ancestral oak carvings, rude brass repousée platters—a thousand anti-quarian interests in this gray land. But it is a bright one withal. The fields of yellow colza stretch over the landscape in broad patches of glory ; the red-cheeked cider apples glow in the orchards. The chestnut-trees in the grounds of the old feudal château, its fleched gables dimly visible, hang gratefully over the high bounding wall, above the roadway. The peasants still wear the picturesque Breton dress, tasselled hats, embroidered short jackets, and knee-breeches for the men, great white caps and elaborate kirtles for the women. Along the coast the surf beats in a line of angry light upon the rocks, and shows white, in the midst of the blue, around the islets out at sea. And the old fishing villages look as if they were but flotsam and jetsam cast up by Providence around the gray, weather-worn church that has taken them to its bosom.

For a few days after they left Dinan Kent noticed a change in Clytie. She was reserved, thoughtful. It was not until she appeared to have thrown off the weight of an obsessing idea that she grew buoyant and frank again. An incident unknown to him had occurred at Dinan, shaking the girl's heart to its depths.

Her bedroom in the hotel opened, like the others on the same floor, on to a small balcony, the spaces in front of each room being separated by a light iron bar. She was dressing one morning when her attention was aroused by voices in the next room, near the balcony. Her own French window was open. The air was sunny and still, and the voices struck clear.

" And that is your last word ?" asked a woman's voice in French. She used the familiar *ton.* Her accents were tearful and pleading.

"Yes," replied a man's voice brutally. " There, there !

Do not make any scenes. I go because it is my good pleasure. What have you to say against it?"

"But I love you, I love you, Armand!"

"Bah!" laughed the man, "they say that always. Here are the thousand francs."

Clytie, who had involuntarily overheard this scrap of the conversation, hastened to shut the window. The sounds died away into murmurs dimly perceptible through the partition wall. Then she heard the room door slam violently and a heavy step tramp down the passage.

Some two hours later she was sitting in the salon of the hotel, reading the papers and looking idly out upon the market-booths in the little *place*. Kent and Farquharson had gone out together to devote a scientific forenoon to the monuments of the town, and Caroline was writing letters in her own room. Clytie was alone. Suddenly the door opened and a woman, scarcely more than a girl, appeared on the threshold. She made a step forward, but perceiving Clytie by the window, she hesitated, irresolute whether to advance or retire. Clytie looked up quickly, caught a glance which she interpreted as one of appeal.

"Oh, enter, mademoiselle," she said, with a smile.

The newcomer murmured a "*Merci*," entered, closed the door, and sitting down on the faded sofa by the wall, commenced turning over the pages of an old illustrated paper. Clytie went on with her *Figaro*. Presently her ear caught a little sniffling sob. She turned round. Her companion was squeezing a wet rag of a handkerchief in her hand, her head turned away towards the paper; she was crying. Clytie rose, moved softly across the room. But as she was going through the doorway she saw the girl, abandoning herself to her misery, bury her face upon the sofa cushion. Clytie was touched. She went back to the girl, laid her hand softly on her shoulder.

"Mademoiselle!"

The girl started, raised a pretty, tear-stained face, looked at Clytie wistfully out of her light blue eyes, her lips quivering.

"You are in trouble," said Clytie.

"Oh, mademoiselle, you are very good," cried the

other—"*oui ; je suis bien malheureuse.* But you must leave me. You are a young girl well brought up, whilst I—— *Merci*, mademoiselle ; you can do nothing."

The voice struck a chord of association. Where had she heard it recently? Quickly it flashed upon her, the scrap of dialogue she had overheard that morning. The girl again hid her face. The low-cut dress, beloved by Frenchwomen, disclosed a shapely neck, on which clustered coquettishly a few tiny madcap curls below the smooth, upbrushed, fair hair. Her figure was young and graceful, relaxed now in the attitude of abandonment.

Clytie looked down upon her wonderingly, her heart beating. Her maidenhood urged her to fly ; a higher sense of life bade her stay a moment by the sobbing figure. She had never, to her knowledge, been near to one of the great unclassed—still less spoken. She remembered the few cynical words of the man ; they seemed to give her a pain at the heart akin to nausea. She remembered the pleading tones : *Je t'aime, je t'aime bien !*" and her pity went forth upon the woman.

"I don't ask you to tell me," she said very gently. "But we may talk a little, mayn't we ? Perhaps it may ease you—a woman—the same age,"—Clytie stumbled in the foreign language,—" and perhaps not so well brought up—after all, a woman."

"Oh, mademoiselle, you do not understand. This life !" her shoulders shivered expressively. "After all, it is bearable ; but when, with all that, one loves—ah !"

"He is not worth it," cried Clytie. "He is a scoundrel—I know what he is !"

The girl raised her face quickly.

"You know him ? You know Armand ? Ah, no ; you spoke at random. Yes, he is base, cruel, but that does not prevent it. Mademoiselle, you are good, you are sweet. It is not many who would have spoken. You will let me sit here near you for a little ? Ah, *mon Dieu*," she went on rapidly, " you cannot imagine what it is—never, never to talk to a woman whom one can respect, and who may not betray you ; and then the only persons one can respect are the men, who despise one. And even they—one can love them, but they are cowardly, hard, selfish !"

" There are some good men," observed Clytie.

" That may be," returned the other, finally drying her eyes, and putting up her hand to her hair in tidying touches—" that may be, but we don't often see them. Oh, mademoiselle, I know well that I should be ashamed of showing you what I am, but when you touched my shoulder it was like a good sister of the convent,"— Clytie smiled in spite of herself at the comparison,— " and it touched my heart."

" And I too have a confession to make," said Clytie, gently interrupting. " This morning—I overheard—my room is next to yours——"

" Ah, it was you who shut the window ? "

" Yes.   So I know, mademoiselle—at least I can judge. And are you quite alone now ? "

The girl shrugged her shoulders.

" What would you have ? He has gone, and I must go too.   One does not amuse oneself here alone."

" And where are you going ? "

" To Paris.   In the middle of summer.   It is not gay. Everyone will know *qu'il m'a plantée là*. But one must live.   Ah ! you are happy, you other honest women ! "

She talked on, in half-cynical, half-artless confidence, as is the way of her race, forgetting in her need of expansion that her hearer was the English girl well brought up.   She dilated on her present trouble, her life in Paris, her creditors, the spitefulness of women, the brutality of men.   Clytie listened with mingled feelings of horror and pity.   She was so young, this girl, so fresh for all the soil of Paris, and yet taking, from use, the whole horror of her life as a matter of course, realising it only in rare emotional moments.   Here was a rejecter of formulas, of a race that has thrown off convention ever since Rahab harboured the spies ! Too fragile, delicate she looked for this social warfare. Whither was she tending ? Clytie had a supreme, lurid moment of introspection.   Only two or three such come in a lifetime.

At last the girl rose from the sofa in the quick French way.

" Forgive me, mademoiselle, for talking like this.   I had forgotten.   You see well that you could not have helped me otherwise than you have done by sitting by my side. I must not encroach upon your time. Adieu, mademoiselle, and thank you; oh, a thousand times, thanks. I shall not forget you."

She was going. Clytie rose and went towards her, her face a little flushed, but kindness in her eyes.

"You will shake hands, *à l'Anglaise?*" she said.

The girl looked her quickly in the face, and then impulsively seized the proffered hand in both hers and kissed it twice rapidly. Then she ran from the room.

Clytie went back to her seat by the window and looked out upon the market-sellers. But she did not see much, as tears stood in her eyes and rolled down her cheeks.

She did not tell Mrs. Farquharson of this incident, but kept it in her heart as a secret and strange revelation of life—something precious, mysterious, awful. During her drive with the others in the afternoon she was strangely silent. Kent rallied her on her depression in his bluff, kind-hearted manner. She smiled absently, complained of a headache, then shivered with a wave of recollection. For days the spectre haunted her, sometimes looking at her through the light blue eyes of the girl, and sometimes taking a dual form, in which the coarse drudge features of the mother of Jack, the model, were dimly visible. And a question hummed in her ears : "Was this the aspect of life that men kept so jealously hidden from women ?"

But Clytie was young and vigorous, with fresh bright blood leaping in her veins. The thrill of the salt breeze and the whole-hearted laughter of her friends soon prevented these imaginings from becoming morbid, and gradually the first sharp impression dulled more or less down to the level of her other experiences of things. She gave herself up again to the freedom and gaiety of the trip, to the unfeigned delight of Kent, who had been beginning to wonder whether, for unknown reasons, some coolness had arisen between them.

He forbore to allude to the subject until the night when they were all returning together from St. Malo to Southampton. He had found her a sheltered corner of the upper deck, rigged up a screen of rugs, comfortably established her in a canvas chair with many wraps. Most of the passengers had gone below. They were almost alone. The voices of two men in an opposite corner came vaguely out of the darkness. All was still save for the continuous rattle and wash, which at sea forms a strange kind of silence in itself.

"Aren't you sorry it is over?" asked Clytie from the dimness of her wraps. "We did nothing very wonderful, but it has been very pleasant—a thing to look back upon."

"'A garnered joy for after-time.'"

"You are waxing poetical."

"Oh, that's Wither. He was poetical in his youth. You would hardly think it of him. I have always thought that line rather pretty. Anyhow, it is true in the present case."

"And we haven't quarrelled," said Clytie, "in spite of the maxim, 'If you want to lose a friend, travel with him.' But I don't think I could quarrel with you. You wrap yourself round with such imperturbable superiority."

"The metaphor is mixed, but proceed," interrupted Kent.

"Well, it's not worth while playing to such a bad house."

"I don't see what we should have to quarrel about," returned Kent, laughing. "We each give the other credit for independent opinions; and as for action, if you wanted to go to the right and I to the left, I suppose I should give in and let you have your way—if it were not contrary to common sense."

"And if it were? If it were simply idiotic?"

"Perhaps I should go with you then, to keep you out of harm's way."

"Thank you," murmured Clytie rather touched, looking up restfully at the stars.

There was a little silence. Kent puffed at his pipe. The glow attracted George Farquharson, who had just come up on the deck and was groping about for them in the darkness.

"Going to stay here all night?" he asked.

"Most of it," replied Clytie.

" Kent making you comfortable ? "

Clytie murmured an easeful affirmative, and Farquharson, nodding a good-night, disappeared into the
darkness.

" Apropos of quarrelling," said Kent after a while.
" Do you know, I thought once, for a few days, you
were vexed with me for something—after we left Dinan.
Were you ? "

Clytie felt the words like a touch of ice. Why had
Kent blundered so tactlessly ?

" Oh, why do you mention that ? " she cried. " The
only painful thing in all the trip. Something that I saw
at Dinan—I was put out. Was I very disagreeable ? It
did not refer to you in any way, dear friend."

" Pardon me if I have touched on a sore place,"
replied Kent. " I find I have a good deal to learn in
these matters. Will you make a compact with me to tell
me if ever I offend you ? Your friendship has grown so
valuable and dear a thing to me that the idea of running
the risk of losing it makes me—what shall I say ? Well,
I couldn't bear it. I don't often talk like this,—sentiment comes out of me very awkwardly,—but when I do
say anything of the sort I mean it. Believe me."

Clytie put out her gloved hand and touched him
lightly on the arm. She, too, felt that she had certain
need of him. A little thrill of tenderness passed through
her as she turned her head towards him to reply.

" Didn't I call you ' dear friend ' just now ? And I
meant it, too. You are too honest, too single-hearted,
ever to offend me, as you say. If I am ever rebellious
with you it will be my own fault, and I shall know it.
And as I really have got some common sense, I shall be
sorry for it. But you won't expect me to tell you so
every time, will you ? You will have to take it for
granted."

" You always make yourself out worse than you are,"
replied Kent. " Very few people know you. The Farquharsons, myself, Winifred, do. I should like to go
with you wherever you go, and tell folks not to believe
you, to prove to them what a——"

" Oh, stop ! stop ! " cried Clytie, with a little laugh.
" This sojourn in the land of compliments has infected

you. Oh, no ; I am ordinary ; not bad, not good.
You see, if I had had anybody to care for specially, and
who cared for me, I might have shown up differently. I
have hardly had a chance of seeming otherwise than
selfish. Opportunity makes the saint as much as it
makes the thief."

Kent meditated, framing a reply. The right words
would not come until it seemed that too long an interval
had elapsed. There was another silence—one of those
pleasant ones between friends when they feel in sympathy. Clytie at last broke it.

" Would you have had such a conversation as this
with a man friend?"

" No—at least—well, no. Why ?"

" Oh, nothing. The idea occurred to me," replied
Clytie.

CHAPTER IX.

The long autumn months rolled on, bringing little new to Clytie or to Kent. Clytie continued to paint her small *genre* pictures, but with a more certain touch, a restraint which a deeper insight into life compelled. They did not satisfy her now, however, as they used to. She had more articulate longings after an art which should be higher, more comprehensive, more responsive to certain subtler and at the same time more stirring impulses within her.

" I want to paint something that may live," she said to Kent, " something I can throw my whole soul into, something I can look at when it is finished and say : ' There, that is final ; that expresses consummately everything I have ever felt and dreamed.' "

" If you can ever say that, you will cease to be an artist," he replied in his matter-of-fact way.

" Perhaps so. But I must try. And the subject, the subject ? "

" Wait," said Kent. " If it ever comes, it will do so of itself."

Clytie waited, but the subject did not come. Meanwhile she had her hands full with orders, both for pictures and for magazine illustrations. Her life was full, as far as work could make it. Winifred came regularly to the studio, as usual, cheering her with sweet companionship. She had spent her summer holiday at the seaside, treating out of her own purse her two little brothers to a holiday. She came back with glowing reminiscences of her adventures, the humorous naughtinesses of the children, the odds and ends of character she had met with. Her only regret was that her dear Clytie had not been there too.

" I should have thrown those horrid children, Reggie and Arthur, into the sea ! " exclaimed Clytie.

"Oh, no, you wouldn't. They simply adore you. They are nice children, aren't they, now?"

"You little goose!" cried Clytie, kissing the warm brown cheek. "They are like you, the sweetest little children in the world. When are they coming to tea?"

These teas in the studio were red-letter days for Winifred's brothers and sisters. They worshipped Clytie, who had keen sympathy with the unconventionalities of childhood. She made grotesque caricatures of them, at which they screamed with laughter, or sat on the hearthrug with them and talked the nonsense that bright children love. Their joy was complete if Kent came in. They called him "Kent," took complete possession of him, presented him to Clytie as a pet trifle they carried about with them. He, too, was fond of these debauches, and seldom missed attending them if he could leave the Museum in time. He loved to see Clytie take her part in them. She seemed to him even more sweet and womanly than Winifred when she had a child on her lap, and her dark red hair was touching the black ruffled curls. He told her so one day, and the colour came into her cheeks as she laughed.

Another occasional visitor in the studio was Treherne, the young clergyman whom Clytie had met at the Farquharson's numismatic dinner-party. Kent and herself had run across him at a Bond Street gallery where some paintings by the impressionists Degas and Monet were on view. He was looking ill and overworked. He replied to their inquiries that he had been forced to give up his North London parish and take lighter duties near Victoria. As he lived in her neighbourhood, he hoped that Clytie would allow him to call one day and see her pictures; "Jack" at the exhibition had aroused his admiration. Clytie readily gave him her "day," when Miss Marchpane and herself were at home to their friends, and hoped he would come. He called, found a certain charm in the bright talk of the studio, exhilarating after the dull rounds among his parishioners, and soon became a constant visitor. Perhaps the charm of a pair of soft brown eyes attracted him more than he thought of confessing. Towards the end of the year, however, he bought, through a dealer, two of Winifred's dainty pictures.

The days shortened, the painting light grew less and less, and the time came for Clytie to pay her Christmas visit to Durdleham. She had not been there for a year, and her heart longed at times for the familiar faces and the voices of her own kith and kin. She thought that, perhaps, now she had grown older, her father and sisters would think her mode of life less unnatural, less likely to result in moral shipwreck. The letters, too, she had been receiving from them lately were kinder, more affectionate in tone. Mrs. Blather longed to have her dear Clytie back amongst them once more, and Janet wrote touchingly of the vacant chair at the dinner table. Clytie anticipated much quiet pleasure from her visit. The need of an attitude of rebellion was past, and she could throw herself lovingly, with no fear of compromising her independence, into all the mild interests of the household. There were times when a tenderer, softer chord vibrated in her heart, suggesting sadly the sweetness of home and loved family ties. She was human, with the foolish human craving for things that are not. She could not abandon her free artistic life ; but if she could fill it with gentler, softer graces ! In these moods she clung to Winifred, loving her for this element of sweet womanliness she brought into the rooms in the King's Road that were her home. It was with this range of feelings uppermost in her heart that she went to Durdleham.

For the first few days after Clytie's departure Kent laboured honestly and doggedly in his old way. But gradually he began to feel a lack of interest in his pursuits, to be vaguely conscious that the conditions of things were upset, and then he wished that Clytie had not gone.

One evening he was sitting in his room with a litter of proof-sheets lying idly before him. He felt depressed. It was a new sensation. It puzzled him, annoyed him, made him angry with himself, like a man's first unsuspected attack of the gout. He rose and walked about. His fire had nearly gone out, his lamp had been flaring and the room was filled with its acrid smoke. He could not open the window, for the sleet and rain were beating against the panes. He stopped for a moment watching

the water dribble outside down the glass. Then he
turned away impatiently, seeking solace from his book-
backs and pictures. But they seemed to look back
upon him unsympathetically, as if reproaching him for
the bare floor, the untidy dresser, and the cheerless
hearth. He rekindled his fire, filled a pipe, and sat
down to think.

Kent was not given to introspection. His external
interests in life were too engrossing for him to think
deeply or continuously about himself. Such a habit of
mind he used vehemently to deprecate as morbid, ego-
tistical. But now this strange depression, this vague
sense of loss, compelled him to account for it to his
reason. He began in a sober, materialistic way to
review his general health (there are philosophers amongst
us who refer all moods to the liver, not looking upon it,
however, like the ancients, as the seat of the affections !),
to question some little disappointments he had had with
regard to his great work, and to dwell upon the futility
of existence—the suggestion of which he should have
been logical enough to see was the result and not the
cause of his state of mind. But he was not logical.
Few men are when the great facts of inner life are in
question ; for in the course of logic " none of us would
see salvation," as far as this world's happiness is concerned. Gradually a truth dawned upon him. He
missed the ever-ready companionship he had enjoyed
for nearly a year. He missed Clytie. He found that
for the first time in his life since he was a baby he had
been depending for something on a woman. He had
never realised until then the strength of that unknown
subtle influence, the withdrawal of which left him so weak,
so unable to put forth all his powers. At first he thought
that it was merely the abrupt interruption of pleasant
habits, the sudden jerk out of a well-oiled groove.
Telling himself he was satisfied with this solution, he
resolutely went back to his writing and began to correct
his proof-sheets. But gradually his attention wandered
again. These sudden impulses to work against the grain
soon spend themselves out and produce greater lassitude
than before.

He tossed down his pencil in disgust and swung round

towards the fire. It was Clytie herself, then, that he missed. He missed her in spite of her being a woman, he told himself. And yet the picture rose before his mind of Clytie's dainty room and Clytie sitting there opposite to him, her hand, with falling lace at wrist, pressed into the softness of her hair. Why had she not written a line to him?

Yes, he missed her. But why should that make his work distasteful? He was puzzled. One thing alone was clear, his loneliness was growing intolerable. He threw on his waterproof, and, leaving his work, trudged through the rain to the " monastery," at South Kensington.

Wither was alone. Fairfax and Greene were dining out. The little man had been too lazy and sybaritic to face the cold and wet outside. He had clad himself in pyjamas and dressing-gown, and was reading a French novel on the couch drawn up in front of the fire. His diminutive figure looked absurdly small and wizened in his loose wrap. He nodded affectionately at Kent, explained briefly the fact of his being alone, and, while Kent was hunting in a familiar corner for the pair of slippers always there in readiness for his use, went on with his reading.

" Get me some whiskey, old chap," he said without looking up. " I have been dying for some this last hour and I have been too lazy to stir off the sofa."

Kent, as usual, supplied Wither's wants and poured out a glass for himself.

" Lazy little beggar," he said kindly as he sat down in the great saddle-bag chair. " How do you manage to get through your work?"

Wither laughed.

" I thought you knew better than to ask me that."

It was a tradition in the " monastery " that Wither never did any work. They paid him at his office for lending it a gentlemanly tone. As a matter of fact, like most clever, lazy men, he generally did an ordinary man's day's work in a few hours.

He stretched himself out luxuriously and lit a cigarette.

" Have you ever read this? " he asked, holding up his novel. It was Bourget's " Cruelle Énigme."

Kent nodded.

"I skimmed it through here one night while waiting for you. I have no patience with that sort of thing."

"Possibly not," remarked Wither, "but that's a fact about yourself, and not about the book."

"I don't believe it is human life," replied Kent. "People can't make animal passion the keynote of their lives nowadays."

"Why not nowadays?"

"The conditions of life prevent it. The savage has furious brute instincts, which he gratifies occasionally, when his mind is not taken up with fighting and hunting for his food. It may be the guiding principle in a splendid barbarism like some Eastern courts, where men have little else to think of. But in our modern civilisation there are other interests too absorbing. The hurry of life is too great."

"What about the empty-minded women you are always railing at?"

"They are all absorbed in their futilities—at least most of them," he added, correcting himself; "but even when idle they are not beasts. Now this woman you are reading about is a beast."

Wither eyed him curiously.

"You are talking nonsense, old chap. If she had been simply that, she would not have been a problem to the psychologist. The enigma was the sudden burst into animalism in the midst of a love that was almost idyllic."

"Bosh!" said Kent. "It was the same old hideous adultery."

"Oh, well! if you go on those lines, I am done," replied Wither, shrugging his shoulders. "I thought we were a little more advanced in our ideas in this establishment."

"You know I don't mean that," said Kent, puffing violently at his pipe. "The legality of the connection has nothing to do with it. It is the eternal coupling of the male and the female that revolts me. Pah! They might as well write a novel on the loves of the pastures."

"If I could write French, I should like to try it," said Wither. "It would be interesting."

"There is too much of that sort of thing written and

talked about," said Kent. "It's sickening. It's degradation of humanity."

"Well, it's not uncommon," said Wither, with a sphinxlike smile playing round the corners of his mouth as he gazed upwards at the cigarette smoke.

"Look here, Wither," said Kent ; "I have a higher faith in humanity. You profess to be a cynic, a man of the world, and you delight in calling yourself non-moral. That's all foolishness, I know. You are the kindest hearted little chap in the world. But can you, as a man of intellectual tastes, sympathise with all this animalism ?"

Wither threw away his cigarette, and bending forward laid his hand on Kent's knee.

"My dear old boy," he said, with more earnestness than he generally displayed, "I do call myself a man of the world, for I'm in it and I love it, and I have a very decent bowing acquaintance as well with its pals, the Flesh and the Devil. I know something of men, and as for women, it has been my lot to have been petted by a good few—my size lends itself to that sort of thing. In fact, Gulliver with the Brobdingnag maids of honour is not in it with me. I know all about 'em ; and I tell you, old chap, that the Beast, sometimes with a big B and sometimes in diamond type, lies in the nature of us all. There is not a living being with pure blood in his or her veins who is not overmastered at times by the principle of sex. You scoff at Bourget as a writer of morbid and impossible fiction. Look at your daily papers. Don't you see parsons of hitherto blameless lives running off with their cooks, virtuous women ruining their lives and their husbands' for the sake of some Hercules of a scoundrel—just as the patrician ladies in Rome went mad over the charioteers in the circus ! Man alive ! it is the Beast, the Beast that may slumber in an old maid's bosom until she is sixty and then drive her into the arms of her footman. How otherwise have you accounted for these things ?"

"I have not tried," replied Kent simply. "They have not interested me. They are diseases of the brain, for the physiologist to study, like suicide and murder. I don't believe in them in normal everyday life."

There was a long pause, broken only by Wither's request that Kent should put some coals on the fire, and the rattling of the operation. Wither resumed his reading and Kent pulled at his pipe in silence. At last the former looked up and said suddenly :

"Why do you think people marry ?"

"That's funny," replied Kent, with a slight start. "I was just wondering myself. I don't know : money, companionship, family, idiocy—God knows what."

"It has always struck me that you would be the first of us to go," said the other in pure, idle maliciousness.

"I ?" cried Kent, with a gesture of disgust. "I marry ! give up my work, procreate children I couldn't support ! Have to kiss and pet and fondle a woman——"

"Well, you need not do that unless you like," replied Wither, laughing in his gnomelike way. "She might expect it, but she would be soon consoled by the blessedness of pure spirituality."

Kent's reply was interrupted by the return of the absentees, Fairfax, the doctor, and Greene.

"I am so glad you fellows have come back," said Kent ; "Wither has been drivelling on his favourite topic until I was begining to loathe him."

"He's an immoral little wretch," said the doctor, throwing his greatcoat on Wither's curled-up body—"a pocket Mephistopheles. We keep him here as a kind of Familiar. Oh, what rot dining out is !" he added, with a yawn and a stretch as he seated his burly form on the foot of the couch. "I wish I had stayed at home."

"I wish you had," said Kent. "Let us have just one rubber before I go. There is time."

But Kent walked home that night with a new trouble at his heart that kept him awake a great part of the night.

Meanwhile Clytie was not enjoying herself at Durdleham. At first there were eager embraces, trifling tendernesses and solicitudes. The dear prodigal had returned, but the fatted calf was killed discreetly, lest it should convey a husk-flavoured reproach. Grace and Janet bubbled over with light Durdleham gossip, seeking to interest, and Clytie earnestly and sympathetically sought to be in touch with her surroundings. It was a real heart-felt effort on both sides towards harmony. But it soon became patent that these efforts were unavailing. Clytie saw the old prejudices barring her at every turn. She recognised with the bitterness of disillusionment that she was the bit of grit in the family machinery, stopping the smoothness of its working. As long as she identified herself with Durdleham interests things went well; but as soon as she, in her turn, ventured to sketch the bright incidents in her town life she felt a check in the current of mutual sympathy. If she was reserved, her sisters complained. They ought to know something of her friends, her occupations. When she was expansive they shrank cold and crablike into their mail of prejudice.

Her intimacy with a strange Bohemian man was a thorn in the side of the family. Mr. Davenant considered it extremely injudicious, and Mrs. Blather whispered to him that she scarcely thought it moral. Janet was too horrified to allude directly to the circumstance. But, in her neat, prim bedchamber, she prayed to the Almighty to lead her erring sister out of the paths of temptation. She duly informed Clytie of this act of piety, and when Clytie burst into laughter that was nearer to tears than to merriment, left the room in virtuous indignation.

Clytie could not help confessing to herself that she longed for Kent's companionship, with its broader sympathies and inspiring influences, but the view the household took of it pained her with a sense of aching discomfort, and made her feel a strange diffidence in writing to him as she had promised. She at last addressed him a short little note, stiff and constrained, which reached him the morning after his conversation with Wither and did not help to cheer him. Too proud to wait for an opportunity of posting this letter herself, she placed it on the hall slab together with the rest of the outgoing correspondence of the family. Although a hundred letters might have lain there for post without any one of them attracting Mrs. Blather's attention,—she was too pure-minded a gentlewoman for idle curiosity to be one of her failings,—it was too good an opportunity for the imps who seem sometimes to regulate human affairs to let slip, and as a matter of course Mrs. Blather's eye fell upon the address.

"So you are keeping up a violent correspondence with that man," she remarked acidly to Clytie. It is the way of some women to exaggerate.

Clytie bit her lip, checking an impulsive answer. What was the use of a retort?

Women of broad, liberal education, with interests beyond the nursery, still-room, and the afternoon-tea table, are known to live together, like men, in comparative harmony. They have learned the lesson the higher, broader life teaches of rising or declining instinctively to another being's plane of thought or feeling. It is hardly a fault of sex that women are petty, spiteful, and intolerant. When the conditions of life are narrow and illiberal any human being, man or woman, runs the risk of being shaped by them. And that is why Mrs. Blather and Janet, good, upright women according to their lights, subordinated their affection to their principles, and stood away shocked from their sister. Their traditional ideals of femininity had been sinned against. The crime was all but unpardonable. It was always present with them, always assuming fresh, distorted shapes. They were on a different plane from Clytie, and viewed all her actions in a false perspective.

Clytie was hurt, wounded in her womanly pride. She knew that there was much clay in her composition, and often felt with chastening self-abasement how much nearer the angels Winifred was than herself. Yet she was accustomed to live in an atmosphere free from reproach. Winifred, Kent, the Farquharsons, and others of her friends might touch with light, tender finger on here and there an imperfection in her character or conduct; for this she was grateful, knowing the deeper feelings of esteem and respect that prompted. But to move in a circle where she was looked upon as a black sheep, as a girl on the path to unutterable abysses, galled her to the quick, sent the hot blood mounting in stinging waves to her cheek, leaving the heart cold. Yet she had learned not to blame her sisters over much. She had lost her militant scorn of Jacob. Kent had taught her that although Esau might possess the higher birthright which no bartering of pottage could alienate, there was still saving grace in the stolen birthright which Jacob guarded so jealously. But this knowledge did not make her heart less sore.

The happiest time in this Christmas visit was when she could get away into the old lumber-attic in which she had dreamed so many girlish dreams. It had long been dismantled of the Liberty curtains, Persian rugs, and cheap Japaneseries that had lent it the suggestion of artistic atmosphere the girl of eighteen had craved. It was bare now, except for a table and chair and a few odds and ends of artist's materials, but a fire could be laid in the grate to make things look cheery, and there was still the deeply recessed attic-window where she could stand and look out over the same drear landscape. It was only the ordinary midland succession of fields, now black with winter, and pastures through which the river ran, its course only indicated by the fringing line of pollards and willows. Away on the slope to the west rose a clump of trees from which peeped a few houses and a church spire, the little village of Wexwith. In the foreground ran the highroad skirted with new red-brick cottages, a touch of sordidness added by man to the ungenerous dreariness of nature. Once this had affected Clytie with a sense of the unutterable melancholy of things. The young are prone to be so affected. They are rather proud when they realise it ; it is a kind of youthful vanity. But Clytie, like the wiser among us, sought brightness as she grew older, and although she could not consider the landscape cheerful, looked at it only through the memories of five years. Every spot had associations for her. There was the cottage where she had seen the little bully strike his playmate, the original conception of the picture that had helped to cause her welcome banishment from home. Next to it used to live the old beldame who threw out of doors the custards and jellies that Janet with angelic perseverance used to take her. What cruel mockery she used to make of Janet in those days ! Now she submissively helped to carry the custards. Behind the swelling uplands over the village the sun set, a red ball in the wintry sky. For how many wild fantastic daubs had not that formed a background !

It was during these reveries that the picture subject she craved commenced to haunt her as it gradually shaped itself into definiteness. Since her singular interview with the French girl at Dinan a lurid gleam streamed from the gates ajar of mysteries that had baffled her. She had read widely and deeply; but books are only the gloss of life, they are not the text. Its secrets must be read in the living world, with much pain and sleeplessness and wearied eyes. The throbbing page had been presented to Clytie for one sharp moment, blazing, the while, in letters of flame. Such knowledge changes lingering girlhood into womanhood without the aid of passion. It changes sex-pride into sex-sorrow —in higher natures, be it understood. And this sex-sorrow runs in channels hollowed out by ever-varying circumstance and temperament. It flows in the patient, all-enduring devotion of the sister labouring among outcasts, in the militant enthusiasm of the social reformer. It quivers in the hearts of teachers like George Eliot and Elizabeth Barrett Browning. It lives in the souls of some mothers who tremulously watch the shaping of their daughter's destiny. With Clytie it ran confluent with her artistic impulses. It had influenced them vaguely, dimly, hauntingly for months, but now, at last, stirringly, proclaiming itself, insistently demanding expression.

The subject was found : Faustina in her innocent maidenhood. The problem : how to manifest the foreshadowings of passion on the young, clear face ?

Clytie spent hours in her attic trying to fix the summer lightnings of features that flashed elusively before her mind. She wished she were in London, to go abroad in the highways seeking after a face. It seemed to her that in the great city she would find the one she wanted, in the park, at the theatre, perhaps among the subdued black rows of women—lines of suppressed volcanic workings—in some great shop. But in Durdleham volcanoes were extinct or regulated by formula to erupt with mild propriety. She began to feel the frenzied weariness of helplessness. If only she could talk to someone—to Kent.

One day Mrs. Blather came into the attic. Clytie

was dreaming before incoherent charcoal streaks. The fire had burned low and the draught of the opening door made her shiver.

"Why, Clytie, child, you are blue with cold," said her sister, wrapping her gray woollen shawl more tightly round her thin shoulders. "Why do you mope up here?"

"I am not moping, Gracie," replied Clytie; "I am only working—conceiving a picture, that's all."

"Oh, but you oughtn't to do any work. Have you not come down for a holiday? What's the good of burning the candle at both ends? Come down to the drawing-room and talk to the Howatsons; they are inquiring after you."

"But I am in such a mess!" laughed Clytie, showing her blackened finger tips.

"Well, come down and tidy yourself in my room; there is a fire, and you can warm yourself for a few minutes."

Clytie followed her sister down the stairs to the latter's bedroom, where a cheerful fire warmed the cold clean chintz of the hangings. Mrs. Blather sat down by the hearth, while Clytie washed her hands and touched her hair.

"Why don't you tell us more of your work, Clytie?" she said propitiatingly. "Here you are being criticised in the newspapers, quite like a famous person, and we at home know nothing of it."

"Why, Gracie, I thought it did not interest you much."

"We would take an interest if you would only let us."

"But, you see, I paint such queer pictures. I don't think they are your style. And then pictures are not portable like books. If I wrote poetry, you could be deluged with presentation copies; but even we ourselves lose all the result of our work when the picture is sold."

"Of course, but you might write and talk more. And with regard to the 'queer' pictures, don't you think, if you made us your confidantes, the pictures might be a little less—'queer'? You see, Clytie, you are young, and it is your nature to run into extremes. If you were just a little bit restrained by older folks, would you not get what you are so fond of talking about—'truth'—in your work?"

Clytie was somewhat puzzled at Mrs. Blather's conciliatory tone. Was this an effort towards a better under-standing, or was it a disguised lecture? She finished her hasty toilet and went and stood by the fire near her sister, her foot on the fender.

"Thank you very much, Gracie," she said, "but would you always understand? Perhaps," she added, smiling, after a pause, "you would want to restrain too much—and where would the picture be?"

"Well, why not try? What is the picture to be about that you are working at now?"

The blood rushed to Clytie's cheeks, which, bent down, caught the added glow of the fire—a contrast, with her rich colour, to the clear, waxen, negative face of her sister. She broke suddenly into a nervous laugh.

"There! Even from the beginning I couldn't discuss it with you, Gracie. It is only a girl's face—I can't tell you anything more about it."

"Well, that's what I complain of," said Mrs. Blather with growing acidity. "You keep your own sisters in ignorance of your life, and confide everything to this Mr. Kent, who is nothing to you."

"How do you know I have told Mr. Kent about this picture?"

"I was not referring to this one, though by your manner I see you have."

"Well, yes, I have," said Clytie, "because—because—he has the artistic temperament—and he can seize an idea—in fact—why are you saying this to me, Gracie?"

"Because you are not going the right way, Clytie ; and it is my duty as your elder sister, who has looked after you since you were so high, to make a last effort to bring you within some restraining influences. We don't like your intimacy with Mr. Kent. It is not what we have been taught to think right. I know you look down upon us as narrow-minded at Durdleham. I think it is better for us. We are shut in, perhaps, between high walls, but the high walls keep us safe."

They were silent for a few moments, then Clytie said :

"Gracie, don't you think this subject has been enough discussed? It is wasting words and spoiling good intentions. Suppose we go down to the Howatsons."

CHAPTER X.

One day, about this time, Kent was walking home from the Museum. His spirits had by no means lightened since his conversation with Wither, and he strode along moodily, trying to fix his attention on the arrangement of that evening's portion of the great work. He had gone back to it resolutely and doggedly, and was conscious that it was progressing not badly, but at the same time he had a troubling sense that he was treating it less as an aim than as a cure for existence. Fairfax, the doctor, told him he was overdoing himself, that the strain of double work was telling, advised total idleness, and if possible a change of air. Kent gave the prescription a trial, and went down to the Isle of Wight for a week-end, where he tramped himself utterly tired during the day and bored himself exquisitely during the evening. Then he came back rather worse than when he went. No ; he was suffering from change, and not from the want of it.

London was in a pitiable condition. It had snowed, then thawed into slush, and now a hard black frost had set in, rendering the roadways like glass. Already during his walk home Kent had seen four horses down. On the first two occasions he had lent a helping hand. After that it began to grow monotonous, and he hurried past the accidents, anxious to get home out of the sullen iron-bound streets. At the corner of Sloane Square and the King's Road he saw a familiar girlish figure coming towards him. It was Winifred, her dark cheeks glowing with the exercise of walking ; but he noticed a look of trouble in her eyes.

"I am so glad to have met you, Mr. Kent," she said; "I want to speak to you. Can you walk a little way with me ? "

"Of course, as long as you like. What is the matter ? You are not yourself."

"No.   I have been upset, so upset; you would hardly think it.   Come and I will tell you."

They crossed the road and went on down Lower Sloane Street.

"It's about Jack—Jack, the model, you remember. He has been run over!   Oh, it's horrible!"

"And you are going to him?" asked Kent, noticing for the first time a little basket hanging over her arm. "Give me that," he added, taking the basket, which she out of habit surrendered to him.   "And these are jellies and what not for him?"

"Yes.   Will you come with me and see him, see what can be done for him, rather?   His mother is so harsh, so stupid."

"How did you come to hear of the accident?"

Winifred's cheek paled a little and she turned her head from him.

"I saw it myself.   Oh, I shall never, never forget it! just outside Sloane Square station; I was coming home, yesterday.   The ground was just as slippery as it is now.   Oh, how can I tell you!   It makes me shudder to think of it!"

"Take your time," said Kent good-naturedly.

She was silent for a few steps.   Then, nerving herself, she went on with more coherence.

"He was just in front of me when I came out, and as he saw me he ran away, frightened—like a little scared animal; you know his ways.   And crossing the road, not looking where he was going, he turned his head round as if to see I was not following him, and then he slipped—oh-h!   under the hoofs of a horse—in a hansom.   And the driver tried to pull up sharp, and the horse came down too—on top of Jack!"

"Good God!" said Kent.

"A crowd at once collected.   I rushed through—I must have screamed a little and cried that I knew him, for the people made way for me.   It all seemed like a horrid dream.   I can't tell what happened, except that I found myself kneeling on the ground with the poor little mite's head on my lap.   Then someone was talking to me, who said he was a doctor, and began to examine the boy's injuries."

" Is he badly hurt ? "

" The doctor does not know yet. No bones are broken—the injuries are internal."

" Is he at the hospital ? "

" No. At his own home. I gave them the address, and told them his mother would care for him—why, I don't know. And then they got a stretcher from the police-station and carried him home, and I went with them and broke it to his mother. But, oh ! Mr. Kent, almost the most awful part of it is that it seems as if I was the cause of it."

" Nonsense, my dear child," said Kent in rough earnestness.

" Oh, yes, it is. If it hadn't been for me he would not have run across the road in a fright. Oh ! I can see it now—the horse plunging, his hoofs over the child —and then the collapse, and the child hidden under the horse ! "

They turned down a side street and then another, sinking into the squalour that still remains in that vague river district between Pimlico Pier and Milbank.

" Poor little chap ! Punishment has come at last," said Kent. "It has a kind of way of doing so. What does Clytie think of it ? Have you told her ? "

" I only wrote to her yesterday. This morning I got a telegram. I think I have it with me. It is Clytie all over ! "

She opened the purse she was carrying inside her muff and drew from it a crumpled telegram. It ran :

Dreadfully distressed. Get the best of everything, nurse, doctor. Find money to go on with in drawer at once. I must feel that I am doing something. Will write.

" Yes, it is like her," said Kent, with a smile, as he handed it back to her.

" I wonder whether you would mind doing something for me, Mr. Kent ? " said Winnie after a pause. " Get the money out of Clytie's drawer for me. I have been so busy all day. Reggie is in bed with a bad cold and the house is upside down—and of course I have to come here. You see, I must use the money, or else Clytie would be hurt ; it seems to me to be a matter of conscience."

"Or a matter of Clytie's telling you?" said Kent.

"Well, perhaps it's that. One always does what Clytie says. So do you, Mr. Kent. Anyhow, I should like to have the money for the sake of obeying her wishes. Could you get it for me?"

"Of course, if you will tell me how."

"Oh, that's easy. I have the key of her secretaire in my purse. She keeps her cash-box there. You can let me have it as it is. Will you?"

"Of course. I will bring it round to-night."

The early winter twilight had fallen and scared shivering indoors the brood of unwashed children that possess these gray, sordid streets. Here and there women stood at the doors, their hands folded in their aprons, with little ones clinging to their skirts, chaffering with a costermonger, or exchanging shrill confidences with a neighbour. Most of the front parlours on the ground floor were lightless, with drawn blinds. Here and there a public-house beer-can gleamed white upon the railing spikes. Workmen lurched heavily along, now and then followed by shawled, bare-armed wives, vituperative. For it was Saturday afternoon, when the businesslike wife looks after her husband. Here and there from a suddenly opened doorway came the smell of many weeks' cooking. The poorer classes despise fresh air in their rooms—perhaps because they get it for nothing.

Winifred stopped with Kent at a dark-fronted, dingy house, the facsimile of the forty other houses in the dingy row and of the forty opposite across the narrow roadway. A little girl answered her knock.

"Mrs. Burmester in, my dear? Come, Mr. Kent, if you don't mind. I know the way."

Kent followed her up two flights of stairs, and into Mrs. Burmester's room. It was less squalid than he had imagined. A fire was burning in the grate, with a saucepan simmering. There were fairly substantial chairs, a table, and the ragged remains of a carpet. On a big bed by the side of the wall, not uncomfortable-looking nor unclean, lay Jack, tossing his wild elf head in delirium. By the side of the bed sat a nurse, whom the doctor had sent. Mrs. Burmester was spreading out the tea-things on the table. Her red, heavy face brightened momentarily when Winnie entered.

"How is he now?"

"Oh, mortal bad, miss. He hasn't had his senses all day."

"And the doctor—does he say anything?"

"He said he would like a consultation," replied the nurse, "but he did not know exactly whom to refer to."

"Why, to me, of course!" replied Winnie. "He knows my name and address. If you see him before I do, say I authorise him to do anything he thinks right. We are willing to—that is, he need not be hindered by questions of expense."

Winnie turned to Mrs. Burmester with the basket, which she had taken from Kent's hand. The mother thanked her, almost monosyllabically. She was too dull for emotions of any kind. Kent watched her with interest, for Clytie had often spoken of her, hinting at her own puzzle.

There was a lull in Jack's ravings as Winifred and Kent stood over the bed looking at him. The expression of sullen ferocity had gone from his face, which now seemed refined and gentle. He smiled at Winifred, not recognising her, murmured something incoherent about arithmetic. His mind had wandered back to his earlier school-days. He had been fond of a teacher there, his mother explained. Her name was Miss Jones. She wished he was fond of anybody now. He was a sore trial to her. The floodgates of dull speech were opened and a slow stream of joyless anecdote poured forth— a jeremiad of Jack's iniquities. Winnie stopped her gently.

"We must not think of that now, Mrs. Burmester," she said. "We have to get him round again; and then we will see whether we can't make a good boy of him for you."

"Ah! You won't do that. He is too much like his father."

They stayed a little longer, talking. Then they went, as Winifred had to be back among her own family responsibilities.

"By the way," said Kent as they were walking homewards, "this must be Treherne's parish—in fact, I am sure of it.   Has it not struck you ?"

"No, it never occurred to me."

"Well, he ought to know.   I'll send him a line.   He knows all about this sort of thing."

He walked with her as far as the door of her own house.   There she gave him the key of Clytie's secretaire.   Mrs. Gurkins kept the room key.   He left her and turned homewards, striding along rather fast, eager to execute Clytie's commission.   He was filled with a foolish pleasure at her impulsive telegram ; touched also at Winifred's implicit obedience and confidence.

"She's a queen among women !"

The silly phrase passed through his mind and he caught himself repeating it with his lips, half aloud.

"Bosh !" he added with some impatience.   And he stopped to look in at a shop-window to divert his mind. It was a boot-shop.   He ran his eye mechanically over the rows of commonplace, cheap boots, and then it fell upon a little pair of tan shoes, with broad silk laces. Before he realised how his mind was working, a picture rose before him of Clytie wearing a similar pair during the summer trip abroad.   He remembered bending down one day when a knot had slipped and retying it for her.

"I am becoming a positive ass !" he said to himself, with an angry jerk away from the window.   Then he redoubled his pace, as if in defiance, but the silly phrase rang in his ears :

"She's a queen among women !"

He obtained the key from Mrs. Gurkins, and entered the tenantless room.   The blinds were down, the curtains undrawn.   It was just dark.   He lit the piano candles and looked about him.   How dreary the room seemed ! The fireless grate, the coverless table (the cloth had been thriftily put away by Mrs. Gurkins), the absence of the feminine litter with which Clytie was wont to strew the room—all made his heart sink for a moment beneath the weight of a great longing.   He remembered, too, the room by that dim light—on the evening of Clytie's submission.   He saw her again lift her arms to unpin her hat from behind, the proud young figure standing out free as she looked at him half playfully, half seriously, her ripe, full lips parted in a smile. His breath came quickly as a flood of self-knowledge swept over him. He had felt puzzled then—at vague inarticulate desires. Now they were gathering a terribly real, objective shape. He grew dizzy, hot and cold, half terrified at himself.

With shaking fingers he fitted the key in the lock of the secretaire. In the drawer was a heterogeneous collection of odds and ends—letters, keys, ball-programmes, receipted bills—which he had to thrust aside so as to withdraw the little japanned cash-box. As he lifted it out a handkerchief came with it, caught by its lace edge, and after dangling a little fell at his feet. He picked it up, kept it in his hand, soothed at the softness. A faint odour of perfume rose from it, subtle and delicate—the well-known perfume that Clytie always used. It was like an emanation from herself. It grew over his highly strung senses like a breath of her own personality, sweet, intoxicating, overpowering. His brain swam. With a kind of groan he staggered to the sofa, threw himself upon it, burying his face in the little handkerchief, kissing it madly.

Now all was clear, waves of lightning flashing the truth through him. He loved her, passionately, desired her with a passion all the fiercer for its long restraint. Yet he could not think coherently. One thought, one utter realisation, overpowered all others. At last this great surging sex-tumult was sweeping through his veins.

"Oh, my God, I love her! Oh, my God, I love her!" That was all that he could groan out as he lay upon the sofa.

The creak of the door made him start up. On the threshold stood one of Mrs. Gurkins's curly-headed little children. She looked for a moment, rather frightened, at his haggard face, and then ran away. Thus aroused to a sense of external things, he locked up the secretaire and went out, taking the cash-box and handkerchief with him.

On the slab outside his rooms he found a letter in Clytie's familiar handwriting. He went into his room, and sitting down before his writing space, spread the letter out before him.   It ran as follows :

My Dear Friend Kent :

If you ask me why I have not written to you for such a long time, I must shrink within my shell of femininity and refuse to give you reasons.   For I have them, and they are compounded from a recipe handed down from Mother Eve.   Well, I write to you now because I must.   That reason I make you a present of.

I want to be in town again, in the King's Road, and to see you by the fireside, ready to be asked questions and to answer them, and to comfort your erratic friend Clytie with your kindliness and wisdom. She is looked upon as a bad girl here, and pines for someone who thinks her human, and who also thinks her art human, and can help her in it.

Listen, now ; I have got *the* subject at last ; it is eating my heart out almost, I have to keep it hidden so to myself.   I must tell you— for the sake's sake.   "Faustina as a young, innocent girl, with the foreshadowings of passion on her face."   There !   Now you know. What do you think of it ?

Do you remember my depression at Dinan ?   Well, I think it was there I got the conception.   I can't tell you more.   But it is haunt- ing me.   I feel what I want to do, but I can't get a face.   What shall I do ?   Tell me.   You know, dear Kent, in our talks, we have often disregarded principles that move the world pretty potently. But as an artist I am bound to recognise the part that passion plays in the tragedy of things.

> " These things are life :
> And life, some think, is worthy of the Muse,"

as Meredith says in " Modern Love."   (Do you remember our read- ing it together ?)

I can't write properly about it.   I long for a talk with you.   I shall break away soon and come for it.   So be prepared with all your sympathy.

Do you miss me just a little bit ?   I often fancy my perverseness must give a little wholesome irritation to your life, and you are very good not to mind it.   I always seem to be coming to you for help and sympathy.   When can I ever do anything for you ?   You must tell me, dear friend, when the time comes.

I should like to tell you to give Winnie a kiss for me, but that is idiotic, isn't it ?   Yet you know what I mean.   See that the dear child is not wearing herself out.   There !   I am asking you to do something else for me.   Do write a long letter, full of yourself, with just a paragraph about the needs, artistic and otherwise, of

Your friend,
C. D.

Kent took some time to read this.   The letters swam a little before his eyes.   Then he laid his head upon his arms and thought, in dumb agony.   Clytie's letter,

sisterly and trustful, soothed and goaded him at once.
" The part that passion plays in the tragedy of things ! "
God !   Had a fleeting thought never struck her what a
part it might play in their lives' tragedy ?   How could he
answer that letter, addressed to a friend, received by a
lover in the hot flush of newly awakened realisation ?
How could he meet her bright, frank look with this
burning demon within him ?   It was base, horrible.   His
mind wandered to a German print he had seen somewhere, a goat-footed satyr kneeling and leering at
Psyche.   He shuddered.

It is given but to few men to know this terror of love :
only to those who, like Kent, have hitherto expended vast
animal and moral energies in non-sexual enthusiasms,
and have rebelled with almost passionate repulsion
against the assertion of the sexual principle.   To some
men love dawns like a sweet, fair star—the storm comes
later on.   To such as Kent it comes in terrific forked
lightnings and crash of thunder, overwhelming the soul
with terror.   To Kent's excited fancy it seemed that the
Beast, such as Wither had spoken of, had entered into
him.   He had betrayed the compact of friendship, her
sisterly trust in him.   Fool that he had been !   Why
had he not recognised it before ?   Now all was over
between them.   The future seemed nothing but black,
rolling darkness.

The solitary gas-jet that he had lit on entering flared
high and strident over the mantelpiece above the black-
ening fire, and Kent lay with his hands on his arms,
his morbid brain at death-grapple with love, he himself
heedful of nothing external—not even of a gay whistle
and a quick, springing tread on the uncarpeted stairs.
The door burst suddenly open.

" Come out, you fusty old hermit——"

Then Wither stopped.   Kent raised a drawn, rather
ghastly face and stared at him stupidly.

" My dear old chap, in the name of Heaven, what's
the matter ? " cried Wither, putting down his hat and
stick and coming towards him.

" Oh, nothing ! " said Kent, who pulled himself together with an effort, rose, and broke into a forced
laugh.

Wither looked at him steadily while he slowly drew off his gloves.

"That's nonsense!" he said quietly.

Then his sharp glance fell on the little crumpled handkerchief that lay beside the open letter on the table. His quick sense, aided by certain opinions he had formed long since, grasped the main feature of the situation.

He went over to where Kent was standing by the fireplace, and laid his hand on his shoulder.

"Never mind, dear old man, it will all come right."

"It will never come right," groaned Kent absently.

"It must. She must care for you in time."

"How do you know what I am thinking of?" Kent burst out rather fiercely.

"I guessed. Besides—the handkerchief. It is not your own. Yours are a little more businesslike."

"Oh, well!" said Kent a little huskily, and throwing his head back with a gesture of impatience, "I can't hide it. What would be the good? I have found out that she is a friend no longer, that what you were saying the other night is true—and I feel a brute! My God, what a brute I feel!"

Wither's mental balance was for a moment upset. He righted it after a moment with considerations of his friend's character. In many fragile, nervous bodies there is a delicacy of perception which often remains all the keener when protected by a shell of cynicism.

"You want to be reasoned with gently, friend John," he said. "You must not feel a brute when you love a woman as a man like you can love. It's the best and holiest thing on God's earth, believe me."

"But, Teddy, she is so frank, so trustful, so proud of our friendship—it can never be the same again—if I should tell her, she would hate me——"

"You can bet your life she wouldn't!" murmured Wither.

"She would go out of my life in indignation, and she would be right," Kent went on. "She would scorn me for the feelings that I know now I have had all along for her. No; it is all over, all over. I can't meet her again. I think I shall go mad! I shall throw up everything and go away."

"You dear, foolish old chap," said Wither, "can't you see that very little would make her in love with you, if she is not so already? Why should you two not get married ? "

"I marry ! " gasped Kent, as if struck by a new idea. "I ask Clytie Davenant, with her beauty and intellect and genius, to come and share—this ! Clytie Davenant marry me ! Why, the idea is ludicrous—preposterous ! "

"If I were she, I should not think so," said Wither affectionately.

Kent shook his head gloomily, and kicked the smouldering coal into a fitful blaze.

"No. Until she shows me unmistakably—which can be never—that she cares for me in that way, I would sooner bite my tongue out than tell her."

"Until she asks you to marry her, in fact ! John Kent, you are two years older than I am, and three times as big. But verily you are a little child ! And if you weren't," he added impulsively, with a soft glitter in his elfin eyes, "you would not be the lovable old chap that you are ! Good-bye ! "

"Oh, stay a little, Teddy ! " cried Kent. "I'm not much company, but I——"

"Come round with me and have some dinner, then," interrupted Wither. "It will occupy your body—if not your mind. And it will be better for you than the bottled beer and sardines which you usually feast upon. I shall be quite alone and you can do some work for me."

"All right ! " replied Kent dejectedly. "It does not matter what I do."

Wither turned his face to the fire, while Kent prepared to go out. When he turned round Kent was holding the cash-box in his hand. The handkerchief and letter were gone from the table, and Wither smiled inwardly. He had himself disposed of many such trifles in a similar way. Men are very much alike in several matters.

CHAPTER XI.

THE atmosphere of Durdleham was uninspiring.
Clytie could make no progress with her picture, and at
last she laid it aside in despair. She had set her heart
upon painting it, and the thoughts of it worried her,
prevented her from sleeping. Not only would it give
her fame, satisfy her ambition, stimulated by the success
of "Jack," but it would satisfy certain cravings of her
soul. And yet she was conscious that only when these
cravings found articulate utterance could the haunting
shadows be fixed. The lack, therefore, seemed to lie in
herself : whether in her spiritual nature or in her material
experience of the world she could not tell ; perhaps it
was a subtle combination of the two. She could not
bring her lens of introspection to a focus. What she
saw through it was blurred and inchoate.

She had looked forward to Kent's reply to her letter.
His sympathetic common sense might help her. When
his answer did come, after some days' interval, it was
strangely cold and dispiriting, just two sides of notepaper barely filled with sententious enigma.

"If the painting of it will bring you joy, paint. If
not, you are grasping at shadows."

That was the gist of it. What did it mean ? Clytie
was inclined to be indignant. Her own letter had been
written out of the friendliness and needs of her heart, and
the reply seemed almost like a rebuff. She did not know
that the writing of it had caused Kent two hours' perplexed
wretchedness. Even the finest feminine perception
cannot pierce through a millstone. The little feeling
of resentment towards Kent took the keenness of edge
from her anticipated pleasure of seeing him again ; at
least so she told herself when she packed her boxes at
the end of her visit to Durdleham. But as the train
brought her nearer to London her spirits rose. She was
free once more to live her own life, without fear of com-

ment or criticism. It was simple, laborious, and innocent enough, and she desired little more at present ; but there was the exhilarating sense of freedom, of perfect liberty to be outrageous, reckless, if such was her good pleasure, wherein lies much of the sweetness of independence.

She found her sitting-room tidied, neatly arranged, looking as nearly as possible as if it had never been vacated, and Winifred, a transforming fairy in the midst of it, eagerly awaiting her. Clytie sighed a little as she listened to Winnie's gossip. The latter looked at her with reproachful inquiry.

"I was only thinking, dear, that this is more my home than the house at Durdleham, and you are dearer to me than anyone there."

Winifred stroked her friend's hand in girlish fashion and turned away her head. She knew Clytie too well to make any reply. Then she spoke of Jack, who was in a fair way towards recovery. She had been very glad of Clytie's money, she confessed, with a deep blush, because things at home—well, Clytie knew. And Mr. Treherne, with whom Kent had communicated, had been very kind and helpful. He went round to Mrs. Burmester's every afternoon to cheer up the invalid.

"And I suppose you go round pretty often?" said Clytie.

"Of course — every afternoon," replied Winifred simply.

And Clytie, as she smoothed the shapely head lying in her lap, smiled to herself a little mysterious smile.

Mr. Kent, too, Winifred continued, had been invaluable to her. He had brought the boy picture-books, toys—had sat up with him one night whilst the nurse rested, the mother being quite helpless, and sleeping in an adjoining room which they had rented for the time between them. Never had street arab been so petted, so preciously guarded. He was growing quite human under the treatment. Kent and Treherne had managed to get him a nomination to a decent school-home, which would assure him an honest career in after life. Winifred was enthusiastic. She had never known before what a good, beautiful world it was, how filled with good and beautiful people !

In reply to a question of Clytie's she said that she had seen little of Kent lately ; that he looked overworked, worried, on the rare occasions when she had exchanged a few words with him.

"He is doing too much. I must speak to him about it this evening," said Clytie.

She took it for granted that he would come, if not at the present hour, while they were sitting over the tea-cups, at any rate after dinner, to discuss in cheery, familiar fashion the events of the past month. But the moments slipped by and his footstep was not heard on the stairs.

"Are you sure that he knew I was coming back to-day?" asked Clytie.

"Of course. He inquired twice of me," replied Winifred.

Winnie went away, and Clytie dined, took up a book, and waited. But Kent did not come. Clytie felt hurt. If he had been engaged, he might at least have left her a word of welcome. It was unfriendly, unlike him. Surely she could not have offended him in any way. She grew interested in her book, sat up till a late hour finishing it. As she neared the end she heard the well-known footstep coming up the stairs. She laid her book down, expecting to see the door open, but though she thought she detected a faint pause outside on the landing, the sound of the tread did not cease, but continued up the next flight until it was lost. Then she went to bed, somewhat angry.

She was in her studio betimes in the morning setting things straight. Orders had come in for a couple of small street-urchin pictures. She had to make arrangements for setting to work upon them at once. Her mind was intent upon the matter when she heard Kent pass down the stairs on his way to the Museum. Ordinarily he was accustomed, if he was not pressed for time, to thrust his head in at the studio door as he passed, nod good-morning, and perhaps receive some small commission to execute at the colour man's in Oxford Street.

"Perhaps he has grown tired of our intimacy," thought Clytie, "and is taking this opportunity of breaking it off." The thought was a whip to her pride. It sent the blood rushing in fierce waves to her cheeks. She was alone, an angry woman, not fit company for herself. She felt humiliated, insulted, and encouraged herself in the feeling, baring her shoulders to the lash. It scarcely occurred to her then to inquire into the justice of the suggestion—the mere fact of the suggestion presenting itself was sufficient to make her burn with indignation.

After lunch she took a cab and drove to Piccadilly to look at the shops and the people. Town was filling again, the afternoon sun shone brightly. Clytie's spirits rose. She went with light, defiant tread down the Burlington Arcade, flashing a contemptuous glance upon admiring loungers, bought herself gloves and odds and ends of millinery, crossed over to Bond Street, looked in at Dowdeswell's to see a picture on view in the gallery, and then, after an interview with Burrowes, the dealer, in Oxford Street, she turned into Regent Street, prepared to enjoy the contemplation of the miscellaneous crowd forever moving up and down its broad pavement. Perhaps the wished-for face would meet her there, she thought, smiling to herself; in which case she determined that she would stop, pass it and repass it, fixing its features in her memory. She amused herself thus for some time, scanning the faces of the passers-by, inventing rapid histories to account, here for the after-light of laughter in a young girl's eyes, and there for the lines of pain round the corners of an older woman's lips. She paused before a shop-window to observe a ragged little arab who was flattening a nose, already much snubbed by previous applications, against the glass. To gratify a whimsical artistic fancy she entered the shop on a trivial pretext so as to obtain from the other side of the pane the aspect of the urchin's face. Then, after making a mental note of it for future use, she went on her way. It was exhilarating, this bright London, with its manifold variegation, after the dull uniformity of Durdleham. This perpetual stimulus was necessary to her art, which drooped helpless in the quiet country town. And with the thrill of artistic quickening came the buoyant, vigorous pulsation of youth. Her tread was elastic, her cheeks and eyes animated. She had forgotten her irritation of the morning in the sense of vitality and enjoyment. It was a good thing to be young, with a purpose in life and the freedom and strength to carry it out. Clytie tasted a rare happiness that afternoon, one of which the high gods are very sparing.

Suddenly she felt a touch on her arm, and a voice exclaimed :

"My dear Clytie! What are you wandering about here for?"

She turned round. The speaker was Mrs. Farquharson, merry and smiling. They shook hands and walked leisurely down the street together.

"When did you get away from that dreadful place, and why haven't you been to see us?"

"This is my first day of freedom," replied Clytie, "and I was just thinking of coming round to Harley Street."

"That's right! You will come round with me when I have finished my shopping. I was wishing for you. I have a little—no, a big treat for you."

"Is it nice to eat? I looked in longingly at Charbonnel's as I passed down Bond Street, and I am hungry."

"It's Thornton—at last," said Mrs. Farquharson with a little air of triumph.

Clytie was interested, and forgot Charbonnel's.

"When did he come?"

"He has been in England some weeks, but only a few days in London. Do you know, he is going to settle down. Won't that be delightful? I do hope you will like him."

"And he is going to give up fighting and exploring and all that?" asked Clytie.

"So he says. But I don't believe it. He will get seized with the fever after a time and then off he will go again. That has always been his way. But at any rate we will have him with us for a season."

"Is he staying with you?"

"Oh, dear, no! We wanted him to, but he is too wild a creature. Besides, he knows the half of London, and is in demand everywhere. He is quite a personage."

"Then where does the treat come in?" asked Clytie, laughing.

"Why, he comes to Harley Street this afternoon for tea, you obtuse girl," cried Mrs. Farquharson. "And that is why we had better make haste to get back, as it is growing late."

Clytie had often heard Mrs. Farquharson speak of this cousin, Thornton Hammerdyke, and was half doubtful whether to allow herself to be infected with her enthusiasm or to prepare herself to find him commonplace, as one generally does find the particular heroes of our intimate friends. Caroline was never tired of talking of him. He was a hero, a latter-day berserker. She was proud of him, treasured up paragraphs in the newspapers in which his name was mentioned, wove a woman's web of romance around his brilliant exploits. She had often waxed eloquent over his fame, his personal charm, his physical strength and beauty.

"But all this can't be contained in one poor mortal," Clytie would say sometimes, teasingly.

And Mrs. Farquharson would reply, without any of the banter that generally characterised her personal gossip:

"Wait until you have seen him, my dear."

To the imaginative there was much that was heroic and romantic in the record of the active life of Thornton Hammerdyke. He had entered the army shortly after leaving school, but, wearying after a couple of years of the dulness of a garrison life, had resigned his commission. An exploring party to Thibet was afoot. He joined it, quickly became its leading spirit, and when the chief of the expedition was incapacitated through illness he undertook the command. This brought him into public notice. When the Soudan War broke out he joined Lord Wolseley as a volunteer, and made himself conspicuous by his daring and his marvellous feats of bodily strength. His name was known all through the army. He courted danger, especially where it took the form of hand to hand fighting. An eye-witness of the scene had told Caroline how once, when attacked by three gigantic Soudanese, he had shorn one clean through the body, lost his sword, leaped from his horse, wrenched the spear from one of the others with a force that made the man's arm snap like a twig, turn on the other—while the broken-armed savage leaped upon his back and tried to throttle him—and how before there was time to follow his movements both were lying dead at his feet. He had fought side by side with Burnaby in the rash conflict when the author of the "Ride to Khiva" fell pierced with Soudanese spears. He had been in evidence in every skirmish. When the war was over he remained in Africa, on the Soudan frontier, in command of some Egyptian cavalry, maintaining a guerrilla warfare until the troops were recalled. And then he plunged into the interior, exploring on his own account, with a nominal authority from the Belgian government. And it was on this part of his career that his reputation chiefly rested. Certainly ugly stories against him of undue harshness, even ferocity, were afloat at one time. But he laughed at these rumours on his return to England, and sarcastically observed in a letter to the *Times* that, given a community consisting of a judge, a prisoner, and a hundred howling, savage maniacs, it was a matter of some difficulty to form an impartial jury.

When Mrs. Farquharson and Clytie arrived at Harley Street the short January day had nearly drawn to a close. In the drawing-room the gas had not been lighted, and by the dull glow of the fire objects were only dimly visible. Two men rose from either side of the hearth as the ladies entered. The long ungainly figure Clytie recognised as Mr. Farquharson, the other as Thornton Hammerdyke, from Caroline's description of his great powerful frame. His face she could not distinguish; only a large, finely shaped head, and white teeth gleaming under a heavy moustache as he exchanged laughing greetings with his cousin.

Mrs. Farquharson performed the little ceremony of introduction. Then tea was brought in.

"You will excuse this outer darkness, Clytie," said Caroline. "George thinks it soothing. You know his ways. You see what a poor woman has to put up with!"

"I agree with him," said Clytie. "It is cosy, and it seems to sanction foolish gossip."

"Did you ever hear me gossip?" asked Mr. Farquharson severely. "I like it, Miss Davenant, because it induces a meditative frame of mind."

"And slumber," murmured his wife as she dispensed the tea.

The talk continued light and easy, on the topics of the day, the studios, Thornton's plans for the enjoyment of civilised life. He spoke brightly, in a deep, resonant voice, that of a man assured of himself and of the interest afforded to others by reference to his own doings. Although the subject was trivial, the others listened amusedly, carried away by the influence of a strong personality. Clytie glanced at him from time to time, trying to measure him, to sum him up in the instinctive feminine way. But he was sitting far back from the fire, in the gloom, and she could only gather a general impression of physical size and vitality. She was conscious too, that, as she was sitting with her face in the direct glow, she was visible to him, and that he was looking at her quietly as he smoked his cigarette and talked. She picked up a newspaper from a little table by her side, and held it before her face as a screen. His glance, which she felt rather than met, embarrassed her, she scarcely knew why. Gradually the talk drifted into a slight discussion between the two men. Mrs. Farquharson took advantage of it to draw her chair near to Clytie.

"And all this time I have scarcely asked you a question about yourself. Come, account to me for the six weeks you have been away."

Clytie dutifully went over the main incidents of her stay in Durdleham, making light, in her pleasure at being in London again, of the little wearinesses and depressions of the past. A faint cloud came over her gaiety when Mrs. Farquharson asked her suddenly :

"And Kent? What has become of him ?"

"He is still alive," said Clytie.

"Do you know, he has not been near us all the time you have been away. He has treated us very badly. You must scold him for me. What has he to say for himself ?"

"I don't know ; I haven't seen him yet, and I have scarcely heard from him. I shall have to scold him on my own account," she added, brightening.

"That's odd of him," said Caroline. "You are such inseparables that I thought he would have been waiting for you with a bouquet in each hand when you entered the house."

Clytie laughed at the idea of Kent waiting for her with Covent Garden tributes.

"I would just as soon think of him reading me a sonnet. But I did expect him to come down to tell me I had been wasting my time, and to draw out a scheme for the better occupation of it."

"Take care that he has not gone and fallen in love with somebody whilst he has been left to his own devices," said Caroline teasingly.

"Oh, how can you say such wicked things?" cried Clytie. "Of course he hasn't!"

"One never knows, my dear. Men are the most unreasonable beings in the world. With a woman, now, if you know just the least little bit about her,—it isn't everybody, of course, that does,—you can always tell what she is likely to do. But with a man—never. Do you think I know whether that husband of mine is going to be pleased with his dinner to-night? No, not one scrap. And Kent's a man—just like the rest of them."

"Are you talking about Kent?" interposed Mr. Farquharson. "I saw him the other night at the meeting of the Numismatic Society."

"There, now! How like a man! And you knew I wanted to know what had become of him. What had he to say for himself?"

"That most of the rude coins marked with the name of Alfred were in reality imitations made by the vikings during their periodical visits to this country. His remarks were very interesting, my dear."

"Thornton," said Mrs. Farquharson in her blandest tones, "would you be so very kind as to light the gas?"

Her husband chuckled to himself, and Hammerdyke rose to comply with her request. During the operation all the three mechanically watched his movements.

"There!" he said, turning to face them, "I think that is better; we shall be able to see one another."

As the full blaze fell upon him Clytie could not repress a little feminine thrill of surprise. Seen in the vague darkness she had imagined him quite different. He seemed to spring out of it a perfect type of physical manhood. He bore with him an atmosphere of splendid animalism. The artist in Clytie, trained to detect beauties of limb and set and fall of muscle, scanned him for a second with involuntary admiration. Although he was dressed with a fashionable tailor's perfection of fit, which generally gives suave uniformity to strong and puny, his clothes could not conceal the evidences of a magnificent strength—deep chest, arms that seemed to fit tightly the coat-sleeves, broad, massive shoulders, thick, powerful neck. He held his head high, commandingly, which gave him the appearance of tallness, although he was not much above medium height. Short-cut brown hair, clinging close to his head in crisp waves, a broad forehead with two thick vertical veins, added to this impression of strength. In spite of his thirty-four years the blood showed beneath his bronzed skin, on which there were few lines. His features, although on a large scale, were saved from coarseness by regularity. His under jaw was slightly heavy, but in keeping with the massiveness of his limbs. His eyes were dark and lustrous, with a light burning in their depths ; his teeth white and even.

"When Hammerdyke is fighting he is all eyes and teeth," was a saying that had come to Mrs. Farquharson's ears ; she had repeated it long since to Clytie, who remembered it now as she beheld this hero of Caroline's for the first time. He was not fighting now, but laughing, talking with a certain daring charm of manner, almost boyish sometimes. The time passed quickly. When the little clock in the corner struck six Clytie rose in some confusion. She had promised to spend the evening with Winifred and the children. She took her leave hurriedly.

A little later she was sitting in the Marchpanes' drawing-room, with the children clinging around her, a block of paper and a pencil, as usual, in her hand. And led away by a sudden fancy she drew pictures for them of the wild deeds that she had heard tell of Thornton Hammerdyke. This was quite a novelty to the children, who were accustomed to street arabs and grotesque caricatures. They were delighted, hung on her lap, demanded more pictures of soldiers and camels and a great man in a helmet killing savages. To satisfy them she had to draw extensively upon her imagination, sometimes upon theirs. Winifred's suggestions were scouted as being too mild. The final picture was a great triumph. It represented the same man in the helmet dancing upon a struggling heap of savages, transfixing one with a spear held in his left hand, whilst with a sword in his right he clove another in twain. Nothing is so fascinating to children as the grotesquely horrible ; Clytie herself was carried away by their enthusiasm.

Meanwhile the subject of this picture history had remained at Harley Street for a short time after Clytie's departure.

"So that is the Clytie you used to write to me about in Africa ? " he said. "No wonder you like having such a splendid thing about the place, as a kind of inter-mittent fixture."

"I am so glad you like her," said Caroline.

"I didn't say I liked her. I don't give myself away so soon as that. But, by Jove ! I liked looking at her. Where is she generally to be found ?"

"Either here or, if you make yourself very civil to her, she may let you go round to her studio—on her day, you know."

"Oh, she runs a day, does she ? These young women are getting very emancipated."

"They are," said George Farquharson, lighting his pipe. "So much the better."

"I don't know so much about that," replied Hammer-dyke. "If they are too emancipated, they get an idea that their own way is everything in the world, and grow devilish hard in the mouth when the time comes for them to be pulled up."

"What a contradictory creature !" cried Caroline. "Only yesterday you were railing at the well brought up drawing-room young ladies you were having to take in to dinner."

"I should think so : the things that draw, recite, and play the fiddle, and rush about to lectures. I am getting a bit too old for that kind of young animal. I'd sooner spend a week with the wife of a camel driver than with any one of them. She would be just as intelligent, somewhat funnier, and the advantage would be that you could lick her into shape without alarming absurd prejudices. No ; the drawing-room young lady is distinctly ' off,' just as much as the over-emancipated."

" Well, what kind of a young woman are you looking out for ? "

" I never look out for anything, my dear Caroline. I take what comes—if it pleases me."

" Then I hope Clytie will please you, Thornton. She is quite different from any other girl I know. And it's just her little airs of emancipation that give her charm. I wish there were more like her."

" So do I, by Jove ! There would be some pleasure in looking around a theatre or a ball-room."

" Yet I should think that was rather a relief after Central Africa."

Thornton broke into a gay laugh.

" Unsophisticated woman has her good points, you know ! "

" Um ! " said Farquharson, pulling at his pipe.

They chatted for a little while longer. Then Hammerdyke pulled out his watch.

" I must go and dress for dinner."

" Oh, by the way, Thornton," said Caroline, " did you not tell me you had an appointment at six ? I hope we haven't kept you from it."

" Oh, yes," he replied cheerfully as he gathered up his hat and stick. " It's only Field. I dare say he's waiting for me now. I shan't turn up at the club, though. He can rip. When he is tired of kicking his heels and drinking small whiskeys he can curse the waiter and go. I must be off now. Let me know when Clytie is on view again and I'll throw over anybody."

Mrs. Farquharson smiled indulgently. In her eyes there was no one like Thornton.

" Thornton is a bit of an egotist," said George mildly to his wife, later in the evening, when they were alone together. He was not addicted to the hyperbolic, like Caroline.

"Oh, but, George, he is such a dear good fellow—and such a splendid man!"

"'Quem sese ore ferens! quam forti pectore et armis!'" murmured her husband.

Now George Farquharson knew that if there was one thing his wife disliked it was that he should quote Latin at her. It generally occasioned a distraction. If it failed, he translated. The effects of that were certain. This time Mrs. Farquharson was content to allow his remark to remain " veiled in the obscurity of a learned language."

CHAPTER XII.

"I DO wish you would cheer up, old chap," said
Wither sympathetically. "You are getting uncomfortable—like Mr. Mantalini's body, in the midst of our
joyousness."

He was lying curled up, a susual, on the sofa, smoking a cigarette. Kent was brooding over the fire. Fairfax had been rallying him from a doctor's point of view,
and he had answered vaguely, striving not to let his
friend's rough kindness jar too unbearably. He felt
relieved when the doctor was called out to see a patient,
and Wither and himself were left alone together.

"I suppose I am making an ass of myself. I have
never felt miserable before in all my life, and it must be
that I am unused to it——"

"It gets in your way like a man's court-sword on the
first time of wearing," said Wither.

"Somewhat," replied Kent, with a short laugh. He
did not mind Wither's jesting. It came spontaneously
from the small, bright-eyed man—was in fact his natural
language. "Perhaps it does. I'll get over it some day."

"It will be all right when she comes back."

"She has come back."

"When?"

"Nearly a week ago."

"And how are matters going between you?"

"I haven't seen her yet," said Kent moodily, staring
into the fire. "That is to say, I have seen her. I have
lain in wait for her, so as to catch a glimpse of her as
she passed by. But I have not met her."

"And when do you propose going to see her?"

"God knows! I don't."

"I don't know whether this is *fin de siècle* or whether
it belongs to the glacial epoch," said Wither, drawing
a breath of bewilderment. "At any rate, has it never

struck you, friend John, that being in love with a woman is no reason why you should be rude to her?"

"I have scarcely thought of that."

"Then, by Jove, the sooner you can get it into your muddled head, the better. What have you been doing with yourself these evenings?"

"Anything to keep away. A meeting of the Geological, another of the Numismatic—a theatre, where there was just such another ass as myself. I couldn't stand it, so I went out and turned into the Empire and tried to find comfort in performing dogs. I have also dined out."

"You must have been a cheerful lot. What did you say to your partner?"

"Nothing. She wanted to babble on, and I let her babble. Curse the whole thing!" he cried, smiting a block of coal with the poker, so hard that the chips flew over the hearthrug; "To think that it should be my fate to meet the only woman in the whole world who doesn't babble!"

"I should consider it in the light of a privilege," said Wither.

The next morning, after a night's agony of indecision, he plucked up courage and tapped at the studio door. He entered. Clytie was alone, busily preparing her palette. She paused with the half-squeezed tube in her hand, and looked up at him without rising, her brows slightly knitted. He remained motionless, too, on the threshold, after mechanically shutting the door behind him. He tried to utter the little address of lame excuses which he had framed, but the words stuck, somehow, in his throat. He was only conscious that she was there, in the same room with him again, looking bewilderingly fresh and beautiful in her dark dress, with its dainty painting-apron, too simple almost for the rich colour of her eyes and hair and the stately bend of her neck. Yet even then he noticed she was a trifle paler than usual.

"I meant to have come to see you before," he stammered.

"Why didn't you? I rather expected you," she replied calmly.

She finished sqeezing her tube, and taking up her palette-knife, went on with her occupation. Kent, instinctively conscious that it is a disadvantage to stand, when morally wrong, before a sitting person who is in the right, drew Winifred's painting-stool away from the easel and sat down.

"You might have come in, if only for five minutes," said Clytie, as he made no reply. The hand holding the palette-knife trembled a little.

"I wanted to," replied Kent, finding words with difficulty. "But I couldn't. I am very, very sorry if I have been rude. I am always doing things of this sort."

"It is not very pleasant for your friends; and I suppose we have been friends."

"Yes, we have been friends," he replied, "and I hope we shall continue so—if you will forgive me."

His voice sounded strange in his own ears. In Clytie's it sounded cold and formal. She was puzzled.

"Oh, of course I forgive you! You have made your apology."

"Believe me—things have happened. I could not come before, indeed I could not."

"I never doubted your word, Kent," said Clytie, with a touch of her old soft manner towards him. "Only it seemed strange not to see you. One gets into a certain groove, and a change from it jars. You see how easy it is to become a Philistine. You are much more a child of the light than I am, in that you have got out of the groove quite easily."

"You have no right to say that," said Kent, rising.

"Well, perhaps I have not," said Clytie, bending intently over her palette. "Anyhow, the fact remains that we parted friends before Christmas, and now that I have come back you are changed. I am very sorry—sorrier than I can say. I have valued your friendship and the help it has given me—I am unchanged, I think so—and, to be franker than my sex generally is, I may say, I am hurt."

Kent misunderstood. He could not help it. He thought she was grieved at his friendship having changed to love, which the tone in her voice told him could not be returned. All had happened just as he had anticipated. She spoke more in sorrow than in anger ; that was the only difference.

"If you would prefer that I did not see you again—or so often," he said, twisting the brim of his hat.

The words estranged them still further. They were pathetic in their ludicrous inappositeness.

"That you must please yourself about," replied Clytie, with a quick flush. "I have said all that my pride will let me say in the matter. If you prefer to break off our intercourse, well—so be it ! "

"You know that I don't wish to do that," he said in a low voice. "Let me see you sometimes. Could I see you this evening, for instance ? "

"No ; I am sorry, I am going—I am dining out. Some other time. You know my hours."

He stepped forward and shook hands with her to say good-bye, thus breaking through an established custom between them of non-handshaking. He reflected on this a moment afterward. It seemed an omen of the dissolution of their friendship.

When he had gone Clytie felt as if she would like to cry? What did it all mean ? Why did Kent wish to break with her? She put down her palette and sat in her chair near the stove. She felt unhappy, lonely. She was in that strange state of uncertainty about the present, which often takes the form, with women especially in certain moods, of a presentiment of future trouble. "I wish Winnie would come," she half repeated to herself. But almost on top of the thought entered one of Mrs. Gurkins's curly-haired children bringing her a note. It was from Winifred, who was suddenly called out of town on business and could not come on that day to the studio. Clytie mechanically tore up the note and scattered the pieces over the coals. She was not subject to fits of personal depression—independent entirely of the artistic side of her life. But the air seemed charged with disturbing, conflicting elements.

Soon she roused herself and went over to her easel, where for some time she worked steadily. A lay-figure clad in a child's ragged frock stood near by and she painted in the lights of the skirt, with mechanical precision of touch. But her thoughts were far away. Then the face that she had painted attracted her attention. It was that of a child—merry and smiling—but with the little London street girl's precocious wisdom. It was cleverly executed. Clytie had seized the suggestion of the everlasting feminine in the face, accentuating it ever so little. It seemed to laugh mockingly at her, out of the canvas, as who should say—"Look at me. Child as I am, I am as old as the world, and I can tell you secrets that you know not of."

"You wise little witch," said Clytie, after a while, standing back, with head inclined in critical surveyal of her work. "I wish you could tell me what is the matter with Kent."

And then for the first time Mrs. Farquharson's idle, jesting words came into her mind :

"Take care that he has not gone and fallen in love with somebody ! "

And the child's old face seemed to add a mocking confirmation.

This would explain all : his sudden change, the stiffness of his letter ; his shrinking from seeing her ; the awkwardness of his apology ; the vague phrase, "things have happened," which had puzzled her. The more she thought of it the more probable did this solution seem. It caused her a little heaviness of heart. Certain strange imaginings had come to her, too, this week. She needed the strength of Kent's friendship.

There are no persons harder to read and easier to misunderstand than those of whom we are fondest. There are two common causes of mutual miscomprehension. First we take it too much for granted that we can read the heart of another human being ; and secondly, we are too apt to conclude that affinities sharpen perception to such an extent that the unexpressed becomes luminously expressive. This is a curious fact, too little recognised in our minor problems in social statics. Clytie had fallen into the one error, Kent into the other.

For the first time in her life Clytie felt afraid. The sense of what was missing in her life dawned, half shadowy, before her. She was different from other girls of her age, more advanced, as the phrase goes. For the majority of women come in ignorance to emotion ; they feel, before they realise that they are learning. But Clytie in her eager search after the roots of existence had learned much, with feelings as yet untried.   In this knowledge, if as yet there was no sorrow, there was fear. If Kent had come to her at this moment with a passionate avowal of his love, she would have yielded to him.   Her fear would have melted away into joyousness, the rich springs of her nature would have been opened, and her destiny would have been accomplished.   But neither of them knew this.   He was engaged in the humorous task of trying to kill love, and she was half consciously tending along a path strangely diverging from his.

She dined that evening at the Farquharsons'.   Hammerdyke was the only other guest.   It was a bright, cosy meal, and Clytie soon forgot her depression of the morning.   Caroline was at her merriest, proud of her three companions—of each in an especial manner. George was mildly satirical, as usual.   He wore his velvet jacket, in which he found more happiness than in his ceremonial dress-coat.   His dry touch of humour was pleasantly antagonistic to Hammerdyke's stronger personality and downright views of life.   The latter laughed heartily, almost boyishly at his rebuker, like one who is accustomed to indulgence on the part of others for caprices of action and language.   These, coming from a lesser man, might have been repugnant to the sensitive ; but from him they seemed to bear a physical justification.

As he sat opposite her, talking in off-hand, picturesque fashion of incidents in his adventurous life, Clytie could not help looking with a feeling somewhat akin to awe at the man who had gone through such things and could speak of them so lightly.   She listened, interposed a question here and there, wondered what it would feel like to treat those memories in so familiar a fashion.   A new page of life seemed to lie open before her, quivering with sensations beyond her ken.

" Didn't you ever feel horribly afraid ? " asked Caroline, while he was sketching some of his more recent exploring experiences.

" I did so," he confessed frankly, "but I had my

devils well under control. I had the power to string a
mutineer up on the nearest tree or to pot him with my
revolver, and somehow they rather funked me. If it had
entered their woolly heads to go for me all together they
would have made short work of me—but no one liked
to take the initiative."

"Did you ever try kindness, on these expeditions—
by way of experiment?" asked Farquharson.

"Not much. You can't afford to fool away your life
for the sake of an experiment. Oh, no! my dear sir, the
noble savage does not swarm much round about the
slave tracks in Central Africa. The Zulus may be
different. I don't know—I've never seen much of
them—but Fuzzywuz and his neighbours can only understand brute force."

"I don't quite see, now, how you got all that power,"
said Farquharson. "Did you establish yourself as a
little king—or what?"

"Oh, no!" returned Hammerdyke, laughing. "When
I had finished with the Soudan I wanted to while away
a few months in the interior, and as the Belgians wanted
a road made through the forest I offered to see things
were done straight for them. As for the authority—
judicial and that sort of thing—one takes that as a matter of course. The niggers don't know anything about
it, except that there is a white man bossing them. They
think it's all right, so what does it matter?"

"Then you hire a set of woolly-headed navvies, and
if they lapse from your standard of virtue, you shoot
them—is that the idea?"

"Somewhat. In mere slips one employs the *argumen-
tum ad bacculinum*. It isn't pleasant, but it's the only way."

"You are not going back again, are you, Thornton?"
Caroline asked, wishing to turn the conversation. She
believed in Thornton, in his power by divine right to
blow all the tribes of Central Africa from the cannon's
mouth if it so pleased him, but she saw that George was
not sympathetic. It was a sore little point with her that
her husband did not share all her enthusiasm for Thornton. "You are going to settle down now, really?" she
added.

"Who knows?" he replied. "All things become

monotonous after a time—even playing potentate. That's why I am here—with the intention of giving civilisation a chance. Some fine morning I may wake up and think that it would be nice to have a little excitement, and then I may pack up my things and start for No Man's Land again."

"It must be a stirring life," said Clytie half aloud, with a quick glance at Hammerdyke.

"It is the best life. Action, excitement, keen enjoyment of everything ! You should take a ·turn at it, George."

But George shook his head.

"I have a wife dependent upon me. Otherwise you may be sure I would leave this effete and effeminate civilisation and start to-morrow."

"I don't think you would do much good out there," said Mrs. Farquharson candidly.

They finished dinner early and went up to the drawing-room, which not long afterwards was filled with the heterogeneous crowd that the Farquharsons loved to gather round them. This reception was instead of the ordinary Sunday one, and was in Thornton's honour, although it was not unusual for Caroline thus to change her evening, scattering warning post-cards the day before. Kent, being on the list, had received one that morning, and before he saw Clytie had been half wondering whether he should go to Harley Street. So he had put his question as to Clytie's evening engagement tentatively. Her somewhat evasive reply had decided him. He would not inflict his society upon her. As Clytie's eye wandered over the familiar figures in the drawing-room, she involuntarily sought for Kent's. It seemed strange that he should not be there, for during the autumn he had scarcely missed a Sunday. One or two friends came up and asked after him. On the occasion of one inquiry, Mrs. Farquharson and Thornton were standing by her.

"Who is Kent that everybody is talking about—if I may ask ?" said Hammerdyke.

"Kent ?" interposed Caroline. "Oh if you know Clytie, you must know Kent. They are a kind of Mentor and Egeria combination."

"That's lucid," said Hammerdyke, laughing. "I hope you will present me to him one of these days, Miss Davenant." Clytie replied with a commonplace, smiling absently. She was sad at heart about Kent.

Soon Redgrave, the R. A. who had given Clytie her first encouragement in her art, came up to talk with her. He had been following her career with some interest. Since the exhibition of "Jack" he had not seen her, and he took the opportunity of offering his congratulations, criticising the picture favourably. Then he inquired after its successor.

"But I don't think you will ever become a great artist, if you keep to that semi-impressionist style."

Being a portrait-painter of exquisite finish, Redgrave was prejudiced against the school of Degas. He mentioned his name with some acerbity.

"Talking treason again, Redgrave?" asked a thin, wiry man in gold spectacles, who had overheard. "Don't listen to him, Miss Davenant. He is archaic and eating his soul out with jealousy. There's no one in England who can touch you in your particular line. You stick to it!"

"You are quoting the rubbish you wrote in your paper, French," said Redgrave, laughing. "Now, whom are you going to believe, this newspaper man or me?"

"Whoever will help me best to sell my pictures," laughed Clytie.

"Then leave your future with me," said Mr. French, rubbing his hands as he moved away.

"You didn't mean that?" asked Redgrave.

"A little. One must live. Higher art, to use the cant phrase, would satisfy one's soul's needs better—but it would not those of the body."

Redgrave looked at her for a moment, as if meditating over her rich colouring and fine vitality. A body such as hers had its needs. He smiled a little sadly and shook his head.

"You would not sacrifice your life for your art?"

"No," replied Clytie, with quick frankness, "I wouldn't. The fuller one's life, the fuller one's art. The one is a reflection of the other. At least it is so with me."

"I'll paint your portrait one of these days for nothing," said Redgrave somewhat irrelevantly.

Clytie flushed a little at the compliment.

"What are you going to put into me ?"

"The question whether even the most emancipated of young women ever has art in her soul," said Redgrave, with a quiet smile.

"I am going to paint a picture some day that will astonish you," replied Clytie, with a laugh.

"Ah ! So is everyone. When will that some day be? I hardly know a painter or a writer or a musician that has not something he is going to do some day—a three-act drama all ready, bar transcription on paper—a masterpiece all complete, bar the mechanical transference to canvas."

"Oh, Mr. Redgrave, if you are going to moralise like that, I'll report you to Mr. Farquharson. You had much better sit down and take me round the studios."

But Redgrave was carried off before he had time to begin, and Clytie joined a large group standing and sitting round the fire. They were the younger, less responsible members of the company, and were talking nonsense. Singleton, a clean-shaven, red-faced man and a minor poet, was explaining what he called the Physical Basis of Life. Professor Huxley, by the way, has treated the subject differently.

"The man who cannot dine," Mr. Singleton was saying, "cannot feel. He has not his proper equipment of senses. He is an imperfection, a waster."

"That does not apply to women, I hope," said Mrs. Tredegar, a languid, well-preserved woman, who was suspected of hankerings after a long defunct æstheticism. "I have been feeling all my life—and I can't remember to have ever dined."

"I did once—at the Café Anglais. By Jove, it was good !" interpolated a fair-haired youth, who leaped eagerly at objectivities in the conversation.

"Your enthusiasm does you credit !" said Singleton. "You'll die yet, of a hopeless passion."

Then, turning to Mrs. Tredegar :

"Of course it applies to women. *La femme qui dîne,*

aime. Put it into French, and you see the force of it at once."

"Ah, but if you put it the other way about. *La femme qui aime——* It is horrible; it takes all the romance away," said Mrs. Tredegar.

"Oh, dear!" sighed Mr. Singleton, clasping his little plump hands resignedly. "Are we still to adore the well-conducted person who goes on cutting bread and butter? Oh, believe me, Edwin Smith and Angelina Brown can't love, any more than they can appreciate Château-Mouton. They possess for each other a faint current of sexual attraction, which produces between them a mild excess of amiability. A lot of vanity comes in, as they like to parade the possession of each other before the envious. They call themselves lovers, and follow the traditions they have been taught in the novels they have misunderstood and the hints they have received from observance of their friends. The furthest they can go is to clasp hands limply under a sofa-cushion, when they think no one is looking."

"That's humbug," said the youth. "I have been in love myself."

"Precisely," said Mr. Singleton, "and you know nothing at all about it. Cultivate all your senses first, my young friend, and then you may fit yourself for falling in love."

"And how is one to begin?" asked Mrs. Tredegar.

"Well, first cultivate a choice taste in food, wine, and cigarettes. Then disabuse yourself of the idea that the angelic, either in man or woman, is in any way desirable; purge yourself of that clog to all true appreciation of sensation—that interfering bugbear which still survives with an effete superstition—known as a conscience; get into an Hellenic state of mind by joyous perception of the beautiful, and realise that the supreme cultivation of the *ego* is the *ultima ratio* of existence."

"But then we should only love ourselves," observed a dissentient.

"As self-knowledge is the beginning of all wisdom, so is self-love the beginning of all passion," returned Mr. Singleton oracularly.

During the frivolous chorus that followed this remark,

Hammerdyke crossed the room and sat down by Clytie's side.

"You seem to be very merry over here. What is it all about?" he asked.

"It's only Mr. Singleton trying to play with paradoxes," Clytie replied, laughing. "He is a chartered libertine, and nobody minds him."

"That always strikes me as so odd when I get back to civilised life—the tremendous amount of talking one has to get through—and no one seems to get any further with it. Everybody seems bound to provide himself with a theory of life, as they call it—either sincere or paradoxical. Why do they do it?"

He had pulled his chair a little aside, so that, when Clytie turned round, they were cut off from the main group close by. She replied laughingly to his question, and the conversation took a light, personal turn.

"I seem to have known you so long," he said after a while, "and yet this is the first time I have been able to say a word to you by yourself. I used to hear of you, you know, in Africa, when Caroline sent me a budget of news. I used quite to wonder what you were like."

"Caroline and I are great friends," she replied. "She has been very, very kind to me."

"Yes—a good sort, isn't she? She used to keep me posted up in all kinds of things, as I say—you amongst them. At last I built up a little romance about you!"

"What a crash it must have come down with!"

"I am not so sure of that. Time will show. It was just after one of her letters that I read the story of 'Marjorie Daw,' which some good people sent me down with a package of books from Cairo. Do you know it?"

"I have read it, but forgotten it," replied Clytie.

Now, she remembered it very well. The words had come almost involuntarily. She was a little angry with herself. But it was pleasant to lean back in the arm-chair, amidst the babel of voices and heavy cloud of cigarette smoke, and be talked to thus pleasantly.

"It's a pretty little tale," said Thornton. "A man writes letters to amuse a sick friend—broken leg, I think—and describes an imaginary young lady living opposite him. And the broken-legged man falls violently in love with this Marjorie Daw and starts off to see her as soon as he is well—and is moved to much wrath when he finds out the truth. Well, I am afraid I must confess that I made a kind of Marjorie Daw out of you—although I haven't exactly come over in search of you. So you see that we are old acquaintances—on one side, at least."

" Caroline must have been saying very foolish things about me," said Clytie. " I remember Marjorie Daw now. I am not the least bit like her."

" I never said you were," he returned, looking at her boldly, a smile playing about the corners of his mouth. " I did not think so then, either. And since I am in for a kind of confession, I may as well say it did not occur to me that I should ever meet you. Now that we have met—under my cousin's wing, so to speak—I hope we shall make friends."

" You speak as if we had quarrelled," said Clytie.

" Well, I thought perhaps you might have been a little vexed at my confession. Are you ? "

" No," said Clytie, looking at him in her quick, frank way. " Why should I ? "

Hammerdyke did not reply, but smiled and shrugged his shoulders a little.

" Well, since you are so particular as to the wording, let us *be* friends. For Caroline's sake," he added after a short pause.

" Very well, for Caroline's sake," repeated Clytie. " Only, you know I am a very humble person."

" Oh, no ! I know too much about you. You are by way of becoming a great artist—and it would be a privilege for an uncultivated barbarian like me. Tell me, how could we begin being friends ? "

" Well, suppose you tell me some of the wonders you have seen."

" ' Anthropophagi, or men whose heads do grow beneath their shoulders ' ? Very well—and you shall show me your pictures. Will you let me come and see them sometime or the other ? Do ! "

He spoke low, with a touch of softness in his voice. Clytie felt flattered, touched. It was a little tribute to her womanhood to be pleaded with, especially by a man who, in the eyes of the world, was a recognised heroic figure.   There was a latent light, too, in the depths of his dark eyes, a sign of reserved power and strange, unknown forces, that pleased her strangely.   All the day she had felt sore, ill at ease, with a little aching, chafing sense of loss.   The time had seemed woefully out of joint, and the setting of it right again utterly beyond her powers.   But now the world's equilibrium seemed more stable.

"I am not sure whether you would care for my pictures," she said.

"Oh, I have seen those that Caroline has," he replied. "I made her show them to me.   I don't know what your art word is—but they seem to me to have a grip upon life that I like."

He could not have chosen words more flattering to Clytie.   They summed up bluntly the whole of her ambitions.

"You see, I like real things," he went on.   "Something I can catch hold of.   All this talk of Art with a capital A, and metaphysical preciousness, is so much froth—at any rate to me.   But perhaps you put a capital to it?"

"I do, sometimes."

"Well, then, you will teach me what it means.   Will you?   It will be a way of teaching me something about yourself."

"Oh, I am not worth your learning," replied Clytie, with a laugh.   "But you can come and see my pictures, if you like."

"Thank you," said Hammerdyke, as he rose in obedience to a beckoning glance from Mr. Farquharson, who was sitting on the other side of the room.   "I will come as soon as you will let me.   To-morrow, can I?"

He looked at her pleadingly, admiringly.   Clytie was suddenly brought in contact with a new force, against which she felt powerless.

"Yes, you can come to-morrow," she said

CHAPTER XIII.

IT was an evening in mid-February that Clytie went to a dance given by the Redgraves in their large house in St. John's Wood. Redgrave met her almost as soon as she arrived in the dancing-room.

"So you have come at last—we had almost despaired of seeing you. I think there are a good many men you know—all dying to dance with you."

"Oh, give me a little breathing time," laughed Clytie. "You have had time to fix on your cap and bells, let me adjust mine."

"Don't touch yourself or you would spoil the effect," said Redgrave, mixing the metaphor for the sake of an opportunity of expressing his admiration of her beauty. "I wish I could paint that portrait of you now : 'Clytie, woman and artist.' There is one advantage about that combination—it assures perfect taste in dress."

He looked her up and down critically, stroking his long gray beard.

"I am glad you like me," said Clytie. "It cost me sleepless nights, I assure you. Didn't you know it was my serious occupation in life?"

"Well, my dear, I hope you will have your reward," replied Redgrave, laughing—"only you won't find anybody who admires you and your genius half as heartily as I do."

He nodded, smiled, and left her as one or two men came up to her, programme in hand. She gave them the dances they requested, and took a seat near the door by the side of some ladies of her acquaintance, watching animatedly the waltz that was in progress.

"Good-evening, Miss Davenant," said a voice, deep and resonant, that made her start and the colour mount into her cheeks.

It was Thornton Hammerdyke.

"You see I procured the invitation, and here I am. Where is your programme?"

He took her card attached with its bit of silk to her fan, and scribbled recklessly.

"You have nearly filled it all up!" she exclaimed.

"Naturally," he replied. "Let us dance out the fag-end of this."

She took his arm gaily, and with him entered the whirl of dancers.

"You are looking dazzling to-night," he said. "What witchery have you to make your eyes so blue and your hair so glorious?"

She shook her head and smiled half inwardly, thinking of Redgrave's late compliment and differentiating it from this. Each man was honest, in his own way.

"I put myself down for all those dances," he went on, "because there is not a woman in the room fit to look at after you. I couldn't dance with them, and I should have been bored and irritated with standing and watching you dancing with other people. Then we can get away and sit by ourselves."

"But what are all the men to do, to whom I have to be polite?"

"They must give way to the man to whom you are always fascinating. I scarcely saw you at all yesterday. Now is my chance, and I am going to make the most of it."

"Yes, but there are the sacred conventionalities."

"I thought you went in for being superior to them."

"So I am in a general way; I attach no intrinsic value to them—but they are useful as counters in one's dealings."

He laughed; pressed the fingers that he held in his left hand.

"To-night no checks are taken! It must be all solid gold—the true, real Clytie. As for people talking, you are glorious enough in your beauty to defy them. What can you and I care for idle gossip?"

The words thrilled through her. Womanlike she had humbled herself before his greatness. To be raised thus by him to his empyrean, whence they could look down upon the rest of earth-bound mortality, in common grandeur, made her heart swell with a not ignoble pride.

"We shall do whatever you like," she whispered.

To this pitch of intimacy had the past three weeks brought them—a long enough period for an infinite number of things to happen—none the less real for being subjective. Nothing had changed in their external lives. Hammerdyke went into society, read a paper here and there on his travels, digested many bad dinners and worse flattery, played cards, smoked, and drank with his fellows. Clytie painted assiduously, read, exchanged visits with her friends. Kent was missing from her life. She saw him rarely, at odd moments, when they talked commonplaces and avoided by tacit consent the subject of their disunion. They were "league-sundered by the silent gulf between." He told her that he was thinking of accepting an offer privately made to him by one of the heads of his department, of leave of absence for three months for the purpose of studying the numismatic collections of certain foreign capitals. The prospect was enticing, as he could thus have the run of the continental libraries, whereby his own great work could be considerably advanced.

Clytie listened kindly, wished him good luck. He went from her sad at heart, and she was angry with herself and humiliated at feeling somewhat relieved at the idea of his absence. It was not that she regretted the old life less. Its memories were still precious. But Kent's departure would clear the way to a better understanding of herself.

Much had happened during the past three weeks—the discovery of a new world for Clytie in which all was strange, beset with vague dangers, vibrating with a tremulous joy akin to terror. She had been lifted off her feet, hurried against her will into a whirl of new sensations. At first she resisted with fierce virgin pride ; then gradually she began to close her eyes for a short sweet spell and allow herself to be drifted by the current ; finally she gave up struggling. The history of most women at their first contact with passion.

The story of this period is very simple. In its first

developments love is usually not ultra complex. Given a man and a woman and conditions for meeting freely alone ; further, a sudden overmastering passion on the part of the man, a half known, unfulfilled need in the woman ; given these premises, and a child can deduce the result. It is the fundamental law of sex. Only when the sentimentalities and more delicate affinities come into play, when the needs of the finer animal man begin to cry after their satisfying, does love leave its simple phase and gird itself with its infinite many-coloured web of complexities. At first the mind may see the web glimmering in a far-away twilight—but heeds it not as long as the sense is held captive.

Two remarkable personalities had met, Thornton Hammerdyke and Clytie. With the intensity of a strong animal nature he had fallen in love with her, with her beauty, charm, and directness. Her magnificent vitality drew him, compelled him. He shut his eyes to every other interest. The sense that he wanted her was sufficient justification for setting all else aside. He never even thought of marriage in the first flush of his passion. But that was the result of habit. Passion is a very different thing from the serene considerations that, according to the Book of Common Prayer, induce people to enter into the holy state of matrimony—and Thornton was quite free from any considerations of the kind. So that when marriage dawned upon his mind as a necessary condition, he accepted it, as a reckless sacrifice, as a means to an end, not as an end in itself. He was a man whose life had been passed in hot, headstrong action. Desire imperiously compelled immediate gratification. Since loving Clytie entailed marriage, he resolved to marry her forthwith.

He informed Mrs. Farquharson of the fact, in his masterful manner.

"I am going to marry Clytie—so get yourself a wedding garment." Mrs. Farquharson jumped up, clapped her hands. She would not have been a woman had the possibilities of this match not occurred to her seductively. The announcement, however, anticipated her hopes.

"Oh, Thornton," she cried, "I am so glad ! I have

been longing for it. You two are made for each other. I must go down and see Clytie this afternoon!"

"Better not," said Thornton. "I'm going. Besides, I don't think Clytie knows it yet."

Caroline's face fell a little. "Oh! I thought you meant you were engaged, and that sort of thing."

"That's a detail—it doesn't matter. She's going to marry me, and you'll come and dance at the wedding."

Caroline kept her counsel, but she worked steadily in Thornton's cause, sang his praises to Clytie, invented many occasions for bringing them together. She believed with all the fervent loyalty of her nature that this marriage was an ideal one for her cousin and her friend, and had at heart equally the interests of each.

Thornton very quickly constituted himself a factor in Clytie's life. She saw him almost every day in Harley Street, at home, or at the houses of common acquaintances. His influence grew strong upon her. Glimpses of the physical joy of life flashed before her like revelations. For the first time she doubted the possibilities of the artistic life. They seemed shadowy, unsatisfying.

From Thornton seemed to come realisation that something stronger, more real, positive lay beyond them— the delight of living in pulse and nerve and bodily fibre. Yet, unlike a man, a woman cannot live by sense alone. Sentiment invariably plays its part. This in Clytie's case was fed by the glamour of Thornton's heroic history, so different from that of ordinary men, whose lives, compared with his, seemed tame and colourless. The glow of his personality bathed magically all his actions, all his words. In his superb manhood he stood before her eyes as the incarnation of physical force, the victorious protest against the shams of art, culture, and other pale shades of our morbid civilisation. When she was lifted high with him in this triumph, sense and sentiment were fused together and she was wholly at his mercy. Thornton had come into her life at the most delicately critical moment of a woman's career, when the current of her nature, checked at the turning-point between friendship and love, struggles tumultuously for some other channel into which to empty itself.

" We shall do whatever you like," she said to Thornton, during their waltz. It was the first definite surrender she had made to him. She was surprised that it cost her so little, seemed so sweet and natural.

" Then you and I will defy the world ! " he replied.

They paused to rest for a moment, leaning against the wall. An elderly man came up, shook hands with her, and opened a desultory conversation with Thornton. Clytie looked amusedly at the animated scene, tabulating mentally, by force of habit, the types that passed and repassed before her. Seldom had it struck her before so forcibly how few of her fellow-creatures possessed the secret of the joy of life. How many of the couples circling round, backing, glissading in that dizzying mass of motion were really gladdened by what they were doing ? Stout men puffed around with a serious air of responsibility. Tall men, with drooping moustaches, paced languidly in time, scarcely heeding their partners, who expressionlessly suffered themselves to be guided hither and thither through the throng. The robust youth of either sex seemed to look upon dancing as an athletic exercise, and waltzed with the intent fervour of tennis players on their mettle before a big gallery. Only here and there did a girl, safe in the arms of a good dancer, half close her eyes and surrender herself to the sensuous charm of motion in perfect time with the throbs of music. Mankind is astonishingly ignorant of the essential qualities of many of its habitual pleasures. So thought Clytie, in the thrill of her new knowledge. The orchestra began the opening bars of the *coda.* Thornton turned away from the elderly gentleman, and putting his arm round Clytie's waist led her away, without a word, to finish the waltz.

" How delightful it is to dance with someone who is not bored by it ! " she said, when the music stopped and they were pushing their way through the crowd towards the door.

He laughed in his boyish way, throwing back his head.

" I had better not answer that remark," he replied.

" Why ? "

She looked askance at him as she asked, just as any little peasant girl would have done. Certain conditions bring all humanity to one level. He pressed the hand that was on his arm lightly against his side.

"Let us get away by ourselves, and I will tell you," he said.

But this opportunity did not occur. Thornton was captured by his hostess for introducing purposes, Clytie waylaid by brother artists for dances. When Thornton and herself were able to find seats the music struck up the prelude of the next waltz, and Clytie was discovered and led off by her partner. Only three men, exclusive of Thornton, had been fortunate enough to find places on her programme.

The hours passed away swiftly. She forgot her life, her responsibilities, her needs. During the three dances with the fortunate—which were early in the evening— she flashed with wit and merriment, her partners thinking with masculine self-esteem that they were the fine steel that had caused these scintillations. But more than one woman there that night observed how Clytie's eyes ever and anon caught those of Thornton, who was standing by the doorway. When the two danced together, men watched them curiously.

"If the principle of natural selection could always be carried out like that!" said French, the journalist, to Redgrave.

"Physically, yes ; but——"

"But what? If the human race sprang exclusively from such parents, what a glorious race it would be! "

"It might be a very good thing for the race," replied Redgrave drily ; "but I was thinking of the parents— at least of one of them."

"Nonsense! a marriage like that would be ideal," said French.

Redgrave shook his head.

"I doubt it," he said, with some earnestness. "I know a little of Clytie Davenant. I may claim to have discovered her. She has the blood of life in her, it is true—but she has the finer artistic temperament as well. Mark my words, French ; if she marries that man she will lose her art clean—clean ; and not another 'Jack' will she ever be able to paint. Many of us men artists are ruined by marriage. A woman artist, to whom it means fifty times more, runs fifty times more risk."

"Well, perhaps we are a bit previous," said French laughing, and turned the conversation.

Later in the evening Thornton and Clytie came out of the dancing-room. She was flushed, dazed with the music, the noise, the electric light and the heavy scent of cut flowers; confused, too, by Thornton's presence, by the after-pressure of his arm around her waist, over-wrought a little by his personal magnetism.

They threaded their way through the crowd that lined the passage and the stairs, went through the brilliantly lit studio with its polished oak floor and wealth of hang-ings and costly decoration, into the models' dressing-room beyond, that had been turned into a small boudoir for the occasion. Many couples were wandering about the studio, examining the pictures and the china, but the dressing-room had escaped notice.

"This is soothing after the glare," said Clytie, sitting down restfully on a divan.

Great palms screened the door, the room was hung with dark, heavy drapery, and between them shaded electric lamps shed a subdued light. Thornton sat down by her side. After a while the steps and talking in the adjacent studio ceased, and there rose from below the faint strains of the music and the dull rhythmic thud of the dancers.

"What were we talking about? I forget," said Clytie, after a short silence, and then, meeting his eyes fixed upon her, she turned away her head :

"Don't! I can't bear it," she murmured involuntarily.

Then he caught her hand : "Clytie, you are adorable, glorious, bewitching ! " he cried, and kissed her quickly, twice, on the corner of her lips. She snatched her hand away and started to her feet, pale and trembling, her eyes blazing.

"Why did you do that? You have no right to do that ! "

He rose, went to her, caught her wrists again—but this time she was powerless to withdraw them, and he spoke in a quick, deep voice :

"I have the right to kiss you—to kiss you and kiss

you till the world's end—for I love you—and I would
sacrifice all I have got—my life itself, for one kiss from
you—I loved you, wanted you, from the first time I saw
you—when the suddenly lit light revealed your beauty
to me, and you sprang glorious, bewildering out of the
darkness."

"Let me go, let me go!" she murmured, faintly struggling.

"Not until you tell me that I have the right to kiss
you—I know you will give it, you must! Clytie, I am
stronger than most men, and my love is stronger than
most men's and will not be denied—I will make you,
force you to love me as passionately as I love you.
Look at me. Speak! say just a word!"

She flashed a swift, sidelong glance at him, and met
his eyes with the light burning in their dark depths.
His passion intoxicated her.

"You know," she murmured. The words came
almost without volition.

He released her hands. She remained standing for
a moment, motionless with downcast eyes. Then she
lifted them once more shyly, met his, and uttered a short
gasping cry as he caught her in his arms and kissed her
passionately.

"You will be my wife, and let our whole lives be one
long kiss?"

"Yes," she said, below her breath.

A little later Thornton put her into a cab, and she
drove home. The cold night air invigorated her relaxed
body, but seemed to benumb her mind. She could not
think—only feel Thornton's kisses upon her. The rest
of the subjective and objective universe was a blank.
Only when the cab stopped and the driver asked the
number of her house through the trap-door in the roof,
was she conscious of external things. Then she found
that he had driven a long way past the familiar door.
As he turned round grumblingly, she was aware of being
chilled through from her drive across London, and longed
to get indoors.

It was not until she told Winifred the next morning
that she realised the great change that had come over
her life.

"I am going to marry Mr. Hammerdyke."

The commonplace statement, thus uttered for the first time, seemed like a cold decree of fate, inevitable, irresistible. Winifred cried a little at the thought of losing her.

"But you will be happy, my darling," she said, smiling through her tears. "He is so brave and strong and handsome, and he must love you better than his life."

"Yes, dear," said Clytie, gently stroking her friend's brown hair (Winifred was sitting at her feet) and looking tenderly at her pure, upturned face. But her own, bent down, was aflame with reminiscence.

"When is it to be? Not for a long, long time, I hope," said Winifred.

"Almost immediately—he wants it—there is no particular reason for waiting."

"I felt it was coming some day," said Winifred; "but I did not expect it so soon."

"It is best," said Clytie—"best that it should be at once; the interval between the old life and the new would be too trying if it were drawn out."

"You always do what is best, dear," whispered Winifred in her trustful way. "Oh! you must be happy, very, very happy, Clytie dear."

Clytie leaned back in her chair, caressing her friend's cheek with the back of her hand, and looked around the studio. It came almost as a shock to her to realise that in a short, short time she would have to bid farewell to all that had grown up around her artistic life. The grotesque caricatures on the walls stared at her like meaningless shadows. Her palette, brushes, and paraphernalia of rags and turpentine bottles lay strewn about like the properties of a forgotten comedy. The unfinished pictures on easels and stands lost their fascination. Only Winifred's little study on the other side of the studio seemed unchanged—retaining its virginal freshness and purity. But the sound of a step on the landing outside, buoyant, elastic, dispelled all wistful regrets. She sprang to her feet as Winifred rose, and listened, transformed into a radiant woman, with quivering depths in her dark blue eyes, her red lips parted in a half smile, her chin raised showing the full neck.

A moment or two afterwards Mrs. Gurkins appeared at the studio door.

"Mr. Hammerdyke, miss. I have shown him into the sitting-room," she said, and then retired.

"I knew it was he," said Clytie.

"Go, dear," said Winifred, putting her arm round Clytie's waist and moving with her across the studio to the door.

Clytie kissed her laughingly and disappeared. But two tears rolled down Winifred's cheek as she went back to the chair by the stove; and then she flung herself down where she had been sitting, and burying her face in her arm, began to cry bitterly.

"I don't like him, I don't like him; he will spoil my darling," she moaned.

Sometimes knowledge is given to those who seek after it least.

CHAPTER XIV.

THE unexpected always happens, often inopportunely. Winifred had risen from the ground by the stove and was standing miserably before her easel when a knock was heard at the studio door. She cried, "Come in!" and Kent entered. He was looking rather pale and worn out, his beard sinking ever so little into his cheeks; his eyes were tired. On seeing him Winifred could not restrain a start of surprise.

"Why, Mr. Kent! you here at this hour of the day!"

"Yes; I have just come back from the Museum. I went up to tell them I wasn't coming, as they say in Ireland. The fact is I am feeling lazy and want a few days' slackness."

"You have been overworking yourself, that's what you have been doing," said Winifred with kind severity. "Come and sit down by the stove and rest yourself. You want someone to look after you."

She pulled the chair that Clytie had been occupying a little forward, by way of invitation.

"What a good little creature you are, Winifred," he said as he sat down. "You always think of other people. Men don't seem able to do it; they are too much wrapped up in themselves. How are you all— you and the children? You must make them invite me to tea soon. I have not seen them for ages."

"Oh, they are quite well again," replied Winifred, brightening, "and they have been clamouring for Kent, as they call you. I'll tell them to send you an 'At Home' card. And it must be soon, for you are going abroad. When do you think of starting?"

Kent sighed and looked into the fire.

"I don't quite know yet; I wanted to see Clytie first. Where is she?"

"She has a visitor—in her sitting-room," replied Winifred somewhat shortly.

But Kent was too absorbed in his own affairs to notice the change of tone.

" Will she be engaged long ? "

" Probably."

" I wanted so much to see her."

Winifred looked at him for a moment and then came and put her hand lightly on his shoulder.

" You seem so unhappy. Is it about Clytie? You and she have quarrelled or had some difference,—she has not told me what it is,—and I have been so grieved. If I knew, perhaps I might bring things straight."

" Would you, Winifred ? " said Kent eagerly.

" Of course. Don't I love Clytie better than anybody else—and haven't you been a good kind friend to me ? I haven't asked her—nor you—why you have stopped being friends, because one shrinks from asking such questions, but I have seen it, and I have been so, so sorry."

The gentle sympathy touched him. The realisation of the feminine had come to him of late powerfully enough to have overset his old one-sided theories. He knew the value now of a tender word from a woman, and his nature hungered for it.

" Winifred," he said, half turning in the chair and looking up at her in his honest way, " do you think Clytie could ever care for me—not as a friend—as something nearer ? "

Winifred fell back, looked at him aghast, unable to speak, as the light dawned upon her. He mistook her movement, rose, and began to speak hurriedly, pacing the room.

" I couldn't help it—how could I help it ? I have struggled against it with all my might. I know I am a fool to think that she can love me, and you are surprised and dismayed, as she was when she saw that I loved her. I would have bit my tongue out then rather than tell her, but I saw she guessed—and that is why our friendship has been broken. I have kept away from her to spare her the pain of it. But it has nearly driven me mad. I can't go abroad with the weight of it upon me. I must see her and let her know everything. Tell me, Winifred, you who are so fine and delicate, I did not wrong her

and our friendship by growing to love her better than
anything life has. She won't think me unworthy of the
trust she gave me, and despise me ? "

"Oh, no, no, no !" said Winifred half chokingly.
"Your love would honour any girl. Oh, why did you
not tell her and plead with her before ? "

"Then do you think, Winifred——" began Kent with
a sudden joy in his eyes.

"Oh, don't !" cried the girl, interrupting him ; "I
can't bear it. It is too late ! I hate to stab you like
this, but you must know it. Clytie is engaged to be
married."

There was a long silence, during which neither looked
at the other. Kent was stunned, dazed. He had come
prepared for a refusal, but not for such an absolute
shattering of all his hopes. He grew very white and
stood with his hand on the back of a chair, as if steadying himself.

"How long has she——" he said, at length, huskily.

"Only last night. She told me of it this morning."

"And the man ? "

"Mr. Hammerdyke—Mrs. Farquharson's cousin."

She went up to him, took his hand, and turned her
pure face up to his, the tears standing in her eyes.

"I won't say you will find someone more worthy of
you, because you couldn't."

"I am not fit to tie her shoe-strings. I know that
very well," said poor Kent.

"Oh, that is foolish," she said, with a wan smile. "But
there isn't another girl like Clytie in the world ; and
you will always think kindly of her, and help her if she
wants help, won't you ? You won't turn from her and
hate her, as I have heard men often do — for I don't
think you are like such men."

"I would give up everything I had in life to save her
one hour's pain," said Kent. "I have been a fool,—I
see it now,—oh ! not in having loved her—not that. It
is a blessed privilege — I can't explain, for you would
not understand. I shall always love her, Winifred ; no
other woman can be to me what Clytie has been—and
might have been. I shall leave by the early boat to-
morrow morning, so you will not see me for three or

four months. When I return—perhaps you'll let me come and talk to you a little sometimes."

"Oh, it will comfort me," said Winifred, "for am I not losing her too?"

He bade her good-bye, exacting before he left a promise that she would not let Clytie know of what had passed between them.

He went downstairs, anxious to escape from the house, to get into the open air. In the entrance passage the side door leading into the shop was open and Mrs. Gurkins was standing by the threshold. Kent stopped for a moment to acquaint her with the fact of his sudden departure next day. He would keep on the rooms, which must be scrupulously locked up during his absence. Since his first intimacy with Clytie he had imperceptibly grown more amenable to feminine interference in his domestic arrangements, and Mrs. Gurkins no longer had her former terror of invading his domain. But she was still in enough awe of him to promise faithfully to execute his desires. To talk on these trivial matters was a relief from the terrible strain of the last few moments, although he wondered a little how he could lend them coherent attention. He was listening with waning interest to some final irrelevancies on the part of his landlady when a man ran down the stairs and strode quickly past him in the passage. A glance was sufficient to tell Kent who Clytie's visitor was—it had not occurred to him before to conjecture. His heart sank as he realised the splendid physique and proud, masterful bearing of his rival. Ordinarily the least observant of men in such matters, Kent noted the careless ease with which he wore his faultless attire. The patent-leather boots, the new silk hat, the well-cut frock-coat with an orchid in the buttonhole, the new gray Suède gloves grasped along with a gold-mounted malacca—all seemed to belong to the man naturally, to be the world's fit adjuncts to the gifts of nature. Smiling to himself and humming a song, he seemed the personification of the joy and strength, the success and luxury of life.

"I am not that man's match," thought Kent bitterly, thus falling, as all men must do at times, a little below himself.

The front door slammed behind Hammerdyke. Kent waited for a moment, gave a few vague general directions, and then went out into the street. He felt stronger now that he had to struggle against real and tangible trouble instead of the intangible doubts and fears that had set him off his balance. The single-hearted loyalty of his nature, that had caused him to regard his love for Clytie as treason against her unsuspecting friendship, and had thus placed him in the weakness of a false position, now gave him strength to face fearlessly life and its responsibilities. But time alone could assuage the pain and bitterness of it all. He strung himself together and walked briskly through the bright, frosty air towards the home of his mother and sister in Notting Hill. There was sincere affection between mother and son, sister and brother ; but neither of the quiet, contented women knew much of his life or sympathised with his ambitions. Mrs. Kent's hopeless wish was that he would marry some good, sensible girl who would keep his house tidy, provide him with decent meals, and bring bright children's faces around his knee. This conception bounded her horizon of a man's happiness ; as she knew that her son would never appear within it, she regarded him with wistful, unhelpful affection. Agatha, with the younger generation's superior grasp of things, looked upon him as a soft-hearted eccentric who deserved to be humoured. For many years, therefore, Kent had ceased to share with them any of his inner life, not because he loved them less than during his boyhood, but because their mental attitudes precluded confidence. They were women, they could not understand. When he entered the house he left his own interests outside and plunged, in his rough, hearty way, into theirs. He gave his whole attention to accounts of Cousin Henrietta's baby, Uncle William's gout, the leakages of the cistern, and the turpitudes of the cook. In matters such as the cistern he gave practical help ; in others, such as the baby, he overflowed with sympathetic though alarming suggestions. His own life was seldom touched upon. With finer natures—Clytie, Winifred, Wither—that divined the strong purpose underlying his eccentricities, and met him halfway with their sympathy, he was generous in his confidence ; but to others, proud, shy, and reserved. So Mrs. Kent and Agatha knew nothing of Clytie, little of his scientific work, and only vaguely of his duties at the Museum.

He walked up Sloane Street and through the park, thinking of his great loss, trying to scheme out his future, in which Clytie would only be a memory. When he arrived at his mother's house he paused for a moment, as if literally to unstrap the burden of care from his shoulders and leave it outside the front door. Then he entered and greeted his mother and sister in his bluff, cheery way. He remained with them a couple of hours, during which he performed a few odd jobs about the house which he had promised to attend to, and then took his leave. Mrs. Kent was solicitous as to his health, besought him not to work too hard nor to come back with a German wife. She could not quite see the reason of his sudden departure. Why the country should waste its money in sending him abroad to study old coins she, in her placid utilitarianism, could not imagine. However, she bade him a motherly farewell, hoped from her heart that he would have a pleasant holiday, although she could not refrain from expressing a regret that he would not return in time to superintend the spring-cleaning.

When the door closed behind him he picked up his burden and walked doggedly away with it, mechanically, not heeding his direction. He suddenly found that he had come, contrary to his intention, diagonally across the park to Hyde Park Corner. It was past five o'clock. Wither would be in his club. He would go and say good-bye, for Wither was very dear to him.

The little man was giving some directions to the hall porter when Kent appeared.

"My dear, good creature!" he cried, "what have you been doing to yourself? You are as white as a ghost. You want some whiskey or brandy, probably both. Come down to the smoking-room and have some."

"I am a bit overdone," replied Kent, "and perhaps I have been walking too much to-day. But I don't want any brandy."

"Oh, but you've got to," said Wither, and entering the smoking-room, he gave the order to a waiter.

"I have come to say good-bye, Teddy," said Kent as soon as they were seated in a quiet corner. "I am off to-morrow morning."

"The deuce you are! Well, so much the better. A sound friend abroad is more comfortable for all parties than a sick friend at home. Have they given you your three months?"

"Yes—on full pay."

"Lucky dog. And while you are flirting around the capitals of Europe we poor devils will have to be slaving away in this grimy and sooty metropolis. In the good fortune of one's friends there is always something devilishly obnoxious. Why is the eternal order of things so mismanaged that you should have a good time and I not? Here is your brandy. Drink it and look more human."

Kent did as he was bidden. The stimulant, which he needed, revived him. Wither guessed that something untoward had occurred. He had a woman's intuition, this bright-eyed, cynical little being, and he rattled on in his light way to save Kent the strain of making conversation.

"Have a cigarette?" he asked, taking out his case. "No? Well, smoke your pipe. I can't understand how anyone but a horny-palated son of toil can smoke a pipe. By the way, what do you think a girl sent me by way of a present this morning?"

"I don't know," said Kent. "A hymn book?"

"No; a cigarette holder—mouthpiece, you know. I wrote and told her it was very pretty and I would keep it in memory of her to my dying day; but as for using it, I should just as soon think of kissing her through a respirator."

"That was unkind," said Kent, laughing in spite of himself, tickled at the idea.

"Lord bless you, no," replied Wither oracularly from the depths of his armchair. "It is wholesome to check this frenzy of profusion now and then. When a woman once begins to give she never knows where to stop. When she has exhausted her imagination she gives away herself. It's embarrassing sometimes, for one can't put half a dozen women away in a drawer with the rest of the odds and ends. Oh, no ; a little fatherly repression does a world of good to the ingenuous and enthusiastic. I don't pretend to be moral, but I am not without kindly instincts."

He chuckled sardonically and began to turn over the pages of *Punch*. Kent smoked on in silence, cheered a little by the familiar chatter.

"Teddy," he said at last, "you seem to hear all the gossip about town ; do you know anything about a man called Hammerdyke ? "

"Thornton Hammerdyke — man from Africa — explorer ? "

" Yes."

" Yes, rather. One of the greatest devils unhung," replied Wither cheerfully.

" What do you mean ? " cried Kent in an agitated voice, starting forward and gripping the arms of his chair. " Take care what you are saying. It is a matter of life and death to—to somebody. What do you know about him ? Tell me."

Wither arched his eyebrows in surprise, and became serious. Then his quick intuition supplied him with the reason for Kent's agitation.

" I only spoke idle gossip," he said, " and I have the misfortune to be hyperbolical at times. The man has had some dealings with our office and that is how I come to know anything about him. Don't you remember he got into a row for wholesale slaughter of niggers on one of his expeditions ? He cleared himself all right, of course, by proving mutiny, self-defence, and that sort of thing."

" I remember the incident now," said Kent. " It was in the papers."

" Well, his public character is cleared," said Wither, " and he is a good deal of a lion these days ; but fellows who have served with him take the niggers' side of the question, and wonder how he remained a day among them without being torn to pieces. That's all I know about him, which you see is not much. My dear old boy," he continued earnestly as Kent sat silent, staring in front of him, " is that the reason why you are starting so suddenly ? Is it all fixed up ? No chance ? "

Kent nodded moodily.

"I suppose not. I was going to ask her this morning when I learned she had engaged herself—only last night—to this man. And I have seen him. Devil or not, he is a man."

Wither bit his lip. For the moment he was at a loss for an expression of sympathy, somewhat uneasy·as to the line he should adopt. What was the use of making Kent more miserable by telling him other ugly stories he had heard concerning Hammerdyke if either were powerless to prevent the marriage from taking place? Besides, it was only idle gossip after all, and in the serious affairs of life Wither was honourable and conscientious.

Suddenly Kent broke out :

"Oh, my God, Teddy, I don't care a little damn about myself,—I can worry along, as I did before—better, for it is something to have loved her,—if only she is happy. But if this man is not fit for her, if this horrible gossip of yours is true, she will be entering into a life of misery,—I know her,—and I shall feel as if I had not put out my hand to stop her."

"Everyone must dree his own weird, my dear old boy," said Wither. "And while he's doing it neither you nor anyone else can interfere with much profit. Make your mind easy about yourself and your responsibilities. You could not go to her and say, ' I hear the man you are going to marry is a blackguard ; have me instead.' In the first place, your pride would not allow you, and in the second, if she cared about him, she wouldn't believe you, but would marry him all the sooner to prove her faith in him. It is the way of women when they are worth anything."

"Yes ; Clytie would do just that," said Kent. "I think even a man would, if he loved a woman."

"Well," said Wither, "it is no use making yourself miserable about it. The wise man guards against indulgence in things that upset his moral as well as his physical digestion. But wisdom was never much your forte, friend John."

Kent stayed and dined with Wither and then returned alone to the King's Road. He had already made certain preparations for travel; the few final arrangements did not take long. As he passed by Clytie's sitting-room door he noticed that it was ajar, a sign that she was out. In the old days,—less than two months ago, but far away for all that,—he had been accustomed to run down on such occasions, at about half-past ten or eleven, and stir up the fire. Since her return from Durdleham this little token of intimacy had gone with the rest. But on this evening the desire came over him to perform this service for her once more, for the last time. He crept down the stairs on tip-toe, in case she should have come in without his knowledge. But the door was still ajar, the room was vacant. The fire had burned down very low, only a few glowing coals at the bottom of the grate. He returned to his own rooms and fetched some wood and paper, and kneeling down, built up a satisfactory fire. At first, however, the wood would not burn; it had to be dried by repeated conflagrations of paper, and the blaze had to be induced by much cunning coaxing. It was just beginning to flare merrily up the chimney when the sudden slam of the street door below aroused him to a sense of his position. He left the room and fled quickly up the stairs. Outside his door he listened. It was Clytie, arriving home somewhat early. He was disappointed, a little humiliated. The freshness had gone from his sad little pleasure, for he had not wished her to guess that he had been down. Now the act seemed clumsy, in bad taste, as if he had been forcing his attentions on her. He went into his sitting-room with a heart heavier than before, and continued his preparations for departure. He had packed up his portmanteau and was now stowing away his papers and valuable odds and ends that he wished to remain under lock and key during his absence.

Suddenly a step was heard on the stair that made his heart stand still, and Clytie appeared at the door.

"Can I come in?"

He could scarcely find words to greet her. Now that their good comradeship was at an end, above all, now that she was lifted beyond his sphere, she held a different position in his eyes. She looked beautiful, queenly. Her rich hair and colouring, the pale blue of her dress, struck a note of exquisite brightness in the gloomy, half-dismantled room.   He removed some books from his writing-chair and pulled it towards her.

" How good of you to come ! " was all he could say.

" How good of you to look after my fire ! " said Clytie.

" I did not want you to know——"

" Why not ? "

" Oh, a sentiment," he replied.   " We are governed a great deal by such things."

" It touched me so," said Clytie.   " I could not help coming up to thank you, as you are going away early in the morning."

" Ah !   Winifred told you ? "

" Yes ; she said you had come to bid good-bye."

Kent felt bound to fall in with Winifred's friendly fable, although his honesty shrank a little from accepting what was not its due.

" There is always something sad in leave-taking," said Clytie.

The remark was trite and commonplace ; but so is a kiss or a grasp of the hand or the words " Good-bye, dear," themselves.   The original generally brings more titillation than comfort.

" This leave-taking is sadder than most—to me," said Kent.

" And to me too," said Clytie.   " It marks the end of the old life—a very pleasant one.   Kent," she went on after a short reflective pause, " I want to tell you something : I reproached you a little in my heart—last month. I don't now.   I haven't the right.   Winifred said she had let you know of my engagement.   If our parting had not come from you, it would have come now from me."

" I see now ; it was bound to come sooner or later," replied Kent, much moved.   " Oh, my God ! what puppets we are.   But I wish you happiness, from my heart, in your new life.   You will always be to me the one woman whom "—he was going to add, " I could love," but he checked himself and quickly substituted, " who has taught me what there is in women."

" Ah, my dear Kent," returned Clytie with a touch of

her brightness and charm, "there will be someone nicer than I who will teach you better. You, too, must have happiness, you know. You will marry soon——"

"I marry!" cried Kent, wheeling round to face her. "How can you say that!"

They looked at one another, each misunderstanding. He was wounded at her treating his love as a thing of no account. She was puzzled at his implied contradiction of her theory.

"I thought I had discovered the reason for your wishing to break off our intimacy—but I find I was wrong."

"I don't understand," said Kent, agitated. "I acted foolishly, very foolishly and rudely. Yet I only did it to save you pain. To break with you cost me the dearest thing I had in the world. Surely you must be aware of that."

"You did not break it because you suddenly—during my absence—wished to form other ties?"

A light broke upon Kent, like a flash of lightning over a desolate wilderness. All of this heart-burning, then, was for nothing. She had never suspected that he loved her. A sense of the futility of things crushed him for a moment.

"I am not a man to fall in love readily," he replied in a low voice.

"Then," said Clytie earnestly, "I am at fault. Why did you not answer my letter? Why did you shun me? Why were you so constrained when we met? Why did you tear yourself out of my daily life?"

Kent turned away his face, so that she should not see him as he fought out within himself a great battle. Had these words only been spoken a day or two ago he would have poured out his love to her in all its honesty and strength. But now she was bound to another irrevocably—now indeed it would give her pain to hear what he foolishly thought would have given her pain to hear before. Then he was restrained by misinterpretation of the meaning of the passion that had come surging into his blood. Now he was held back by finer feelings, ignorant perhaps, quixotic, but such as work in man to the shaping of his nobleness.

"It was something I would rather not speak of," he

said at last—" something in my own life. I might have told you then ; I was wrong not to ; I did it for the best. I can't now. This seems like a cheap way of making mysteries,—perhaps it is one, not very big,—but it is better that it should be one to you. It was no fault of mine, believe me. You do believe me, Clytie, when I say that it was bitter for me to give up your friendship, don't you ? "

" Yes, Kent," exclaimed Clytie, " I do believe that you are everything that is true and tender and loyal. You don't know what strength and comfort your sympathy and your brave, frank way of looking at things have been to me. I have wronged you—forgive me."

She rose, held out her hand to him. He took it and raised it to his lips very gently. Her eyes grew a little moist.

" You are treating me like a foolish woman, and not *en bon camarade*," she said in a low voice.

" You are no longer my *bon camarade*," he replied. " You are my very dear lady, whom I will serve till the hour of my death."

A moment or two afterwards she was gone. The next morning Kent left England.

CHAPTER XV.

A great writer has remarked, that between the acting of a dreadful thing and the first motion, all the interim is like a phantasma or a hideous dream, and that the state of man under those circumstances, like to a little kingdom, suffers the nature of an insurrection. Although the step that Clytie was about to take was not of the character that Brutus contemplated, it was sufficiently serious for the interval between her engagement and her marriage to be a time of great mental and moral upheaval. Her "genius and mortal instruments" had periods of fierce council, in which the latter always obtained turbulent victory. Dreading these inner conflicts, she shrank from introspection. When doubts began to creep over her she shook them off, and sat down and wrote letters to Thornton which she burned an hour or two afterwards. But it was only when she was alone in the studio hastily finishing the orders she had in hand, or during the few lonely evenings that she passed in her sitting-room, that these torturing misgivings arose. When Thornton was near she forgot that any had ever come to her. He overpowered her will and her senses, dominated her with a caressing word, a touch of the hand, a glance from the depths of his dark eyes. In the lucid intervals between these periods of dizzying surrender she did not recognise herself. It was almost as if some Morgan le Fay had cast around her a spell of woven paces, and changed her into she knew not what, while she saw the old Clytie fading like a dream-shape away. To women of finer temperament marriage looms shadowy, formless, a great enchanter that will change all things, deliver into their keeping the secrets of pain and delight. But to Clytie it was something less and something more. Its material responsibilities were less of a mystery to her than to most girls of her age, owing to the peculiarities of her self-training ; but its spiritual and moral results were hidden from her in a cloud, denser, more lurid, more extensive. She loved Hammerdyke, not indeed as she would have loved Kent had he made one little effort to turn the wavering friendship into love—for then passion would have been finely tempered with tenderness, trust, and generous sympathy ; but still certain chords of her nature vibrated fully in response to the touch of the man she was about to marry. The one might have, as it were, awakened the full organ, but the single diapason that was pulled rang out none the less true.

During the short period of their engagement Hammerdyke was unceasing in tokens of his love. It was the nature of the man to throw his whole being into the delight or danger of the moment. Many a woman who cares lukewarmly, perhaps reluctantly, is fired with a gratitude akin to love by unending, passionate devotion. All the more responsive is the woman of full blood and emotional temperament who already cares greatly. Thornton gave Clytie no reason to doubt his affection ; if anything, he frightened her by its excess. She yielded to him in all things, sometimes half dreamily, indifferently, without regret and without sweetness ; sometimes the surrender was infinite joy.

In one matter, however, she was called upon to exercise her will : Thornton did not care how or where the marriage was performed. A man loathes weddings, particularly his own. It is only the barbarian that lingers, as people say, in the heart of woman that demands ceremonies and pomps and vanities ; a man, finer in some things, strangely enough, sees a certain indelicacy in the brazen publicity of the wedding rites. True, this view never presented itself to Thornton, who merely wanted to call Clytie his own and looked upon the formality of the marriage bond as a necessary nuisance, but it came vividly to Clytie, and caused her, as she was called upon to decide in the matter, to choose as quiet a wedding as possible. She shrank with repugnance from the meaningless ordeal of bridesmaids, favours, and a wedding-breakfast. It was only in deference to Durdleham susceptibilities that she did not entertain the idea of a civil marriage before a registrar.

The announcement of her engagement caused a flutter of excitement in the family. Mrs. Blather and Janet could not understand a girl's art life, but they could understand a wedding. They settled it between themselves that Clytie and her *fiancé* should come down to Durdleham to be there married in the orthodox fashion. They had already drawn up a list of guests and a scheme of wedding arrangements when a letter arrived from Clytie saying that she was to be married almost immediately, and that on no account could the ceremony take place at Durdleham. The sisters were disappointed. Mrs. Blather remonstrated, adding arguments and entreaties that brought tears of desperation to Clytie's eyes. She hated the thought of willingly giving pain to her father and sisters, but a family ceremony was more than she could bear. By trying to explain the inexplicable she made matters worse. If Mrs. Blather and Janet had failed to understand her simple needs of a free, untrammelled girlish life, how could they unravel the tangled complexities involving her repugnance to their proposals? At last she wrote that the day was definitely fixed, and that if her sisters would not come to town, no one but her friends the Farquharsons and Winifred would be present at the ceremony. To journey up to London for the purpose of standing in a bleak, empty church on a dismal March morning just to see Clytie married in a travelling dress was a prospect not pleasing enough to be entertained. The sisters resigned themselves with a sigh to circumstances and to a catalogue of Clytie's eccentricities from her earliest years. Mrs. Blather sent Clytie a pair of silver candlesticks, Janet sent her a tea-service, and old Mr. Davenant, who had been courteously addressed by Hammerdyke on the subject of the marriage, sent her a check for one hundred pounds. And that ended the matter.

Winifred spent the night before the marriage with Clytie.

"Do come, Winnie dear," the latter had said. "I shall be so lonely and miserable."

So Winnie came like a spirit of peace, and the two girls

cried a little in each other's arms, and it was the weaker who comforted the stronger.

"I shall keep on the studio," said Winifred,—"I am getting quite rich, you know,—and then you can come sometimes and take off your things and make believe to be back again. And I shall come and see you in your big house—if you will tell your big husband not to frighten me away."

"You will always be my own sweet Winnie," said Clytie tenderly, "and you will always get the very best out of me even if I change utterly to everybody else."

"But how can you change, dear?" asked Winifred in her simple faith. For she had lost her first instinctive distrust of Hammerdyke in the glamour of Clytie's love for him. "How can you ever be different from what you are and what you have always been?"

"Oh, I may grow very, very wicked and selfish one of these days, and not care for simple things any longer; and then you might be hurt, and you would know how unworthy I was that you should care for me, and you would shrink from me."

"Oh, Clytie, darling!" cried Winifred, throwing her arms about her neck, "how can you say such things?"

"It is silly, I know," said Clytie; "but I sometimes feel that I might do something very wicked without much compunction before I die."

"But you are going to lead a splendid, beautiful life!" said Winnie. "You will live in a great house, and have at your command the most brilliant society in London, all the clever, artistic people—just what you like. And you won't have to paint for orders, so you need never have to cramp your genius, dear. Oh, Clytie, you will simply be overflowing with happiness all your life long."

Clytie sighed. The independence of her half-Bohemian life was very dear to her. This was the last night on which, if it so pleased her, she could go forth into the streets, uncontrolled, whither she would. Henceforward her actions would have to be referred to an authority. To-morrow she would even change her name; be transformed from the Clytie Davenant whom she knew into Mrs. Hammerdyke, a vague, mysterious entity, with whose nature she was unfamiliar. No matter how glorious the future, there is always some regret in leaving forever a past phase of life :

> At leaving even the most unpleasant people
> And places, one keeps looking at the steeple.

But this was a pleasant place Clytie was about to quit, and she looked back upon its associations with a sigh.

In the morning a commissionnaire sent by Thornton came and fetched away her trunks, for the newly married pair were to start for the Continent immediately after the ceremony. When these were despatched Clytie stood for a moment before her glass, adjusted the clasp of her cape and the set of her broad gray beaver hat, and turning to Winifred, said quietly : " Let us go, dear."

They drove together in a hansom to St. Luke's Church, close by, where Thornton and the Farquharsons were waiting for them, in the porch. It was a bright morn‑ing, warm for the time of year, and the sparrows and a stray thrush plucked up heart of grace and twittered cheerily from the trees in the churchyard. Two little street children, with arms about each other's necks, stood by a near gravestone and looked at the little group with somewhat disappointed eyes. They had expected a bride in a long white veil and orange‑blossoms, a costume always mysteriously fascinating to the unsophisticated. Perhaps it was only a christening after all, one remarked to the other. But where was the baby ? The interior of the empty church was more cheerful than empty Protestant churches are wont to be. The slanting sunlight streamed many-coloured through the stained windows across the nave, and a broad shaft poured in from the open south door upon the vacant pews in the aisle. From outside came faintly the hum and rattle of the King's Road. The influences were peaceful, encouraging, and Clytie, sensitive to impres‑sions, felt grateful. The two little children, with their eyes on the verger, peeped in through the door and satisfied themselves that it was a wedding after all.

They whispered together with many smiles and nods, guessing at the *dramatis personæ*. Clytie noticed them, smiled back and nodded. It was as if a bit of her past life had come to bid her be of good cheer. The party stood for a while in the body of the church, talking gaily in low tones. Mrs. Farquharson was radiant at the prospective accomplishment of a dear wish.

"You must be proud of your bride," she said to Thornton. "Is she not looking beautiful?"

And she whispered to Clytie :

"You must be proud of your husband. Have you ever seen a man to compare with him?"

Thornton held his head erect as he gave Clytie his arm and walked up to the communion rail. He was proud of her. The quiet gray of her broad hat and her cloak threw into relief the rich colouring of her hair and eyes and lips. The past two years had completed her womanly beauty. Irregularities of contour below the eyes had been toned down, the delicacy of modelling of her face had been accentuated, and the new emotions of the past three weeks had filled her great dark blue eyes with a new, mysterious light. Thornton pressed her hand against his side, and whispered, "My darling," so close to her that she felt his breath warm upon her ear. She looked at him for a moment, her full lips quivering ever so slightly.

"I should like to kiss you," he whispered again. "You are so beautiful."

In a few moments it was over. The words compromising a lifetime had been said. The wedding ring gleamed upon her finger. As she passed with the others into the vestry she looked down at it in a daze. There it was and there it must remain till death parted them, a token of submission and obedience. In the vestry there were embraces, congratulations. Thornton kissed her after the gallant fashion of a man who can afford to wait for a warmer caress. Winifred threw her arms round her neck, weeping. Mrs. Farquharson kissed her in her affectionate, motherly way. George kissed her gravely on the forehead and dipped the pen in the ink for her to sign "Clytie Davenant" for the last time. Then they found themselves in the porch again, saying farewell. Caroline laughingly called her "Mrs. Hammerdyke" as they finally parted. And then the little knot of three waved their handkerchiefs as the cab drove off that took her husband and herself towards Victoria.

"You are mine now, my darling," he said, taking her hand. "All that is most mine."

"I am glad," she murmured, returning his pressure. "Yours for always."

The commissionnaire met them at the station. He had taken their tickets, settled their luggage, engaged a carriage. A bouquet of violets lay upon the seat. Clytie flashed a quick glance at her husband.

"Thank you for thinking. I love them so much."

He arranged her hot-water can and her rugs and sat down by her side, thrusting up the dividing arms impatiently. As soon as the train had moved out of the station he put his arms around her and kissed her, and spoke to her in tender, passionate words. The stop at Croydon broke the continuity of this first wedded embrace. On the platform outside the carriage window a loud altercation was in progress between the ticket-collector and a young couple who objected to pay for the ticket of a tiny terrier the woman was carrying. They were of the lower middle class, both in their Sunday clothes. She was a fair, delicate woman of some refinement ; but the husband was coarse, vulgar, with the stamp of sensuality on his sharp, somewhat handsome face. Moreover, he was slightly intoxicated, and used a foul expression to qualify the collector after the official had departed. A flush rose to the young woman's forehead.

"Don't, John," she pleaded. "He's in his rights."

But the cad consigned his rights to perdition, and moved off vulgarly proclaiming his own.

Clytie had heard this small scene in a life's drama and she vividly constructed the miserable tragedy. When the train moved on again she shivered, with a nameless, indefinable sense of fear. Three months ago she would have noted the scene for vigorous transference to canvas. Now the woman more than the artist was stirred.

"Please don't talk—just for a little, Thornton," she said as he began to speak.

He looked at her somewhat reproachfully. She drew off her glove and put her hand into his.

" You can't understand—it all seems so strange. Let me gather myself together for a moment—darling."

She trembled on the last word. It was the first time she had used it to him.

He pressed her hand and leaned back on the cushions. Clytie looked out of the window at the telegraph poles and trees and broad fields swaying past. Whither was this tearing train carrying her ? Out of her life into a new, strange world whose habits and customs and laws and speech were all foreign to her ? She was married. She no longer belonged to herself. Her independence was gone. She had promised to love, honour, and obey this man by her side until death should part them. That would be a long time—many, many years. The thought frightened her. Until then she had scarce realised what married life meant, in this respect. Why had she married this man ? As this question passed through her mind her husband raised the hand he held to his lips. The blood rushed hot to her cheeks, she did not finish the mental question, but turning quickly, looked at him for a moment, and falling under the spell of his eyes, yielded to his arm, forgetting all things. He had the power of drowning in a more lurid blaze those glimmerings of self-revelation. She whispered so to him laughingly, and he accepted it as a man generally does accept such things — not seeing that it was of deeper significance than a woman's ordinary tribute of tenderness.

"You are my beautiful Clytie," he said, kissing her, and for a season she was content with the response.

There was a lover's silence between them, which she broke at length by saying :

" Don't you think it would have been much nicer if we could have had one another on trial—say for six months ? "

" So that you could all the time be thinking whether you should repent of your bargain ? Oh, dear, no ! "

" Ah ! you say that ; but would it not have been better, if we grew to hate each other, to be able to shake hands and say good-bye ? For we may quarrel dreadfully, you know."

He answered her with tender assurances, laughed at her fears.

"We shall never quarrel if you are a good little girl and do as you are told," he said.

Clytie laughed, seeing only jesting in the remark.

"And we shall never quarrel if you let me go where I like and do what I like and say what I like."

"But you will always want to go and do and say as I like, darling," said Thornton. "So we shall never quarrel."

"Then you will never want me to be severely respectable?" asked Clytie, with a touch of insistence.

"I shan't allow you to flirt with any and everybody, if you mean that," he replied, showing his white teeth as he smiled.

"I didn't mean that—for the simple reason that I have a certain amount of brains."

"There have been many coquettes with magnificent intellects."

She made no reply. Then, seeing that he had ruffled her, he adroitly turned their talk into less dangerous channels.

They stayed in Paris a couple of days and then continued their journey to the Riviera. It was Clytie's own desire. In the first flush of his passion all places were alike to Thornton, provided she were with him. But she longed to get away from England, to cut herself adrift for a while from all old associations, to surround herself with new conditions, so that nothing should disturb the wonder of this new love. And when, with a lover's hyperbole, he had bidden her choose any spot on the whole terrestrial globe for the passing of their honeymoon, she had selected the Mediterranean.

They went to the little Italian town of Bordighera, hidden away at the foot of the mountains amidst its palms and olive trees. Besides being one of the most beautiful spots on that beautiful coast, it has the charm of quiet. There is no casino at Bordighera, no public garden, no municipal band. It holds out to visitors no attractions but its own loveliness—hence the absence of the banal, the rococo. A few villas are dotted round it, away from the sea. One long, straggling street of shops, narrowing gradually, leads up to the old, picturesque, evil-smelling town on the hill.   And this with its narrow sun-less streets flanked by high, dingy, gray houses, between which the sky above seems a narrow strip of Prussian blue ribbon, its crooked byways and basement loggie of cool malodour, its cobble pavements on which great entrance gateways gape like dark, noisome caverns, offers few attractions other than those of quaintness and curi-osity to any but its own inhabitants.   It is a quiet place, devoid of the cosmopolitan *tohubohu* of Mentone or Cannes.   An index of this is the fact that, save the com-moner qualities of the Italian *regie*, cigarettes are not to be bought for love or money in Bordighera, and these in the greasiest ramshackle shop imaginable.   If you want civilised shops you must go to San Remo.

Thornton and Clytie spent the earlier portion of their honeymoon here in unbroken happiness.   Beyond casual gossip with their table d'hôte neighbours they held inter-course with no one.   All fears, doubts, flutterings of regret, vanished from Clytie's heart, together with all sense of subjective life.   She was tasting the physical joy of existence as it came to her in the passion, sunlight, colour, warmth, and scents of the south.   She had chosen with unconscious wisdom.   The intensity of the beauty of the Mediterranean, its positivism, its splendid denial of the melancholic and mysterious, held her being in tone with the love with which Thornton had inspired her. It intoxicated her with a complementary passion.

They drove one day from Bordighera through Venti-miglia to Mentone.   Halfway they stopped at a way-side inn, and breakfasted under a trellis of grape-vine. On the one side was the dazzling white road, flanked by the terraced hill of olive-trees, the white underparts of their leaves flashing like silver ; on the other, below, the gold sand and the purple sea.   And the sun streamed through the vine, checkering the table and their hands and faces.   The fare was poor and the Asti none of the best, but the wine sparkled and bubbled in the thick tumbler they used in common, and brought a keener sparkle into Clytie's eyes, and a more joyous abandon-ment into her laugh.   When they had resumed their drive, and a turn of the road brought them into sight of

Mentone, her heart leaped at the suddenness with which the blaze of colour was revealed. Below, over a declining foreground of olive and orange gardens, lay the white town in a setting of bright green foliage, stretching from horn to horn of the bay. Behind the eastern horn projected dark and bold the promontory of Monaco with the flashing white of its castle. Behind the town rose the two bare peaks of the Berceau standing out in deep blue-gray against the intense violet sky. Before it swept the broad belt of yellow sand, on which lapped, in little idle waves whose ebb left a delicate fringe of white, a still, unbroken sea of lapis lazuli, melting through infinite gradations of blue streaked with arbitrary purples into the deep ultramarine that met the paler sky far away on the horizon. The burst of intense colour of sky and sea and land, glowing as far as the eye could sweep, drowned Clytie's being in a sensuous flood. It was, as it were, the projection of physical passion into something visible, thus baring to the eyes its wonderful beauty. She uttered a little inarticulate gasp, a catching of the breath. They were quite alone, the coachman half asleep in the sun on his box. Thornton put his arm round her and drew her to him. She turned, closed her eyes. All creation, from the world of wonder before her to the tiniest quivering fibre within her, vibrated with an intoxicating thrill of delight. She caught his hand, drew his arm tighter, and lifted her lips to his in a long, long kiss.

Thenceforward her stay on the Riviera was one uninterrupted delight. It was a dream in which the mind lay subject to the sense. She was in a blue mist, which hid impenetrably past and future, and informed the visible area about her feet with unutterable sweetness. " Don't expect me to write letters," she said in a hastily scribbled note to Caroline. " This is a land in which words have no part. You might as well expect me to talk the ' Moonlight Sonata ' to you." And Caroline, being a wise woman, smiled. Yet, after all, her wisdom had nothing to do with it—for anything feminine would have divined. The days flew on wings of fire. She never read, never worked ; her sketch-book remained empty. Often they sat at their sitting-room window, looking out on to the Strada Romana, hand in hand, without speaking, save for a murmured caress, for an hour together. Or they walked up between the olives, past the famous high wall with its gorgeous coat of mesembryanthemum, through the narrow, crooked town, down the rugged descent to the surf-beaten shore, where the great white solitary *casa* stands, and there sat down in the shade of the big rocks and watched the glowing "countless laughter" of the sea. Often they rambled through the cool, sunless olive gardens, rising terrace after terrace apparently into the deep violet sky. The scent of the rosemary and wild thyme beneath their feet rose penetrating and filled the blood, and Thornton would pick a handful, and laughingly hold it between them above their lips as he kissed her. And when they reached the top of the hill they sat under a tree, and Clytie rested her head on his shoulder, and let her eye wander over the low-lying ridges of the Maritime Alps rising in endless soft-rounded undulations, like the many-breasted mother of men, in each bosom nestling a compact white townlet gathered around the slated cupola of its church; and the soft sunlight lay over all, transfused through the blue atmosphere. Then she would say : " Don't let us talk, Thornton "; but there was a different meaning to the words from that which they had when she uttered them in the train as it left Croydon.

Sometimes they went away from Bordighera for two or three days ; visited Nice, Cannes, Monte Carlo. At Monte Carlo Clytie won three or four hundred francs at the roulette tables. Gambling had never come before within her experience of things. She plunged into it with childish recklessness, looking round with glowing face and laughter in her eyes at her husband when she won, and drawing a short little breath of dismay when the croupier raked in her stake. The game, the intensity of the strange faces, seen nowhere else,—faces which bore the stamp of combinations of the seven deadly sins taken from two to half a dozen together,—the subtle working in that great, glittering room of all the passions under heaven, attracted her, fascinated her. The artistic temperament caught the impressions, instinctively, unconsciously registered them, thus widening and deepening her conception of life. It was a luxury of sense to leave the babel passion of the Casino and to walk arm in arm on the terrace or in the grounds. There the music came faintly and mingled with the far-off splash of the sea away below them and the rustle of the palms and drachinas. On the right stretched out Monaco, clustering like a group of fireflies below the white bastioned castle. Behind them rose the black mass of the Maritime Alps with the Mont Agel towering distinct above. The air was soft and warm, recovering from the sudden shock of sundown. What they said to one another matters little. He saw that she was beautiful and filled with the sense of his love, and he was happy. To Clytie life meant unutterable things.

On the third morning of their stay at Monte Carlo Thornton returned from a short stroll and came into their room.

"A man I know has just come by the train and I fled from him," he said ; "let us go somewhere else."

Clytie was pleased.

"I am glad you still want us to be quite, quite alone," she replied. "But you are sure you are not a little bit weary of me ? "

He answered as many millions of men more or less sincere have answered. And Clytie thought neither of believing nor of disbelieving him, as many millions of women have done. The subjective is apt to crop up afterwards and it generally causes trouble. But in the passion of a kiss woman, being, like man, of flesh and blood, and not an abstraction, does not calculate remote psychological contingencies ; if she does, the kissing is all a mistake. Once, towards the end of their honeymoon, Clytie did touch upon the subjective. They were sitting by the ruined tower on the hill above the Strada Romana. Clytie was heated and had taken off her hat, and the breeze ruffled her hair as she leaned against the trunk of a tree. Thornton sprawled by her side, resting his chin on his hand and looking at her.

"I always grudge your wearing a hat," he said. "Your beautiful hair ought not to be hidden. You look much lovelier now that it is free for the wind to kiss."

She laughed a contented little laugh, throwing her chin up, according to her way.

"Do you know, Thornton," she said with a little hesitation, in which there was much charm, "being called beautiful every day is one of the great novelties of the situation. I always knew I was good to look upon, and sometimes I really was very pleased to behold myself. But before I knew you, dear, it never made anything of a factor in my daily life. And now I almost begin to think it's the only quality I have."

"Given that, you can let all the others go—— " He waved his hand vaguely, consigning them to the *Ewigkeit*.

"But that's not all that you love me for, is it, dear?"

An idle question, with an unsuspected fear lurking in its heart.

"I don't know why I love you. It has never occurred to me to investigate the matter."

"Well, try. It will be like playing the game, 'I love my love with an A'!"

Thornton shook his head boyishly, and laughed.

"It would spoil it all!" he said—"to go worrying about what lies under that sweet face of yours. Can't you understand, darling? What do your qualities matter to me? Provided I can take you in my arms and kiss you as much as I like, what concern is it of mine whether you are acquainted with the cookery book or spell art with a capital A? Don't you think it's more satisfactory to lie here and look into your great blue eyes, and your hair with the sun and wind playing hide and seek in it, and your bosom rising and falling, than to speculate whether you are even-tempered or vindictive or ambitious or fond of Adelaide Proctor's poetry?"

"What a boy you are!" she cried light-heartedly, stretching out her hand so as to run her fingers over his crisp brown hair. "So my face has been my fortune!"

"And your figure," he remarked critically. "The whole of you!"

"Tell me," she continued, "what would you have done if I hadn't married you?"

He started up to a sitting posture, and his eyes flashed.

"I should have gone straight back to Africa and played the very devil there! But you were bound to marry me, you know; and if you had been already a married woman, I should have got to you somehow. I have been hit before in my time, over and over, but never till I met you did I think a woman worth the marriage service. But you're a witch, Clytie," he added, resuming his former attitude, "the Belle Dame sans Merci."

"Poor fellow," said Clytie, "poor knight-at-arms! And you do look ' so haggard and so woe-begone,' don't you?"

She laughed as she looked at his great frame lying at her feet, and his strong, handsome dark face, with its health and masterfulness. Then she continued in the lightness of her heart:

"But seriously, now, Thornton, very seriously. You do want me to be a little help to you in your life—in other ways—don't you? In your ambitions, your work in the world generally. We must begin to talk about such things soon, you know."

Thornton laughed lazily as he lit a cigarette.

"My work in the world is to love you, my dear, and I'll promise to let you help me in that as much as you like."

But Clytie insisted. Sometimes the subjective gets too much for a woman.

"Ah, Thornton dear," she said. "I want to feel that we are much more than lovers. That will wear off after a time. Oh, yes! don't tell me it won't; a woman learns things all with a rush, you see. And I want to feel that we are one in everything, in all our sympathies and views of life, our ambitions, in all the high and great things that lie before you. I want to be in touch with everything you do and think—to be a real helpmeet for you."

He took her hand and kissed it, laughing.

"I have got a lot to learn in the way of connubial responsibilities," he said. "You'll have to train me, my dear. But allow me to remark that the sun is just going to dip over there by the Nervia, and if we want to get in by sunset we shall have to run like the deuce!"

As this was a serious matter,—on the Riviera it is one of the grave responsibilities of life,—Clytie let herself be lifted to her feet, put on her hat quickly, and holding her husband's hand, ran merrily with him down the hill. The exercise and the laughter drove things subjective out of her head for a season. But in the after-time the ghost of this little conversation came and sat at the head of her bed, making mock at a few others who sat on the foot-rail. A thing does not require to be as objective as a murdered monk to have a little ghost all to itself.

CHAPTER XVI.

Perhaps if they had remained in Bordighera the intoxication would have lasted longer. But as our lives are hemmed in by infinite possibilities, to each of which is strung its infinite ramification of consequences, it is somewhat rash to predicate *ex hypothesi*. At any rate so long as they were at Bordighera there seemed to be no reason that the continuity of the charm should be broken ; whereas it did suffer a change during the railway journey from Bordighera to Paris. And this railway journey was a kind of neutral ground in their married life, separating the dream from the reality. On entering the train they were lovers. On leaving it they were a married couple. Wherein lies somewhat of a difference. They were not conscious of the change. Realisation of this mysterious operation is fortunately denied to human beings, seeing that they turn their eyes inwards rather too much as it is already. Nor do they recognise what has happened until some time afterwards, as the old influences still remain lingeringly ; but then they can generally look back to the point of transition, and set it up as a forlorn landmark in their lives.

Why they did not remain longer in the south they themselves could scarcely explain. They had arranged to spend a month there, and then to proceed to Paris to wait indefinitely until their new house in the Cromwell Road should be ready to receive them. There is nothing so irrefragable as an arbitrary programme. Even the most emancipated enslave themselves to it sometimes, as in the present case did Thornton and Clytie They possibly lost a good deal,—the flowers of life seldom grow along the beaten track,—but they never thought of attributing it to the fixity of their programme. They were in Paris, then, living under totally fresh conditions. Thornton found there a succession of friends and acquaintances, and was pleased rather than otherwise to meet them. At Monte Carlo he fled from Carteret of the Hussars ; on the Boulevard des Capucines he greeted him heartily and carried him off into the American Bar. Besides discovering acquaintances daily in the hotel list, Thornton was not unknown in general Parisian society. His name could procure him admission into most circles that he cared to enter. He was put up at a couple of clubs and received invitation cards by the dozen.

To please him Clytie went with him a little into society. He was proud of his beautiful wife, loved to watch the effect produced as she entered a drawing-room upon his arm, and the eager admiration on the faces of the men who crowded round her chair. In fact, Clytie had a small social success—and a paragraph in the *Figaro*. It was a new sensation for her; but in these early days of her married life she would have preferred a quieter, less conspicuous existence. But Thornton, just as he had sought in the south to keep her and her beauty to himself, now seemed to wish to exhibit it abroad.

"I seem to wear you like a decoration, darling," he said once.

At first Clytie flushed with pleasure at the little flattery. Then she thought over it for a bit, and it did not please her so much. But she did not confide this to her husband. She had already begun to discover that for the safekeeping of many little matters her own heart was the best place.

They had a set of rooms in a hotel in the Champs Elysées with a balcony overlooking the Grande Avenue. Clytie loved to sit there with Thornton in the quiet half hour before dinner watching the stream of vehicles, fine and vague far away by the Arc de Triomphe, then gradually broadening, till fashionable Paris returning from the Bois blazed beneath her in its movement and gaiety. They seemed to her so alone up there, above the whirl and the glitter and falseness. It was a return of the hours of the month in the south, and happiness fluttered tremulously around her—like a butterfly, ever so elusively. When she leaned over the balcony by his side many people looked up admiringly at them. When she saw one woman twitch the arm of her companion in a victoria, and both shoot swift feminine glances up at the balcony, she could not help feeling a little thrill of pride in her husband. And then she would remember the morning's solitary ramble among the sculpture of the Louvre (Thornton and herself were less dependent upon each other now for entertainment), and reflect, with a sense of pleasure, that she had seen no antique ideal that could compare with him in splendid manhood. He, too, had done heroic deeds, she would think, and she would move nearer to his side and be glad that he was there. Yet the butterfly happiness was just beyond her grasp.

Some such thoughts were passing through her mind one afternoon as they stood together on the balcony. He broke a short silence by saying :

"We are getting quite an old married couple, Clytie !"

"What made you say that ?" she asked, smiling.

"Oh ! I hardly know. I have got so used to having you by me. It seems as if I had been married ever since I was born."

"It does seem a long, long time ago that we first passed through Paris. But I can't say I am quite used to matrimony yet. Do you know, I have sometimes hoped that I never should be."

"Why ?"

"Can't you guess ? At present, dear, it is all glamour and mystery, and when you get too familiar with the glamour it turns into the commonplace. That's why I am just a little bit sorry we left Bordighera."

"It was certainly very jolly," he assented reflectively. "But we are having as good a time here, aren't we ?"

"Well, I like these little half hours best," said Clytie, "when we are alone together. When we are parted it seems as if I am suddenly called upon to live as an individual and do not quite know how to begin. You see, when I am alone with you I know how to behave as Clytie Hammerdyke, but not yet when I am by myself or with other people."

Thornton laughed, as a man in love laughs when he thinks he is replying to an idle, pretty remark.

"You have always Clytie Davenant to fall back upon," he said.

"Have I? That's just the question I have been putting to myself. But I can't explain it to you. I don't think you would understand."

"Of course I understand!" he cried quickly. "You have to mix with people as a married woman, and you are a bit shy at first. But you'll pull through all right, dear. Why, as it is, you are superb."

"Oh, come," she said, laughing. "I can talk to people without blushing and morally biting the corner of my apron. I meant something a little more subtle than that. You see, after all, you don't understand. I can never, never be Clytie Davenant again. She was buried for good and all at Bordighera."

"And my sweet phœnix has arisen out of her ashes," said Thornton.

"If you like—and the phœnix hasn't quite got the sense of her environment yet."

"All this is very pretty, my dear," said Thornton, with a laugh. "But I can't quite see what we are driving at."

"Have I been talking such great nonsense, then? Perhaps it all tended to express the fact that when I am with you I don't think of myself; when we are apart I am confronted with myself, and feel embarrassed. You see, Thornton dear," she went on, "I have lived a queer kind of life, full of such different hopes and dreams. I scarcely thought about marriage in those days. I knew that love would come to me some time or the other, but then it seemed as if it would all be mixed up with my art, whereas now—— Oh, you can't see how different it is!"

There was no tone of sadness or regret in her voice as she said this, but a touch of tenderness, a tribute, as it were, to his influence.

"But there's nothing to hinder you from amusing yourself with painting pictures, is there?" asked her husband lightly. "You have no call now to earn a livelihood, but you can paint all day if you like, my dear."

"Of course I shall paint—I could not live without it—

except perhaps such a month as last.   But, don't you see, my art was once the guiding principle of my life.   Now I have my art and my love, and they seem to have nothing to do with each other.   They are on different planes, so to speak.   It is all that that makes me feel I don't quite realise myself yet when I have to leave the love plane for a little."

"Don't leave it," said Thornton.

"Ah ! we have done that by going away from Bordighera, and leading this dissipated life here," she replied, laughing.   "But we can get on and off whenever we like, you know.   That is one comfort."

"Well," said Thornton, lighting a cigarette, and speaking between the first few whiffs, " marriage must make some difference.   You have lived a free and easy, emancipated life among artistic people, and now you belong to somebody else—a wild barbarian, who could no more tell you how to paint a picture than how to cut out a dress.   Of course it makes a difference in your way of viewing things.   It has made a difference in mine too, by Jove !   When a yearning for Africa comes over me I have to say : No ; I have a wife, with her arms,—the roundest in the world, my dear,—about my neck.   And so I have got to settle down to politics and domesticity in the Cromwell Road."

"But you don't regret it, do you, Thornton ? " she asked, womanlike.

"Look at me and see if I do," he said.

Clytie obeyed him, half shyly, feeling, as she always did since her return to Paris, the fascination, half pleasant, half painful, of his eyes.   He loved her.   There was no doubt of that.   Yet the nature of his love sometimes frightened her a little if she strayed for a moment off the " love plane."   Her own responsiveness she never questioned, preferring to shut her eyes and let the current of his love carry her whither it would.   But at times now, during her solitary walks through the Louvre, the thought obtruded, What would the new life be like ? Not these early days, which were holidays from the seriousnesses of existence, but the life in the years that lay before her, of whose responsibilities she had as yet but vague premonitions.   How would her art be affected ?

Would it lose or gain in that breadth and insight that it needed ? Would she continue to reckon herself an artist at all, or would she only degenerate into the amateur—painting little meaningless pictures for amusement ? And at the end of a year would she not stand face to face with a new Clytie, paler, more shadowy, and therefore less insistently demanding self-expression ? Even these few weeks had changed her : what would she be at the end of one year, two years, twenty years ? Happier, with all her old cravings satisfied, with her individuality worked out to its fullest, with the riddle of life joyously solved ? Or else—— She scarcely dared think of it. She looked at what had been written in her Book of New Formulas, and found that the marriage service had been omitted. It merely said that marriage was unformularisable, an easy way of curving a contumelious lip at the old formulas which she had rebelled against, but scarcely satisfactory in her present position. Now, in the Old Formulas, marriage was minutely, scrupulously regulated by the most definite of rules. Although they broke up the poem of life into a disjointed copy-book, or at best into a collection of elegant extracts, still they presented a homogeneous scheme. Should she at last have to accept this, confess to Mrs. Blather smiling complacently that the Durdleham philosophy was the only one ? But then she would look at her husband and take a measure of comfort. Such a man could not come out of Durdleham.

That was her consolation in the perplexities that the problem of her married life caused her. She took refuge from herself, her thoughts, her forebodings, in his grand strength and personal magnetism. It was intermittent intoxication, this long Paris after-honeymoon, rather than continuous charm, and the intervals of soberness had their wearinesses. She had thrown her cap over the windmills. Sometimes she regretted it.

On the evening after the above conversation they went to the opera, where they had taken a box with the Claverings, army people with whom Thornton had been intimate in Cairo. Clytie had met them only for a moment the day before, and had not been favourably impressed. However, they were Thornton's friends, and it behoved her to appreciate them. Mrs. Clavering passed for being a clever woman by virtue of a plain face and a vivacious manner ; also because she ruled her husband and had a cultivated taste in sherry.

Thornton had admired her some years before. Mammas with marriageable daughters put it in that way ; those who could afford to be independent put it in another. Whichever way they put it in no wise affected the parties concerned. Mrs. Clavering was too superior a woman to allow idle gossip to influence her or her husband. Now she was eight-and-thirty, she had seen the world and had preserved few illusions, least of all any respecting Thornton Hammerdyke. She met him with a cynical encouragement, which to some men is flattering.

Clytie was quick to notice her manner towards Thornton, and resented it. There was a touch of banal familiarity, too, in his talk with Mrs. Clavering that jarred upon her. The tone was undignified, suggestive of the falser strata of regimental society, in which frankness stands for scarcely veiled mutual contempt.

He was sitting behind Mrs. Clavering, who smiled in a superior, half-patronising way at his remarks. Clytie listened to the music absently, wished they had come alone. The house was crowded, and the air was stifling. She found the opera, " La Juive," uninteresting.

" I am going to carry off your husband to the terrace, Mrs. Hammerdyke," said Mrs. Clavering at the end of the second act, " and I leave you mine in pledge. I hope he will take good care of you."

He was a heavy but honest Briton, who idolised his wife, his dinner, and the British Constitution. As neither the opera nor Clytie came within this area of adoration, he treated them with a polite though somewhat embarrassed indifference. Still he acquitted himself of his charge satisfactorily and entertained Clytie during the *entr'acte.* After a tour round the house he found a seat for her in the Salle des Pas Perdus and talked with solemn fitfulness. Then it occurred to him that it was oppressive indoors and he took her out upon the terrace. Clytie did not wish to stay there long—only for a moment to get a breath of fresh air. She remained for a little leaning on the broad balustrade and looking at the scene in front of her—the broad *place* below with the continuous passing to and fro of vehicles crossing each other in all directions, the Café de la Paix on the right with its crowded tables far out on the pavement and tray-laden waiters hurrying between them, the glittering vista of lights in the Avenue de l'Opera, the duller line of lamps in the Rue de la Paix with the Vendôme column towering high in the dim moonlight. It was so instinct with gaiety and movement and the brightness of life that a little thrill of its gladness passed through her, ending in a strange kind of sob that filled her throat. She took her companion's arm, and went across through the stream of loungers back into the heavy air of the Salle des Pas Perdus.

Meanwhile Thornton and Mrs. Clavering had established themselves in a corner at the end of the terrace.

"It seems like old times — on the veranda — at a regimental dance," she said. "At least that is what you were going to say, I suppose. I never yet met an old admirer but what he made some remark of the kind. So I have saved you from the commonplace."

"I was meditating some politeness of the sort," replied Thornton carelessly. "I thought you would expect it."

"I hope you will always have the same delicate consideration for others, Mr. Hammerdyke. How long are you going to be good and domestic?"

"Always, I suppose. I am going to run politics and that sort of show."

Mrs. Clavering laughed lightly.

"Ha! When I see you at it I'll believe it—unless you have changed extraordinarily since I last knew you. And you don't look much changed. Perhaps matrimony will work the miracle. Ha! ha! Pardon my laughing, but it seems so ridiculous to see you, of all people, married."

"I suppose I have human attributes somewhere about me," he said.

"Too vastly human, my poor friend ; that is where the danger lies. To err is human, you know. I hope your wife will do the divine part of the business, as women generally do, and forgive. By the way, I have not made you my compliment, as they say in this country. I think your wife simply perfect."

" We agree there for once," replied Thornton drily.

" Tell me all about it. Can't you see I am dying to know? That is why I brought you out here. Who is she? Where did you meet her? Were you long engaged? And I know you too are dying to talk to someone about her. You may as well gratify the craving while you still have it."

" I believe you are madly jealous, Clara. Pardon my frankness. But you and I always went in for being frank with one another."

" Call it amiable brutality—it would be better."

" As you like. I never went in for splitting hairs. I suppose it's brutal to say you are jealous."

" It is simply idiotic. Therefore I bear you no ill will for your saying so. I honestly admire your wife, and think you have got very much more than you deserve, and I am femininely curious. Now perhaps you will tell me."

" Well, I met her at a cousin's house. She is, or rather was, an artist."

" I appreciate the distinction. Proceed."

Thornton threw himself back with a great laugh against the balustrade, his elbows resting upon it, his hands in his pockets.

" I think you are just a little bit jealous," he said. " Well—to finish my story. She is of an old Buckinghamshire family, and we were engaged about a month. And then we were married. But tell me, by way of changing the conversation——"

" Which may be painful."

" Precisely. How long are you going to stay in Paris?"

" I don't know. As long as Paris pleases me. Am I going to see you any more, or are you too much engrossed? I don't want to take you away from your duties."

" I don't think you are likely to, Clara."

" Possibly not. Your wife will keep a tight rein upon you. She looks that sort. But I don't know why we should be talking in this strain the first time we have had a word together for—how many years? Four? Five? We have quickly dropped into old ways. But then you were a fire-eater, a chartered libertine, independent, a bird of freedom. Whereas now — my poor friend!"

"By George!" cried Thornton, starting forward, with some excitement in his eyes that glowed in the dimness, "don't fall into any delusion. If you think I am going the way of another poor friend of ours who can't call his soul his own, you are devilishly mistaken. I married because it happened to strike me that I wanted to do so. But I run the concern, and my wife's a sensible woman and recognises the fact. And whatever I want to do I am going to do. I have generally done it, and don't see why I should break through my habit now."

"And your wife?"

"How—my wife?"

"Is she going to enjoy a beautiful independence likewise?"

"No. It isn't good for women."

"Thank you. You always were a delicate judge in things feminine. Did you ever read 'As You Like It'? 'Lock the door on your wife's wit and it will out at the casement.' Have a care, my friend. I am about the only woman you have tried to make a fool of and haven't succeeded, and so you perhaps have a kind of respect for my intelligence, and I give you warning."

"I burned some of your letters the other day," said Thornton cynically.

"That was wise. Suppose we go in. The act must be about commencing."

The curtain was already up. Major Clavering was scanning the house drearily through a pair of opera glasses. Clytie was looking at the stage and thinking of her husband, wishing he would come in. When the door behind opened she turned round, and with an eye trained to catch fleeting expression, noticed a look upon Thornton's face,—the after-light, as it were, of a sneer, before the features had time to reset,—that she had never observed there before. The change from this to his usual gay smile was so rapid that she thought she had been mistaken, and attributed it to an illusion produced by the shadow at the back of the box. But the impression of it remained and it was unpleasant.

During the next *entr'acte* the men went out, leaving Clytie and Mrs. Clavering alone together. Either through the mere social desire to please or through a feeling of compassion proceeding from conscious superiority, the elder woman sought to make an agreeable impression upon the young wife. But Clytie had wrapped herself up in a strange veil of reserve and her attitude was unpropitiatory. Mrs. Clavering's falsetto voice struck upon her nerves, the confident air of patronage irritated her. She longed to be away from the heavy, acrid atmosphere, the artificiality of the opera, the society of Mrs. Clavering. She felt self-conscious, was angry with herself. She had the keen feminine sense of a false position and longed for extrication. She was glad when her husband and Major Clavering returned.

"I have been telling Mrs. Hammerdyke about old times in Cairo, and singing your praises," said Mrs. Clavering. "Are you not grateful to me?"

"I am flattered," said Thornton somewhat ironically.

"That is always the way to make a man grateful."

"It is the same with us. I don't suppose there is much difference in that respect between men and women," said Clytie, for the sake of saying something.

"I am not so sure of that," replied Mrs. Clavering ; "women can generally sift the grain from the chaff— only, poor things, they too often take the chaff by preference."

"I hope you are not alluding to me, my dear," said the major, who was given to saying stupid things by way of showing that he followed the thread of his wife's conversation.

Thornton chimed in with his deep laugh.

"That is one for you, Clavering. Perhaps one for me too. Anyhow, the curtain is going up and that saves us. Make room for me by you, Clytie, and tell me about what's going on."

He edged in his chair between Clytie and Mrs. Clavering. The major lounged behind, with his hands in his pockets, very much bored. He was hoping to escape soon.

" Are you enjoying it ? " whispered Thornton to Clytie.

" Moderately. It is a dull opera. And it is so unbearably hot."

" It is not entrancingly interesting. Would you like to clear out after this act? I should."

" And the Claverings ? "

" They are a bit tired of it. Shall we all go back together to the hotel and have supper? "

" I'd sooner we were alone together, Thornton dear—this evening."

He made a little gesture of impatience.

" Of course we won't ask them if you don't want to. But then we must stay this thing out."

He leaned back in his chair and looked at the mass of heads in the opposite tiers, vague in the dimness, and drummed with his fingers on the rails of his chair.

" Sh ! " said Mrs. Clavering. " That's one of your old tricks. You never seem to think that people have nerves."

Clytie caught the words, although they were whispered. She turned her head round quickly and stared at the stage for the rest of the act.

When it was over Mrs. Clavering solved the question of departure.

" I think we all want to go," she said, rising. " My husband is suffering acutely, and yours I know is not very musical. When shall we see you again, Mrs. Hammerdyke ? Will you come and dine with us some evening, quietly—when we can talk better? I'll let you know what evenings we are free. Will that do? That is your wife's cloak, not mine, Mr. Hammerdyke."

A few minutes later Thornton and Clytie were driving back to their hotel in the pleasant Paris victoria. It seemed a superb night. A slight breeze had risen, and the leaves in the Champs Elysées rustled pleasantly. Clytie leaned back with a sense of relief, physical and moral. They had both been rather silent since they left the opera house.

" Don't let us go in," said Clytie suddenly. " Let us drive about a little, along the quays—anywhere."

" I was just going to suggest it," said Thornton.

He gave the order to the coachman, who turned back through the Place de la Concorde and took them past the Tuileries and the great mass of the Louvre and along the quays in the direction of Auteuil.

"What do you think of the Clavering woman?" asked Thornton. "Not much, eh?"

"I can't say that I like her. Perhaps I oughtn't to say it, as she is a friend of yours, but—she doesn't please me."

"Well, I can't say that she does me now. She never was a beauty, but she has sadly fallen off the last few years. She thinks herself so deuced superior. And she isn't, by Jove! Still she is amusing, you know, and that is a quality that covers a multitude of sins. But other women can't understand her. She was loathed by them all in Cairo, so you are not alone in your antipathy."

There was a long silence. Thornton drew her closer to his side and took her hand in his. Clytie felt somewhat hurt. It was not flattering to be grouped with the other women in Cairo, however estimable they may have been in their non-appreciation of Mrs. Clavering. They drove on, and began to talk of different subjects, disconnectedly, without much interest. Finally Thornton came back to the Claverings.

"By the way, I suppose you'll dine with them, as they were civil enough to ask us."

"Certainly, if you wish it and it gives you any pleasure. Perhaps I may like her better when I know more of her."

"You see, you can't drop people because you don't happen to take a violent fancy to them," he said rather lamely. And then he added:

"I wish you had let me ask them to supper."

"Why?"

"It would have livened us up a little."

"Perhaps it would," answered Clytie almost wearily. "I half wish you had."

The evanescent charm had gone from the drive. The weather, too, had changed. Clouds, that had imperceptibly gathered, covered the moon. The quay looked desolate, the water black and lifeless, on the other side

the great buildings loomed forbidding in the darkness.
An air of disenchantment was over all things.

"Will monsieur turn back? It is going to rain," said
the cabman, lounging sideways and looking down at
them.

They turned off through the narrow streets, on the
nearest way back to the hotel. The cab horse was tired
and jogged on painfully, indifferent to the loud-cracking
whip and the "*hués*" addressed to him in the driver's
raucous voice. Clytie shivered a little at the sudden
fall in the temperature. She was chilled too—ever so
little—at her heart. She drew away slightly from her
husband, who held her hand mechanically. When she
withdrew it he did not seem to notice. He had discovered that he was annoyed about the supper.

Suddenly the horse, overdriven, stumbled, tried to
recover himself, and then crashed down helpless, snapping
the shaft. The victoria lurched violently on the side
where Clytie was sitting. To save herself she jumped
out quickly, but her foot slipped on the kerb and she
nearly fell. Thornton sprang out and raised her, and then
turned to the coachman in a sudden frenzy of passion.
He stood there moving his arms about and cursed him
in English. Clytie was shocked to the heart. She was
thankful that she could see his face but dimly in the bad
gaslight. The cabman shrugged his shoulders as he
bent down to loosen the traces. Some people came up,
chiefly from a small *brasserie* whose few tables were just
visible some yards further along the street. Another
cab arrived and paused, interested and expectant, watching the scene : the little group round the fallen horse ;
the stately figure of the girl in white dress and rich opera-
cloak standing by the upset cab ; the great figure of the
man, stamping with rage, pouring forth a torrent of
oaths. It all happened very quickly.

Clytie touched her husband's arm quietly.

"Stop, Thornton," she said. "He does not even
understand you."

Thornton looked at her for a moment, then at the
group. Then he burst into a loud laugh, pulled a ten-
franc piece from his pocket and threw it to the cabman,
who picked it up with an ironical, "*Merci, bourgeois.*"

They entered the other cab and drove quickly homewards. Thornton seemed to have forgotten his rage, for he laughed in high spirits over the incident. He apologised gaily for his loss of temper and language. He was still infected with his years of savagery, he pleaded. He had been so accustomed to rule men by terror that he forgot himself sometimes. Often he had been the only white man among hundreds of fierce, lawless savages, over whom he had despotic authority of life and death. If they had not feared his rage and violence, his life would not have been worth a moment's purchase.

He had regained his old manner, the daring personal charm that had swept her along in spite of herself into marrying him. The glamour of his fame, his power, his heroism came over her and hid the sordid scenes of the evening. When they reached the hotel they were lovers once more.

As Clytie alighted from the cab her foot gave way beneath her. It had been hurting her since her slip on the kerb, but she had scarcely noticed the pain. Now she found that she could not walk. She had sprained her ankle. She limped into the hotel with Thornton's aid. Then she stood at the foot of the stairs and looked at them helplessly. It was an old-fashioned hotel, without a lift, and their rooms were on the third story.

"I'll carry you up," said Thornton.

He took her up in his arms, and mounted the stairs with a step as light and springy as if he had no burden to carry. Until then Clytie had not realised his marvellous strength.

"I feel like the fairy princess being carried off by the giant," she whispered.

CHAPTER XVII

CLYTIE was confined several days to her room through her sprained ankle. It was not an unqualified affliction, as it solved the question of her dining with the Claverings. Thornton went alone, carrying with him his wife's excuses and regrets, and returned to her in high spirits. When she was able to get about again the Claverings had left Paris for Homburg, where they were going to stay for a few weeks. "And when they return to London we can see just as much or as little of them as we like," said Thornton.

The forced confinement also brought Clytie a little more solitude than usual. Thornton found a race meeting or two to go to, and a nominally bachelor supper party, and he laughed, in his gay manner, at this resumption of bachelor habits. Clytie was rather glad, on the whole, to be left to her own society for a little. She was gradually awakening from the dream, realising herself. Very often in the ordinary, sober moments of life Thornton jarred upon her. His absence often was a relief. She hated herself when this unwelcome and unbidden thought came into her mind ; but it came for all her hating. The sprained ankle marked definitely the end of this second or false honeymoon in Paris, whose glamour was the lingering twilight glow of the real one in Bordighera. It was then that Clytie first thought of the railway journey as a landmark. After her recovery Thornton continued his bachelor habits as a matter of course, and as a matter of course discontinued his playful apologies. Still he took Clytie whithersoever she expressed a desire to go, and gladly, proud of having his beautiful wife by his side. Only, if she elected to remain at home, he went out equally cheerfully by himself.

Occasionally they drove in the Bois in a neat phaeton

and pair which he hired for her from a livery-stable, and he would point out to her the celebrities whom they passed by. Some of these she had herself met or seen at the various social functions to which they had received invitations. They themselves, too, had become known and were pointed out with some curiosity,—*le beau couple*, as the phrase went,—even by those who were unacquainted with their name or position. Thornton was always in his gayest humour on these occasions as he sat by his wife's side and guided his pair through the crush of magnificent equipages ; and she felt glad too and elated, pleased by the vivid flashes of colouring in dresses and parasols, and the vague perfumes that filled the air, and the half-caught scraps of conversation and laughter. Her girlish delight at the gladness of life came back to her fresh and untainted. She indulged her old habit of speculation on the life that lay beneath individual faces, which she stored up in her memory for rapid sketching when at leisure, and she would draw Thornton into her vein, and then there were arguments without end. These were some of her happiest moments in Paris, when she recovered her old self, bright, satirical, paradoxical, and felt no cold hand on her heart.

One day, towards the end of their stay in Paris, they had drawn up in the block of carriages by the side of the promenade. The sun was powerful, and the glaring colours in the carriages contrasted with the cool tones of white and gray in the deep shade under the chestnut-trees. Clytie was animatedly observing the bright scene when her eyes met those of a woman, quietly though expensively dressed, seated in an open carriage quite close by. For a moment they looked at one another in silent inquiry, and then came a flash of mutual recognition. It was the girl whom Clytie had met the summer before in the hotel at Dinan. The scene, with its mingled associations of wonder and pity, came back to her, and moved by a strong impulse she smiled and moved her head slightly. A look of eager wonderment came over the other's face as she returned Clytie's greeting. And then she turned quickly away to talk to a man who had just come up to the side of the carriage.

"Confound it, Clytie!" cried Thornton, setting the horses in motion, "you must really make sure who people are before you bow to them. Do you know who that woman is?"

"Yes," said Clytie, "that is to say, I know what she is. I don't know her name."

"She is one of the most notorious women in Paris, Loulou Mendès. You mustn't go playing the fool like this! What did you bow to her for?"

"Because I know her—a little."

"You—know—her?"

"Oh, yes, Thornton dear; it is somewhat of a story. I met her accidentally last year in Dinan. She was in trouble, and I took a fancy for her, and seeing her suddenly here, I showed her that I recognised her."

"I sincerely hope you won't do such a thing again," he said shortly, giving a vicious cut to the horses that sent them spinning down the *allée.* "And please to remember that you are not an amateur Bohemian any longer, but my wife."

"Oh, Thornton, you mustn't say things like that!" said Clytie, with a queer little catch at her throat. "They hurt me!"

"Well, you mustn't deserve them," replied Thornton. And then, mollifying at the sight of her distress: "You don't understand these things, little wife."

"Well, never mind, dear," said Clytie. "Perhaps it was foolish of me. I ought to have considered you; I didn't think of it. She kissed my hand the last time I saw her, and it would have seemed base and hypocritical to have cut her dead to-day. It seemed such a little matter. Why hurt the girl's feelings? That's why I did it."

"Feelings?" echoed Thornton, with a laugh. "Bah! my good child, you are talking nonsense. She put her feelings up the spout years ago to get herself champagne and diamonds and the rest of it. With her soul sold to the devil and her body to men, what the deuce is she going to do with feelings?"

"What I saw of her was very human, Thornton. And if such women are brutes, it is men who make them so. If men were only kinder and tenderer——"

" Like the sentimental idiot in ' Jenny.' That's a poem about it, you know."

" Yes—Rossetti; I am very fond of it," she replied, with a half smile, wondering somewhat at his explanation. Then she added : " But surely there's humanity in every human being."

" That's a very sweet, innocent belief, and you had better keep to it, my dear."

" Oh, Thornton, I'm not an ignorant little schoolgirl," she said, with hurt vanity. " I have learned something of the world. Perhaps I have been too eager to acquaint myself with things."

" Anyhow, you can't know much about them," he replied shortly. " Leave such things alone. They don't concern you, so what's the good of prying into them ? "

" They have concerned me," she insisted. " Believe me, Thornton, it was something deeper than ordinary morbid curiosity that led me to them."

" But I can't see what the deuce the Social Question has to do with girls," he said. " That is what licks me. What the dickens has it got to do with your life ? "

" But you mistake, Thornton," she replied eagerly, with a return of her old earnestness. " It is not the Social Question. Indeed not. I never have any call to look at things in that aspect. I am neither a sociologist nor a reformer. I am an artist. I have to express certain truths about human beings,—the little talent I have lies entirely that way,—and in order to express the truths I had to set to work to learn them. How all this corruption affects society, how it is to be done away with and so on, does not come within my province. But to get to the hearts and inner feelings of individuals, to see how society affects them, what justification they have in their struggle with it, how they contemplate life, what elements of emotion, or passion, or weariness, or what not form essential parts of their beings that do not form essential parts of mine—to try to do that, Thornton, *has* been my business, and, till I knew you, was the dearest motive of my life. Don't you see ? "

" And when you have done it what good will it do to yourself or anybody else ? "

" To answer you I should **have** to appear conceited.

It would be answering the question, What is the good of art at all ?"

" Well, all said and done, what is the good of it ?   To make pretty and amusing things to look at.   All the rest is cant and humbug—including your desire to scrape acquaintance with loose women for artistic purposes. Look here, little wife "—and he turned round, with a sharp smile that showed his white teeth more than usual—" I didn't fall in love with you because you were an artist and held highfalutin' theories about artistic ideals and so forth, but because you were the woman whose loveliness appealed to me and always fascinated me.   And now you are my wife you have other things to think about."

" I know that, Thornton," she replied, staring a little wistfully in front of her.   " Tell me.   What is our new life going to be like ?   You speak so little of it that I scarcely know."

" Oh ! what's the good of worrying yourself about it yet ?   I'll tell you when the time comes.   You'll have our position in society to look after, keep things going straight for me in quarters where a woman can wheedle out more in an hour than a man in a twelvemonth.   I have definitely taken up politics, you know.   Things were settled this morning."

" Oh, why didn't you tell me before ?" she cried involuntarily.

" I never thought of it, my dear.   Well, Hernshawe has asked me whether I would care to be his private secretary.   His present man is in the Civil Service and is resigning owing to some office promotion, so when the House meets after the Whitsuntide recess Hernshawe will be free to take me."

" I don't quite understand," said Clytie, to whom these details were all new.   She was vaguely aware that Thornton had intentions of aiming at a parliamentary career, but as he had volunteered no confidences, she had shrunk from soliciting them.

" I don't understand," she repeated, " why you should take a private-secretaryship.   You want to enter Parliament."

" Of course.   But I am so out of things that I want to get into training, so to speak.   I shall be this session, perhaps next, with Hernshawe and learn all the ropes, and then he will run me for a suitable vacancy. It is as simple as good-morning, as they say in this country. I must do something, and politics seem about the only mildly exciting thing to go in for in this severely flat and respectable continent. But beyond looking after the society side of the matter, I don't see why you need worry your pretty head about it."

"Then don't you want me to become a bit of a politician, so as to help you, and understand you in your career?"

"Oh, of course, to a certain extent," he replied with cheerful offhandedness. "But for God's sake, my dear child, don't become a political woman. If there's one kind of a woman I bar more than another, its the female politician. Of course you'll have to go round canvassing for votes at the election, and to humbug people in society, but all that is rather sport than otherwise? Never mind, little wife; you'll have a ripping good time in London when the show begins."

He laughed, in gay good humour again. Clytie echoed with a faint smile.

"Thornton," she said after a short pause, "I don't want to bother you about politics if you don't like it "— she felt now a strange hesitation in speaking to him— "but you know you'll have to convert me, dear. It has been on my mind for some time. You are a Tory, you know, and I have been a Radical hitherto in feelings and sympathies."

He burst out laughing at her little air of seriousness. Perhaps if he had known how he hurt her, he would not have treated the matter so cavalierly. This difference in political views had been a question of some concern to Clytie, who was aware of old-fashioned Tory prejudices. And Thornton took her Radicalism as a jest, attributing no importance to the difference of opinion.

"You'll change when we get back and become a shining light in the Primrose League."

She was too depressed by the whole of the foregoing conversation to pursue the subject any further. Thornton started the lighter topic of personal criticism of their new acquaintances in Paris, and rattled on in great spirits. He had forgotten entirely the argument that Clytie's somewhat unconventional action had occasioned, and was as boyishly gay as ever. But men forget things much more easily than women, especially when they have no object in remembering, nor any reminiscent twinge of susceptibility.

That evening Clytie spent alone. Thornton was dining at the Café des Ambassadeurs with some men from the Embassy. He had kissed her before he started, called himself a selfish brute for condemning her to a dull evening, and went away humming a café-concert air. She did not mind his leaving her, took it now as a matter of course that each should be to a certain extent independent of the other; for the glamour of the south had departed, and the practicalities of life had begun to assert themselves. But it was the first wretched evening of her married life. She would have liked to cry, but as she was not of those who cry easily, she sat with eyes all the more painful for being strained and tearless. She had received a great shock. Ever since she had rebelled against the Durdleham formula that men were to descend from their intellectual sublimity when they spoke to women, lest like Semele the latter should be consumed in the Jovian blaze, she had been accustomed to meet men freely on an intellectual level. To find herself in a society where this particular formula was unknown had been one of the earliest joys of her emancipated life. She had very little vanity in the matter of her own attainments, but she took it for granted that her associates should recognise in her a woman of ordinary culture, capable of forming rational opinions. Her intelligence was keen, her judgment fine. She had read, thought, observed. Her art was to a certain extent a matter of intellect as well as of instinctive feeling, and in this respect had been stimulated by her intercourse with Kent. In the glow of her young, ardent nature she had committed many extravagances, but they all had borne the indubitable stamp of a mind strenuous in its endeavours. None but fools had ever thought of condescending to Clytie because she was a woman.

And now for the first time she was coolly shown that

she was a woman, that her opinions were not worth serious consideration, that she must not trouble her pretty
head about things that were too deep for her. And by
the man, above all, whose life she shared. They were
hours of dull, dazed humiliation that she spent alone
that evening ; hours that were not lost even in the pain
of her after life. Over the absence of sympathy with her
own pursuits she was only a little regretful. It would
have been nicer if Thornton had been able to take a
pleasure in her art. But she was too large-natured not
to be able to bridge over this small gap between them.
She was ready to sacrifice her art entirely to her love,
was eager to throw herself into his interests and ambitions. But she demanded a full, vigorous share. To
live an empty life was with her an impossibility. And
to this life Thornton, in his good-natured contempt for
her powers, was condemning her. She was puzzled,
humiliated, frightened.

There is a vague mystery of woe in the dawn of a
dreary day.

Meanwhile Thornton was enjoying himself amazingly.
The dinner was one which, as Heine says, " ought to be
partaken of kneeling," and the wine was excellent ; the
party well chosen, the talk essentially, broadly masculine. There is a certain type of man whose conversation is wholly made up of sport in its various aspects,
women, shop, and crude personal gossip—a type which
numbers its tens of thousands in English society. It can
be met with, to utter weariness of the soul, in any
heterogeneous gathering of upper- and middle-class
Britons. They are God's creatures, it is true ; many of
them are possessed of estimable qualities, some of them
have performed deeds of heroism. But as a type they
are a glaring satire upon the vaunted culture and refinement of our civilisation. And it is a remarkable thing
how little their power and influence are recognised by
writers in their analysis of the spirit of this dying nineteenth century. This vast overwhelming type does not
read, does not think, does not care for art or music, has
no power of penetration to the heart of delicate things.
It is dull, brawny, selfish, and a pillar of the Church and
State. Its main subjective characteristic is the brutality

of its views concerning women—varying from the kindly disdain of its highest members to the degraded brutality of its lowest.

Of this type, with all his physical charm, his brilliant personality and splendid capacities for action, was Thornton Hammerdyke. The man whose magnetism had drawn Clytie irresistibly, headlong into his arms was only, after all, a representative of this ignoble, commonplace order of men. The love that had flooded Clytie's being with wild surging tumult was only, after all, the commonplace, ignoble passion of his type. There are some things so elementary that analysis quickly comes to an end. Put in a strip of litmus paper and it is done.

He was honestly glad to be free of Clytie. With unconscious cynicism he never sought to disguise it from himself. With Carteret of the Hussars and Swithin and Holyoake of the Embassy he was in his proper sphere. They were of the type. He had interests in common with them. The fact that he was a man of high distinction was neither here nor there. Over the fish and *entrées* they talked of racing and shooting ; over the game they wandered along the upper galleries of the Cloaca Maxima of Paris ; over the peaches and Château-Mouton they told foul stories. An ignoble, commonplace dinner party.

And Clytie was alone in her room at the hotel staring at an unknown future.

CHAPTER XVIII.

The last three days of their stay in Paris were marked
by a return on the part of Thornton to his old devotion.
He declined invitations ruthlessly, spent almost the
whole of his time with his wife. In all outward and
visible signs they were lovers again, but the inward and
spiritual grace was a bit vapoury. They went on excur-
sions together, to Fontainebleau, Melun, Passy. One
day they wandered about the forest of Vincennes and
he kissed her beneath the trees as he used to do at
Bordighera. They had gay, laughing meals together at
little riverside restaurants. He was passionate in his
expressions of endearment and in his delight at her
beauty. With the negative tact of passion, he avoided
all subjects that could jar upon her. For three days he
was the Thornton of their honeymoon.

Clytie at first could not understand this sudden
change. She asked him the reason tremulously.

"Can't you see, you silly girl," he replied with masterful frankness, "that I love you and we have only three
more days' idleness?"

And then she let the spell come over her again and
surrendered herself to his mood. But now, instead of
entering with spontaneous joy a world of laughter whose
magic gates lay open before her, she crossed the threshold with deliberate step. She had to choose whether
to laugh or cry. She was young, she wanted to love her
husband; so she chose to laugh. It was an act of
reason. But woe to love when reason has to find its
argument !

By Whitsuntide they were in London, installed in
their house in the Cromwell Road. The three days'
passion had cooled down, and the atmosphere was colder
than before. But Clytie for several weeks was so busy
that she had not time for much consideration of trou-

bling questions. First, the house required her attention. There was much supplementary furniture to be chosen, many minor schemes of decoration to be carried out in accordance with her own artistic tastes.

Thornton gave her a free hand in these matters, and, beyond taking it for granted that the house should be fitly arranged, never troubled himself about details. He attended two or three picture sales with Clytie, where he bought a few pictures on her recommendation, ordered some great leather armchairs for his smoking-room, and then transferred his attention to concerns of more serious interest. So Clytie, left unhampered, succeeded in arranging the house to her own satisfaction. This occupied a great portion of her time ; the rest was almost entirely devoted to her social duties.

She found herself in some small position in society, as the artistic wife of a distinguished soldier of fortune with a considerable income, and it was Thornton's special ambition for the time being that this position should be maintained and secured, in furtherance of his own personal projects. Whilst contemplating marriage, or rather after he had, in his fierce impetuous way, decided upon it, he had sought around after some practical interest in his new life. He had forsworn Africa, with a virtuous sense of self-sacrifice. What remained worthy of a man's serious attention? He did not consult Clytie. It scarcely occurred to him that the subject concerned her. Of the few careers that presented themselves he selected two, the turf and politics, and wavered for some time in his choice. At last he tossed up for it, as he had often done at the fork of two paths in the forest. The coin came down with the Queen's head uppermost—and that meant politics. He was a Tory of the fiercer school. Even if family and professional tradition had not influenced him, a lengthy course of despotic authority enforced by the halter and the butt end of a musket is not favourable to the cultivation of Liberal suavities and amenities. And again, the "type" is almost always Tory. He was even out of touch with the broader Conservativism of our day, between which and modern Liberalism he failed to appreciate the distinction. In fact his political ideals, such as they were, belonged to the beginning instead of the end of the century, but he expressed them with a fervour that left no doubt as to their genuineness.

He had no difficulty in setting at work the machinery of social influence, and the result was the offer of a private-secretaryship on the part of an under-secretary of state. He accepted it. It would not only afford him an insight into the practical working of politics, but would give him an opportunity of making himself known to the chiefs of the Conservative party and securing their influence when he should seek to enter Parliament. When everything was settled he informed Clytie casually in Paris of his new ambitions. She, too, had wondered what outlet this man of restless action would find for his energies, and, shrinking from inquiry, had been filled with vague uneasiness. Now she felt that he had made a worthy choice and in spite of dubious encouragement strove to identify herself with his interests. True, she contemplated with a little dismay the abandonment of her own pet social theories, which tended towards an advanced and somewhat inchoate Radicalism, and the espousal of a cause forming part of a scheme of life against which she had so passionately rebelled. But she wilfully, almost desperately, shut her eyes against all this. She would give her heart and soul to Thornton's glory, and the sacrifice of principle on her part would only accentuate the triumph. But this sacrifice Thornton did not concern himself to realise. Very few men ever do. As we have seen, he laughed at it.

He entered upon his political duties as soon as they returned to London, led a busy life of work and pleasure, throwing into both the energy of his strong vitality. He was not a man to wait. Social position, power, must be wrested from the world by force of arms. The sooner the struggle began and the fiercer it was fought the sooner would come success. It behoved Clytie, therefore, to enter upon it with him at once. Before she could realise herself as mistress of a large house, as cut off from the old habits that had invested London with earnest charm, as sundered from Kent and Winifred, as deprived of her art and her dreams and ambition, she found herself caught up in the whirl of London society, bidden to cultivate its conventions, flatter its weaknesses, intrigue, gossip, dance, drive, rush, without a moment's pause to think.

And thus began her new life. It was not the one she had dreamed of. In fact she hardly recognised herself in her deliberate subordination to a nature dominating hers. She let herself drift, abandoning herself to the current, clutching hold of her love towards her husband as the only plank saving her from destruction.

Winifred she saw occasionally. She had no time for anything beyond a half hour's gossip, and then she forgot her own hopes and fears in the happiness of her friend, who had just become engaged to Treherne. She saw nothing of Kent. A feeling she could not analyse restrained her from writing to him, ever so formally. It was analogous to the whimsical shrinking from sketching his portrait when she had first met him. She heard of him, however, through Winifred. He came down to the studio still occasionally, and chatted over the teacups— " chiefly about you, dear," said Winifred, " and the old days and your present life."

"And is he changed at all?" asked Clytie. " It seems centuries since those same old days. I feel almost like asking whether he has a gray head and carries his years well ! "

" It does seem a long time," said Winifred reflectively. " But it really isn't, you know, and Kent is just the same as ever. His trip abroad has done him so much good. Do you know, dear, except Victor—and Mr. Hammerdyke, of course—I think he is the best man in all the world."

Her brown cheeks flushed as she spoke, and Clytie bent down and kissed them.

"Oh, Winnie darling, I wish everybody were as true and loyal as you," she said.

A great sob was in her heart, and she would have given much to have buried her face in Winnie's lap and let the tears come how they would. But she mastered herself, and before the other had time to hear the echo of the chord that was struck she went on :

"Tell me, Winnie, how is his great work getting on ?"

" Rapidly, I believe," answered Winifred. " He seems to have nothing else to live for now. I think he misses you, dear, and plunges into it as a kind of consolation. He has had a great compliment paid him—have you heard? He met a great Austrian scientist, Herr—— I can't remember his name—it doesn't matter. Anyhow, he showed this professor his work, and talked to him about the difficulties of publishing, expense, and all that, and a few days ago he received an offer from the University of Vienna to translate what was already done into German and publish it there. He says it is a most distinguished honour."

"I am so glad, dear," said Clytie. "I feel proud of him, and I wish I could see him—to give him my congratulations. You will tell him that I asked after him, won't you, Winnie?"

"Why, of course!" said Winifred. "Don't we always talk of you?"

Mrs. Blather was anxious that Clytie and her husband should come to Durdleham to stay there after the season in town was over. But Clytie replied evasively to the affectionate invitation. She shrank from Durdleham even more than from herself. Mrs. Blather, now that the soreness as regards the wedding had worn off, was delighted at the brilliant match—just the very marriage one could have wished for Clytie, as she remarked over the Durdleham tea tables. Besides, it was definite settling down for Clytie, saving them from that shadow of scandal that had always seemed liable to be cast over them through her unprincipled behaviour. There were no longer any fears. And Mrs. Blather had her own little triumph in another way. She remembered now she had prophesied years ago that Clytie's desire to live her art life in London was a craze that would not last long—like Janet's transient enthusiasm for cookery classes. Both Janet and herself took it for granted that Clytie viewed her past errors with the same indulgent retrospective smile, and wrote her complacent letters based on this assumption. And Clytie found it harder than ever to write to them naturally, to answer these letters in the same tone. If her sisters had failed to understand her when to her her young, earnest self was brightly intelligible, how could they do it now when she saw herself vaguely, dimly, wrapped in impenetrable vapours? A visit to Durdleham, under the circumstances, seemed almost an ordeal. Yet Thornton's presence there might make some difference.

She spoke to him very little on the subject. He broached it himself one day at breakfast, almost the only time now, except late at night, that she saw him alone. It was nearing the end of July and the session of Parliament was on the eve of closing.

"When are you going to see your people, Clytie?" he asked, looking over his paper.

"I thought I had told you. They want us to come for a week as soon as we can leave town."

"Us?"

"Yes; won't you come?"

"Oh, no, thanks. It would not suit me at all. You go and make an excuse for me."

"Things are not gay there, I know," said Clytie, "but I should like you to come with me."

"It can't be done, my dear," replied Thornton. "You had better have a quiet time there by yourself, while I go up to Scotland——"

"I thought you would have liked me to go to Scotland with you—we have seen so little of each other lately. You don't want to stay up there all the autumn without me?" she added half pathetically.

"Why, my dear Clytie, you can come if you like," said her husband, drawing back his chair from the table. "Only you won't find much fun in a little shooting-box in the middle of a glen in the Highlands. Look : you go and see your people for a month, and then, if you like, you can come and join me there—that is to say, if Carteret has any of his women folks staying in the house, which does not seem to be quite settled yet. If he hasn't, naturally you can't come."

"In that case I shall not go to Durdleham—I couldn't. You would not understand why. I shall stay in London, and mind the house."

"I should not like you to do that," said Thornton.

"Why not?"

"Because I had rather you did not," he repeated, with a gathering frown.

"How long do you contemplate being away?" asked Clytie quietly.

"August and September, perhaps—I can't quite tell yet."

"Do you propose, then, that I should go and stay in Durdleham for two months with my people?"

He had not contemplated it, but he was irritated at her show of opposition. He lost his temper and said sharply:

"Yes. Or with any other friends you like. I am not going to have you remain here all by yourself."

"Will you tell me your reasons, Thornton?" asked Clytie.

He crumpled up his paper angrily and thumped it on the table. The veins in his forehead stood out. His face grew ugly.

"When I say a thing is to be done I mean it," he cried, "and I am not accustomed to be asked for my reasons!"

"I shall leave you until you have recovered yourself," said Clytie with dignity, and she left the room.

This was the first real quarrel between them. The blood had often rushed hot through Clytie's veins and set her pulses tingling, but hitherto she had restrained herself, feeling that the first revolt would mark the beginning of the end.

She passed a miserable day. When Thornton came home in the afternoon to dress for dinner he was in one of his light-hearted moods. He had backed an outsider some weeks back at very long odds. The race had been run that day and the outsider had won, bringing him a couple of thousand pounds—a windfall that relieved him of certain temporary embarrassments. Hence his buoyancy that afternoon. He had apparently forgotten the morning's difference, and called Clytie "little wife" again, and promised her a victoria to supplement the modest brougham with which they had begun. He put his arm round her and kissed her, praised her beautiful hair, the roundness of her arms, her dress. He told her the gossip of the day in his bright off-hand manner, made her laugh in spite of her weariness. But when he kissed her she shrank a little. In the elation of his victory he did not notice her lack of responsiveness; besides, he was not over-sensitive at any time. When they returned home at night from the dinner-party to which they had gone together, Thornton was still in pleasant mood. Nothing more was said respecting the plans for August and September.

The reconciliation did not last long. Clytie strove with an earnestness that was torture to keep the peace between them, but sometimes her nature clamoured within her and broke out in self-assertion. Only four months married, and already the breach between them was perceptible, slowly widening. And it was Clytie that drifted away from her husband. If she had been a lesser nature, she might have retained the love on both sides. A woman of a lower type would have been able to flatter, soothe, cajole, yield, and thus have kept Thornton at her feet. The patronising contempt for her own needs, which lashed Clytie to the soul, she would have treated lightly, as the natural and foolish vanity of the superior being; and she would have found in a sudden demonstration of passion full compensation for previous indifference. But Clytie was not only unversed herself in the arts of seduction, but despised them fiercely in other women. And she began also to dread Thornton's fits of affection as much as his fits of anger.

He left her one morning quivering with mortification and suppressed bitterness. He himself was not conscious of the slight he had inflicted, and he went away in gay spirits. Their talk had turned upon a Cabinet Minister named Godderich, whose influence Thornton was anxious to acquire. Now it had so happened that this same Godderich had succeeded in making himself vastly obnoxious to Clytie. She told her husband this, giving him the reasons.

"I have not been accustomed to that kind of admiration," she said, "and I don't like it."

But Thornton laughed his great laugh, called her "his unconventional prude," and went on to show her what an invaluable ally Godderich was.

"You must swallow your dislike, Clytie," he said. "Why, God bless my soul, if ninety-nine women out of a hundred had that chance, they would get the eyes out of his head."

"Would you so much desire me to be like ninety-nine women out of a hundred, then, Thornton?"

"Oh, nonsense, Clytie; you know what I mean. Come! Don't you see that here's a way of pushing things on a bit? What does it matter if the ass is attentive? You can laugh at him. But keep him in hand a bit until we want to let him loose. Do you see? Of course I trust you, and all that sort of thing."

"I thank you for your confidence," she replied. "But I don't think you will need to exercise it much."

"What do you mean?"

"Oh, never mind. Do you really want me, Thornton, to encourage this man to make love to me, so as to get a hold on him for other purposes?"

"I never saw anyone like you for the dotting of i's," said Thornton, amused. "But that's about the size of it. Don't you see what an infernal ass we can make of him? Well, think it over, little wife. Good-bye."

He opened the front door,—this little conversation had taken place in the hall,—and ran down the steps very well pleased with himself.

But Clytie's heart turned from him and she passed a wretched day—all the more trying as she felt in honour bound to sing antistrophe of praise of Thornton to the strophe of Mrs. Farquharson, with whom she was lunching.

In the evening they were going out together. He came home late from Westminster, dressed hurriedly, and went down to the drawing-room, where Clytie was waiting. She was wearing a low-cut dress. Her arms were bare. A tiny diamond clasp to a thin gold chain flashed on her bosom.

"By Jove! You're looking lovelier than ever!" he cried. "Come, let me kiss you."

He drew her to him, kissed the upper part of her arm, and then her lips. But she made no response. She shrank, and this time he noted it. His arm still round her waist, he held back his head and looked at her.

"Clytie!"

He spoke with loverlike reproach, and kissed her

again, and again she shrank. And then he cast her aside roughly, and stamped his foot.

"Damn it! Clytie," he exclaimed, showing his teeth, "you are a perfect icicle!"

Clytie made no reply, but turned to the window and buttoned her glove. Thornton rang the bell violently, and when the footman appeared asked him why the devil the carriage had not come round. Then he flung himself into a chair and turned over a book. And thus they remained without speaking until the brougham was announced. On their way to their dinner-party they did not speak. He was in a fit of furious sulks, and Clytie's heart was too heavy. Afterwards he went off to his club and she drove home by herself.

And this at the end of only four months' wedded life. What would it be at the end of four years, fourteen? Clytie strove for a little to blame herself for supersensitiveness, egotism, coldness. But her self rose in arms against this charge. For, like the unfolding of a horrible story, the nature of Thornton's love for her, the nature of the place she really occupied in his estimation, gradually broke upon her. The meaning of light remarks, trivial jests, careless actions ; the meaning of caresses now half contemptuous, now passionate—all came to her in full light, in all their crudity, out of the gray darkness in which she had instinctively kept it hidden from herself. She stared at it—not in ignorant surmise as she had done in Paris, but with a ghastly sickening of soul.

Oh, the degradation of it! What was she to her husband but a possession, a toy, a woman, to suffer his caresses when it so pleased him to bestow them, a mistress whom he had taken it into his head to bind legally to himself, so that she might serve certain purposes of his in society? What little better was she to him than the women whom men buy,—Loulou Mendès, for instance,—save that he reckoned,—he had told her so,—on her fidelity to him? Things she had tried to ascribe to the careless familiarity of love blazed insultingly before her, scorching her, making her writhe in her abasement.

Naturally satiety had come to him. He was indifferent whether he saw her or not for a season. Only in his absence she was to obey blindly his caprices. If only she was his wife, she thought bitterly, in the humdrum Durdleham way, where at least she would have had the conventional position in their conjugal relations! Either that or the wild independence of a Loulou Mendès, carrying her will in her hand, free to choose her own way among the groves of the satyrs. For even there the free path smells sweeter than the one of servitude.

Just before the session ended Clytie came to a definite understanding with her husband. It is surprising what pain can underlie this mutual adjustment of two intelligences.

The scene was again the breakfast-room. Each was reading the morning's correspondence. Thornton tossed a letter across the table.

"Carteret's women folk can't come," he said. "Devilish sensible women—they don't see the fun of it. So it's settled. I go up as soon as this wretched grind is over."

"Very well," said Clytie calmly. "I hope you will have a good time."

"Thanks," he replied in his careless way. "It will be like old times again. And you will put in a good, quiet couple of months with your people."

Clytie bit her lip. Her heart beat a little faster. She was going to set herself in opposition to him. She glanced at him before she spoke; he hardly seemed to expect an answer, but continued reading another letter. He looked kind and frank, she thought, a husband for any woman to be proud of. In his morning freshness, clean-shaven, groomed, trimmed, he seemed handsomer than ever. His close brown hair had not a touch of gray; scarcely a line showed on his forehead or beneath his eyes; and the dark rich colour was visible beneath the bronze on his cheek. He broke into a laugh, buoyant and careless, over his letter, and looked up at Clytie. Then, his glance meeting hers, his face grew more serious.

"What are you gazing at me for with those great blue eyes of yours, Clytie?"

She bent forward, rested her cheek on her hand.

"In regard to what you have just said—my going to

Durdleham—I am not going for many reasons. I told you so, Thornton, the other day."

"I am quite aware of it," said Thornton. "But you are going."

He looked her full in the face, and she returned his gaze calmly and unflinchingly.

"Don't let us quarrel, Thornton," she said. "It is so sordid and petty. Let us try quietly to understand one another."

His glance fell first, and he threw himself back in his chair with a laugh and unfolded his paper.

"All right—we'll bar scenes. Only don't say anything too severe or you'll spoil my breakfast."

"Thornton," she said, not changing her attitude, "I think I know what my duty is towards you, and I try to perform it. Has it ever struck you that you may have some duties towards me?"

"I can't say it has," he replied.

"I don't think you understand me, Thornton. I will try to make it clearer to you. As far as you will let me take an interest in your life, I do so. I am more than willing to make any sacrifices—to give up everything for you. But when you do not want me, as this autumn, I surely may remember that I have a life of my own to lead."

"And suppose that life does not suit me?"

"That is the point, Thornton. If you wished me, out of love for you, to do anything, I would do it. But this is a matter in which love has no place. Provided I am scrupulous in all my duties towards you, I have a right to my own life, to my own antipathies, to my own favourite pursuits—in fact to myself as an individual, and it is your duty towards me to recognise it."

"I don't quite see what you are driving at," said Thornton. "You can dislike sweet champagne and paint pictures and read Schopenhauer if you like. Who is preventing you? But in certain matters, as you are my wife, you have got to do what I tell you."

"To take an extreme case, by way of argument : Suppose the fancy seized you to order me to remain in my bedroom all day—you would expect me to obey you?"

"By God ! I should think I would !" cried Thornton,

starting to his feet, with blazing eyes and the veins standing out on his forehead.

"It seems, Thornton," she said very quietly, "you have married the wrong woman."

Then she rose, too, from the table, moved towards him, and laid her hand on his arm. He shook it off with an impatient oath, and turned away, fuming, to stare out of the window. She was too well accustomed to his fits of passion to resent the indignity. She mechanically picked off some withering leaves from some flowers on the mantelpiece, and waited for him to speak. At last he turned round again, and asked her sullenly:

"Have you any other pretty remarks to make?"

"If you will listen to them quietly."

"Well, what do you want? I grant I was a fool to marry you. Let me hear the consequences of my folly."

His face was set in a sneer, an ugly expression. She had seen it several times since that evening at the opera in Paris. The tears sprang into her eyes as she glanced at him.

"Oh, don't speak and look like that!" she cried. "I cannot bear it. I did not intend to say anything hard just now. I only meant that you had mistaken me, and my needs, and my nature. I have tried to look upon marriage from your point of view for four months, and I can't do it any longer. You say I must obey you blindly in everything, even your arbitrary fancies, subordinate myself absolutely to you. Thornton, believe me, where your interests or love are concerned I will do it; but where they are not I can't, and it will be happier for both of us that I should tell you so frankly. If you go your way alone, I must go mine."

"That means you set yourself in defiance to my wishes?"

Clytie checked an impulse of impatience.

"If you won't understand me, and insist on putting it that way—yes."

They looked at each other for some time. And then Thornton ground his teeth and glared at her.

"You can go your own way if you like, but I warn you one of these days there will be the devil to pay!"

And he strode out of the room, cursing, and slammed the door behind him.

Clytie sat down by the window. The tears would come in spite of her pride. She had gained the victory. But there are some victories that have all the aching sense of defeat.

CHAPTER XIX.

ON the day after this conversation Clytie was surprised by an announcement from Durdleham that Mrs. Blather and Janet were suddenly coming to town and would avail themselves of her often repeated invitation to pay her a visit in her new home. Janet had been ailing for some time past. The over-refined Davenant blood had never been vivifying at any time, and now, as there were sudden dangers of a grave kind, their Durdleham doctor had advised her consulting a London specialist. They hurried to catch the great man before he left for his summer holidays. That was their apology to Clytie for the shortness of their notice. Ordinarily on their rare visits to town they put up at Durfey's Hotel in Albany Street. Their father and grandfather had put up there from time immemorial, and they spoke of Durfey's with solemn familiarity, as if it were the one hotel of London. On this occasion, however, they came and stayed with Clytie.

Their presence in the house was a relief to her, even though it was by way of counter-irritation. Thornton showed himself in the light of a charming host and delighted his sisters-in-law. They could not find enough felicitations to bestow upon Clytie. They forgot the old misunderstandings, took it for granted that Clytie had finally settled, was happy, without any ulterior desires. They went round the house, Mrs. Blather manifesting mild enthusiasm over the more solid arrangements in the way of furniture and domestic appurtenances, Janet going into little ecstasies over the decorations.

" I never thought you had such a talent for house management," said Mrs. Blather after an inspection of the linen-cupboards and china-closets.

" I hardly think it requires absolute genius," replied Clytie, " to see that sheets are folded up properly and that plates are not put away dirty."

" Ah ! " said her sister, with a philosophic sigh.   " So many young wives are so inexperienced."

It was a delight to Mrs. Blather to see Clytie in this aspect.   She could talk to her now on common ground ; Clytie had become an ordinary sensible woman, who could discuss the things that fill the ordinary sensible woman's life : housemaids, fancywork, and the price of fish.   Mrs. Blather knew that Hammerdyke was fairly well off, but she thought it her duty to give Clytie many valuable hints as to household expenditure, to which Clytie listened with suave distraction.   She also gave her recipes for cooking, and the washing of lace, and infallible methods for removing wine stains from table-cloths ; also neat little formulas for the management of a husband.

" But yours is simply perfect," she added, with refer-ence to this last.   " Oh, Clytie, you are a lucky girl ! "

To Clytie there was something pathetically humorous in the aspect she presented to her sisters ; in finding her-self, for the first time in her life, perfect in their eyes ; in their changed relations.   It was amusing to be the lady of the house, and to make plans for Gracie and Janet's entertainment.   She brightened under the sense of it, and though many a misconception on their part caused her a sharp twinge of pain, she allowed them to purr on contentedly, taking a small measure of enjoy-ment from the comfort thereof.   Besides, she felt that it would not last long.   Their stay was limited to three days.   A week of it would have been intolerable.   For this reason she declined to accompany them back to Durdleham.   At first Mrs. Blather was rather hurt at her refusal ; but Clytie gently smoothed over the matter, tactfully avoiding to give specific reasons.

Although Thornton was amenity itself in his inter-course with Clytie when they met in her sisters' pres-ence, in their private relations he showed a certain sore-ness—the result of the process of understanding.   She tried to heal this, to win back from him, if not love, at least gentleness and courtesy.

" I must thank you, Thornton, for being so nice to my sisters," she said once.

" I suppose I know how to behave myself in my own

house," he replied coldly, and Clytie retired, and listened, with an ache in her heart, to Mrs. Blather's epithalamion.

Still it comforted her to see Thornton his old bright self again, as she had known him before her marriage, even though she knew his brow would darken on the departure of her guests. It gladdened her to hear him talk animatedly to Janet of the wonders of the forest and the romance of war. The hall, the staircase, and the walls of his smoking room were lined with curiosities of travel : spears and skin-covered shields, swords, wooden maces—a whole armoury of savage weapons. There were feathered headdresses, great rings roughly wrought of virgin gold, strange garments, some stained with blood. On the landing above the hall stairs hung an evil wooden yoke with pendent chains which he had lifted from the necks of two dead slaves, left by the caravan to die and rot by the way ; and, flanking it, two great lions' heads glared defiantly. To each relic a history was attached, now commonplace, now ghastly. Clytie knew them all, but she accompanied her sisters as Thornton took them round, a perfect cicerone, and she was pleased to see his face light up and his eyes glow with the reminiscence of dangers and brave deeds. It brought her a glad memory of the past and a little hope for the future. She was grateful, too, to Thornton for thus effectually hiding from her sisters any signs of their recent differences and divergencies. She could receive their congratulations with a sense of grim humour. Anything approaching pity, with whatever delicate sympathy it might be conveyed, would have made her wince with pain. Even Mrs. Farquharson, who had sharp eyes and many kindly affinities with her, shared Mrs. Blather's unquestioning belief in the happiness of her lot. Before others Thornton was still the gallant lover and courteous husband, and Clytie was not unthankful. When questioned as to Thornton's plans for the autumn she answered vaguely. The session had worn him out. He was going up to Scotland for the grouse shooting. She herself was going to take care of the house until his return. She preferred staying in London in August to going anywhere without him. And Mrs. Blather, quite satisfied, paid her a little compliment on her wifeliness, and suggested various household improvements to occupy her time during her grass-widowhood.

So Mrs. Blather and Janet went back to Durdleham, to raise a flutter of excitement at the Durdleham tea tables over their accounts of Clytie's moral and material prosperity and her husband's manifold perfections. But the old man, Mr. Davenant, shook his head and sighed. Slow to receive fresh impressions, he could not conceive Clytie other than wilful and paradoxical. And he was suspicious of the brilliant soldier of fortune. He would much have preferred his daughter to have married a steady-going country gentleman or professional man. Still no fault could be found with Hammerdyke, who had treated him with every courtesy.

Before Thornton's departure for Scotland a kind of reconciliation was patched up between them. The first overtures had come from Clytie. After all, he was her husband. They were bound together, for better or worse, till death parted them. It was only common sense to struggle that it should be for better. She humbled herself, then, a little, confessed that she had been unreasonable in some things. He happened to be in a softer mood, and encouraged her to tell him she was sorry if she had been cold and selfish. Unconsciously she made him feel quite magnanimous. He kissed her gaily, bade her think no more about it, and even condescended to say with regard to the main point at issue :

" Well, perhaps you are about right in not caring to go to Durdleham. Your sisters are not rapid."

A remark which, although it jarred somewhat on Clytie's strung nerves, she nevertheless accepted as a token of peace.

This was the second time in her life that she had deliberately humbled herself before a man. She thought of it with a queer little pang. When she had put down her young pride so as to retain Kent's friendship and esteem, on the day that Jack had destroyed Winifred's picture, it had been all gladness and triumph. She remembered how happily she had gone to sleep that night, in pleasant subconsciousness of certain feminine workings. It had been a joy to surrender then. But now ? She shrugged her shoulders, tried to dismiss it from her mind.

In the middle of August she found herself alone in the great house, enjoying the leisure and solitude, the independence, the freedom from friction. She devoted most of her time to her painting, which had been sadly neglected since her marriage. Her studio was a pleasant room, with a good light. It had not the severe, business-like air of the one in the King's Road ; it was warmer, heavier with velvet hangings, richer in quaint furniture. Instead of the whitewashed walls scrawled over with grotesque caricatures, it had a delicately toned Morris paper. The floor was polished, strewn with thick rugs ; a great white bearskin lay before the hearth. The piles of canvases stretched upon rough wooden backs that used to lie stacked up in odd corners Thornton had had framed for her, as a surprise to greet her on her home-coming, and now the best of them were hung round the room. Some of her cherished possessions found a place—the etching by Rupert Kent, two or three of Winifred's delicate studies, and an exquisite Jacquemart that Kent had given her long ago. But otherwise all was new, luxurious, separating her from the old associations of her art life.

Whilst searching for a subject she took out her studies for the Faustina picture. But she put them aside with a shudder. She was painting merely for amusement, to gratify the artistic impulse that urged her to create. But the hope, by which she had been gradually rising towards the goal of her ambition, the hope of fame and full accomplishment, was gone, apparently beyond recall ; and she mused upon it sadly. This sense of finality is characteristic of youth—its one governing pessimism. Yet she was cheerful enough, glad to feel the brush between her fingers again, and to smell the familiar odour of turpentine, and to see her fancies take visible form under her touch. The artist within her asserted itself, though vaguely, as from some depth where it lay buried. It was undergoing a subtle change, and its weak, inchoate manifestations were those of a period of transition. But Clytie knew it not.

The Farquharsons returned to town towards the end of the month, and Winifred also, after her annual seaside holiday with the children. And many of Clytie's other friends remained in London, and welcomed her back among them. It was like a return to her old life. Only Kent was absent from her circle. She missed him, sighing a little for the impossible.

Thornton wrote from Scotland with affectionate brevity. He did not know that he could have missed her so much. He had bagged so many brace that morning. He longed to see her. He thought he might as well stay on with Carteret so long as there was any sport forward. His letters, dashed off with a broad quill pen in a great, bold hand, covered four sides of notepaper, and came once a week. Clytie had no reason to complain of lack of attention on the part of her husband. Consequently she looked forward to less troubled days when they should lead their common life together again.

An occasional visitor that she had during these weeks was the boy Jack. He had been for a term at the industrial school to which Treherne and Kent had procured him admittance, and now passed as a reformed character amongst his enthusiasts. The teachers at the school, with vivid memories of stormy scenes, might have demurred at this opinion ; but they were miles away holiday-making, and for the time blissfully oblivious of Jack. Four months over a spelling-book and a carpenter's bench, even though the latter may be situated amid pleasant fields, are not long enough to purify the blood from the wildness of London streets ; and a lifetime so spent cannot wash out hereditary taint ; but they can teach the use of soap and water and a suitable adjustment of garments. And Jack was clean, and his wild elf locks were cropped into compulsory smugness, and his clothes conformed to a strictly conventional order. This external revolution was so startling that an accompanying moral reform seemed unquestionable. Even his mother's dull pessimism was affected by it. When she returned from her work she bribed him with bread and treacle to sit in a chair where she could admire him, instead of sending him out of her way into the streets as she had been wont to do. But Jack ate the bread and treacle and then sauntered into the street of his own accord. He did not admire his mother, and only heeded her blandishments when they assumed an objective form. He admired one person, and that was Winifred. With her the young animal was tame, almost docile. It was merely owing to lack of special instinct that he did not lick her hand. He was often in the studio, where he had been constituted general factotum during his holidays. He swept the floor, cleaned the windows, set the brushes and paints in order before Winifred arrived, ran messages for her, and whenever she permitted would sprawl on the ground by her side, following her movements with his great brown eyes. To prevent him from wasting his time and energies in this passive adoration, Winifred often invented commissions for him which he executed with proud despatch, disregarding all allurements to eat the lotus of the gutter and holding his person sacred as Winifred's messenger. It was in consequence of this that he found his way to Clytie's house, acting as postman for his patroness. At first he was shy. He had not lost the feeling of awe with which Clytie inspired him, nor had he forgotten the dread picture of her anger on that day when she had summarily dismissed him from her service. It was only his devotion to Winifred that had induced him to put, as it seemed to him, his head in the lion's mouth. But when he found that the lion was kind and roared as gently as his own dove, and further, gave him various unimaginable dainties to eat and odd shillings to spend in surreptitious tobacco, the house in the Cromwell Road became invested with pleasant associations.

It was after Clytie had had two or three visits from him that the idea occurred to her to paint the portrait of the reformed Jack. The sittings continued long after the necessity for them had ceased. Jack came of his own accord. At last one day he astonished her by refusing the shilling that she held out to him.

"I didn't come for that," he said bluntly. "I come to see you."

Clytie and the urchin in industrial school corduroys looked steadily for some seconds at one another, and both in their respective ways were conscious of having added to their sum of knowledge. Then they became real friends. Clytie looked upon him with a new interest, taking herself severely to task for having summed him up in the past with such scornful superficiality. She atoned for it now by seeking to interest herself in his life, to give herself a little place in it, whereby it should receive some individual colour. This was all the easier now, as Winifred had smoothed down many of Jack's social asperities. Albeit not refined of speech, he no longer used profane language in the studio, nor did he entertain her with sanguinary details of cat murder. When the time came for him to return to school Clytie felt quite sorry.

CHAPTER XX.

THORNTON returned in due time. The autumn session began. The weeks and months passed. Their relations remained the same as when they had parted in
the summer. Towards Clytie he manifested a kindly indifference, so long as she obeyed his wishes. When she
went counter to them he flared up, showed his teeth, and
swore ; on which occasions Clytie would draw herself up,
and, with her chin in the air, leave the room and retire
into her studio. Then, after two or three days of evil
sullenness, the fancy would take him to kiss her, and
lightly swear that she was the loveliest woman in the
world. But Clytie had lost all responsive feeling. She
met him not wholly unaffectionately, but calmly, presenting an obedient, passionless check. Thereupon he
would either storm again or laugh, reminding her of a
time when her lips sought his, asking her why she
had frozen, where was the Clytie of their bridal month.
And if he pleaded gently, womanlike, she would relent a
little, yield to him, striving to blot out the objects that
met her sight as she looked back towards the past. Then
there would recur the season of indifference, which
Clytie had grown to welcome.

The daily life went on, she scarce knew how. Visiting, entertaining, painting, filled her days. And she
dreamed wistful little dreams.

And then there came to Clytie a great calm, a new,
strange happiness, in the midst of the life she had thought
to be broken. She would sit by herself and think, with
a smile playing round the corners of her lips, and a light
in her eyes. Again the order of things seemed changed.
Again a newer life, with newer hopes and responsibilities,
lay before her. For the time her art, her needs, were
forgotten. Trifling, dainty occupations absorbed her as
she sat in the solitude of the studio on the chilly autumn

days, her feet luxuriously buried in the bearskin before
the great fire. Sometimes Mrs. Farquharson would
come and help her, with a yearning hunger in her eyes
that Clytie knew the meaning of ; for Caroline was a
childless woman. And then Clytie would kiss her
silently and Caroline would shake her head and laugh,
and talk in her bright way of the wonder that would be.

Only at times did a wave of bitterness pass over her.
If all that had happened in her married life since the
train had carried her out of Bordighera station had been
different ! If only she could see her husband as she
saw him that day, by the ruined tower, when she passed
her hand over his hair and thought him all that could
suffice a woman's needs ! Sometimes she looked at him
now, furtively, when his face was in repose. He seemed
the same, handsome, brave, ideally perfect in manhood.
Why had not the glamour lasted ? Why should the
" dream be better than the drink " ? And then she
would turn away and the thought would rise :

" Why did I not continue blind ? Would to God this
knowledge of him had never come ! "

He grew a little kinder to her, however. It was a
rough, patronising tenderness, it is true, but yet Clytie
felt grateful. A little act of forethought and consideration softened her towards him much more than it warranted. Perhaps in spite of all he might have won her
to him again, and brought her lips to his in a kiss of rare
meaning—for at certain times there are wondrous tendernesses and wondrous powers of forgiveness in woman.
But Thornton lost the golden chance, being busy with
his muck-rake.

He came home one afternoon, in an evil humour.
Clytie, prepared to welcome him, looked up kindly from
her lounge-chair as he came into the studio, but as she
saw the blackness of his face, her heart sank. A foot-
stool came in his way, and he sent it, with a kick, sliding
along the polished floor.

" Why do you litter up the place with these infernal
traps, Clytie ? " he asked crossly as he came up to the
fire to warm his hands.

Clytie, like a wise woman, held her peace. Silence
is a very good friend sometimes. But as he remained

there moodily, without saying a word, and the silence was growing uncomfortable, she asked him what was amiss.

"Everything's amiss!" he replied roughly — "all through your silly folly. Read that!"

He drew a letter from his pocket book and threw it into her lap. It ran:

DEAR HERNSHAWE :

As I think Simmons would be a more satisfactory man for Burchester than Hammerdyke, I have suggested the former to the local Conservative association. As they seem rather at a loss for a suitable candidate, I think they will accept my nominee.

Yours truly,

E. GODDERICH.

"I am sorry, Thornton," said Clytie, laying the letter down on the afternoon tea table by her side. "But you hardly expected to have a chance so soon."

"Do you suppose I am going to slave away at this hack's work for two or three years?"

"No; but this is only the second or third vacancy that has occurred."

"What does that matter? Godderich promised to run me as soon as he saw an opening. Hernshawe was amazed at this letter this morning. Don't talk of what you know nothing about. It's simply infernal spite on Godderich's part! Who is Simmons? A damned cheesemonger with a jubilee knighthood, and as much brains as a double Glo'ster! Godderich has the reputation for this sort of thing. That was why I wanted to keep in with him. If you had taken a ha'porth of interest in the matter, it would not have happened. You have treated the man in your confounded icy don't-address-me-or-I'll-petrify-you kind of way, and you have put his back up against us!"

"I always treated him courteously," said Clytie.

"Yes, by Jove, I know what that means!" sneered Thornton. "And now you can have the satisfaction of seeing how your courtesy has played the fool with my plans."

"I can't understand you, Thornton," she replied wearily. "I should have thought you of all people would have preferred to win your own battles."

"So I shall in future. I shall take jolly good care not

to ask you to help me any more! After all your fine professions of identifying yourself with my life and that sort of rot I really thought you would be willing to help me—in about the only way a woman can."

" By a silly, ignoble flirtation? Would you really hope to win success by your wife's dishonour?"

" Oh, rot!" cried Thornton savagely. " Who the devil talked about dishonour?"

" Well, then, we don't see things in the same light," said Clytie quietly. " And I am very glad you have lost Godderich's influence, if that is what it depended upon."

He turned and faced her, in one of his blind rages.

" Why don't you say at once you don't care a little damn about me? It would be nearer the truth. What the deuce did I marry you for, when there are thousands of better women in the world who are to be had for the asking? About the only thing I have ever asked you to do for me was to employ a little womanly tact, and then you get up on the high horse, damme! and talk about dishonour! One would have thought you had been bred in a nunnery instead of the disreputable gutter in the King's Road I found you in!"

" Oh, stop!" said Clytie, rising. " If I were well, perhaps I might be angry and amuse you with a row. But I am not equal to it at present, believe me. I'll see you at dinner."

She walked towards the door, but Thornton intercepted her with three or four quick strides.

" I'm hanged if you do!" he said. " I have too much respect for my digestion. I'm not going to stay in the house with you!"

And he strode out of the studio, slamming the door.

"Thank God!" said Clytie to herself.

And so the film of reconciliation that new circu...stances had begun to spread was rudely torn asunder, and the breach beween them grew greater than before. For several days Clytie suffered. Then she resigned herself to the inevitable, and in her thoughts drifted away from her husband. For they were sweet thoughts, full of unspeakable consolation. And the weeks wore on, and the evenings grew shorter and shorter, and the

little pile of dainty needlework grew higher in the press.
Thornton rarely disturbed her; the time that he could
spare from his official duties he passed as a man about
town idles the hours away. A man with the least domestic tastes in the world, he found no especial pleasures
in his house. His wife did not amuse him; the cooking
at his club was more to his taste than that which
awaited him at home. There was no earthly reason why
he should use the house for any other purpose than
sleeping, breakfasting, and the occasional entertainment,
which was now discontinued for a season. He lived his
own life, more or less satisfactory to himself, and left
Clytie to her own devices. Wherefore she not unfrequently thanked the Almighty. She lived practically
alone. Winifred came to see her from time to time.
Mrs. Farquharson was often with her. The shrewd eyes
of Caroline saw that there was something wrong in the
marriage of which she had augured such fair fruits.
But as Clytie proudly kept all her troubles to herself,
Caroline could do no more than surround Clytie with
her mute sympathy. This gradual discovery was a
shock to her faith in human nature. One of the two had
failed; which one was it? Her instinct told her that it
was not Clytie; her husband unequivocally affirmed that
it was Hammerdyke. When her instinct and her husband differed she sometimes trusted to one and sometimes to the other, by way of giving a certain variety to
life. When they coincided she had no option but to believe. So, although giving up her hero cost her a great
pang, her heart went out more than ever to her friend.

It was a period of strange new happiness for Clytie.
It showed itself outwardly in her art. No one but herself
has ever seen the pictures that she painted during this
time—not even Caroline. They were all unfinished,
sketched in the hurried, semi-impressionist manner with
which from her early girlhood she had been wont to give
objectivity to her cravings and imaginings; but they were
dainty, laughing, tender things, a world of waxen touches
and sweet hopes. It would be hard to say how many small
panels she covered with the promises of this new life.
Sometimes, when she was quite alone, she would lock the
door and take them out and arrange them along the wall

on the ledge above the dado, and gladden her heart with them. After which she would collect them hastily and lock them up, with a smile at her own foolishness. She meditated now and then, before the fire, with closed eyes, turning over the leaves of her Book of New Formulas, which had grown somewhat tear-stained and dusty ; but she found in it nothing relating to present things, and she laughed quietly at the omission, resolving to rectify it by and by. It was strange that she had not included this in her scheme of life. And yet, after all, was it so strange ? She could not quite decide. But the future she never questioned. The evolution of her own individuality seemed in no wise to concern her. She had projected herself into another life. And she looked at the world, and again she saw it fair ; and peace rested on her eyelids as she slept. And the weeks went on.

One evening in the middle of December Thornton and herself were alone together. They had finished dinner and he was smoking a cigar with his coffee in the dining-room. Relations between them were beginning to grow kindlier again. That is to say, he curbed his temper, inquired after her health, and occasionally spent an evening at home. They had not spoken much during the meal. Now that they had so few interests in common, their conversation was generally desultory. The one great and precious bond that was to be between them was rarely mentioned. It was too deeply rooted in the holiest place of Clytie's soul for her to discuss it in the commonplace interviews she had with her husband, and his interest in the matter did not go much beyond a rather irritating sense of responsibility. Some feeling of the sort prompted him on this evening to allude to the subject.

" I heard from the Claverings this morning," he said, knocking off his cigar ash into the fender. " They want us to go and spend Christmas with them in their new place in Hampshire."

" Oh ? " said Clytie politely.

She had seen Mrs. Clavering several times during the summer in town, and futher acquaintance had only increased the antipathy she had conceived in Paris. Thornton, however, had been pretty intimate with them

during the latter part of the season, and he had met
Major Clavering again in Scotland.   Hence the invitation.

"Well," asked Thornton, "what shall I do? Of
course your going is out of the question."

"Naturally," replied Clytie, glad that that point was
settled without any discussion. "Why do you ask
me?"

"To know what your wishes are as regards myself.
Clavering has got some good shooting, I believe, and his
wife always keeps a decent house.   I don't see what
good I should be here ; but still, if you would like me to
stay on and see you through, I don't mind a bit."

He meant to be magnanimous.   Perhaps he expected
his wife to be duly grateful ; as it was she only replied
somewhat wearily :

"You must do whatever you think best, Thornton.   I
should not like to keep you here on my account, while
you might be having a good time with your friends."

"Oh! it's all the same to me," he said.   "It's just as
you like."

Clytie shook her head despondently. If there could
have been any pleasure to either of them in his staying,
these questions would have been impossible.   It was love
and not politeness that should have kept him by her
side.

"You are very kind to think of it, Thornton," she
said, "and I thank you for asking me ; but you couldn't
do much if you stayed, you know."

"I think I should be somewhat in the way," he said
good-temperedly.   "That sort of thing is not much in
my line.   However, I did not like to accept without asking you.   Are you sure you don't mind?"

"Oh, quite sure!" said Clytie suavely.

So the point was amicably settled, and Thornton went
down to Hampshire to shoot Clavering's pheasants and
to be led cynically captive by Clavering's wife.   To
avoid giving the latter a gratuitous loophole for sarcas-
tic attack, he forbore to hint at the cause that prevented
Clytie from accompanying him.   He said vaguely that she
was with her people.   Mrs. Clavering did not press the
point in any way, as she reciprocated Clytie's dislike, and

was perfectly indifferent as to what became of her. In fact she was greatly relieved when Thornton announced that he was coming alone. Him she could manage as she liked—or thought she could, which comes to the same thing.

The house which the Claverings had taken for the winter was one that appealed to the quieter tastes of a man like Thornton. There was good hunting in the neighbourhood, and the stables were well filled with hunters, some of which Major Clavering had hired for the season. Over the estate attached to the house was excellent partridge shooting, and the covers were stocked with pheasants. The house itself was straggling—as a country house should be—roomy, and capable of accommodating comfortably the large party that was assembled for Christmas. It contained two billiard tables, a concert room staged for private theatricals, and a magnificent club-furnished smoking-room with a specially made baccarat table. Among the party the masculine element greatly preponderated, but the few women who were there had been carefully selected by the hostess to maintain a nice equilibrium. The major invited the men, and his wife, running over the list, had settled upon the women. She was doubly grateful that Clytie had thought fit to decline.

On the evening of his arrival Thornton came down early after dressing and found Mrs. Clavering alone in the drawing-room, reclining luxuriously before the blaze under the great marble chimney-piece.

"Clavering must have come into a pot of money in order to run this," he said, parting his coat tails. "I have just been round the place. I had no idea it was such an extensive development."

"Yes. It's better than soldiering. Tom's looking out for a place of his own something after the style of this. The Dynevors wanted to go to Australia, and so they have let it to us cheap."

He nodded, not very interested, and twirled his moustache in silence.

"You are not making a very good start by way of being amusing," said Mrs. Clavering. "How is your wife?"

"Oh, very well. But I don't see how that topic could amuse you. Matrimony isn't very funny."

"Glad to get out of the toils, I suppose."

"Passably. It leaves me free in the society of the only woman I have reasonably cared for," he said, without changing his attitude.

"Have you come down to play at that sort of thing again?" she asked, arching her eyebrows, with a little supercilious curl on her thin lips.

"That's what you wanted me here for, I suppose."

"You came to shoot little birds on the invitation of my adoring husband."

"Perhaps the motives were mixed. You wouldn't believe me if I told you I had come to see you. That was my main inducement. I suppose I ought to have begun better and told you of my longing and despair. Let me make my declaration now, Clara."

"Bah! my friend. What is the meaning of all this?" she said cynically. "You don't care a straw for me—you told me yourself I had gone off lamentably. And I don't rate you a halfpenny above your worth. You are a fine-looking man with impulses and animal passions instead of brains and heart; and if you were to die to-morrow, my delicate appreciation of my dinner would not be impaired. So why in the name of common sense have we revived this miserable farce?"

"It's a kind of absinthe. We like it."

"If I could pump up any enthusiasm about you," she went on, not heeding his epigram, "I could understand it. But you are bad all through. You would not even be moderately faithful to me—as you are not to your wife."

"What the devil do you mean?" asked Thornton quickly, showing his teeth. But Mrs. Clavering laughed.

"Do you take me for a fool, or a woman of the world, my friend? I have eyes and I have ears. I'll go into particulars if you like."

"That would scarcely be interesting," he said.

He looked at her for some moments and then burst out into his resonant laugh, expecting boyish indulgence for his peccadilloes. His whole-hearted animal laughter was irresistible. The woman joined in.

"I don't know which is the worse of us two," she said. "Perhaps I.   I forgive you."

The piquant cynicism of this revived liaison attracted Thornton, was an enjoyable complement to the essentially masculine side of that country-house life.   He was a keen, brilliant sportsman, a famous shot, a perfect though reckless rider, standing out in all physical qualities far above the other men of his type who were his fellow-guests.   By them he was flattered, in an honest British way, his acts were applauded, and his opinions received with respect.   In the slaying of creatures, brute or human, he was an indubitable authority.   And although he was accustomed to a certain shade of deference from his associates, it never failed to gratify his somewhat barbarous nature.   Much of him had remained undeveloped.   Small things pleased and captivated him.   To be the central figure in this tiny world of sport was unalloyed pleasure to the man of fierce passions and heroic courage.   And the bitter philandering in his relations with Mrs. Clavering amused, stimulated, irritated, and fascinated him.   In his own way, therefore, he was enjoying himself exceedingly.   Beyond writing Clytie a hurried note on the second day after his arrival, he scarcely recalled to himself her existence. When he did it was with petulant annoyance.   He wished to God he had not been such a fool as to marry. And now what the deuce was the point of having children?   But that was his wife's concern after all, for which he cordially thanked the wise contriver of the human mechanism.

Christmas came, was celebrated with much festivity. On Boxing Day there was a big partridge drive over a distant corner of the estate.   It had been carefully saved for this one day's sport and the birds were accordingly plentiful.   The best portion of it—a field sloping from a ridge and skirting a pine wood and then merging into a wide gorse-covered pasture tract—was reserved till after lunch.   But the sport was good in the outlying approaches to this, and it was not without some irritation that Thornton tore open a telegram which a breathless messenger brought up.   It announced the birth of a son.   Thornton went on with the line across the wet, ploughed fields, but until they halted for lunch luck did not come his way.

Mrs. Clavering and the other ladies had walked over with the luncheon-baskets. The day was warm and relaxing. They lingered over the meal longer than they had intended. When a keeper came up and suggested that if they wanted to shoot the slope before dusk they had better be starting, the men sprang up in a hurry and betook themselves thither. Thornton was the extreme man, on the right, near the pine wood, which was being beaten. His ill-success in the morning had piqued his vanity. He was not accustomed to be second or third in matters of prowess. After he had brought down his first brace his whole frame was kindled with the desire to slay. Even partridges he could not kill calmly. Covey after covey was driven out of the wood, and as he had the first chance, his bag increased speedily. They had thus proceeded halfway down the long, straggling slope. The keeper by Thornton's side had just handed him his gun, and was watching the wood with intent, outstretched hand. A covey was being driven. At that moment another messenger, a boy, ran down the slope and put a telegram into Thornton's hand. With an impatient oath he stuffed it into the pocket of his shooting-coat, just in time to be able to fire his two barrels into the whirring flight of birds. The next man to him fired simultaneously. Two birds fell. The warm dispute that arose caused Thornton to forget the existence of the telegram in his pocket. And the continuance of the drive kept his mind entirely from it.

But when the party arrived home, and were standing for a moment in the hall, Mrs. Clavering came up to him and asked whether he had received his second telegram safely. Then he remembered. He drew it out, read it.

"Damn!" he muttered under his breath, and crumpling the flimsy sheet into a ball, threw it with a gesture of impatience into the fireplace. Then he turned and talked with Mrs. Clavering until he went upstairs to change.

As chance willed, the crumpled telegram had not fallen into the blazing wood fire, but had struck upon a log and dropped on its unkindled side. And chance willed that Mrs. Clavering should have noticed this. Women of her type are cynically unscrupulous. As soon as the hall was clear of men she picked up the telegram and read it. Her face, which when she was by herself was somewhat faded, grew a little grayer. She put the telegram in her pocket.

Chance willed also that Thornton and Mrs. Clavering should find themselves alone for a long spell after dinner in the little withdrawing-room, where smoking was permitted. Most of the men were tired. One or two of the women had gone up to their rooms. The rest were playing billiards. Thornton was in gay spirits, talking recklessly, giving her openings for sarcasms, and then closing in upon her with a brutality. It was an amusing game.

Suddenly she asked him irrelevantly :

"When are you going back to London ? "

" You're a wise woman," he replied, leaning back in his chair. " But what do you mean ? "

" I asked you a question—a simple one. Are you going to London to-morrow ? "

" No ; why should I ?—unless you are getting sentimental over me, and would prefer the illusion of my absence to the disenchantment of my bodily presence. If you mean it as a hint, of course I'll go."

" I do mean it as a hint," she said with a hard kind of drawl. " I didn't know you were quite such an unreasoning brute. Hadn't it occurred to you that it was only common decency to go off and help bury your new-born child ? "

She rose, and gathering up her skirts, left him before he had time to recover.

CHAPTER XXI.

Thus it had happened with Clytie during Thornton's absence. There came a morning at the end of the Old Year when the snow and sleet dashing against the window could be dimly heard in the heavily curtained room, and Clytie feebly whispered : "Give me the child." Gently they told her that the life had merely fluttered on the threshold and passed back into the silence whence it came. And she sank back on her pillows, struck to the heart with a dumb, hopeless heartsickness.

Recovery was slow. Clytie lay for many days quite listless, the tears rolling down her cheeks, physical weakness aiding to make her feel a great self-pity. The long waiting, the fear, the pain, all had been counted as nothing if at the close there could have lain in her arms a little child—one whose touch would draw all pain from her heart, make her forget every sorrow. And the passionate child hunger, begotten of the pangs of maternity, woke within her and cried for satisfaction.

The whole weight of the world's misery crushed down upon her. She awoke to a gray world. Its glory had departed. There was nothing left to live for, and a great despair came over her. What was the use of dragging out this broken, colourless existence until the time,— hopelessly remote it seemed to her, now that the blood ran again strongly through her veins,—should come for her to die ? She passed through the phase common to all strong natures in supreme moments of weariness, when death seemed the only solution. One little draught out of a phial, an agonised convulsion, perhaps, and then eternal nothingness. She did not fear the annihilation which her materialism had taught her was the end of things. She had no eschatological sentimentality. But the full-pulsed animal's instinctive clutching after life held her back ; the fit passed off, and she decided to live through another act of the dreary tragedy.

All feelings of tenderness, trust, common confidence in her husband, were swept away forever. The faintest breath of the old attraction caused her to shiver with repulsion. Henceforward they were mere acquaintances, who subsisted from a common fund, lived under the same roof, and performed certain conventional actions in common, for the sake of their own relations with a society that demands a certain outward show of harmony between husband and wife. Thornton had come to town from Hampshire in the vilest of tempers. For a day or two he positively hated Clytie. Then the seriousness of her illness had awakened in him a superficial sympathy. But as soon as she was out of danger he regarded her with cold dislike. She had abruptly terminated his pleasant holiday. She had gravely endangered his liaison with the only woman by whom he had been otherwise than purely sensually attracted, wherein lay an odd fascination, and in thus compelling him to her side she had sharply reminded him that a married man, if he wishes to keep in with the world, must not parade himself too conspicuously as his own master. And Thornton had his own reasons for not wishing to openly outrage society.

As soon as she was able to travel Clytie went to Durdleham, for the first time since her marriage. The quiet, easy life soothed her for a while. She was in that condition of hopelessness when inaction seems the highest good. Mrs. Blather attributed her dejection to the objective cause, and sympathised with her as one woman can with another, and strove to cheer her ; but still she privately thought this long brooding somewhat morbid. Clytie always went to extremes. But although she naturally was unconscious of the subtleties of dreariness in the causation of her sister's state, she was none the less helpful with her sympathy—and sympathy very often is all the stronger from the narrowness of the channel in which it flows.

February and March passed in the quiet, monotonous Durdleham way. But as the spring grew into her blood Clytie felt the tingling of life once again, and the period of inactivity was over. She was not of the temperament to sit long with folded hands and lament over the futility of things. The old restlessness of her girlhood, though strangely modified, again urged her towards a fuller, more vivid existence. Again she looked out upon the world and its mysteries with a knowledge begotten of sorrow, and again vague longings took possession of her. She faced the new condition of things bravely, resolved to struggle towards a newer, better content. If the short dream had come true, she would have found happiness in the guidance of another life ; but the high gods had ordained otherwise. As before her marriage, her only problem was the working out of her own individuality ; for henceforward Thornton would be her husband only in name. In what direction should she carry herself so as to prevent the fulfilling of her needs from developing into ignoble egoism? As a girl she had studied life eagerly, had painted from artistic impulses, from desire for fame, and from material necessity. Her enthusiasms, the intimacy of her odd social life with Kent and Winifred, had kept her pure and fresh. Now all was changed. She was alone. She had learned many things : the touch of the fire of passion, the taste of the waters of bitterness. Definite enthusiasms seemed to be wanting ; only the artistic impulse urging creation remained to her—together with mechanical skill. How was she to occupy her life to a fair and noble purpose? She tried to solve the problem calmly, was wise enough to smile when she discovered that she failed. One cannot range a row of potential enthusiasms in front of one, like oranges, and select in cold blood. So Clytie determined to have faith

> " . . . large in time,
> And that which shapes it to some end."

As soon as she had arrived at this decision she threw off her moodiness and became bright again, to the great joy of Mrs. Blather, who was sighing for her to join in such Easter dissipations as Durdleham society offered. In obedience to her sister, therefore, Clytie burst upon Durdleham like a revelation. During her girlhood Durdleham had regarded her as odd, refused to accept her as conducive to social amenities. Now it worshipped

her with dazzled eyes—the whirligig of time thus bringing
in its revenges. The irony of the position amused her,
but at the same time it brought out in her much that
was good and whole-hearted. She saw, perhaps for the
first time, that much of the decorous dulness that had
once chafed her to frenzy proceeded from an almost
childlike ignorance of the possibilities of enjoyment.
For a wild moment the idea entered her head to convert
Durdleham to epicureanism. Janet, to whom she confided this visionary scheme, stared at her open-mouthed,
and Clytie burst out into genuine mirth. Durdleham
was willing to be amused, eager to be brightened by a
brilliant woman ; but it would not be convinced. It
held by its principles, would not yield an iota in a single
formula. Still it could be brought to treat a paradox as
a joke instead of brooding over it with the stolidity of a
hen sitting on a china nest-egg. And that much Clytie did
accomplish during the short season of her social triumph.

In the middle of April she was requested by Thornton
to return to London. He had thrown up the private-
secretaryship, as his purpose in accepting it had been
already served. By dint of self-assertion he had identified himself with the non-parliamentary chiefs of the
Tory party, and during the early spring had rendered
efficient electioneering services. His chance of a candi-
dature was therefore only a question of time. But as
he wished to neglect no means of keeping himself in
evidence, he still felt bound to call upon his wife to aid
him socially—that is to say, to preside at his table and
receive his guests. This Clytie was not disinclined to
do, especially as his summons was couched in pleasant
and courteous terms. So she bade farewell to Durdleham
and returned to London.

When her train arrived at Euston she was surprised at
seeing Thornton on the platform. He wore a gray frock-
coat with a dark rose in the buttonhole, and lavender
kid gloves. He came forward and greeted her, raising
his hat before he shook hands.

"Have you had a tiring journey? You are looking
very well. As I was paying a call near Primrose Hill,—
ghastly place to live in, isn't it ?—I thought I might as
well pick you up here with the brougham."

"That was very kind of you, Thornton," she said.

They talked of indifferent subjects during the long drive to South Kensington : the theatres, odds and ends of gossip. When they got home he accompanied her into the drawing-room and drank a cup of tea.

"You're a deuced lovely woman, you know, Clytie," he said, his great bulk sprawling over a small drawing-room chair, his hands in his pockets. "I have half a mind to fall in love with you again. If you had not turned into absolute ice, perhaps I should. You've got that same devilish witchery in your skin that made me go wild over you a year ago."

"Oh, please don't talk of that, Thornton. It is the past," she said, with a tremor.

"Well, upon my soul!" he said, gathering himself together. "I don't see why it might not be the present. I was going to unfold to you a little scheme by which we might live politely together, but, by Jove! now I look at you and reflect that you are my wife after all—you're so gloriously beautiful, Clytie!"

He rose, but she was on her feet before him, having sprung up with a beating heart. She looked at him with a fearful surmise in her glance, and as he made a stride towards her she recoiled in a terror she had not known before.

"Oh, no, no, no! For God's sake!" she cried, catching at her breath, instinctively putting out her hands to keep him off. "That is all over. We loved one another once. A horrible mockery of it is more than I can bear."

"Confound it, Clytie!" he exclaimed, clenching his hands and showing his teeth, "you're my wife, and, by the Lord! I'll kiss you if I choose!"

The flash of his brown eyes that had once overpowered her will now made her shudder. She stiffened into a woman of iron, with bloodless cheeks. Standing up perfectly rigid, she closed her eyes, and hung her hands against her sides.

"Kiss me, then, since you claim the right," she said in a choked voice.

For a moment or two he stood looking at her. Then with a loud laugh he flung himself back in his chair.

Clytie with shame and horror in her heart rushed from the room.

It was not an encouraging home-coming. The incident, though not repeated, upset many of her plans for the reconstitution of her existence. It added a new dread. For she had counted upon the continuance of the entire indifference with which Thornton had grown to regard her. A sudden outburst like this had not occurred for many months. What guarantee had she that this was not the beginning of a series of spasmodic rekindlings of a fire she had thought dead? For some days anxiety lay heavy on her mind. But human nature is very elastic; if it were not so, God help us all! After a while she recovered and was able to talk calmly to Thornton, who began by treating her with an ironical politeness, and then relapsed into his usual cheerful indifference. Once while discussing their mutual relations she broached the subject of separation.

"I won't consent," he replied. "As we can't be lovers, we may as well be friends. You would gain very little by it. Besides, people would talk, and for me that is an important consideration."

"It hardly concerns me," she said, with a touch of cynicism that was new to her. "Still, if you wish it very much, I will remain."

"I do wish it, Clytie," he said in a softened voice. "You can go your way, I will go mine. But we must live together as far as the world sees us."

Clytie yielded with some misgivings, and set herself to work to discover interests in life.

The society life of London, in which she was free to play an important part, did not satisfy her. She saw too deep below the surface of things to be guilty of the silly cynicism that finds society hollow, its aims futile, and its morals corrupt. There is earnestness even among cultivated men and women. But society is formal, conventional, and in the external rules of life differs only in degree from Durdleham. True, it has a far wider intellectual scope. Contrary to Durdleham, it permits the possession of ideas, but it is just as punctilious as to their correct expression. The elaborate ceremonial of society weighed upon Clytie. She preferred a simpler,

directer life. There were so many wrappings of convention to be pierced through before she could get to the
heart of a thing or a person, and they wearied, irritated
her. And now, as Thornton seemed to care very little
whether she placed herself in evidence or not, beyond
playing the part of hostess in his house, she consulted
merely her own desires in her acceptance of invitations.
But as the circle from which these mainly proceeded
was that into which her husband's reputation, tastes, and
political aspirations had led her, she did not find in it
the interests which particularly affected her. It was
beyond her power either to feel or to simulate an interest
in Thornton's ambitions. Nor did she feel called upon
now to profess the tenets of Thornton's political creed.
She was a solitary, unconventional Radical in the midst of
the most uncompromising Torydom, which is an unen-
viable position even for the least rabid politician. The
political section, therefore, of her social circle she studi-
ously avoided. The purely fashionable, frivolous element,
that goes to Hurlingham and Ascot, and makes itself
merry over material things, had attracted her the previous year with its graceful epicureanism. She had still
been proud of her husband and his boyish zest in amusement, and she had caught from him the spirit of laughing Babylon. But now it was pain to be with him when
he chatted and jested with pretty girls and idle young
men. His light-hearted gaiety jarred upon her. She
saw that men and women were affected by his charm,
and she had half longings to tell them it was a lie. So
she withdrew herself from their midst as much as possible. By this process of elimination Clytie's circle
became conveniently limited. She was sick at heart, and
she turned more and more to the friends of her girlhood.

Mrs. Farquharson's Sunday evenings became pleasant
spots in her barren week. She went there alone, as in
the old days. Nothing was changed there : the same
faces, the same bright, eager talk, the same welcome.
Clytie became her old self, was astonished to find how
many enthusiasms she still retained. She almost forgot
that she was married, and had said farewell to theories
of life and such like vanities. Only at times, when her
own art came within the range of a friendly arrow, did

she wince and remember with a pang that Clytie Davenant was dead. Redgrave, whom she occasionally met, forbore, with a portrait painter's intuitive delicacy, to question her upon the progress of her art under its new conditions. He divined that his prophecies had been correct, and he was sad ; because he had had great hopes of Clytie. In a tentative way he spoke of it to Mrs. Farquharson, who confided to him her own surmises as to the dubious success of the marriage. Then Redgrave brightened, and declared that there was hope yet.

"What do you mean ?" cried Caroline with a touch of indignation ; whereat Redgrave smiled in his serene way.

"I mean that hitherto she has tried to look at life through her art. Now she will be able to look at art through her life."

"Then her art will be very feeble and miserable !"

"Clytie's life has never been feeble and miserable," he replied. "I feared it was going to be so—in a special sense, you know ; I feared that she would be overpowered by the physical element her husband would bring into her atmosphere, and that she would develop into the fashionable married woman, and thus, at the same time, suffer in spirituality and lose her grip upon the subjects that form her artistic range."

"I can't see how an unhappy married life can help her," said Caroline. "If such a deterioration is possible, it has taken place already."

"Doubtless it has," Redgrave replied earnestly. "But it is not final. If she lives within herself again, she will recover spirituality and grip — both strengthened by experience and suffering. That is the most precious knowledge, Mrs. Farquharson, which we have bought with sorrow."

"Then mine must be very worthless," cried Caroline. "And I'm very glad of it. I would rather be ignorant and happy than wise and sad. And I could wish the same for poor Clytie. I can understand the good and beautiful things of this world as well as most people, but I don't believe in art to all that extent. I may be a Philistine,—God forbid it, but perhaps I am,—and I like to see people happy."

" That depends upon what you call happiness," said Redgrave.

But Caroline was not to be led into an argument. She had her views and expounded them.

" I mean common, all-round human happiness," she said, " that makes you laugh to yourself when there's no particular reason for it. And I'd sooner Clytie have that and never touch a brush than paint the most world-convulsing pictures and be wretched."

" But if she painted world-convulsing pictures, as you call them, she would be happy—much happier than under the other conditions."

" Oh, no, she wouldn't ! " she replied, with a conclusive nod. " You are quite wrong, my dear good friend. It is a secondary consideration to a woman whether she convulses the world or not. It might amuse and gratify her to do it *en passant*, but it is only *en passant*. Believe me. I don't give my sex away as a general rule, but I make you a present of that ! So if you're glad," she added with triumphant feminine logic, " that Clytie has made an unhappy marriage, I think it is simply detestable of you ! "

So Redgrave, routed, retired in confusion ; but he took his own ideas with him.

One Sunday evening, early in July, Mrs. Farquharson ran into the room where Clytie, just arrived, was taking off her wraps.

" I have been waiting by the window ever so long, watching for your carriage. You are quite late. I wanted to see you before you came into the drawing-room. Who do you think is here ? Guess ! "

Clytie saw at once by Caroline's face. A little thrill of gladness sent the colour to her cheeks and caused her eyes to sparkle as she paused with one glove half off and looked quickly at her friend.

" Kent ? "

Caroline nodded, glad at seeing that Clytie was pleased.

" I wanted to drop you a line, but how could I on Sunday in this postless town ? George only condescended to tell me last night that he was coming. If we had as little sense as men, I wonder how on earth we should get on ! He met him out a week ago and persuaded him."

" It will be quite like an old evening, dear," said Clytie. " I shall be so glad to see him."

" It is strange you should not have met," said Caroline ; and then she added reflectively : " Well, perhaps it isn't."

She had her own theories on the subject. And to say a woman has her own theories is to say a good deal.

" But I don't see why he should have let us almost lose sight of him," she continued.

" What reason does he give ? "

" Oh, the reason that makes one so helpless, you know. A man you like comes to you and says : ' I have sinned against you without any cause whatever. It was just my own badness, and nothing else, and now I am humble and repentant '—and what are you to do but forgive him ? He's very penitent now and vows amendment."

Clytie completed her little toilet arrangements and went downstairs with Caroline. On their way Caroline asked her where Thornton was.

"He's at Goodwood, staying with some people there. He went down yesterday for the races."

" Wouldn't it have brightened you up to have gone too ? " asked Caroline with deliberate tactlessness, darting a quick feminine side glance. But Clytie broke into a laugh.

"Oh ! good gracious, no ! I didn't even know he was going till yesterday, when Roberts asked me about something he was to do during the master's absence. We are quite old married people now, Caroline, and we each go more or less our own way. It saves a lot of trouble. You see, he knew I wouldn't care for Goodwood and the set he's in with there—the Claverings and such like."

" Yes, I think you are better off here," said Caroline.

" I know I am," replied Clytie, taking her arm. And then they went into the drawing-room.

Clytie's first impulse on entering was to look round for Kent. She met his eyes fixed upon her from the other side of the rather crowded room, and she gave him a

little nod of greeting. He rose and joined the knot of
people who were surrounding her. Both were self-
conscious to the extent of knowing that, as they had
once been a familiar couple in that company, it would be
inexpedient to allow it to be noticed that their meeting
was an event to them. They shook hands, with a friendly
commonplace, and joined in the general conversation.
Redgrave, French, the journalist, Mr. Singleton, Mrs.
Tredegar, were there—most of the old faces, a few new
ones. To see Kent's among them was a joy to Clytie.
She had never understood why he had broken from her.
Now and then the true solution passed through her mind,
but she rejected it. It was incongruous with his action.
Love begets wants, and it is the nature of man to clamour
for them. This was her hasty conclusion. But she had
avoided thinking very deeply upon the subject, instinctively deeming it wiser to refrain.

He had not changed, she thought; and wondered
whether he would notice any change in her. She found
herself listening again to him as he talked, in his downright, earnest way, quickly noting familiar turns of
thought and expression, admiring the thoroughness of
his unconventional enthusiasm. The old contented
humility of spirit came back to her. How much more
real than hers was his life! How much she had learned
and could learn from him! And for a short, swift
moment the laughter and talk sounded dull in her ears,
and all the objects around, all the faces save one, melted
away into the blue cigarette smoke, and that one face
remained—sitting at a table opposite to her, the lamp
between them—and the brows were intent on the sheet
over which a quill pen was scratching assiduously ; and
the surroundings shaped themselves into her old rooms in
the King's Road. Then, just as swiftly as it had come, the
dream vanished, and Clytie sighed. The talk languished
a little. Kent looked somewhat wistfully at her. She
leaned forward and beckoned him with a smile and a
little upward movement of her chin.

"Come down and give me some supper," she said.
" I did not eat anything before coming out."

" That was foolish of you," he said involuntarily.

Then they both laughed.

"You are just the same as ever," she said. And they went downstairs.

It was a tradition in Harley Street that on Sunday evenings a cold supper should be laid in the dining-room from half-past eight onward, so that guests could go down whenever it so pleased them. To break up the continuity of the evening by a formal gathering around a supper table was opposed to Caroline's notions. Besides, irregularities in meals were one of the features of the house. You need never be in time, and there was always food when you wanted it. To the erratic and unregulated visitor it was paradise. Caroline paid her servants extra wages to insure satisfaction in this respect. So Clytie's little manœuvre was quite in accordance with the recognised order of things.

They found the dining-room unoccupied. She sat down near the end of the table, while Kent, a little way off, gravely carved some chicken, which he brought to her together with some salad and a jug of claret-cup. Then he sat down by her, at the corner.

"But aren't you going to eat anything yourself?" she asked, laughing.

"I am not hungry."

"Oh, that doesn't matter. Do go and get something, to keep me in countenance. How can I eat when you are sitting watching me like that, with your elbow on the table?"

"I have done it so often before. It seemed natural to sit by you while you had your meal. I was forgetting. You see my manners have not improved. However——."

He rose for the purpose of helping himself to some food, but Clytie stopped him, made him sit down again.

"There! It was silly of me," she said. "I did not think of it. Don't be any different from what you used to be. Let us imagine that this evening is one of the old Sunday evenings here. Ah! If you only knew how glad I am to see you. What an eternity it has been since we met."

"Eighteen months," said Kent laconically. "The longest eighteen months I have ever lived."

"Why?"

" Don't you think I have missed you ? "

" So much as that ? "

" Yes ; so much as that."

" My poor Kent ! " said Clytie, troubled. " I wish I could do something for you."

" Ah, *es ist vorbei,*" he said, puckering his brows, as he watched the rings he was making in the damask with an inverted wineglass. Then his forehead suddenly cleared, and he looked up with his frank laugh.

" You see I am just as much of a bear as ever. Instead of telling you what a delight it is to be with you again, I come to you complaining, and I ought to have every reason not to rail at fortune."

" You are doing great things, I hear," said Clytie. " Tell me about them."

" Oh, they are neither great nor much worth telling. The *opus* is being translated into German, and part of it will be soon published by the University of Vienna."

" That is a feather in your cap."

" A big one. I don't think I am given to running after notoriety and that sort of thing, but it is gratifying to be recognised a little. It encourages one."

" Ah, it does ! " said Clytie with more meaning than she intended.

" So I have been working away at it harder than ever."

" I wish I had your enthusiasm," she said. " And your power of work. Do you remember your lectures ? "

They talked a little about the old days, half sadly, half tenderly. Those memories were very pleasant. Then they came back to the present.

" Winnie tells me you are a great man now at the Museum. I am so glad."

Kent waved his hand deprecatingly and laughed.

" Winifred is quite an Iris," he replied. " For she comes down to earth sometimes and tells me things about you. Yes, I am quite a man of affluence these days. I am the head of the department. I have got so much money I don't know what to do with it."

" I hope you employ some of it in giving yourself proper meals," said Clytie. " Or do you still have your extraordinary suppers ? "

" Oh, I live just the same," said Kent. " If I began

to be respectable in one thing, I should gradually become so in all."

" And the rooms are just the same as ever ? "

" A few more pictures and odds and ends. And I have got a carpet. That's Wither's doing. He came to see me in the winter and caught a cold, due to the bare boards, so he said. When he had recovered he made me go and buy a thick Turkey square. After that I had serious designs of forbidding him the rooms lest he should turn them into a boudoir altogether."

They laughed over this idea. Clytie asked him whether he still kept the tripods before the fireplace, and whether the paraffin oil can in the corner harmonised well with the carpet. It was like a breath of fresh air to meet Kent again.

Suddenly he pointed to her plate.

" You are not eating anything."

" I am not hungry," said Clytie with some demureness.

" But if you have not had your evening meal, you'll get faint. What did you come down for, if you merely wanted to pick at the wing of a chicken and to put hardly any of it into your mouth ? "

Then Clytie burst out into merry laughter. He was so downright and honest. Just the same as ever.

" Oh, you foolish Kent ! I should have thought even you could have invented that."

" Did you really want to see me ? " he asked, brightening.

" Why, of course ! Do you suppose I am devoid of human attributes ? "

This brought them nearer than they had been since the time that Kent realised he loved her. To Kent this meeting was enchantment. To see her sitting by him, bright, laughing, her old self, was enough to make him lose sense of the past eighteen months of hopeless longing. He thought to himself that it was better she had not learned, since her ignorance gave him this sweet half hour.

" I suppose we must be going upstairs soon," she said, with a little wistful wrinkling of her forehead. " When shall I see you again ? "

Kent started at the question. It troubled him. He did not know what answer to make.

"Within less than another year, I hope," he said.

"Oh, yes, Kent. We mustn't be strangers any more. It's not good for us. Would you care about seeing me very often?"

"I am not coming to call upon you," he replied bluntly.

The actual words were ungracious. But there was a flash of eager longing in his eyes that lent the words a subtle meaning. And Clytie rose from the table with a little gasp of pain as the truth burst upon her.

"Oh, Kent, Kent!" she cried, greatly moved.

Their eyes met, and this time there was no mistake. He knew that she had guessed. But with a great effort he evaded the appeal.

"No; I can't come to your house to see you," he said huskily. "There you are Mrs. Hammerdyke, and I shouldn't know you. Your home is full of interests and associations in which I could only be a stranger and an intruder. To me you are Clytie, the Clytie whose daily life I used to share—and only as Clytie can I bear to see you."

"Would it help you to see me as Clytie?" she asked.

"Yes, dearly," he said.

"Then you can always come in to the studio when I am with Winifred, and I shall always be here on Sunday evenings. Don't you think I want to see you too—as Clytie!"

"Thank you. Thank you," he said in a low voice, taking her hand. "Now it is time for us to go upstairs."

CHAPTER XXII

EACH lay awake that night, thinking. To Clytie the revelation of Kent's love was dazing. The sense of her own dulness in never having pierced the heart of his mystery was even more confounding. Why should she have divined suddenly the meaning of the light in his eyes, on this first meeting after their eighteen months of separation, when she had been blind to it before? She only half guessed as yet why he had not told her, but she saw that it must have arisen from a rare, strange delicacy in his nature differentiating him from all other men that she had known. Her heart went out in pity for him.

"How he must have suffered!" she repeated over and over to herself. And then scenes between them came before her mind and became clear in the light of this revelation: the strange suppressed interview after her arrival from Durdleham; the last evening he had spent in London before going abroad, when he had lit her fire, and she had gone up to bid him farewell. How had her ears been so dull as not to detect the tremor in his voice when, after kissing her hand, he had said: "You are my very dear lady whom I will serve to the hour of my death"?

And then a little hissing snake of a thought formed itself into a reply; and she shrank up together with a slight convulsive shiver as if something foul had touched her.

After that she could not sleep. She got up, lit her candle, and took a book at random from her shelves. It was her well-worn, girlish Globe Shakespeare, one of the books she had surreptitiously procured when the family Bowdler was included in the category of formulas against which she revolted. She took it back to bed with her and commenced reading where it had chanced to

open. The first words that met her eye seemed like a
voice from the other world :

> Such harmony is in immortal souls ;
> But while this muddy vesture of decay
> Doth grossly clothe it in, we cannot hear it.

They followed so closely on the track of her own
shuddering thought that she could read no more. She
blew out her candle, and remained awake, staring into
the darkness, until the gray dawn filtered through the
blinds, and she fell asleep.

Nor was Kent more restful. He had battled with his
love, and with a strong man's will had brought it under
subjection, making it minister to his happiness in spite
of torturing longings instead of allowing it to darken
his life. It had awakened him to a sense of a world of
beautiful things, given him a deeper understanding and
a wider sympathy than he had before. For him truly
might it be said that to love her was a liberal education.
It gave him the key to the knowledge and appreciation
of women, drew him from his seclusion into the general
society he had formerly avoided. A feminine conclusion
which he would once have pooh-poohed as weak and
illogical struck him now with its intuitive subtlety and
delicacy of point. He learned that what the essentially
feminine mind lacks in breadth it gains in fineness, and
he was amazed to discover what a sensitive touch upon
life is possessed by a cultivated woman. · And mingled
with this new charm was another of an esoteric kind.
No woman he met had all the fascinations of Clytie, but
every woman seemed to possess one of them. He confided
this once in a roundabout way to Wither, who laughed, and
told him he was growing too susceptible and would find
himself married one of these days. But Kent shook his
head. "I could only find a Clytie among them by marrying the whole sex and making an extract of it," he
said with conviction. For not only did the higher qualities of woman's nature manifest themselves to him, but
the minor graces of manner and appearance appealed to
that side of his æsthetic temperament that had hitherto
been under a cloud. It occurred to him then that he
had been living with half his faculties. Accordingly

he felt a peculiar satisfaction in his new powers of perception.

It had cost him a pang to forego the pleasure of the bright society that Mrs. Farquharson gathered round her. At first he had given up going to Harley Street through fear of meeting Clytie, for he shrank from meeting her under the new conditions. Then as time passed on, and he accustomed himself to the idea of Clytie as a married woman of fashion, he wished to go, but shyness held him back. It would look strange to resume visiting suddenly after his apparent rudeness and neglect. Probably the Farquharsons would never have seen him again had not George met him at a learned society's meeting, and given him a hearty and pressing invitation.

But there was a large though somewhat scattered society in which, although the rarest of visitors, he had always been welcome. And now he not only mixed assiduously in this, thereby causing many laughing conjectures as to the reason of his social reformation, but he volunteered occasionally to go out with Wither, whose circle of acquaintance, like Sam Weller's knowledge of London, was extensive and peculiar. A revolution was thus effected in Kent's habits, and to a certain extent in his mode of thought. A new zest was given to life in this enlargement of his horizon. And all through his love of Clytie. The awakening of the dormant sex principle had strengthened his nature, extended his humanity in depth and breadth. In spite of a hopeless, passionate love Kent was still a happy man.

And now this spell of her influence was broken, or at least modified. He had seen her, felt the softness of her voice, the kindliness of her eyes. And he had unwittingly betrayed his secret. She knew that he loved her. She pitied him, promised that he should see her frequently on the basis of the old friendship. It was kind and generous, he thought, to step down from the height of her wedded felicity to comfort him with her friendship and sympathy. An unexpected happiness was in store for him. Perhaps, after all, his loyalty and devotion might be of some use to her.

But strong, loyal man as he was, this sudden meeting troubled him. If only he had spoken at once, before the other had come upon the scene, she might have been won to love him. The old torturing regrets came upon him, and he tossed sleeplessly on his bed. The love which, through its very hopelessness, had all these months given him peace and a measure of happiness now burst forth again tumultuously. It became a miserable farce to lie awake in the darkness. He rose, went into his sitting-room and lit the gas. Then he sat down at his writing space, and, burying his face in his hands, remained for some time in great pain of thought. At last his eye fell upon some notepaper lying invitingly on his blotting-pad. An idea struck him. He would write to her. He covered four sides with a passionate outburst of his love, writing wildly, unthinkingly, as men must write in moments of overpowering emotion. Then he tore up the sheet and began afresh. The summer morning light was streaming into the room through the curtainless window, mingling oddly with the yellow gas, when Kent enclosed and addressed the first letter to Clytie in which he told her of his love. He got up, stiff from his long sitting and somewhat exhausted, and going to bed, slept the sleep of the just until it was his usual hour for rising.

The next afternoon when Clytie returned from a drive she found the letter awaiting her. She took it up to her room, and there, sitting on the edge of the bed, read it with conflicting feelings. It ran as follows :

My Dear Clytie :
  You know my secret. I think so. I saw it in your face. But if I was mistaken, let me tell it to you in so many words ; and as I bring to you what is best and truest in me, it will neither dishonour me to tell it nor you to hear it. And as you in your goodness offer me a resumption of the old friendship, I must say it once and for all. I love you, Clytie, with all the strength of a man who has allowed women to take up very little part in his life. I loved you long before I knew it. It grew up gradually during our intercourse, and only one day when you were at Durdleham a little, little chance circumstance revealed to me that you were not only the grand, sweet friend, but the woman that I passionately loved. And I could not tell you for fear of paining you and destroying our friendship—for what was I to love you ? And I dreaded lest you should think me disloyal to the trust between us. And at last I came, resolved to speak, and it was too late. Winifred can tell you.

From that time I have carried my love with me as the vivifying principle of my life. I thought you would never know, but now I have betrayed myself.

Will it not pain you too much in your present happiness to see me under this new guise ? Ah, Clytie ! tell me frankly as you always used to do.

I shall never, never willingly trouble the serenity of your life. I love you too sincerely, too devotedly ; and my love makes me myself too happy. If you will meet me now and again after this, freely, at the houses of our common friends, you shall only see the old Kent who now and then scolded you, sometimes helped you, and who always held you dearer and higher and grander than all other women ; and yet you must let yourself be loved—that I cannot help. It is fused into my being, and it gives me happiness in my own way. I am an oddity, you know, Clytie, as you yourself have called me, and oddities have their little privileges, and if you know that it makes my happiness, and does not grudge you yours, you will not find it hard to be loved.

If you were a woman of ordinary conventional ideas, I could not tell you this. You would misunderstand it.

There seems but little I could do for you—and I would do so much. But life is full of strange chances, and perhaps my chance of serving you may come, and would then I could die for you to save you an hour's pain.

Yours in all devotion,

KENT.

Clytie read the letter over several times. At first the tears came into her eyes and a lump rose in her throat. This simple, unrequiring love soothed her and smote her at once. The largeness and tenderness of the man's nature came to her almost as a revelation. What was there in her worthy of this sacrifice? How could she tell him, she thought in her broken pride, that she had failed miserably, wretchedly, that she had forsaken the higher for the lower, that this selfless love of his was as far above the sudden intoxication that had degraded her as the spirit is above the flesh? She had thrown away the best, like the shepherd in the German legend, who, in the sensuous heart-leap at the sight of the glittering treasure, disregarded the voice, " Forget not the best," and dropped and trampled underfoot the little blue flower that opened the enchanted hillside. How could she tell him that?

Then, too, the note of unconscious irony in his letter jarred through her painfully. " Her present happiness ! "

"Oh, my God!" she cried at last. "If he only knew how much need I have of happiness!"

And then the strength that had kept the tears back for all these latter months of weariness and disillusion suddenly forsook her, and turning as she sat, she threw herself on the bed in a great agony of sobbing.

A little later she wrote Kent the following reply:

My Dear Friend Kent:

I am not worthy of such devotion. I can only wonder at it and accept it humbly and gratefully. Words like these of yours I never could misunderstand, Kent. If it is a pleasure to you to see me, you need not shun me any more.   CLYTIE.

Kent went into the studio on Monday to tell Winifred of the meeting; on Tuesday, with a vague hope of seeing Clytie; on Wednesday, when Winifred herself expected her, but she did not come. On Thursday, however, he heard her voice from outside the studio door, and his heart gave a great throb. He entered and found himself once more in her presence. Neither spoke of the letters that had passed between them, but the faintest pressure of the hand and a glance from her eyes told him that she understood.

After that they met frequently—on Sunday evenings at the Farquharsons', during the week in the studio, where for some months Clytie had taken to coming very frequently for the comfort of seeing Winifred. Clytie maintained her usual habits; Kent, as far as was possible, resumed his old ones. Sometimes it was strangely like the old days. With a little longing, perhaps, to add to the illusion, and also to give herself some employment while Winifred worked, Clytie began a picture, choosing in a humorous tenderness to take Winnie as her model. The picture never was completed, for Clytie had not the temperament to do justice to the slender figure in its quiet summer dress, and to the soft, dark face bent so earnestly over the palette and sheaf of brushes. But while the painting of it lasted it gave a comfortable air of reality to the revival. It was new life to Kent to come in on his return and once more receive Clytie's friendly nod as she stood by the easel, a painting-apron over her dainty dress, and her hands smudged with char-

coal or daubs of paint. He did not think much of the
portrait, and he told her so with laughing frankness.
But he divined why she was doing it, and while criticising, encouraged her to proceed. His arrival, however,
as it always had been, was a signal for the cessation of
work. Then Winifred cleaned the brushes and put them
in the trays, and gathered up the tubes and rags which
Clytie, with less sense of tidiness, had strewed around her,
and Clytie drew out the basket-table and rang the bell
for Mrs. Gurkins to bring up the tea. Clytie had left
behind her all her small domestic articles for Winnie's
use in the studio. So there was the familiar tea-service,
the Crown-Derby cups and apostle spoons,—a piece of
wicked extravagance on Clytie's part in times gone by,—
the gray Japanese teapot whose wicker handle had still
to be delicately fingered, and the little glass sugar-bowl
that looked so plebeian beside the aristocratic porcelain.
Scarcely anything in the studio had been changed. The
charcoal caricatures on the walls were as sacred in Winifred's eyes as if they had been frescoes by old Italian
masters, and she had issued strict injunctions to spring-
cleaners to leave them intact. Even Clytie's easel was
there now. Kent lived for these afternoons.

One day Kent was going to dine with Wither and
Fairfax. As his road to a certain point was the same as
Clytie's, they walked along together. This was almost
the first occasion on which they were quite alone together. He reminded her casually of the fact.

"Yes," she replied. "And I have been wanting to
see you by yourself. I have not thanked you for your
letter. But you do see that I appreciate it, don't
you?"

"There is nothing to thank me for, since I pleased
myself in writing it. The thanks are from me to you for
treating it as you have done."

"Oh, no," said Clytie, shaking her head and looking
before her. "You can't understand,—and perhaps it is
better you shouldn't,—what a letter like that means to a
woman. Well, it meant a great deal to me. To tell you
so is the only return I can make you."

"Don't let us talk of it," said Kent. "I could not
bear to have you as a friend under false pretences."

After they had walked a few steps in silence she continued the subject.

"Don't you think it would be better for you to forget all about me, and look around for someone who can make you happy—really happy?"

"I'd have to live till the day of judgment to find her," said Kent bluntly.

"That's ridiculous, Kent. But can't you feel that it sometimes pains me to see you sacrificing your life for me?"

"I am not sacrificing my life," he answered cheerfully. "Besides, I don't quite see what it has got to do with you—in one sense. I love you, and I couldn't love anybody else for all the joys in creation. Thank God, you are broad-minded enough to let me tell you this without any chance of misconstruction."

"Ah! That's all very well," she said, with a little sigh. "If I were a saint, I might placidly accept it as my due. Being only a woman, and that none of the best, it seems such a waste of good love, Kent, and love is a rare, rare thing in the world."

"But it would go a-begging if you did not have it," he replied, laughing. "Come, don't let us say anything more about it. You are happy with your own home and interests, and I am happy in seeing you and having your friendship. Of course I have suffered a bit, but it's all over now."

"Ah!" she said. "Life seems to be made up of that."

"Of what?"

"Suffering."

He waved an energetic protest with his ash stick.

"Since when have *you* grown a pessimist? I don't believe in it. Life is made up of responsibilities and interests. There's suffering in it of course; but there are alleviations. It's like cold and frost. If you stood up without a rag on in the snow you'd think the world was made of nothing else but frost. But you put on warm clothing and defy it."

"But the poor, ill-clad, shivering wretches—what about them?"

"I'm talking of people with average material wealth,"

he replied. " That's just it. So can the people of ordinary moral wealth clothe themselves against suffering. I don't like the morbid view of things. It doesn't do any good. Do you remember a passage in Longfellow's ' Hyperion '—a criticism of two German poets—' melancholy gentlemen to whom life was only a dismal swamp, upon whose margin they walked with cambric handkerchiefs in their hands, sobbing and sighing, and making signals to Death to come and ferry them over the lake' ? It's a bit fierce on your pessimists ; but it's a wholesome little passage to remember."

A little while after this they parted. Kent walked on, swinging his stick, convinced of Clytie's happiness, yet wondering at her unusual note of pessimism, and Clytie called a cab, as she was late, and drove home with a world of strange and troubling thoughts.

CHAPTER XXIII.

On the 1st of August Clytie received a visit from the boy Jack, who had just come to London for his summer holiday. He had grown greatly during the past year, had filled out. The taint of the street had gone from him and he was becoming civilised. Clytie leaned back in her chair and looked at him curiously as he sat, in all the self-consciousness of a newly awakened sense of propriety, upon the edge of his seat, twirling his glengarry cap. As an artistic object he had deteriorated. The motive of his worth in that respect had gone with the picturesqueness of his old garments and dirt and wild elf locks ; but he was handsome in spite of his cropped brown hair and the severity of his attire. Indeed there was something incongruous in the corduroy uniform and the refinement of his face, with its bright dark eyes and finely cut lips that disclosed a perfect row of white, even teeth. And yet there was cruelty around the mouth, the sublimated essence of the fierce savagery that Clytie had impressed upon her famous picture. He had been transformed from the animal into the human being, it is true ; but that does not necessarily imply that the human being does not retain many of the passions of the animal. With the old Jack the untamable was degradingly confused with lowness, but it shone out all the clearer now by reason of the humanising of his face. Clytie noted all this as they talked together.

"You are getting quite a man," she said. "When are you leaving school ? "

"Mr. Kent says I'm to stay there another year," replied Jack. "Then I'm to be 'prenticed."

"To a joiner ? "

"I suppose so," said Jack. And after he had scraped a little with his toe on the ground he looked up and added : "Do you think I needn't be a joiner if I didn't want to ?"

"I don't see why you shouldn't be what you like, Jack."

"Really!" and his face brightened. "I have been thinking I should like to be something else."

"What is that?"

"A carver and gilder," said Jack bashfully.

"Where do the especial charms of that trade come in?" asked Clytie, laughing.

"I dunno," said Jack; "I only thought it."

There was a touch of pique in his voice. Clytie noticed it, saw that she had wounded susceptibilities.

"Tell me, Jack, why you want to be a carver and gilder."

"I could make all the picture-frames for you and Miss Marchpane," he replied.

"Thank you, Jack," said Clytie, touched at the boyish idea. "But perhaps we'll make you something better than a carver or gilder. I don't know what you could be. What could we make of you?"

A vague idea of raising Jack above the artisan level had occurred to her during her scrutiny of his face. He was not an ordinary creature. That he should spend his life in the dull, commonplace atmosphere of the British workman seemed a waste of possibilities. There are millions who possess just the qualifications for hewers of wood and drawers of water. Why should a finer organisation not be cultivated, trained, put into an environment where there are conditions for free development? But whether the boy was a potential admiral, Lord Chancellor, or novelist she could not determine. That was why she asked the question, "What could we make of you?" somewhat pathetically. Jack shook his head in reply. He had learned at school that life was a serious thing terminating in apprenticeship.

"I've got to learn a trade," he replied after a little, "and I'd sooner be a carver and gilder than anything else."

"But suppose a good fairy were to come, Jack," persisted Clytie, "and say that you were not to learn a trade, or that, if you did begin, you would work your way out of it, and become a great man, and do glorious things in the world—suppose you were able to choose to be anything you liked—what do you think you would be? Tell me—something great and bright and noble!"

She had grown animated with her enthusiasm, and leaned forward, with her chin raised and lips parted—her attitude in moments of exaltation. The boy looked at her for a few seconds, catching her spirit. Something was at work within him too, for his eyes glowed, and his breath came quickly.

" There is something, Jack. Tell me what it is!"

" I'd like to be a soldier like my father," he said in a low voice, the extravagant, glowing fancies that had haunted him for six months thus finding half-choked expression.

" Your father?" asked Clytie, taken aback, and diverging into the side track of her astonishment. " I never knew you had—I mean, I thought you did not know anything at all about him. You used not to tell me the truth, then, Jack."

" Oh! but I did not know then!" he cried eagerly. " It was only when I come here at Christmas, and you was ill, so I couldn't tell you. He was a soldier, my father, an orficer. And I would like to be an orficer too."

" Really, Jack, this is very interesting," said Clytie. " Aren't you pleased to have a father you can be proud of? Was he a very brave man?"

" He had a sword," said Jack proudly, as if that was proof positive of valour.

" Come and sit down in your old place on the hearth-rug and tell me all about him."

The boy did as he was bidden, sinking somewhat shyly at first on to the great bearskin at Clytie's feet. But after a while he huddled himself up in his old posture.

" Mother didn't tell me much," he said in answer to a question of Clytie's. " I was looking in a chest of drawers of mother's, and I see a photograph—an orficer—all over strings and buttons and a sword and great big moustaches. And I come to mother and says : ' Who's this?' and she says: ' That's your father.' And then she snatched it out of my hand and hit me a clout on the head for going to her drawer. She wouldn't tell me no more ; but I know he was an orficer because he's got a star on his collar. I think I knows orficers when I sees them," he added, with the ci-devant street urchin's knowledge of life. "And I go and look at him now when mother isn't by."

"But you shouldn't go to your mother's private drawers," said Clytie by way of moral precept.

"I've got as much right to look at my father as she has," replied Jack in an injured tone, whereat Clytie laughed a little.

"You are an odd youth. I wish I could make you an officer right away. But I am afraid I can't."

"I believe you could,' said Jack.

There was a world of childish faith in the remark and the manner in which it was delivered. Clytie was both touched and saddened. She regretted that she had raised hopes in the boy that from the nature of things were doomed to disappointment. The overpowering difficulties in the way of her sudden visionary aspirations for Jack's future ranged themselves before her mind. So it was with a sigh she answered his outburst of faith.

"I am afraid I can't, Jack," she repeated. " But you yourself can do a great deal. If you like, one of these days when you are much older, you can enlist in the army, and then throw your soul into your duties, and keep before you at every minute of the day the words, " I am going to be an officer," and if you do this intensely, and never lose sight of it, you will succeed. That's the only way. They call it getting a commission through the ranks. But between now and then there are a great many years, and I'll do all I can for you, Jack. Yet, perhaps, after all, you'd be a happier and more useful man as a carver and gilder. Who knows ! "

Jack did not heed the pessimism of the peroration. His mind was aflame with the possibilities of becoming an officer and he took his leave in high spirits.

Clytie sat for a little musing over the solution of the problem that had troubled her in the first days of her acquaintance with Jack. She was gratified at her intuitions having proved correct. But there was still much that was dark to her. The physiological side of the question, however, was shadowed at present by more practical considerations. Why could she not find a means of giving Jack a chance in life? She looked ahead at the years to come, as she often had done since that dark December morning, and a pain came at her heart as she beheld their blankness. And now fate had thrown across her path this drifting spar of humanity. Jack was hers if she chose to claim him. No one would dispute with her the privilege.

After luncheon she walked to the King's Road and sat with Winifred, in the hope that Kent would look in on his way upstairs. She wanted to take counsel with him. His sturdy common sense would help her. She did not confide her vague scheme to Winifred, because Winifred would have called her a darling, and put her arms round her neck, and made her feel as if she were meditating something peculiarly noble. So she waited for Kent's sobering presence.

He came in at his customary hour, bearing a paper bag of peaches which he had brought for Winifred. He had carried them from some distance through the streets, and there were little wet stains on the paper. But when the fruit was put on a plate beside the bread and butter on a flap of the wickerwork afternoon tea table it looked fresh and inviting. This sudden return of their old intimacy was delightful to all three of them, and they chatted during tea as if nothing had happened to break it.

Then Clytie propounded her case, and they formed themselves into a committee to consider it.

"I don't like social experiments," said Kent. "It's constituting one's self a Providence without Providence's resources. If one bit of the machinery fails, the whole thing is apt to go wrong."

"But I don't want to experiment!" cried Clytie. "It's quite wicked of you to say so."

"How can it be otherwise?" asked Kent. "You want to put an industrial school boy of the most unconventional type and upbringing into the most caste-bound, conventional profession under the sun. It's like putting a bit of metallic sodium into water. A pretty experiment, though rather common; but the result is an explosion."

" But he must be trained and made a gentleman first," cried Winifred, coming to Clytie's assistance.

" Of course," said Clytie. " Should he ever be able to get into the army, he will be by that time quite a different being to what he is now."

" Then you'll have to give him a rigid, conventional training, and so spoil him," said Kent.

" It wouldn't spoil him to learn to speak the Queen's English and the use of his knife and, fork," said Clytie a little defiantly.

" He'd have to learn more than that. Besides, how is he to be taught ? "

" That's what I've come to you for advice about."

Kent mused for a moment and stroked his beard.

" Are you very much bent upon this ? " he asked.

" Yes."

" Then I can only see one way."

" Well—and that ? "

" Adopt him," said Kent. " An industrial school boy can be run by a committee—the experiment is not very dangerous, but a conventional gentleman must have conventional references."

His first words struck the chord she had shrunk from striking herself. It was the formulated suggestion of a vague desire. She was silent for a little. Then Winifred in response to a business summons went out on to the landing, and Kent and Clytie were left alone.

" I am afraid I have been too downright and have hurt you," he said concernedly.

She shook her head and glanced at him smilingly.

" I came to you for common sense. You have given it me. And your conclusion is one that I dared not come to myself."

" That you should adopt him? A *reductio ad absurdum!* "

" Yes, I feel it. I am not my own mistress now. There are difficulties. Oh, Kent, don't let me talk of them ! You see, I came to you for help—to no one else."

" I don't quite understand you, Clytie," said Kent, anxious at her sudden agitation.

She recovered herself, womanlike, and forced a laugh.

" If I were a rich, lonely old woman, I might be able," she said, "but, you see, I'm not. No, no, I can't adopt Jack ; and we'll have to run him by a committee, whatever happens to him."

" Well, what have you decided ? " asked Winifred, coming into the room.

" That it will be fairer to Jack to let him work out his own salvation," said Kent. "Let him work his way through the ranks. If there is anything in him it will come out. You don't think me unkind, do you, Clytie ? "

Whereat Clytie laughed honestly and Kent received much consolation.

They talked a little longer, on indifferent subjects, and then at Winifred's hour of departure they all rose together. Winifred went to the back of the studio and put on her hat ; Clytie and Kent moved slowly in the direction of the door. Kent sighed a little.

" I only seem to have seen you for five minutes," he said, "and I have told you nothing, but given you commonplace advice."

" Had you so much to tell me ? " she asked, smiling, as his unformulated wish echoed within herself. " There is no reason for us to go away because Winifred does. Would you really like to stay a little and talk to me ? "

Before Kent spoke Clytie had not the faintest thought of doing this. But in a flash came before her the long evening she was to spend in the great lonely house. Thornton rarely came home for dinner. He even dressed at his club. Often he slept there. On such occasions the first notice Clytie received of his absence was from the inscrutable butler, who would come into the studio in the morning with : " The commissionnaire for master's letters, ma'am." Occasionally three days passed without their meeting. When they did pass an hour in each other's company sometimes there was calm and sometimes storm. It depended upon his mood. As a general rule he was polite, even bright and entertaining, and life with him under these conditions was just bearable. But now the thought came with some bitterness : What did it matter whether she was at home by seven or eight—or twelve, for that matter ? Why should she not have a cheery hour with Kent ?

His face brightened as she made her smiling offer to stay.

"It is too good of you. Of course I should like to have a talk with you. But you—can you——"

"Oh, yes," she interrupted lightly. "I am not due home at any hour. I want to chat with you myself. Winnie dear, we are going to remain a little. Give me the key and I'll hand it to Mrs. Gurkins as I go down. I haven't asked you, but I suppose we can?"

"Why, of course, darling," said Winnie, coming up and giving her a farewell kiss. "I hate to think the studio isn't yours."

So Winifred went away and they remained as in the old days. The sudden association gave Clytie a pang. A reaction from her enthusiasm about Jack to weariness of spirit made her sink back listlessly in her chair.

"What is the matter?" asked Kent, filling his pipe. "You are not looking yourself. It is this steaming London. Why don't you go and get some country air?"

"Oh, one place is just the same as another. It isn't London and it isn't the weather. It is the world that is out of joint, somehow. I am afraid I have been moping. I think I shall invest in a cat. Then I can pour out my grievances to it. That's the best of a cat: it never mopes. It goes on purring cheerfully so long as it's warm and well fed, and when you feel paradoxical it never worries you to explain yourself. Do you like cats? I forget."

"What are you moping about?" he asked between the first few puffs of his kindling pipe.

"Oh, don't talk in that aggressively cheerful tone, Kent. I have come on all over moods, and I want comforting."

"You should work," replied Kent with some self-restraint. "You have hardly touched a brush in earnest this year. It is the claims of that part of your nature that cry out if they are not satisfied. Why don't you go on painting? What has the fact of your not having to make your living got to do with your art?"

"Everything, in a way," she murmured.

"I can't believe it," said Kent earnestly. "You are not the woman to neglect your art out of pure idleness.

Come, Clytie, rouse yourself and paint a great picture.
The ' Faustina '—what has become of that ? "

"Oh, don't, don't ! " she cried, putting her hands up
before her face. "I can't do that now—can't think of
it. Years hence, perhaps, when I am a middle-aged
woman, if I find it good enough to live till then, I may
try—but not now."

Kent laid down his pipe and drew his chair near to
her. He was pained and troubled. He saw that her
nerves were a little unstrung ; but the Clytie he knew
was the last woman in the world to give way to attacks
of this kind. And then a dreary conjecture dawned
upon him, and his heart sank.

" My poor Clytie ! " he said in his kind way. " You
seem unhappy. I wish I could do something to help you."

" Ah ! it's too late now," she said impulsively, scarcely
heeding the purport of her words. " You might have
done it eighteen months ago—if you had not been
quixotic."

" What do you mean ? " he asked, more and more
troubled and at fault. " Eighteen months ago ? How
could I have helped you ? I loved you and hid it from
you. I could only have caused you pain. I love you
now. I don't hide it. Why should I ? I am ready to
help you if I can. I am stronger, wiser now than I was
then. How could I have helped you then ? "

The simplicity of his short, reiterative sentences and
the sincerity of his tone went to her heart.

" You could have helped me then by not hiding it."

" I don't understand," he said. " How could the
knowledge that I loved you have helped you, unless you
cared for me ?"

" Perhaps I might have cared for you," she said
wearily.

" Oh, God, Clytie ! don't say that. It is cruel ! " he
cried, starting to his feet in great agitation. " I know I
acted like a fool, but it was with true motives. Don't
twit me with them. It is more than I can bear."

Only then did Clytie clearly realise what she had been
saying. The fit of supreme dejection passed off as suddenly as it had come, and she felt keenly the justice of
his words.

"Oh, Kent, Kent, forgive me!" she cried, with starting tears. "I hardly knew what I was saying. You are so noble and true-hearted that you must forgive me. Sometimes when a woman is wretched she has not control over herself, and I am sometimes very, very wretched, Kent. I was thinking of myself more than of you when I said the thing that pained you. Tell me that you forgive me."

The appeal was too human, too unreserved, to be rejected by Kent's tender nature. He sat down again by her and took her hand and kissed it gently.

"I have never seen you like this before," he said. "I wish I could comfort you."

He knew that it was no passing irritation or weariness that forced the confession from Clytie's proud nature. It was something deep and final—something impossible in her married life. Her wretchedness made him forget his own longing in the desire to be of use to her and lighten her lot. He let go her hand, which she allowed to lie on her lap as it fell, with the palms lightly upwards.

"I don't know why I have told you this to-day," she said, not meeting his eyes. "I have never breathed it or hinted it to a living being, and it came upon me unawares. Don't despise me, Kent."

"Clytie!"

"Oh, yes. I know what any outsider would say. I was posing as the *femme incomprise*. I was casting away my womanly pride. Of all persons in the world *you* ought not to have been my confidant. Judged by conventional canons I am to be despised, for what can the world say of a woman who tells a man that still loves her that she regrets she did not marry him? Oh, don't interrupt me. I may as well speak out my true self once and for all to you. You yourself once remarked that if we were superior to conventionalities of habit, we ought to extend our unconventionalities to sentiment. You are loyal and staunch. You can help me by being my friend, for I have no one else to turn to. My life is a dreary mistake. My art does not satisfy me, because I have no hopes. One must have enthusiasms to be an artist, and all mine are dead. Now you know."

There was a certain fierce pleasure in this self-abasement. It was like the vengeance of her higher nature upon her lower, the whip of scorn applied by the spirit to the flesh.

He did not answer, but looked at her with inexpressible sadness in his eyes. She added a few more words.

"If you despise me for telling you, let me know at once. It would be better."

"God forbid!" he said in a low voice. "I shall never apply to you the conventional canons of misjudgment. I take what you have said to me as a sacred trust, and thank you from my heart for thinking well enough of me to give me your confidence. You must never ask me such a question again, Clytie, for it would wound me."

"I believe you, Kent," she said, raising her eyes to his in her frank manner. "And I was wrong to say you *might* have helped me, for you can now. And you will?"

"With my last breath," said Kent simply. "It has been the torturing regret of the last eighteen months that, much as I wished, I could never do a hand's turn for you."

"But what can I do for you in repayment, my poor Kent?"

"Be your own bright, eager self again. Throw yourself into your painting, and the result I will take as my reward. It will be my influence gleaming through your genius, and it will be sweet to me. Oh, Clytie! you are wrong. A life is seldom so wrecked that it cannot be reconstructed, for that implies the utter loss of faith. A grain of faith in anything can move mountains; if one hasn't it, then it is time to put an end to life altogether, it becomes one's duty not to live."

"I came within an ace of that at the beginning of the year," said Clytie, with a sad retrospective smile. "Some time I may tell you why. I thought of dying, but then it seemed cowardly. Perhaps it was I had more curiosity to go on seeing how the world went on than I was aware of. And now, Kent, you have put things in a new light before me, and how can I thank you for all your goodness?"

"I have told you," he replied, with a smile.

CHAPTER XXIV.

The next morning, after writing her letters and attending to her household duties, Clytie went into her studio with the praiseworthy intention of stimulating the artistic impulse that had been flagging for so long. Kent was right, she thought. Her life could be reconstructed. She would begin her laborious art life again, resume it seriously as a profession, put her pictures into the market once more. Amid the many confusing thoughts and emotions resulting from her conversation with Kent, one idea had sprung in connection with Jack. She could not adopt the boy. That was a wild feminine craving, somewhat selfish, springing out of a bitter hour when fairer hopes were crushed. It cost her a sigh to resign ; but she trusted to Kent's judgment, and her mind was so far at rest. Yet if it could lie in her power to help Jack materially in after years, when a little capital would be worth all the world to him, she felt that she would have wrought some good for one human creature at least in her somewhat self-centred life. And then Kent's advice as to her art mingled and combined with these thoughts, and the outcome was the sudden idea that the proceeds of the sale of her pictures would, in course of time, form a very considerable fund. She clapped her hands with delight when this occurred to her. A mountain of weariness seemed removed. In the spontaneity of new workings she scribbled a hasty line to Kent and had it posted with the address scarcely dry.

"I am going to paint *seriously*, and *sell* my pictures, and devote the proceeds to a fund for Jack. Shall I ?"

She was in bright spirits this morning, having discovered an object in life. The future has generally much more to do with our present moods than the past. Yet, notwithstanding this broad truth, the immediate past had a certain influence on Clytie's humour. Whilst she was driving home the afternoon before, the gravity of the fact of her confession to Kent had somewhat weighed upon her. She had spent the lonely evening grappling with a truth that had been taking half-reluctant shape in her consciousness for the last two months, and now rose clear and sharply defined. She had even written to Kent the following portion of a letter which she straightway tore up into the finest of pieces. In fact her intention of sending it to him was from the first of the very remotest. "My dear Kent," ran this singularly feminine effusion. "My words to-day were true. If you had told me you loved me eighteen months ago, I should have realised myself and what it was that I felt towards you. The knowledge of her own heart does not come to a woman with the easy grace that your sentimentalists make out. It is somewhat of a fierce process, Kent. There is no royal road to it. Well, I know my own heart now, and I have bought the knowledge with agonies of suffering. Oh, Kent, my true, loyal Kent! I am tired, tired of hiding facts from myself, of acting in a wilful dream, in defiance of the promptings of my reason. I am a woman, and I ought not to confess things to myself, let alone to you. So people say—and people are so wise, aren't they? I love you, Kent. There, I write it down in black and white. It looks odd, grotesque, horrible, and yet wonderfully comforting. I love you, Kent. Why should I deceive myself any longer? God knows whether it is for my happiness in the future or my misery; but now that the beauty of it is upon me it makes me wonderfully happy. Yes, wonderfully, wonderfully, wonderfully happy."

And then she threw down her pen and shredded the paper with frenzied zeal. But her heart was lighter. The world seemed a clearer, pleasanter place. Her cheeks burned like fire at the thought of Kent ever knowing of this feeling. She arranged in her mind the tenderest and most elusive of relations between Kent and herself. He, a declared lover, should give her all the comfort and kind counsel of a friend; she, his declared friend, would find delicate, subtle ways of colour-

ing and softening his life with her love. A new paradise
of exquisite emotion opened its evanescent portals. For
the first time in her life came the romance of delicate
sentiment, tinged with an innocent pink like the buds in
spring. It is true these same buds, to continue the
analogy, burst into gorgeous, riotous bloom under the
summer sun ; but while the tenderer air of spring keeps
them closed they have a grace peculiarly their own.

Clytie moved about the studio singing, a sign with her
of great content. The window was open and the morning sun streamed in, filling the large and somewhat
heavily tapestried room with gay light. It glorified
Clytie as she passed across the patch of sunlight, falling
upon her hair in a thousand scintillations and revealing
the deep sea-blue of her eyes. She wore a soft cream
morning gown, a golden tasselled girdle round her waist,
an edging of old lace round the somewhat open neck.
The wide, drooping sleeves she had caught up a little for
convenience in working, and her arms were bare to the
elbow. The skirt clung around her as she walked
quickly about the room, with her old elastic tread, making a soft frou-frou that pleased her, she did not know
why. She was happy again, filled with a double sense of
the meaning of life. At last she sat down before a small
easel, on which was put the board with its fair sheet of
Whatman paper ready for the first sketch. In her rapid,
eager way she commenced to indicate the motive of the
picture that had flashed like an inspiration upon her. In
the middle distance on the left a pair of lovers, the
woman looking with upturned face at the man, whose
arm was round her waist. In the foreground, peeping at
them from behind a clump of bushes, a girl of about
seventeen, with a letter in her hand. The contrast
between the two female faces was the motive—the fulfilment of knowledge on the one, the dawning revelation
on the other. The title had come with the conception :
" Maiden and Woman." Clytie worked on steadily with
her *ébauche*, keen, sure of herself, tingling once again
with the excitement of inspiration. She knew she could
put that in their faces which would raise the picture
above the narrative prettiness of Sant and his school.
The accessories were to be severe to austerity. No

elaborate detail in tree painting, no subtle effects of light and shade. The principle of abstraction to be as uncompromisingly carried out as in one of Seymour Haden's etchings. The whole artistic force of the picture was to be concentrated in the awakened and awakening souls.

She was absorbed in her work when, after a tap at the door, Jack came in. Clytie looked up with a smile.

"You here again, Jack! That is good of you. But I can't say a word to you—positively. I am so busy. Sit down somewhere until I have finished."

The boy, used to these fits of absorption in his two artist patronesses, sat down for a little and let his eyes wander round the studio, looking at the pictures and nicknacks. Then he got up to make a closer examination of vases and photographs, and walked about on tiptoe, trying to still the noise of his iron-shod boots against the hard, polished floor. At last he discovered on the bookshelves an illustrated History of England, with which he retired to his favourite place on the hearthrug. And so they remained for half an hour without saying a word—Clytie bending over her study, Jack curled up with his picture-book. It was quite still. A stray bumble-bee looked in now and then at the window, buzzing querulously, as if he had lost his way in London, and then darted off again. From the servants' hall came the just perceptible voice of one of the maids singing a hymn-tune, and from far, far away came the tinkling treble of a piano-organ. And these few sounds, so faint yet so clear, accentuated the summer stillness.

When Clytie had put the last few touches on the portion of her work that demanded all her concentration, she gave a little sigh of relief.

"What do you think of that, Jack?" she said, leaning back with her head critically aslant. "Don't you think that is going to make a famous picture?"

Jack jumped up promptly, leaving his book open on the hearthrug, and came up to her side. He was not a connoisseur, in spite of his associations with art, so he said nothing, but grinned appreciatively, rubbing the calf of one leg with the instep of the other.

"Well," asked Clytie, "why don't you admire?"

"You aint given them no faces," said Jack.

" Ah !   This is to be one face," she said, pointing to a kind of *remarque* at the foot of the sheet. " Or something like it. Now just use your imagination, Jack. This face is to go there—the woman whose whole nature has been awakened, and is shining out of her eyes, and quivering on her lips, and is vibrating all through her frame—all of which is Greek and Chaldee to you, my good Jack ; but I may as well explain. And now I have got to fix a face for this one. What kind of face do you think I am going to give her ? "

" I dunno," murmured Jack. And then after a slight pause : " And what's the man going to be like ? "

" Ah ! " said Clytie. with a mock sigh. " What a little Philistine you are ! The man can be any kind of creature on two legs. What does it matter about the man ? He is a nuisance. I have a good mind to make him awfully ugly with a face like a rhinoceros. See, like this."

She made a few rapid strokes with her charcoal in the oval left for the man's face, and the result was a picturesque monster with a long nose, Mephistophelian eyebrows, and a moustache curling up to his ears. Then they both burst out laughing.

" Let me draw some funny men for you." she said in the light-hearted buoyancy of her mood. " Run and get me that sheet of paper over there."

She pinned the sheet that Jack brought her on to the board and began to draw caricatures.

" You shall choose one for me to put in the picture, Jack."

It was a long, long time since she had indulged this freakish side of her genius. It ran riot now in grotesque exuberance. Here a head with wide, leering mouth and pointed ears, like the devil that looks over Lincoln ; there a snouted monster with cat's whiskers, an eyeglass, and a silk hat ; a lean, cadaverous, equine face with a terrible squint ; a masher, indicated by three or four little dots and lines. Jack looked on in rapture. She had never drawn pictures for him before. He broke out now and then into breathless exclamations.

" Lord, he's an ugly one ! Give him a long nose— longer than that ; and, my eye ! that's a wart upon it. One of the teachers at school has a wart on his nose.

That's just like him !   And where's this one's 'ed ?—he's all body and legs ! "

And then he jumped and clapped his hands when the head was seen to emerge from between the knees after the fashion of the boneless wonders.

When she had filled up the last space on the sheet she tossed the charcoal into the tray, and rose from her seat.

" There, Jack !   There's nothing like going absolutely mad on occasions.   Now if you'd like to keep these pictures and show them to the boys at school, you can."

She rolled up the stiff piece of drawing paper, slipped an elastic band round it in her hasty way, and gave it to Jack, who could only look his delighted thanks.

" Now I must go and wash my hands and get decent for lunch.   Go downstairs and tell Mrs. Pawkins to give you something to eat.   Stay—you had better leave that roll up here ; come in for it before you go."

She took it from him, and laid it on a little table near the door.   She did not desire that the inquisitive eyes in the servants' hall should witness the mistress's frivolity. Jack understood her more or less, but Mrs. Pawkins and Mary and John would have questioned her sanity.

Jack lingered for a moment on the threshold, and then drew shyly from his handkerchief pocket a dingy, whitey-brown packet.

" I came to show you this," he said, putting it into her hand.   " I prigged it from mother's drawer this morning. You'll give it me back, won't you ? "

" I have a good mind not to," said Clytie severely.   " If your mother knew, she would be very angry, and you would catch it.   Still, as you have been a good boy, I'll look at it and give it you back.   Run away, now."

Jack did as he was bid, and Clytie, after a few turns about the room, putting things more or less straight, unfolded the dirty wrapper of Jack's packet, with an amused curiosity as to the features of Jack's father.

But in another second all her curiosity, amusement, idle interest, were fled, and her whole emotive force concentrated into a short, irrepressible gasp of astonishment. It was a photograph of Thornton, her husband.   There was no mistaking it.   She had the fellow to it in her album. One day long ago she had seen it among his odds and ends, and had begged for it, loving it for all that it was so many years old, taken when he was still in the army. He looked so stalwart, soldierly, magnificent in his uniform. It was perhaps the likeness of him that she had cherished most—only too familiar. For a moment she could hardly understand—the shock was so sudden and unexpected. Then with the quick reaction she realised what it meant. Thornton was Jack's father, Mrs. Burmester was his mother. With a shudder of disgust she threw the photograph on the table.

The riddle of Jack's parentage was solved in a way she had not looked for ; the mystery that had lain hidden in strange, unknown depths of passion was now clear to her in all its unlovely nakedness. Her soul sickened at the truth. She had not come to her husband with the helpless ignorance of a young girl. The knowledge of good and evil, to employ the somewhat meaningless euphemism, had come to her through her intelligence by means of books, through her contact with real life. She had grasped the fact of the existence of the Loulou Mendès type with whom love is a trade. That a man should have had a liaison with such a woman she could have understood. In fact she never at any one moment had fancied that Thornton had brought to her the pure ardour of a virgin soul. To have been revolted at the discovery of a mere antenuptial infidelity on the part of her husband would have been to her impossible. It was not noble, it is true ; but it was intelligible. There was certainly for a lower nature a charm, witchery, fascination, in the fleshly beauty of the courtesan. She had heard of many men falling victims to it, and sinking very little into degradation. If Jack's mother had been such a woman, she would have felt little more than the shock of coincidence, a sense of strangeness in her relations with the boy. But Jack's mother was not of this type. She never had charm, witchery, or fascination. She had never even passable good looks. A poor, stolid, dull, animal drudge.

The truth had come upon Clytie ; the truth that had touched her now and then with its bat wings, making her shiver ; the horrible, soul-nauseating truth of the eternal *beast* in man. She knew Thornton now as he was, and her indifference passed into loathing. In Thornton's feelings what difference had there been between this boy's mother and herself?

She walked swiftly up and down the studio, with clenched white hands, her shoulders rising now and then in an involuntary heave of disgust. The glory had gone out of the day. A foul shadow overspread it.

Suddenly Thornton himself appeared with eager face, a telegram in his hand. He had just come in from riding in the Park, and according to the modern fashion out of the season, was dressed in tweed suit and gaiters. He carried a silver-headed riding whip jauntily under his arm. He waved the telegram exultingly.

"They have asked me to put up for Witherby!" he said. "I'll have some lunch on the strength of it. I suppose there's some going."

"I believe lunch is at the usual hour," said Clytie, not looking at him.

He lingered a little, flicking his legs with his whip.

"You might as well congratulate me, if only for the sake of politeness," he said in an injured tone.

"Oh, yes; I congratulate you," she replied.

Her voice sounded strange in her own ears. She felt an almost irresistible impulse to burst forth into a torrent of speech, to say out finally all the bitterness and loathing that were in her heart. She restrained herself, but the effort gave a queer guttural resonance to her words. She turned and looked out of the window.

"What the devil's the matter?" he asked impatiently. "I came in, 'pon my soul, thinking you'd be pleased. It's a safe seat. I'm dead certain to knock the confounded Radical into a cocked hat. Just the moment when I've got what I've been sweating for the last eighteen months, confound it all, I did think you'd be civil for once in a way. But it's just like you; I might have expected it. Well, perhaps it's the truth to say you don't care a damn one way or the other."

He walked to and fro for a little, fuming. Then his eyes falling on the photograph that lay on the table, he picked it up, as an angry man will do, looked at it absently for a moment, and pitched it sharply to the other side of the room. Clytie, startled by the slight click of the cardboard striking against the wall, turned half round and met his eyes fixed loweringly upon her. Each held the other spellbound for a few seconds. Then the door opened and Jack came into the studio, checking his motion forward as he saw Thornton.

"What the deuce is this?" cried the latter.

With a swift, instinctive glance Clytie compared the two faces. They were astonishingly alike. The same finely moulded features, dark lucent eyes, brown crisp hair, white evenly set teeth ; the same lines of cruelty at the corners of the lips. Strange that, much as she had studied Jack's physiognomy, the likeness had never suggested itself. At Thornton's petulant question the boy looked at him half frightened, and then at Clytie, and was about to shrink back. But she called him in.

"Don't go away without your drawing, Jack. This," she said coldly to Thornton, "is a *protégé* of mine. He was once my model—for my picture ' Jack.' Here, Jack, take your drawing. Run home. Thank you for coming to see me."

"And—and the photograph. You said you'd give it me back."

Clytie went to the table where she had thrown it. Not seeing it, she remembered the sound that had startled her, and turning round, perceived the photograph lying face upwards on the floor. She gave a little start of dismay. The situation threatened to become dramatic, and she was unprepared. In her hurry to dismiss the boy she had forgotten the photograph. Now he had called attention to it, and she felt bound to restore it to him to save the poor little urchin's honour and most probably his back. And Thornton was leaning against the mantelpiece, with his hands in his pockets, frowningly surveying the scene. With outward calm, but with a beating heart, she picked up the photograph, wrapped it in the dirty covering, and put it into Jack's hand. Thornton, who had watched her movements with gathering surprise, strode forward with an oath.

"What the devil——"

But Clytie quickly interposed herself between him and the boy.

"Run away!" she said in a hasty whisper, and Jack,

accustomed from his childhood to sudden dartings, disappeared like a flash. Clytie put her back against the door and looked at her husband with strange eyes. It had been done with the speed of a conjuring trick.

"What on earth is the meaning of all this?" asked Thornton; "and what are you giving away my photographs for? Upon my soul, I think you are taking leave of your senses. You'll have to drop this sort of thing. I'm damned if I am going to have my photographs given away to all the street urchins in London. Play the fool yourself if you like, but I'll trouble you to keep me and my things out of it. Have you been giving me away any more?"

"Oh, God! Thornton, you have given yourself away!" she cried, echoing his slang phrase half unconsciously in her bitterness. "I'll tell you, if you like. The photograph belongs to the boy's mother. He is your child."

"What!" cried Thornton in a voice of thunder, showing his teeth savagely.

"Yes, your child," she went on, striving to be calm. "His mother's name is Burmester. You gave her the picture yourself years ago. I had just made the discovery when you came in. Ah—h!" she cried, putting her hands suddenly before her face, "it is horrible, horrible!"

"Ha!" retorted Thornton fiercely. "You are in one of your damned high-horse moods. Well, I did give one of my father's kitchen-maids a photograph, and she did have a child, and I paid her for her trouble, and, damme! what that's got to do with you now is more than I can see. Besides, you never were such a fool as to imagine you were marrying an infernal saint."

"Oh, stop! stop!" she cried. "Don't say anything more. You will brutalise me as well as yourself. I never thought you a saint—even when I cared for you. I know what you are, and, oh, God! this is the end of it. If you had betrayed a sweet, innocent girl, you would have been a villain, but not necessarily a brute—someone charming, pretty, attractive—I could have understood it; but a poor stupid drudge—a kitchen-maid—little better than an animal——"

Thornton rushed forward and caught her by her shoulder.

" By the Lord God ! if you don't hold your tongue, I'll strike you ! "

She saw that she had aroused the devil in him. She had meant to be calm, to tell him plainly the facts of the case and to say that it would be better that they should live apart. But an irrepressible shudder had come over her, and then the brutal cynicism of his confession had caused her the loss of her self-control. As she saw the blazing eyes and white glittering teeth in front of her and felt the grip on her shoulder, she regretted that she had been, in a way, to blame ; but she was no coward, and the threat awakened the fierce old Puritan courage in her nature. She did not flinch, but looked him directly in the face.

" Your striking me would only add to your other brutalities."

" Damn you ! " he cried in blind fury ; and swinging her round, he struck her with the riding whip with all his huge strength, cutting the back of the thin morning gown, that flew open at the gap, showing her bare shoulders. Then he hurled her from him and rushed out of the room.

With an almost superhuman effort of will Clytie sprang to her feet, stood for a moment dazed, stunned, on fire with agony, then staggered forward and threw herself upon the bearskin rug, with the illustrated History of England, open as Jack had left it, beneath her face.

CHAPTER XXV.

Suddenly Clytie rose to her feet and left the studio.
As she moved a strange weight seemed to lie upon her
limbs. It was a physical effort to drag herself up the
stairs to her bedroom. Her heart seemed to be burned
through, a fiery sword to have been thrust through her
temples. It was the supreme moment of the horror and
abasement of her married life. One intense thought
possessed her ; to fly from the house, to escape from the
area of Thornton's influence, to bury herself somewhere
far away. Mechanically she changed her things, choosing one of the simple morning dresses she had retained
since the days before her marriage, and bathed her
feverish face and hands. The cold water refreshed her,
restored adjustment to her quivering nerves, and she was
able to think, form a coherent plan.

She would go forthwith to her old rooms in the King's
Road, which she knew to be vacant. There she would
live again as Clytie Davenant, and shut out of her
memory the nightmare of the past months. The plan
conceived, she hurried to put it into execution. She
would have liked to open the street door there and then,
to cross its threshold for the last time. But the practical side of life asserts itself in the midst of the intensest
emotions. She would have to pack her boxes, select
what things she would take with her. The aid, too, of
the servants would be necessary. After a swift look at
the glass she composed her features, summoned her
maid, gave her orders in a calm, equable voice, as if she
were going on an ordinary visit in the country.

While the servants packed the articles she designated,
she went down to the studio in order to collect a few
of the portable objects that were dear to her : Rupert
Kent's etching, the Jacquemart that Kent had given her,
a book or two, a favourite box of oil-tubes. All the rest

she would leave behind, together with everything that Thornton had ever given her. The maid, an excellently trained servant, packed quickly, but to Clytie she seemed unutterably slow. It was an effort of control to refrain from urging the girl on, from snatching the articles from her hands and stowing them away anyhow, haphazard. Every moment that she lingered seemed an eternity of degradation. In after days she wondered that she had never reflected how far Thornton's possible presence in the house might have affected the ease of her escape. As it happened, he had flung out of doors as soon as he had left her stricken upon the floor; but she, in the fixity of her idea, never concerned herself as to his whereabouts.

At last, when the boxes were packed and locked, the maid, dangling the keys in her hand, asked Clytie when she should order the brougham.

"I shall go in a four-wheeled cab with the luggage," said Clytie. "Go and order one round at once."

The maid retired wonderingly, and Clytie was left alone. She put on her bonnet and sat down on the edge of the bed to draw on her gloves. Then for the first time her eye fell consciously upon her wedding-ring, and thereupon came over her the sense of all that her present action implied : the final renunciation of the marriage-tie, the assertion of her own individuality, the beginning of another life. And yet, in spite of her repudiation, the tie remained, indissoluble except by death, and this little circlet of gold was the symbol. With a twinge of pain she wrenched it off, for it was tightly fitting, and went and threw it in a jewel box containing the jewellery that Thornton had given her. At any rate, she could spare herself the hourly misery of this visible bond. It was a poor kind of relief to leave it there with the other tokens of her wifehood.

Then, as she waited, her crushed pride rose a few degrees. Whatever subsequent steps Thornton might take, her departure should at least not have the indignity of flight. A scribbled line would save her self-respect. When the servants came into the room to take down the boxes to the cab she had written the note.

"I am leaving your house. I go back to my old

rooms in the King's Road, where I shall resume the life
I led before I knew you."

Then only did it occur to her to inquire of the footman whether Mr. Hammerdyke was in. The man, who
was accustomed to the separation between the lives of
his master and mistress, replied, without manifesting any
surprise at the question, that Mr. Hammerdyke had gone
out just before lunch.

"Put this note in his room for him," said Clytie. "I
shall be away some time."

In a few moments she had started. With a little convulsive moan, wrung involuntarily from her lips by her
agony of body and soul, she leaned her head against the
rusty cushions of the ramshackle vehicle and closed her
eyes. The day was still glorious, London bathed in
sunlight, the streets filled with life and motion. For all
the world but her the promise of the morning was kept.
As the cab slackened its pace on crossing the Fulham
Road she opened her eyes for a moment, and looked
vacantly, as if in a dream, out of the window. Then
she relapsed into her darkness.

"And I was so happy this morning," she murmured
to herself. "I could have lived the better life—with
Kent's help!"

Kent! She started, as a wave of blood rushed
to her cheeks. She was going to Kent now, to live
under the same roof with him once more, to see him
daily, to take him more intimately than ever into her life.
Until now she had not realised this coherently. Vague
thoughts of him had passed through her mind, but she
had been too dazed, too sickened, too much possessed by
the overpowering longing for freedom, escape from the
house of bondage, to connect him definitely with her
immediate future. And in the unconscious sequence of
ideas a little self-reproach came into her mind, bringing
with it a sense of soothing. Why had she not thought
of Kent at first, of the true, loyal friend and lover, on
whom she could rely for strength and comfort? How
could she have been so much wrapped up in herself and
her wrongs as never to have given him a place in her
plans? And then the tide of feeling ebbed back again,
leaving her heart quite cold and sad. How could she

meet him? How could she tell him? The eternal woman in her shrank from the confession. If he had been to her but a friend, it had been easy. But she loved him. Had not her heart sung within her that very morning, only a few hours before, at the grace and tenderness of her at last awakened love? And she fought, womanlike, against she scarce knew what, striving to disentwine herself like Laocoon from the coils that love and circumstance had wound, in subtle intricacy of convolution, about her heart. But for all her shrinking she longed for Kent. If only he could understand it all without her telling! If only he could come that evening and sit by her side and hold her hand in strong, mute sympathy! Well, she would conquer her woman's diffidence, and tell him bravely. She felt she owed him a little reparation. The inherent delight in putting itself in the wrong is perhaps one of the most elusive traits of a woman's nature.

The cab stopped before the familiar side door. Mrs. Gurkins, standing beneath the awning of the shop between the stalls of cabbage and fruit, gave a gasp of bewilderment as she saw Clytie alight from the luggage-laden vehicle. She ran round through the connecting passage and opened the front door.

"You are not coming to stay here, miss?' she asked.

It was only in moments of calm reflection that she could bring herself to address Clytie more decorously as "ma'am."

"Yes, I am," replied Clytie in her decisive way. "Can I have my old rooms?"

"Of course, miss—but——"

"Well, have my boxes taken up and get things straight for me, Mrs. Gurkins. You know what an erratic creature I am, don't you? I think I am going to stay a very long time. I'll go and see Miss Marchpane while you do all that is necessary. You'll forgive me for putting you to all this trouble?"

"La, miss—ma'am, I'm that glad to have you back! But Miss Marchpane left early to-day—about an hour ago. You can go up to the sitting-room. I was cleaning it out only yesterday."

Clytie went upstairs to the familiar room, and took off

her bonnet and gloves. In a few moments the boxes were brought up. When she had unpacked these and arranged their contents, and eaten as much as she could of the meal that Mrs. Gurkins prepared for her, the glorious afternoon had melted into night. She sat by the open window and looked out upon the hurrying street below. It was a Saturday evening. The whole population of the district was astir buying their Sunday provisions or their Sunday headaches. Bands of the youth of both sexes clattered noisily past, singing hoarsely or darting from pavement to roadway in loud, dissonant gaiety. Along the kerb stretched the line of costers' barrows with flaming naphtha torches, and the faces of the sellers and buyers stood out clear in the glare. A babel of sounds arose: the confused murmur of private conversations pitched in the discordant key of the unrefined, the raucous cries of the costers offering their wares, the shrill " Buy ! buy ! " of the butcher a few yards away and the rapid click of his steel, the doleful nasal dirge of a tramp woman holding a vague bundle looking like a baby in her arms, the continuous scraping of feet, the roar of the 'buses and carts in the roadway.

Clytie had often before sat on Saturday evenings at her window, lost in the wonder of speculation upon the individualities of the units that composed this hurrying, bawling, laughing, cursing crowd. And now she felt the old fascination creep over her. The noise and movement acted as a counter-stimulus to the fierce whirl of emotions through which she had passed during the day. She lost for the time the sense of loneliness, soul-sickness, and bodily prostration in this external world of tumult. What did it all mean, this hurry and strain ? Looked at as a whole, it seemed to indicate that life was intense, earnest, throbbing with infinite variety of passions, an end in itself, to be carried on, because it was life, to all eternity. It seemed real, practical, objective, obeying inscrutable, immutable laws. The planets circle round the sun ; our solar system circles round another focal sphere. It is great, it is glorious, serving some great and glorious end ; yet what that end is no man knoweth. And so with the collective life that surged beneath

Clytie's window, yielding blindly to the unchanging laws that direct the cosmos. If this movement was meaningless and vain, then did the stars wander futilely in their courses. Sin and shame and misery, love and laughter and happiness, what did they matter in the progress of collective life? They are internal forces affecting its resistless march as little as the incessant motion of men affects the rotation of the earth.

But the individuals, when detached from the conglomerate mass of humanity — what was this life to them? How far was it a gracious thing to yonder bawling cheapjack, with his red, sodden face? And the factory girl, with her feathered hat and deep fringe overshadowing pinched, soulless features, looking hungrily at his Brummagem wares; the fat, unintelligent workman's wife gossiping loudly of sickness, death, and funerals; the besotted navvy stumbling along in the grip of a soberer friend—how far were they intellectually, spiritually, cognisant of life? Again as of old these questions presented themselves to Clytie. During these latter months she had been too closely confronted with the problems of her own personality to interest herself in that of others. But now a newly awakened self-knowledge had given her a key to mysteries to the elucidation of which she had once devoted all her artistic powers. She had arrived at the truth of the relativity of individual life. There was no such thing as absolute fulness of existence. Everyone—coster, factory girl, statesman, poet—was striving, each in his way, after a completer life, but the ideal of completeness was limited by each individual's capacity for action, sensation, and thought. Hence yonder factory girl's life might be relatively as full as her own, the hunger for the unknown that would complete it as loudly clamourous. Clytie was glad for the moment, almost happy. New artistic stirrings seemed to be at work within her soul. Heretofore she had sought a solution for the problems of life through her art. Might not this newer knowledge and more extensive sympathy enable her to present finely perceived truths, thus making her art less self-centred, more universal?

This train of thought was working through her mind as she sat by the window, resting her cheek on her arm.

Gradually, however, the thoughts confused themselves
into a medley of dim associations, which in their turn
became lost in drowsiness. Worn out by the physical
strain of the day, she fell asleep in the midst of the
uproar that arose from the hurrying street.

Suddenly she became conscious of a presence beside
her in the room, and, starting up, beheld Kent looking
down upon her.

" You'll get cold or a stiff neck or something sleeping
by the open window like that," he said in his kindly way.
" And yet I did not like to wake you."

" I do feel a little cramped," said Clytie, rising. " But
the night is hot. Bring another chair and sit down. I
shall not go to sleep again."

Kent did as she bade him, and they sat on either side
of the window, Clytie with face half averted looking into
the street, Kent leaning forward, gazing at her with
troubled eyes. For some moments neither spoke. At
last Kent broke the silence.

" Clytie ! "

" Yes ? "

" Was I wrong to come in ? Do you want to be
alone ? Tell me frankly and I will go."

" No ; stay," replied Clytie slowly, without turning
her head. " I wanted you to come. I don't know why.
How did you find out I was here ? "

" Mrs. Gurkins caught me in the passage. She said
you were staying some time. I knocked at your door,
but you did not answer, so I looked in, saw you asleep
there. I could not resist the temptation of coming
nearer so as to see your face. You look so done up,
you must go to bed early and have a good night's rest."

" Ah, Kent ! How like you ! " said Clytie, looking
quickly round at him. Womanlike, she was pleased
that he had not expressed wonderment at her presence
in the house, and beset her with abrupt questions, but
tried instead with delicate sympathy to put her at her
ease.

" Can you guess why I am here, Kent ? " she asked in
a low voice.

" I dare not try," he replied.

" I have finally parted from my husband."

" Good God ! Clytie, what do you mean ? " he cried, with a leap at his heart, followed by a feeling of great pity for the woman he loved, an aching sense of the irony of things. " It has been a misunderstanding. It will all be cleared up in time," he continued unsteadily.

Clytie shook her head.

" No ; thank God, this is the end. See my hand : that which was there I drew off to-day for the first time. It shall never be there again."

" Clytie, my dear friend Clytie ! " said Kent, very much moved. " What can I say to you ? My heart aches for all that you must have suffered. You told me yesterday your life was not what I thought it to be, for I fancied you happy, with all around you to make the world bright and glorious. I do not know what to think now. Is there no hope for your happiness ? "

" Oh, no, Kent, not that way. Let me tell you at once what I can. Don't judge me severely. I did what lay in my nature to do. I bore things that nearly drove me mad, although perhaps many other women would not have looked on them as burdens. But my marriage was a mistake—for both of us. And then—oh, how can I tell you ? Something happened to-day, the climax, rendering further life there impossible. Oh, I can't speak or even think of it ! "

Her voice ended in a moan and a shivering catch of her breath, and she covered her face with her hands. Kent leaped to his feet quivering with a sudden intuition.

" Clytie, you have been wronged far more than by mere misunderstanding. Did he dare——"

" Yes—yes. Don't think of it. It's all over."

" But I must think of it. It is like a red-hot iron in my heart. I can't bear it. All last night I lay awake thinking of your unhappiness, tortured by regrets, hating the man who made your life a weariness to you. I never thought of this. The coward ! The brute ! Oh, my God ! "

And as he strode up and down the room, with set lips and clenched hands, Clytie looked at him half-wonderingly. She had never seen her calm, strong Kent so moved by passion. She went up to him, with natural impulse, and put her hand on his shoulder and looked into his face.

"You need never speak or think of this again, Kent. It is all over, buried. For nearly a year we have lived almost as separated as we shall do henceforward. I have come to be Clytie Davenant once again, to lead the old life of work and happiness with you and Winifred. I can blot out the past eighteen months like an evil dream in which I have suffered much and learned much. We can work together as we used to do, Kent, and you will find me, I hope, a better, gentler woman, dear. Now forget all about it, as I shall do. Remember what you said yesterday—that no life was so wrecked as to be incapable of reconstruction. You cannot tell what comfort you gave me. And I cannot tell you what happiness I passed through this morning—before—ah, well—— Oh, Kent, my true, loyal Kent! I am a very weak woman, and I want your goodness and help and tenderness. You can do nothing to help or avenge what has passed. You can do all for me in the future if you will."

"What I can do is small enough, God knows!" replied Kent.

"Do you know what you can do for me?"

"Tell me."

"Let me forget myself and my selfish wants in trying to bring some help and gladness into your life. I wronged you deeply once—I wronged myself; let me make reparation."

Kent turned aside and passed his hand across his forehead.

"You must not think of me," he said in a low voice. "I am rough and strong, with no particular burdens to bear. Some day or the other, when you are happy, I will come to you with my little griefs for the sake of having them charmed away by your sympathy; but until then let me think of you—help you if I can. If I can't, Heaven knows it will not be for want of longing to do so."

"Kent," said Clytie very softly, unconsciously moving nearer to him, "I am happy now. Can't you see that I am?"

Kent's heart beat like a sledge hammer ; a wave of passionate love swept through his veins, thrilling him to the finger tips. He was conscious that if he turned his face the hair on her forehead would brush his cheek. Never before had a woman spoken to him in that strange tone. The world stood still for a moment. Then in a blinding daze of light, in which all things in heaven and earth were drowned, he turned, caught her to him, and kissed her.

Slowly Clytie freed herself, held out a restraining hand, and, with steps strangely faltering, moved across the room to the couch, where she sat down and hid her face in the cushions. Kent paused for a moment, steadying his senses still reeling from the shock of the first kiss of love he had ever given to woman. Then he went and stood by her side.

" Forgive me, Clytie. It was base of me. But it was something beyond my will that acted. You forget that I love you. I have wronged you, my queen, my life ! If you can ever trust me again, I will devote myself to making you forget that I have dared to love you. I ask your pardon, Clytie."

He stayed for a moment looking at her bowed figure. Then, as she gave no sign that she was moved by his appeal, he left her, and with a strange mingling of death and gladness in his heart walked lingeringly to the door. But just as his hand was on the knob Clytie rose impulsively from the couch, and with hair ruffled and her cheeks glowing came up to him, and it was she who opened the door.

" You are pardoned, dear, for I love you."

A moment later she was alone. And she resumed her position by the open window, and looked out upon the busy scene. But she heeded it not. Her sight was directed to the mysteries of an invisible world.

CHAPTER XXVI.

CLYTIE'S last words rang in Kent's ears all night.
She loved him. She had surrendered herself to his kiss,
she had told him her heart in plain, unequivocal language.
In the first blaze of this happiness he did not perceive
the gloomy background of their love. All that he could
feel was that Clytie had left the life to which he had
been a stranger, that she had come back to live in his
daily company in the old helpful way, that, furthermore,
her simple friendship had changed into something unutterably sweeter. He looked into the future and found
it glowing with many rose tints of beauty. He saw
Clytie and himself carrying out to its fullest his brave
gospel of work—to its fullest because of their belief and
trust in one another. He saw Clytie painting noble
pictures, drawing strength and confidence from his sympathy—himself stimulated to great achievement, the
prose of life transmuted into sonorous epic, lyrical gladness, elegiac grace. The fever in his blood kept him
awake as image after image passed before his fancy. But
whether the vision was of Clytie walking by his side
through the gaslit streets, or of Clytie's glorious head
strained back to view the effect of brush strokes he had
suggested, or of Clytie sitting by the table as he worked,
the lamp between them, it ended always with the warm
touch of Clytie's lips beneath his, and the low, clear
voice, "I love you."

This exaltation is common to most men when a strong
love comes to them. But to Kent it was all the intenser through the peculiarities of his nature. He had
lived without the sphere of women. The passionateness
of his temperament had thrown itself utterly into another
channel. His work had been his love, his wife, the
centre of all his energies, all his hopes. The craving
for the unknown complement of existence had found
satisfaction in the added line upon line, the growing

bulk of manuscript, the builder's thrill when the creation of his own brain is materialising itself course by course into a majestic edifice. Besides, action, whether it was spending hours in a musty library in the exciting search after a reference, or tramping for miles in the keen mountain air of Norway, always fascinated him and compelled the entire energy of his being. He beheld the earth after his wholesome fashion and saw that it was good. To him life was complete. Things, therefore, not contained within his sphere he looked upon as superfluities. Woman was a superfluity; the impulses of sex repugnant. The very intensity of his nature made him shrink all the more strenuously from the sexual principle upon which love is built. When, however, love came to him, in spite of himself, he was dazed with it, terrified. On that January morning when he buried his face in the faint perfume of Clytie's handkerchief he felt himself overcome with a kind of horror. The fierce consciousness that he would give his soul to hold her in his arms and kiss her hair and eyes and lips was to him a torture of debasement. This morbidness was due only to the violence of the reaction. It lasted but a short while, and toned down into a feeling of disloyalty to Clytie's friendship in daring to love her. But time at last adjusted his moral balance, when it was too late, and Clytie was lost to him. And then his love was purified into a deep, passionate devotion that was its own joy and recompense. If circumstances had remained unchanged, Kent would have carried this deeper than romantic love with him to the grave. It had grown into his inmost heart, informing that subconsciousness that makes a man's individual life. Even during the last few months, when they were meeting in frank, friendly fashion, his love had altered very little in kind. He believed her to be a happy wife, loving her husband, with whom in a moment of bitterness he had once silently measured himself. The precious boon of her friendship was regained, nothing more, and it was given to him, under no false pretences on his part, but all the more tenderly because she knew of his devotion. Secure in the impression of her happiness, he would never have wavered in word or thought from his straightforward, simple loyalty, and his days would have passed in quiet contentment, saddened a little, perhaps, by regrets for what might have been, but never tormented by longings for the impossible.

But conditions were no longer the same. Clytie had renounced her married life. Except as a memory of bitterness it had no place in her thoughts. Except by a legal fiction she was her own mistress once more, free to go and come, think and act. Even in name she would be Clytie Davenant again, and she had spoken to him in that strange tone he had never heard before, and had come nearer to him as her touch lay upon his arm. The whole pent up passion of Kent's life had gone forth into that kiss. For Kent the world was changed, and the night a dream of unutterable things. But by the morning it had brought counsel. This love, acknowledged on both sides—whither would it tend ? A great problem. So great a one, indeed, that Kent was tempted to shirk grappling with it. Courage and a stout heart, he said to himself, and all would be well. But one cannot rid one's self in this easy way of responsibilities. If you shake them from your shoulders, they shackle themselves about your feet. Kent felt thus fettered as he lay awake. Moreover, his early misgivings concerning Hammerdyke came, like the curses in the proverb, home to roost. If he had spoken to Clytie then, before her marriage, possibly she might have been spared all this suffering. He wished that he had obtained from Wither all the particulars of the ugly rumours that had been afloat, investigated them, confronted Clytie bravely with the truth, and so saved her from wrecking her life. And yet he felt that he could not have done so. Well, what was past was past. The present and the future contained enough matter to engage his attention. He lay for some time in bed trying to solve these perplexities. At last, at half-past nine, he rose, dressed, and went into his sitting-room to prepare his breakfast. This was a simple process. On a couple of gas-stoves, connected by india-rubber piping with the two gas-jets in his room, he placed a kettle and a saucepan, the latter containing eggs. Then he spread a little cloth on a clear space of his dresser-table, and brought out his crockery and other breakfast requisites from one of the under-cupboards. A ham somewhat cut into, butter, and marmalade he procured from a safe in a third little room on the landing which he used as a combined larder and lumber-room. For years Kent had enjoyed the simple Bohemianism of this Sunday morning meal. He could linger over it easefully without the weekday glance at his watch, when time was short. There was the Sunday paper, a weekly review or two, the long, undisturbed after-breakfast pipe. It was a time when he could release himself with free conscience from his busy life and enjoy his leisure. But this morning the eggs seemed stale, the ham tasteless, the journals dull, and he found himself looking at his watch. He would go down and see Clytie at eleven, an hour which he had himself arbitrarily fixed upon, and he was counting the minutes. It is surprising how long minutes are when you count sixty of them.

At last eleven o'clock came and Kent descended the stairs. But Clytie was out. Mrs. Gurkins, who answered his ring on Clytie's bell, informed him that Miss Davenant would not be in for lunch. Perhaps she would be back during the afternoon. So Kent went upstairs again, disappointed, and, after vainly trying to occupy himself, seized his hat and went out for a long tramp through Putney and Wimbledon. His heart was full of strange emotions that beset him for many hours, making them seem hopelessly long. Of the two Clytie passed by far the happier day.

In the afternoon, on his return, he heard voices in the studio. He knocked and entered. Clytie was there with Winifred.

"Can I come in?"

"Of course," said Clytie. "Why do you ask? We have been expecting you ever so long. In fact we have kept tea waiting for you."

He put down his hat and stick, nodded as usual to Winifred, and advanced, through force of later habit, with outstretched hand, to Clytie. She laid her fingers in his slowly, looked up at him from her chair by the stove, and laughed.

"You forget I am no longer a visitor, Kent," she said rebukingly.

" Only this once, then," he answered, " to welcome you back among us."

" Where have you learned to make pretty speeches ? " asked Clytie.

She was pleased with the words and gave his hand a sudden pressure.

Kent brought a chair up to where Clytie and Winifred were sitting, tried to talk lightly, and failed. A silence came over the little party. Tea caused a distraction, and they fell to discussing indifferent subjects, odds and ends of gossip, but in a desultory fashion that each found strange. At last Clytie rose, cut the Gordian knot in her impulsive way.

" I am going to do one or two things in the sitting-room," she said. " You two have a talk until I come back."

Kent opened the door for her. On the threshold she turned and whispered to him : " Talk to Winifred a little. You will do each other good."

He closed the door after her and went back to Winifred.

" So we have her with us again."

" Yes," she replied gently, " and I don't know whether to feel sorry or glad."

" Did you know—had you any idea that she was un-happy ? I never knew till yesterday—or the day before."

" I think I knew—before—perhaps because I am a woman. It made my heart ache."

" But she is not unhappy now," said Kent. " There-fore you ought to be glad."

Winifred glanced at him swiftly. In spite of the brown softness of her eyes they were woman's eyes, capable of quick, subtle perceptions.

" But will she be happy, Kent ? " she asked, bending down over her needlework. As she had not been able to paint, she had taken in hand, by way of feminine com-fort, some sewing for Clytie.

" What do you mean ? " he asked, with a man's prefer-ence to answer a concrete question rather than a deli-cately hinted suggestion.

" Will not this tie that cannot be loosed hamper her all through her life ? "

" God knows ! " he said gloomily.   And then, brightening, he added : " But we have her with us for always, Winifred, and we who love her can try to make her forget it."

"Ah, can we, my dear Kent ? " she said, putting her work and both hands in her lap and looking at him. " You love her, but you can't love her as I do.   Oh, no, no," she added as he smiled and shook his head.   " You may think you do, but it is not possible.   You have found faults in Clytie and scolded her—oh, very kindly and sympathetically, I know, but still in your eyes Clytie can do wrong.   In mine she can't—and there is the difference.   Clytie is not like other girls.   She is like no one in the world.   Everything must give way to her.   If Clytie were to do something you would think *dreadful*—commit a murder—I feel that she would be justified in doing it, and I should love her all the more tenderly and dearly."

" God bless your loving little heart ! " cried Kent. " Love like yours could make the most miserable creature on earth happy."

" Ah, no, Kent.   What could I do for her ?   Listen : I was a poor, friendless, ignorant, uninteresting little girl when I first met Clytie.   And she was kind to me.   She seemed so brave and strong and clever and beautiful, I quite shrank from her.   I felt so small and humble beside her.   And she singled me out from among all the rest of the girls at the Slade School, and made me her friend.   I never could tell what she found in me."

" She can tell, and I can, too," exclaimed Kent with abrupt enthusiasm—" the purest, tenderest flower of a soul that ever breathed ! "

" Oh, Kent ! " said Winifred as the colour rose to her dark cheeks.   " You must not say things like that. Clytie has done everything for me, everything— and I——"

" You have helped Clytie as no one else could have done," said Kent, " and you are doing it now."

" Am I ? "

" Yes ; don't you see how bright and happy you have made her ? "

"She is brighter than I should have thought," said Winifred musingly. "But will it last?"

"We must try to make it lasting, you and I," said Kent softly.

He pondered for a moment over the love in each of their hearts, the girl's and the man's. How exquisitely pure and selfless hers seemed to be! He could not realise it in all its beauty, but his perceptions had been refined enough for him to be profoundly touched.

"You have taught me something, Winifred," he said after a pause, during which she had quietly resumed her sewing. "I am happier than I have been all day."

Clytie returned soon afterwards. She looked curiously at the faces of her two friends, and then, divining, perhaps, something of what had passed between them, went up to Winifred and kissed her. After this they talked more freely—of old habits, plans for the future. The latter were vague, for Winifred's marriage with Treherne was fixed for the early part of the next year, and the studio without Winifred was unrealisable. Still the plans were food for much intimate gossip, which some may liken to the very salt of life.

When Winifred had gone, Kent went with Clytie into the sitting-room, where, furnished with hammer and nails, he hung the few pictures that Clytie had brought with her, together with some that had been lying about the studio. It was a delight to him to perform this little service for her, and she too felt the woman's happiness of being surrendered to a man's helpfulness. He fetched from his own rooms a bookstand, which he secured against the wall, a few curios, and an armful of the dainty cushions, chair backs, and curtain sashes with which his sister Agatha in misguided zeal had years ago supplied his drawers and cupboards.

"They are not as artistic as your odds and ends, you know," he said by way of apology. "But until you can get some together they will be more cheerful to look at than Mrs. Gurkins's efforts."

He had just completed his scheme of decoration when Mrs. Gurkins came up to lay the cloth for Clytie's dinner. Clytie detained him as he was about to go.

" Won't you stay and dine with me ? " she said half timidly.

She felt that she could not dismiss him. To do so on conventional grounds would be the silliest prudery. Besides, a sense of helplessness had come over her, and she wanted him by her side, longed for him to think and act for her. The touch of any incident bordering ever so slightly on the dramatic would at that moment have sufficed to free the spring of feminine reserve and loosen passionate expression of her longing for his presence. But the simple commonplace of the situation saved her. Kent's eyes brightened at the invitation.

" And we can have a long evening afterwards ? " he asked half pleadingly.

" Of course, " said Clytie, with an inward smile.

On Monday morning Kent, as he was starting for the Museum, put his head in at Clytie's sitting-room door. She was at breakfast, having risen rather later than usual. By her side was an open letter. As Kent entered she pushed back her chair and looked up at him, a gleam of gladness eclipsing in her eyes a late expression of pain. Kent noticed the sudden change.

" You have been sad, Clytie," he said in his rough tenderness. " That is not right. Did you not promise me last evening that you would be happy, very happy ? "

" So I shall be," she answered, taking his hand in hers and turning away her head. " Only there are things that cut one to the heart. You are a man ; you can't understand a woman—no man can, no matter how he loves her. Look, read that—the end of the sordid story of my latter life. Oh, Kent, I am not worth your love ! This thing has degraded me enough, and this last insult—— Oh, read it and see. It would be better that you should know of how little account I really am."

Kent took the letter which she thrust into his hand, and, without having read it, tore it into tiny pieces which he scattered through the open window to the four winds. Then he came and put one arm around her.

" Because one man insults you, dear, it is all the more reason that I should love and shield you. That part of your life is dead now. You said yourself this letter was the end. Let it be so, Clytie."

His delicacy and tenderness moved her very deeply. Womanlike, she had wanted him to read the paper, and yet loved him all the more for not having done so. The letter was her own note to Thornton, which he had returned with "You can go to the devil!" scrawled across it. The sheer brutality had made her lose, as it were, her self-respect, had presented her to her own eyes as a thing of naught, unworthy of the reverential love that Kent brought her. How could she honestly be to him the brightest and noblest of women with that scrawled thing dragging her down? Accordingly his actions and words gladdened her. She looked up at him, and he read as in some magical book the spell of tenderness that swam in her eyes. Then he threw himself on his knees before her and buried his face in her lap.

"Oh, my love, my love!"

And, stirred to her depths with a passionate thrill that was like a great pain, she threw her arms round his neck and kissed him.

CHAPTER XXVII.

Two years passed, outwardly uneventful, yet momentous in the development of inner life. Her marriage sometimes appeared to Clytie as a far-away episode, a kind of dream state in which she had been invested with a strange, unrealisable personality. Yet influences had remained, impulses had been awakened, that could not again lie dormant; knowledge had come to her that could not lapse into oblivion, leaving no trace behind. In her daily intercourse with Kent her nature expanded. It lost imperceptibly that vein of hardness which her struggle for self-development had fostered, and the disillusions and repugnances of her marriage had gradually been strengthening. Except in a brief interval of intoxication she had never known the woman's sweetness of surrender. The great triumph of surrender had never even then been hers. And this was gradually making itself felt in her heart during the two years that passed from the time of leaving her husband's roof.

They contained hours of sweet bitterness, it is true. Although Thornton had gone out of her life like an evil phantom, yet the legal tie between them remained unbroken. Mrs. Farquharson, who seldom did things by halves, after seeing her idol broken trampled it underfoot into a thousand pieces, and vehemently tried to persuade Clytie to seek after a divorce. She even insisted upon her taking counsel's opinion on the matter. But there was no definite evidence obtainable to support an action at law, and Clytie, sick at heart, was glad to dismiss the question from her mind forever. Yet in the eyes of the world she was Hammerdyke's wife, and so she would have to remain until death parted them. Perhaps when enlightenment sheds a fuller ray upon our civilisation we shall make radical changes in our marriage laws, for they are based upon the sad old fallacy that human conduct and human emotion are indifferently susceptible of regulation. As yet we can universalise only on material things : security of property, full stomachs, and warm backs for the poor. The facts of broken lives and torn hearts we can recognise only in particular instances, as they come within each man's individual sphere. The universality of spiritual, moral, and emotional suffering is as yet far from being a national conception. When this is attained we may hope for social conditions happier than those under which we struggle at present.

Thornton had taken the most effectual steps to become an undisturbing element in Clytie's life. The constituency for which he had intrigued and striven to be nominated did not return him at the bye-election, which took place soon after Clytie's departure, but chose instead a radical lawyer with an insignificant presence and a shakiness as to aspirates. Thornton was disgusted and humiliated at his defeat. Politics lost their charm. An offer from the Belgian government to reform the administration in a wide tract of country whose borders were infested with Arabs came to him at this juncture, and found him in a mood for acceptance. He bade Mrs. Clavering a sardonic farewell and replunged into the wilds out of English ken.

Winifred only remained in the King's Road for a few months. Early in the new year she married Treherne, and Clytie was left alone. The studio seemed very forlorn for some time afterwards, robbed, as it were, of an inherent tender grace, a softening, refining influence that had always been dear to Clytie, even in her days of greatest wilfulness. Yet it gladdened her to know that Winifred was happy—married to a man of fine fibre who could value the exquisite gift that the high gods had given him.

"You are a lucky girl, dear," she said to the young bride one day when visiting her in her new home.

"Of course I am," replied Winifred enthusiastically. "A man like Victor——"

"Oh, yes," replied Clytie drily. "I know. He is all perfection. But the man doesn't live who is fit to black your boots, my child. I did not mean that ; I meant that you were a lucky girl in having eluded your obvious destiny."

Winifred looked at her open-eyed.

"I always used to think somewhat sadly about you," Clytie went on. "I seemed to read in your face and eyes that you would marry a man quite unworthy of you, who would ill treat you, and that you would love him more as he became worse, that your life would be a dreadful, purposeless sacrifice. And now you see how you have escaped. Victor is just the husband I could have picked out for you. So you are a lucky girl."

"I wish you were as happy as I am, darling," said Winifred, looking at her somewhat wistfully through her own gladness.

"Perhaps I am," replied Clytie, with a flush. "Who knows? Utter completion of existence is not possible in this imperfect world of ours ; and if my life has its gaps that ache a little, yet it has its fulness, believe me, dear. I am happier now than I have ever been. After all, the gaps matter very little."

"Now you are getting somewhat beyond me," said Winifred. "I can't quite follow you."

"Ah, you needn't, Winnie dear," replied Clytie. "Only go on loving and trusting me. Don't you see that I am happy because I too have a good man's love ?"

"But if—if you had been—if things were different— you might have married," said Winifred hesitatingly.

"That does not make the love less beautiful and life-giving," replied Clytie.

This and other conversations of a like tenor succeeded finally in allaying Winifred's doubts as to Clytie's happiness. An uneasy burden was lifted off her mind, glad as her heart was in the new joy of her marriage. Henceforth she was content to take Clytie's assurances, and to trust in her own rooted idea that Clytie's deep, complex nature was beyond the reach of her simple comprehension, and ungovernable by the canons that regulated commoner clay. Strong in this faith, she triumphed in the first little conflict of opinion that arose between herself and her husband. Fine and generous as his views were, he had, nevertheless, a strict churchman's regard for the proprieties of life. The recognised intimacy between Clytie and Kent, harmless as it appeared before Clytie's marriage, had begun to cause him certain uneasiness. He was fond of them both, partly for their own sakes, partly on account of his wife. An unkind thought concerning them hurt his sensitive nature, and yet, as time went on, such thoughts began painfully to formulate themselves in his mind. At last his conscience forced him to broach the subject to Winifred. She listened with a little flush of spirit in her cheek, and then broke into such a warm torrent of words that Treherne was fairly amazed. He had never dreamed that his gentle, brown-eyed wife could be capable of such passionateness. Her logic of devotion overmastered his scruples, and he was almost converted to Winifred's unswerving faith. At any rate, from that time forth he was Clytie's firm friend and ally.

During these two years Clytie was in some need of friends. The society in which she had moved during her married life was a world unknown to her now. Only the circle of her girlhood's acquaintances remained, and of these some manifested disapprobation at the mode of life she had adopted. Every staunch adherent was therefore of inestimable value, and half unconsciously she clung to every hand held out in friendship.

The resumption of her life with Kent had produced also great tension in her relations with Durdleham. Finally it snapped them entirely.

" I don't for a moment suppose," wrote Mrs. Blather in the last letter that passed between them, " that everything is not most innocent and honourable on both sides. But your conduct is grossly imprudent and must inevitably give rise to most painful scandal. It is your duty both to the name you bear (painful though the associations connected with it may be) and to that which you had from papa to put yourself beyond the reach of calumny by living no longer beneath the same roof as Mr. Kent. Until you do so papa and Janet and myself will consider that any regard you may have had either for ourselves personally or for our honour as a family has entirely gone, and, I grieve to say it, our doors, though not our hearts, will have to be closed against you."

Clytie read her condemnation very sadly. She could not blame her sister. Mrs. Blather was acting conscientiously, according to the faith and tradition she had inherited from her Godfearing ancestors. Petty and futile as many of the formulas were by which she had been trained to regulate human conduct, yet there were great ones which could not do otherwise than command respect. "Thou shalt not sin," is a formula the obeying or renouncing of which is often a secret for one or two human hearts alone. Its corollary, " Thou shalt not appear to be sinning," is one which must be dealt with openly, under the world's eye. Mrs. Blather's judgment was based on this latter formula, her position unassailable. She had no Winifred to shake with the eloquence of love her faith in the formula's eternal verity. She was supported by the firm convictions of a lifetime, and by the unhesitating assent of her father and sister. The letter cut off all Clytie's hopes of ever being understood by her family. She herself knew their inmost hearts, was conversant with every principle by which they were guided, and she could bear them no ill will. But to them she knew she would be forever inscrutable, and she accepted their judgments with sad resignation.

In point of common fact, she was called upon to make the old, old choice that has been offered to woman in all ages, between her family and the man she loved. Without a moment's hesitation she chose the man, and severed herself finally from her kin. Kent had become the object of her life. She had loved him—she knew that now—before her marriage. She had wronged him, as it seemed to her, by not having realised it, had received notwithstanding a tender, absolute devotion whose brave selflessness had been a revelation to her. No sacrifice that she could make for his happiness was too great for her. She loved him with the whole strength of her full nature. If any sacrifices on her part were not made, it was Kent that forbade them. The less he would accept the more did she find in her heart to offer. That she should remain in what they had begun to look upon as their common home seemed to be a vital necessity to his happiness. The mild, affectionate approval of Grace and Janet could not compensate the great loss that each would sustain in a rupture of their intercourse. Any appeal to her sister she knew would be useless. She was firm in the path in which she had elected to walk, and Mrs. Blather's letter remained unanswered.

But Kent could not take this comprehensive view of humanity. That Clytie should be cast off by her family aroused his indignation.

"They never loved you," he said one day. "You were always a thorn in their flesh, and now they have seized an opportunity of plucking you out."

"You are wrong, dear," replied Clytie. "They loved me in their unemotional fashion, and if I were to die they would shed many tears and wear mourning for a whole year. But don't you see that I am of Samaria? I cannot pray in the temple of Jerusalem, and the houses of Israel are closed against me. It is of their religion to do so. They believe that the 'bread of the Samaritan is as the flesh of swine.' We cannot change their faith. We can only seek in Samaria for freer conditions of life, and the love of those who are Samaritans at heart."

"If I loved you less, I might take up as lofty a position as you," said Kent. "But I cannot bear that even a Pharisee of the Pharisees should presume to judge you."

"They have been judging me rightly or wrongly all my life," said Clytie, with a smile. "It was my own challenge; I gave it vehemently and passionately as a girl when life lay before me like a closed book which they refused to open for me. Now that I have learned some of its secrets I give the challenge with a calm conviction that I am acting in accordance with laws higher than theirs. So do not fret about me, dear." And then she added in a low voice:

"You know I would give up all I could have in the world for you, if you would accept it."

Then Kent put his arms around her and kissed her.

"I accept far too much in my selfishness," he said. "My old lonely life was happy, but it could not be so again. So in spite of all, Clytie, I say, Stay with me."

"I should stay whatever you said," returned Clytie. "Don't fancy that all the giving is on my side."

One sad event marked the mid-time in these two years, robbing Clytie of an external interest that had grown to be very dear to her. The boy Jack died.

The first meeting with him after the terrible scene in her husband's house was in the studio, whither he had betaken himself on one of his frequent visits to Winifred. A sensation of pain caught at Clytie's heart as she marked the lines of Thornton's features wrought in miniature on the boy's face. It only lasted a few moments, and then it melted away into a great pity. Jack was Jack, were Thornton twenty times his father. That he was so parented should make her pity for him all the greater. She never felt more drawn towards the boy than in that first interview. She told no one but Kent of the secret of his parentage, not even Winifred, to whom Jack, in spite of full intentions, never had an opportunity of showing the photograph. For Mrs. Burmester having discovered that Jack had temporarily abstracted it, had cuffed him soundly and secreted the coveted treasure in a secure hiding-place.

Whatever hopes Clytie might have entertained as to Jack's future were cut short by the change in her circumstances. All she could do was to contribute towards his training in the sphere in which the high gods, assisted by Kent and Treherne had placed him. Besides, he had manifested no particular intellectual bent. His gifts were rather those of action ; books wearied him, except such as dealt with wild exploit and adventure. And she shrank now from the idea of his entering the army—a feminine distaste, easily understandable. So she had perforce to concur in the scheme whereby he should remain another year at the school and then be apprenticed to a respectable trade. Kent comforted her with his assurances. If the boy had the fire of success in him, he would rise out of the common ranks. Life was all before him with its endless fortuities. With devoted friends watching and guiding him, it would be a poor world if he did not arrive at ultimate good. And Clytie in her turn comforted the boy, trying to soften and mould his nature with her womanly influence.

It was his last term at the school. He had won for himself the golden opinions of the authorities. The semi-animal little arab of four years ago had developed into a bright, self-reliant lad of generous impulses, subject, it is true, to fits of ungovernable passion, but quick to forgive, repent, and do penance. Suddenly Clytie received a telegram that Jack was very ill. She left her work and started immediately for the school. There she found that diphtheria had broken out among the boys, and Jack's was the most critical case. Day and night she nursed him. But it was of no avail. The boy died, and Clytie returned to London with a cheerless sense of loss. Mrs. Burmester, who came to see her after the funeral, whimpered a little, and hoped that Clytie would recommend her to any of her friends who happened to be in need of a charwoman. And then Clytie looked at the mother, thought of the father. After all, if the laws of heredity had anything to do with the controlling of human destinies, were it not better for Jack to be dead? When the woman had gone she went and stood before the replica of her famous picture which she had painted for Kent, and shook her head sadly.

"What I have painted there," she said to Kent, "the cruelty and animalism that seemed to have gone out of his face latterly, would always have remained. Human nature is a palimpsest, dear. What is written is written forever, though it seem obliterated, and may be called up to the surface at any moment. I call Jack happy, being dead."

With the exception of this episode the weeks and months passed in peaceful uneventfulness. Clytie worked assiduously at her art. At first the studio seemed lonely and dispiriting without Winifred. But other influences compensated her loss. As soon as it became known that she had resumed her profession, orders came in plentifully and kept her busy. And then perhaps Winifred's absence brought her nearer to Kent. If she worked hard all day and failed to reach her artistic ideal, it was deep comfort to know that Kent's whole-hearted encouragement would soon come and cheer her and save her from depression. They had learned to depend much upon each other in their work. In every mood they were constant companions, never weary of each other. Instead of walking home from the Museum, as he had done for years, Kent would hurry back by train from Charing Cross to Sloane Square, so as to shorten her loneliness by half an hour. A cup of tea, a talk over the day's work, perhaps a stroll along the Embankment, dinner, and then the long quiet evening as in the old days—such was the ordinary routine. Certain changes had naturally occurred in Kent's habits—changes for his distinct good, as Clytie used to declare laughingly. He rarely used the attic sitting-room. His scratch Bohemian meals were things of the past. What law of God or man forbade them to eat together? Clytie asked once in the early days when they were talking of household trifles. And then Kent bluntly insisted upon an arrangement whereby they divided equally the rent of the rooms they inhabited. It was not fair, he maintained, that he should give her sitting-room all that wear and tear without helping to pay for it. Clytie yielded, not unpleasurably, seeing that he was bent upon it, but she reserved the studio as her own especial sanctum.

The charm of the life grew daily upon Kent, with its infinite grace of little things. He told her this often, with awkward sincerity, as a man can only tell the woman he loves deeply. And Clytie would laugh contentedly and say :

" But you'll soon get tired of these organised meals and long for your freedom again. Don't you ever crave to be swallowing your coffee as you brush your hair in the mornings ? And doesn't it chafe you all the afternoon at the Museum to think that there is a regular dinner awaiting you when you get back ? "

" No ; somehow I like it," he would reply, laughing. " I believe I am developing into respectability."

Combining their resources they were able to entertain in a modest way those of their friends who perfectly understood their relations—the Farquharsons, the Trehernes, Wither. On these occasions Mrs. Gurkins's husband, a lean, self-effacive man, would wait at table in the severest of black and lend immense dignity to the meal. Wither was a constant visitor. The " monastery " was broken up ; Fairfax had taken a practice in a large country town, Green had taken a wife. Wither complained bitterly, railing at them both for their disgusting selfishness. Clytie learned to love the bright-eyed, gnomelike little being, his cynical, paradoxical talk, his large-heartedness which he was ever anxious to conceal from the world. Often when life seemed to weigh a little heavy, the future to loom somewhat sad, and Kent and Clytie had been sitting alone, a spell of wistful silence over them, Wither would come in unexpectedly, and, with his subtle feminine perception piercing to the heart of their mood, would exert himself to extra brilliancy and dissipate their cloud in laughter. A man by no means requires delicate tact to win a woman's love, but no man who displays it towards a woman can fail of winning a little of the overflow of her heart. Clytie was grateful to Wither. Once, when bidding him good-night,—Kent had gone into the passage,—she added impulsively, "and thank you."

He looked at her in his odd way, with a smile playing around his lips.

"What for? For being miserable and lonely and making use of you to cure myself?"

But they understood one another, and he was touched by Clytie's little tribute. And Clytie had spoken out of her heart.

For, in spite of the helpfulness and comfort of their life together, there were gaps in its plenitude which, as she had said to Winifred, ached a little at times. Kent was tenderness, manly sympathy itself : he would have cut his tongue out rather than formulate a longing that could not be satisfied. But moments came when the irony of life seemed somewhat bitterly mocking, and caused a veil of sadness to be drawn between them. And like people who love deeply each was sensitive to the variations in the other's mood. Then Clytie would yearn for the impossible : to fix forever the light she loved to see in his eyes, to cling to his arm and be acknowledged his wife before all the world. Thus through the midst of their happy, earnest life ran a vein of sorrow.

But the years that had passed, with their manifold emotions, experiences, and disillusions, with their awakenings of passion, with their plentiful gift of tears, with

their later gift of an almost holy communion of souls,
had completed the woman and the artist. One hunger
remained to her—one that had had no place in her
girlish cravings—a woman's hunger that is as a thing
sacred, and wondrously softens her nature. An infinite
compassion took within her the place of scorn. Her
eyes had learned the trick of tenderness which illumi-
nated her bright, fearless face. Her judgments became
less harsh, gained in breadth what they lost in brilliance.
She "saw life steadily and saw it whole." Many of its
mysteries had been revealed to her, and she had learned
the road to the heart of others. The great lesson that
Kent in the years before had suggested to her she
grasped in its entirety, and it revolutionised her artistic
career. No longer was her art a stepping-stone, a magic-
lantern sheet on which to project life in order to realise
its meaning. It was no longer the objective form of a
vague craving, but the idealised record of an experience.
When she painted the wistful, old-world look in a waif's
eyes it was no longer with the impatient, fretful hope
that its significance would be taught her from her own
canvas ; her awakened sight gazed with the sorrow of
knowledge into the young soul, and she used her art to
bear witness to the world of what was there. In a dim
way she was conscious of this change of attitude—seeking within herself for the reason of the deeper, intenser,
calmer feeling with which she approached her work.
There came, too, a sense of responsibility, the necessity of
perfecting whatever she painted in its presentation of
truth. As her genius expanded the inner interpretation
of the formula, " Art for art's sake," dawned upon her in
the realisation of the " sorrowful great gift " whereby
the artist has the privilege of piercing through the media
of sense and intellect and touching the naked soul of
man.

She went, as of old, into the streets for her models,
choosing the side of life least understanded of Philistia,
sublimating that which was spiritual, eternal in abject
and outcast, beggar and courtesan. Strange were the
walks of Kent and herself about the great city, by day
and by night, and strange the spars and fragments of
humanity they picked up in these rambles, who found

their way afterwards to Clytie's studio. They went together to East End music halls, bank holiday gatherings, thieves' kitchens, night clubs in the West End, where ladies are admitted free on a member's introduction, Kent paying his subscription almost at the door. It was towards women that Clytie's sympathy flowed the strongest. Her first contact with one of *ces autres* in the hotel at Dinan had set a chord vibrating within her that now rang out full and true. She could paint these women, young, withered, children on the lurid threshold, old women with charred and blackened past. It is the moralist's part to condemn, evolve the moral ; the artist on the higher plane disintegrates the spiritual from the animal and presents it in the form of Truth. From the comedy of misery, the tragedy of sex, the never ending drama of vice and crime, the one draws groans, the other tears. Each has his place in the cosmos. Thus Clytie, artist and woman, walked through the abomination of desolation and opened the eyes of the world to the glimmering spiritual rays that shot across it.

Once more she took out the studies she had made for the " Faustina " picture. This time she could look on them without a shudder, only sadly. The picture would never be painted. She was no longer in feverish, passionate search after mysteries that had baffled her. The picture now had no artistic reason for existence. It would be a cruel, despairing work, a tragedy of cynicism. Knowledge of the world had given her knowledge of self ; she knew now how blent were the foreshadowings of passion in her own soul with those that she had hungered to express on the young face of Faustina. In those days she could have found a model in her own mirror, and then the personal note dominating the picture would have saved it from heartlessness. For the complete woman to paint it would be the presentation of the damnation of a young soul. But the contemplation of her earlier work suggested vividly the converse of the subject—a Faustina swept away by the whirl of passion with the after-light of innocence in her soul's depths. The conception grew within her, took form, awoke the full artist in the ripe woman. With a throbbing sense of mastery, a quivering thrill of inspiration, new to her as the first love kiss on a young girl's lips, she betook herself to her task.

It was the 5th of August, two years after Clytie had resumed her artistic life with Kent. The afternoon was hot and oppressive. Clytie was tired and lay back on the couch by the window, for she had worked unceasingly all through the summer and the strain was beginning to tell on her.

They had just returned from the West End Gallery, where Clytie's picture had been exhibited during the season. This was the closing day, and they had gone to see the picture for the last time. A wealthy American had purchased it for the art museum of his native city, and to-morrow it would be packed up and sent over seas.

" It's like parting forever from the child that is dearest to you," she said with a little touch of melancholy. " That is the worst of painting. A poet or a musician —even an etcher can keep his work by him, but a painter loses all. Doesn't it seem hard ? "

Kent acquiesced, comforted her, spoke with vague cheeriness of the law of sacrifice which we must all obey. On the other hand, she must think of all that the picture had brought her, the public fame, the homage of those whose opinion was dear to her.

" Yes ; in all that I have succeeded beyond my wildest hopes," said Clytie. " But what is it? At the Redgraves' the other afternoon crowds of people stared at me, whispered each other requests to be introduced to Clytie Davenant. The men praised all the wrong points in my picture, and the women tried to get at the way I did my hair. I know it's flattering to one's vanity, dear, and I like it. I honestly like it. But it is a superficial little gratification. Now it is all over I begin to think of what that picture has cost, what has gone to the making of it. Neither money nor fame can pay me back."

" It has cost you hours of work in which you have found happiness," said Kent. " You must not overlook that."

" Oh, Kent ! " cried Clytie, not seeing for the moment that he had deliberately avoided the deeper elements in her thought. " Don't you know what I mean ? You who have been just now preaching to me the law of sacrifice ! Don't you know that to be the woman to paint that picture there were sacrificed the traditions and formulas of my home—there were sacrificed the first pure flush of a girl's love, the illusions of a wife, the joy of motherhood, the dignity of a proud woman ? "

She raised herself impulsively on her elbow and continued with flashing eyes :

" Don't you see that ? And you of all men who have shared with such bitterness in the sacrifice ! Yes, you, my dearest, my best, my love ! Your life has been sacrificed, your love, your devotion, your nobleness. For once in the world the man has paid, and not the woman. For two long years we have lived together, eating at the same table, living a common life, which, had one great fact been non-existent would have crowned our days with happiness. I am of Samaria—I don't care. I have offered to you to defy the world, to live openly together, to bear your name. You have said ' No,' for my sake sacrificing yourself. Can this life last forever ? Have not the past two years been filled with longings, restraints, bitternesses, regrets, all silently working—you too loyal to utter them, I dreading lest the utterance of them on my part should render you unhappier ? "

" I have been happy," said Kent. " A thousandth part of what you have given me would have made me more than happy."

" But your due is a thousand times more ! " cried Clytie. " I have given you little enough, but I have drawn from you the breath by which I live, the strength, the passion, the will by which I have reached my poor success. It can't be so any longer ; it would be unjust, cruel ! "

" Stop, my darling ! " exclaimed Kent, greatly agitated. " I am a man, and you are saying things a man cannot bear from the woman he loves. Let us finish this before it is too late, and I lose mastery over myself. I have thought over it all—with the fiercest hunger in my heart— even in moments of our love that have been worth a century of misery. I have thought over it all ways. What was impossible two years ago is impossible now.

I will not wreck your life by condemning you to scorn and ostracism and the loss of all that the outside world can give you."

Clytie did not reply, but turned her face towards the open window, looking with knitted brow into the patch of blue heaven that was just visible over the tops of the opposite houses. A great, great longing possessed her, an infinite tenderness towards the man who could speak and act so selflessly. She longed to be able to say three little words, summing up the yearning of her heart : " For my sake." But they seemed unutterable at that hour. Perhaps at another time, in a moment of less vehement tone, when he was unawares, the words could be whispered in his ear. She sank deep into the thought—utter woman.

A long, long silence, which Kent, uncomprehensive, like a man, did not dare to break. A thought had seized him too, a troubling doubt. Would he always be as strong ?

At last he drew mechanically out of his pocket an evening paper that he had bought on the way home, and as mechanically opened it and began to skim the contents.

Suddenly he leaped to his feet with a loud cry :

" Clytie ! "

She sprang up, startled, and saw him standing with white cheeks and shaking hand, holding out the paper.

" Read—he—he—read ! "

Clytie took the paper from him, and her eyes instinctively fell upon the paragraph :

A telegram from Loango announces the death of Mr. Thornton Hammerdyke, the well-known explorer, in a skirmish with some Arab slave-traders. Later particulars will be given in our next edition.

The newspaper fell from her hand, and they remained for some moments facing each other, trembling. Then she lowered her eyes and went to him humbly.

THE END.

Printed ... Billing and ...
BILLING AND SONS, GUILDFORD, SURREY.

Telegraphic Address
Sunlocks, London.

21 BEDFORD STREET, W.C.
October 1894

A LIST OF

MR. WILLIAM HEINEMANN'S

PUBLICATIONS

AND

FORTHCOMING WORKS

𝕱orthcoming 𝖂orks.

REMBRANDT:
SEVENTEEN OF HIS MASTERPIECES
FROM THE COLLECTION OF HIS PICTURES IN THE CASSEL GALLERY.

Reproduced in Photogravure by the Berlin Photographic Company.

WITH AN ESSAY

BY FREDERICK WEDMORE

In large portfolio 27½ inches × 20 inches.

The Collection of Rembrandts in the Cassel Gallery enjoys the distinction of consisting of a group of unsurpassed masterpieces, and of the twenty-one Pictures now in the Museum, seventeen have been selected for reproduction; these will be printed on the finest Japanese paper.

The first twenty-five impressions of each plate are numbered and signed, and of these only fourteen are for sale in England at the net price of Twenty Guineas *the set.* *The price of the impressions after the first twenty-five is* Twelve Guineas *net, per set.*

REMBRANDT:
HIS LIFE, HIS WORK, AND HIS TIME.

BY
ÉMILE MICHEL,
MEMBER OF THE INSTITUTE OF FRANCE.

TRANSLATED BY
FLORENCE SIMMONDS.

EDITED AND PREFACED BY
FREDERICK WEDMORE.

A re-issue in Monthly Parts, price 2s. 6d. net, per Part.

*** A few copies of the FIRST EDITION are still on sale, price £2 2s. net; also of the EDITION DE LUXE (printed on Japanese vellum with India proof duplicates of the photogravures), price £12 12s. net.

The TIMES.—"This very sumptuous and beautiful book has long been expected by all students of Rembrandt, for M. Émile Michel, the chief French authority on the Dutch School of Painting, has been known to be engaged upon it for many years. . . . . Merely to look through the reproductions in M. Michel's book is enough to explain the passionate eagerness with which modern collectors carry on their search after Rembrandt's drawings, and the great prices which are paid for them."

Forthcoming Works—continued.

MASTERPIECES OF GREEK SCULPTURE.

By ADOLF FURTWÄNGLER.

Authorised Translation.   Edited by E. SELLERS.

In One Volume, 4to.

With about 20 full-page and 150 text Illustrations.

A CATALOGUE OF THE ACCADEMIA DELLE BELLE ARTI AT VENICE.

With Biographical Notices of the Painters and Reproductions
of some of their Works.

EDITED BY E. M. KEARY.

In One Volume, crown 8vo.

A CATALOGUE OF THE MUSEO DEL PRADO AT MADRID.

EDITED BY E. LAWSON.

In One Volume, crown 8vo.   Illustrated.

SONGS ON STONE.

By J. McNEILL WHISTLER.

A Series of lithographic drawings in colour by Mr. WHISTLER, will
appear from time to time in parts, under the above title.

Each containing Four Plates.

The first issue of 200 copies will be sold at Two Guineas net, per part,
by Subscription for the Series only.

*There will also be issued 50 copies on Japanese paper, signed by the
artist, each Five Guineas net.*

LIFE OF HEINRICH HEINE.

By RICHARD GARNETT, LL.D.

With Portrait.

Crown 8vo (uniform with the translation of Heine's Works).

Forthcoming Works—*continued.*

LETTERS OF SAMUEL TAYLOR COLERIDGE.

EDITED BY ERNEST HARTLEY COLERIDGE.

With Portraits and Illustrations.

In Two Volumes, demy 8vo.

EDMOND AND JULES DE GONCOURT.

Letters and Leaves from their Journals.
Selected and Edited.
In Two Volumes, 8vo. With Portraits.

SOUVENIRS

OF THE PRINCE DE JOINVILLE.
Translated from the French by Lady MARY LOYD.
With many Illustrations from drawings by the Author.
In One Volume, demy 8vo.

NAPOLEON AND THE FAIR SEX.

(NAPOLEON ET LES FEMMES).
From the French of FRÉDÉRIC MASSON.
In One Volume, demy 8vo. With Ten Portraits.

THE STORY OF A THRONE.

CATHERINE II. OF RUSSIA.

From the French of K. WALIZEWSKI, Author of " The Romance
of an Empress."
In Two Volumes, demy 8vo.

STRAY MEMORIES.

BY ELLEN TERRY.

In One Volume, 4to. Illus'ra'ed.

A 2

Forthcoming Works—continued.

CORRECTED IMPRESSIONS.

By GEORGE SAINTSBURY. In One Volume. Crown 8vo.

ISRAEL AMONG THE NATIONS.

By ANATOLE LEROY-BEAULIEU. Translated from the French. With an Introduction by JOSEPH JACOBS. In One Volume. 8vo.

MANNERS, CUSTOMS, AND OBSERVANCES: THEIR ORIGIN AND SIGNIFICATION.

By LEOPOLD WAGNER. In One Volume. Crown 8vo.

DEGENERATION.

An Examination of the Laws and Results of 19th Century Civilisation. By MAX NORDAU. Translated from the German. Demy 8vo.

ALFRED, LORD TENNYSON.

A Study of His Life and Work. By ARTHUR WAUGH, B.A. Oxon. With Twenty Illustrations from Photographs specially taken for this Work, Five Portraits, and Facsimile of Tennyson's MS. Fourth Edition. Crown 8vo, cloth, gilt edges, or uncut, 6s.

Books for Christmas.

A BATTLE AND A BOY.

By BLANCHE WILLIS HOWARD. With Forty Illustrations by A. MacNIELL-BARBOUR. Crown 8vo, cloth.

THE ATTACK ON THE MILL.

By EMILE ZOLA. With Twenty-one Illustrations, and Five exquisitely printed Coloured Plates, from original drawings by E. COURBOIN. In One Volume. 4to.

LITTLE JOHANNES.

By F. VAN EEDEN. Translated from the Dutch by CLARA BELL. With an Introduction by ANDREW LANG. In One Volume. 16mo. Also a limited Edition on Large Paper.

𝔉orthcoming 𝔚orks—*continued.*

IN RUSSET AND SILVER.

POEMS. By EDMUND GOSSE. Author of "Gossip in a Library," &c. In One Volume. Crown 8vo, buckram.

A CENTURY OF GERMAN LYRICS.

Translated from the German by K. F. KROEKER. In One Volume, fcap. 8vo, 3s. 6d.

THE PLAYS OF GERHART HAUPTMANN.

HANNELE: A DREAM-POEM. Translated by WILLIAM ARCHER. Small 4to, with Portrait and Illustrations, 5s.

To be followed by

LONELY FOLK and THE WEAVERS.

THE PLAYS OF F. C. BURNAND.

Uniform with Mr. PINERO's Plays.

THE PLAYS OF ARTHUR W. PINERO

With Introductory Notes by MALCOLM C. SALAMAN.

VOL. X. THE WEAKER SEX.
VOL. XI. LORDS AND COMMONS.
and
VOL. XII. THE SQUIRE.

Completing the First Series.

Also

THE SECOND MRS. TANQUERAY.

By ARTHUR W. PINERO.

THE FIRST STEP.

A PLAY. By WILLIAM HEINEMANN.

Forthcoming Works—continued.

Fiction.

IN THREE VOLUMES.
IN HASTE AND AT LEISURE.

By Mrs. LYNN LINTON, Author of "Joshua Davidson," &c.

IN TWO VOLUMES.
HER OWN FOLK.
(EN FAMILLE.)

By HECTOR MALOT, Author of "No Relations." Translated by Lady MARY LOYD. Crown 8vo, cloth. 12s.

A DRAMA IN DUTCH.

By Z. Z. Crown 8vo, cloth. 12s.

A VICTIM OF GOOD LUCK.

By W. E. NORRIS, Author of "Matrimony," &c. Crown 8vo, cloth. 12s.

IN ONE VOLUME.
THE EBB-TIDE.

By ROBERT LOUIS STEVENSON and LLOYD OSBOURNE. Crown 8vo, cloth. 6s.

THE MANXMAN.

By HALL CAINE, Author of "The Bondman," "Scapegoat," &c. Crown 8vo, cloth. 6s.

ELDER CONKLIN.

And other Stories. By FRANK HARRIS. In One Volume.

THE POTTER'S THUMB.

By F. A STEEL, Author of "From the Five Rivers," &c. A New Edition. Crown 8vo, cloth. 6s.

BENEFITS FORGOT.

By WOLCOTT BALESTIER. A New Edition. Crown 8vo, cloth. 6s.

A PASTORAL PLAYED OUT.

By M. L. PENDERED. Crown 8vo, cloth. 6s.

AT THE GATE OF SAMARIA.

By W. J. LOCKE. Crown 8vo, cloth. 6s.

A DAUGHTER OF THIS WORLD.

By F. BATTERSHALL. Crown 8vo, cloth. 6s.

EPISODES.

By G. STREET, Author of "The Autobiography of a Boy." Crown 8vo, cloth. 3s. 6d.

THE SURRENDER OF MARGARET BELLARMINE.

By ADELINE SERGEANT, Author of "The Story of a Penitent Soul." Crown 8vo, cloth. 3s. 6d.

CHIMÆRA.

By F. MABEL ROBINSON, Author of "Mr. Butler's Ward," &c.

UNIFORM EDITION OF

THE NOVELS OF BJÖRNSTJERNE BJÖRNSON.

Edited by EDMUND GOSSE.
Fcap. 8vo, cloth.

SYNNÖVE SOLBAKKEN.

With Introductory Essay and a Bibliography by EDMUND GOSSE,
and a Portrait of the Author.

To be followed by

ARNE.	THE BRIDAL MARCH.
A HAPPY BOY.	MAGNHILD.
THE FISHER MAIDEN.	CAPTAIN MANSANA.

AND OTHER SHORT STORIES AND NOVELETTES.

UNIFORM EDITION OF

THE NOVELS OF IVAN TURGENEV.

Translated by CONSTANCE GARNETT.
Fcap. 8vo, cloth, price 3s. net, each volume.

Vol. I. RUDIN.

With a Portrait of the Author and an Introduction by STEPNIAK.

To be followed by

Vol. II. A HOUSE OF GENTLEFOLK.
„ III. ON THE EVE.
„ IV. FATHERS AND CHILDREN.
„ V. SMOKE.
„ VI., VII. VIRGIN SOIL. (Two Volumes.)

The Pioneer Series.

12mo, cloth, 3s. net; or, paper covers, 2s. 6d. net.

JOANNA TRAILL, SPINSTER. By ANNIE E. HOLDS-
WORTH.

GEORGE MANDEVILLE'S HUSBAND. By C. E.
RAIMOND.

THE WINGS OF ICARUS. By LAURENCE ALMA
TADEMA.

THE GREEN CARNATION.

AN ALTAR OF EARTH. By THYMOL MONK.

Other Volumes to follow.

Recent Publications.

MY PARIS NOTE-BOOK. By the Author of "An Englishman in Paris." In One Volume, demy 8vo. Price 14s.

Contemporary France, with the never-failing interest of the period since 1855, is mirrored in the pages of this book with the intimate and at the same time universal knowledge only possible to a man of the world, whose acquaintance with human nature is aided by his skill in noting the salient features both of circumstances and of men.

The anecdotes related are not mere tales of small importance, but are indicative of a keen literary appreciativeness of their bearing on characters or movements.

MEMOIRS. By CHARLES GODFREY LELAND (HANS BREITMANN). Second Edition. In One Volume, 8vo. With Portrait. Price 7s. 6d.

The Times.—From first to last a very entertaining book, full of good stories, strange adventures, curious experiences, and not inconsiderable achievements, instinct with the strong personality of the writer, and not unpleasantly tinged with the egotism that belongs to a strong personality."

THE ROMANCE OF AN EMPRESS. Catherine II. of Russia. By K. WALISZEWSKI. Translated from the French. Second Edition. In One Volume, 8vo. With Portrait. Price 7s. 6d.

The Times.—"This book is based on the confessions of the Empress herself; it gives striking pictures of the condition of the contemporary Russia which she did so much to mould as well as to expand. . . . Few stories in history are more romantic than that of Catherine II. of Russia, with its mysterious incidents and thrilling episodes ; few characters present more curious problems."

A FRIEND OF THE QUEEN. Marie Antoinette and Count Fersen. By PAUL GAULOT. Translated from the French by Mrs. CASHEL HOEY. In Two Volumes, 8vo. With Two Portraits. Price 24s.

The Times.—"M. Gaulot's work tells, with new and authentic details, the romantic story of Count Fersen's devotion to Marie Antoinette, of his share in the celebrated Flight to Varennes and in many other well-known episodes of the unhappy Queen's life."

The Great Educators.

A Series of Volumes by Eminent Writers, presenting in their entirety "A Biographical History of Education."

The Times.—"A Series of Monographs on 'The Great Educators' should prove of service to all who concern themselves with the history, theory, and practice of education."

The Speaker.—"There is a promising sound about the title of Mr. Heine mann's new series, 'The Great Educators.' It should help to allay the hunger and thirst for knowledge and culture of the vast multitude of young men and maidens which our educational system turns out yearly, provided at least with an appetite for instruction."

Each subject will form a complete volume, crown 8vo, 5*s*.

Now ready.

ARISTOTLE, and the Ancient Educational Ideals. By THOMAS DAVIDSON, M.A., LL.D.

The Times.—"A very readable sketch of a very interesting subject."

LOYOLA, and the Educational System of the Jesuits. By Rev. THOMAS HUGHES, S.J.

Saturday Review.—"Full of valuable information. . . . . If a schoolmaster would learn how the education of the young can be carried on so as to confer real dignity on those engaged in it, we recommend him to read Mr. Hughes' book."

ALCUIN, and the Rise of the Christian Schools. By Professor ANDREW F. WEST, Ph.D.

FROEBEL, and Education by Self-Activity. By H. COURTHOPE BOWEN, M.A.

ABELARD, and the Origin and Early History of Universities. By JULES GABRIEL COMPAYRÉ, Professor in the Faculty of Toulouse.

In preparation.

ROUSSEAU; and, Education according to Nature. By PAUL H. HANUS.

HORACE MANN, and Public Education in the United States. By NICHOLAS MURRAY BUTLER, Ph.D.

THOMAS and MATTHEW ARNOLD, and their Influence on Education. By J. G. FITCH, LL.D., Her Majesty's Inspector of Schools.

Volumes on Herbart, and Modern German Education; and Pestalozzi; or, the Friend and Student of Children, to follow.

THE PROSE WORKS

OF

HEINRICH HEINE.

TRANSLATED BY

CHARLES GODFREY LELAND, M.A., F.R.L.S.

(HANS BREITMANN).

In Eight Volumes.

The Library Edition, in crown 8vo, cloth, at 5s. per volume. Each volume of this edition is sold separately. The Cabinet Edition, in special binding, boxed, price £2 10s. the set. The Large Paper Edition, limited to 100 Numbered Copies, price 15s. per volume net, will only be supplied to subscribers for the Complete Work.

I. FLORENTINE NIGHTS, SCHNABELEWOPSKI, THE RABBI OF BACHARACH, and SHAKESPEARE'S MAIDENS AND WOMEN.

II., III. PICTURES OF TRAVEL. 1823-1828. In Two Volumes.

IV. THE SALON. Letters on Art, Music, Popular Life, and Politics.

V., VI. GERMANY. In Two Volumes.

VII., VIII. FRENCH AFFAIRS. Letters from Paris 1832, and Lutetia. In Two Vols.

Times.—"We can recommend no better medium for making acquaintance at first hand with 'the German Aristophanes' than the works of Heinrich Heine, translated by Charles Godfrey Leland. Mr. Leland manages pretty successfully to preserve the easy grace of the original."

Saturday Review.—"Verily Heinrich Heine and not Jean Paul is *der Einzige* among Germans : and great is the venture of translating him which Mr. Leland has so boldly undertaken, and in which he has for the most part quitted himself so well."

Pall Mall Gazette.—"It is a brilliant performance, both for the quality of the translation of each page and the sustained effort of rendering so many of them. There is really hardly any need to learn German now to appreciate Heine's prose. English literature of this country does not contain much prose more striking, more entertaining, and more thought provoking than these now placed before English readers."

Daily Telegraph.—"Mr. Leland has done his translation in able and scholarly fashion."

To be followed by

THE POETIC WORKS OF HEINRICH HEINE.

VILLIERS DE L'ISLE ADAM: His Life and Works. From the French of VICOMTE ROBERT DU PONTAVICE DE HEUSSEY. By Lady MARY LOYD. With Portrait and Facsimile. Crown 8vo, cloth, 10s. 6d.

RECOLLECTIONS OF MIDDLE LIFE. By FRANCISQUE SARCEY. Translated by E. L. CAREY. In One Volume, 8vo. With Portrait. 10s 6d.

PRINCE BISMARCK. An Historical Biography. By CHARLES LOWE, M.A. With Portraits. Crown 8vo, 6s.

THE FAMILY LIFE OF HEINRICH HEINE. Illustrated by one hundred and twenty-two hitherto unpublished letters addressed by him to different members of his family. Edited by his nephew, Baron LUDWIG VON EMBDEN, and translated by CHARLES GODFREY LELAND. In One Volume, 8vo, with 4 Portraits. 12s. 6d.

RECOLLECTIONS OF COUNT LEO TOLSTOY. Together with a Letter to the Women of France on the "Kreutze Sonata." By C. A. BEHRS. Translated from the Russian by C. E. TURNER, English Lecturer in the University of St. Petersburg. In One Volume, 8vo. With Portrait. 10s. 6d.

THE LIFE OF HENRIK IBSEN. By HENRIK JÆGER. Translated by CLARA BELL. With the Verse done into English from the Norwegian Original by EDMUND GOSSE. Crown 8vo, cloth, 6s.

A COMMENTARY ON THE WORKS OF HENRIK IBSEN. By HJALMAR HJORTH BOYESEN, Author of "Goethe and Schiller," "Essays on German Literature," &c. Crown 8vo, cloth, 7s. 6d. net.

DE QUINCEY MEMORIALS. Being Letters and other Records here first Published, with Communications from COLERIDGE, The WORDSWORTHS, HANNAH MORE, PROFESSOR WILSON, and others. Edited with Introduction, Notes, and Narrative, by ALEXANDER H. JAPP, LL.D., F.R.S.E. In two volumes, demy 8vo, cloth, with Portraits, 30s. net.

THE POSTHUMOUS WORKS OF THOMAS DE QUINCEY. Edited with Introduction and Notes from the Author's Original MSS., by ALEXANDER H. JAPP, LL.D, F.R.S.E., &c. Crown 8vo, cloth, 6s. each.

    I. SUSPIRIA DE PROFUNDIS. With other Essays.

    II. CONVERSATION AND COLERIDGE. With other Essays.

MR. PUNCH'S POCKET IBSEN. A Collection of some
of the Master's best known Dramas, condensed, revised, and slightly re-
arranged for the benefit of the Earnest Student. By F. ANSTEY, Author
of "Vice Versa," "Voces Populi," &c. With Illustrations, reproduced
by permission, from *Punch*, and a new Frontispiece, by Bernard Partridge. 16mo, cloth, 3s. 6d.

FROM WISDOM COURT. By HENRY SETON MERRIMAN
and STEPHEN GRAHAM TALLENTYRE. With 30 Illustrations by
E. COURBOIN. Crown 8vo, cloth, 3s. 6d.

THE OLD MAIDS' CLUB. By I. ZANGWILL, Author of
"Children of the Ghetto," &c. Illustrated by F. H. TOWNSEND. Crown
8vo, cloth, 3s. 6d.

WOMAN—THROUGH A MAN'S EYEGLASS. By
MALCOLM C. SALAMAN. With Illustrations by DUDLEY HARDY. Crown
8vo, cloth, 3s. 6d.

STORIES OF GOLF. Collected by WILLIAM KNIGHT and
T. T. OLIPHANT. With Rhymes on Golf by various hands ; also Shakespeare on Golf, &c. *Enlarged Edition.* Fcap. 8vo, cloth, 2s. 6d.

GIRLS AND WOMEN. By E. CHESTER. Pott 8vo, cloth,
2s. 6d., or gilt extra, 3s. 6d.

QUESTIONS AT ISSUE. Essays. By EDMUND GOSSE.
Crown 8vo, buckram, gilt top, 7s. 6d.

       *** A Limited Edition on Large Paper, 25s. net.*

GOSSIP IN A LIBRARY. By EDMUND GOSSE, Author of
" Northern Studies," &c. Third Edition. Crown 8vo, buckram, gilt top,
7s. 6d.

       *** A Limited Edition on Large Paper, 25s. net.*

THE ROSE : A Treatise on the Cultivation, History, Family
Characteristics, &c., of the Various Groups of Roses. With Accurate
Description of the Varieties now Generally Grown. By H. B. ELL-
WANGER. With an Introduction by GEORGE H ELLWANGER. 12mo,
cloth, 5s.

THE GARDEN'S STORY; or, Pleasures and Trials of an
Amateur Gardener. By G. H. ELLWANGER. With an Introduction by the
Rev. C. WOLLEY DOD. 12mo, cloth, with Illustrations, 5s.

THE GENTLE ART OF MAKING ENEMIES. As
pleasingly exemplified in many instances, wherein the serious ones of this
earth, carefully exasperated, have been prettily spurred on to indiscretions
and unseemliness, while overcome by an undue sense of right. By
J. M'NEILL WHISTLER. *A New Edition.* Pott 4to, half-cloth, 10s. 6d.

THE JEW AT HOME. Impressions of a Summer and
Autumn Spent with Him in Austria and Russia. By JOSEPH PENNELL.
With Illustrations by the Author. 4to, cloth, 5s.

QUEEN JOANNA I. OF NAPLES, SICILY, AND

JERUSALEM : Countess of Provence, Forcalquier, and Piedmont. An Essay on her Times. By St. Clair Baddeley. Imperial 8vo. With Numerous Illustrations. 16s.

CHARLES III. OF NAPLES AND URBAN VI.; also

CECCO D'ASCOLI, Poet, Astrologer, Physican. Two Historical Essays. By St. Clair Baddeley. With Illustrations, 8vo, cloth, 10s. 6d.

THE NEW EXODUS. A Study of Israel in Russia. By

Harold Frederic. Demy 8vo, Illustrated, 16s.

TWENTY-FIVE YEARS IN THE SECRET SERVICE.

The Recollections of a Spy. By Major Henri le Caron. With New Preface. 8vo, boards, price 2s. 6d., or cloth, 3s. 6d.

    *** *The Library Edition, with Portraits and Facsimiles, 8vo, 14s., is still on sale.*

THE GREAT WAR OF 189—. A Forecast. By Rear-

Admiral Colomb, Col. Maurice, R.A., Captain Maude, Archibald Forbes, Charles Lowe, D. Christie Murray, and F. Scudamore. In One Volume, large 8vo. With numerous Illustrations, 12s. 6d.

STUDIES OF RELIGIOUS HISTORY. By Ernest

Renan, late of the French Academy. In One Volume, 8vo, 7s. 6d.

THE ARBITRATOR'S MANUAL. Under the London

Chamber of Arbitration. Being a Practical Treatise on the Power and Duties of an Arbitrator, with the Rules and Procedure of the Court of Arbitration, and the Forms. By Joseph Seymour Salaman, Author of "Trade Marks," &c. Fcap. 8vo, 3s. 6d.

THE COMING TERROR. And other Essays and Letters.

By Robert Buchanan. Second Edition. Demy 8vo, cloth, 12s. 6d.

ARABIC AUTHORS: A Manual of Arabian History and

Literature. By F. F. Arbuthnot, M.R.A.S., Author of "Early Ideas," "Persian Portraits," &c. 8vo, cloth, 5s.

THE LABOUR MOVEMENT IN AMERICA. By

Richard T. Ely, Ph.D., Associate in Political Economy, Johns Hopkins University. Crown 8vo, cloth, 5s.

THE SPEECH OF MONKEYS. By Professor R. L.

Garner. Crown 8vo, 7s. 6d.

THE HOURS OF RAPHAEL, IN OUTLINE.

Together with the Ceiling of the Hall where they were originally painted. By Mary E. Williams. Folio, cloth, £2 2s. net.

THE PASSION PLAY AT OBERAMMERGAU, 1890.

By F. W. Farrar, D.D., F.R.S., Archdeacon and Canon of Westminster, &c. &c. 4to, cloth, 2s. 6d.

THE WORD OF THE LORD UPON THE WATERS.

Sermons read by His Imperial Majesty the Emperor of Germany, while at Sea on his Voyages to the Land of the Midnight Sun. Composed by Dr. Richter, Army Chaplain, and Translated from the German by John R. McIlraith. 4to, cloth, 2s. 6d.

THE KINGDOM OF GOD IS WITHIN YOU.

Christianity not as a Mystic Religion but as a New Theory of Life. By Count Leo Tolstoy. Translated from the Russian by Constance Garnett. Library Edition, in two volumes, crown 8vo, 10s. Also a Popular Edition in One Volume, cloth, 2s. 6d.

THE LITTLE MANX NATION. (Lectures delivered at the Royal Institution, 1891.) By HALL CAINE, Author of "The Bondman," "The Scapegoat," &c. Crown 8vo, cloth, 3s. 6d.; paper, 2s. 6d.

NOTES FOR THE NILE. Together with a Metrical Rendering of the Hymns of Ancient Egypt and of the Precepts of Ptah-hotep the oldest book in the world). By HARDWICKE D. RAWNSLEY, M.A. Imperial 16mo, cloth, 5s.

DENMARK: its History, Topography, Language, Literature, Fine Arts, Social Life, and Finance. Edited by H. WEITEMEYER. Demy 8vo, cloth, with Map, 12s. 6d.

*** *Dedicated, by permission, to H.R.H. the Princess of Wales.*

THE REALM OF THE HABSBURGS. By SIDNEY WHITMAN, Author of "Imperial Germany." In One Volume. Crown 8vo, 7s. 6d.

IMPERIAL GERMANY. A Critical Study of Fact and Character. By SIDNEY WHITMAN. New Edition, Revised and Enlarged. Crown 8vo, cloth, 2s. 6d.; paper, 2s.

THE CANADIAN GUIDE-BOOK. Part I. The Tourist's and Sportsman's Guide to Eastern Canada and Newfoundland, including full descriptions of Routes, Cities, Points of Interest, Summer Resorts, Fishing Places, &c., in Eastern Ontario, The Muskoka District, The St. Lawrence Region, The Lake St. John Country, The Maritime Provinces, Prince Edward Island, and Newfoundland. With an Appendix giving Fish and Game Laws, and Official Lists of Trout and Salmon Rivers and their Lessees. By CHARLES G. D. ROBERTS, Professor of English Literature in King's College, Windsor, N.S. With Maps and many Illustrations. Crown 8vo, limp cloth, 6s.

Part II. **WESTERN CANADA.** Including the Peninsula and Northern Regions of Ontario, the Canadian Shores of the Great Lakes, the Lake of the Woods Region, Manitoba and "The Great North-West," The Canadian Rocky Mountains and National Park, British Columbia, and Vancouver Island. By ERNEST INGERSOLL. With Maps and many Illustrations. Crown 8vo, limp cloth, 6s.

THE GUIDE-BOOK TO ALASKA AND THE NORTH-WEST COAST, including the Shores of Washington, British Columbia, South-Eastern Alaska, the Aleutian and the Seal Islands, the Behring and the Arctic Coasts. By E. R. SCIDMORE. With Maps and many Illustrations. Crown 8vo, limp cloth, 6s

THE GENESIS OF THE UNITED STATES. A Narrative of the Movement in England, 1605–1616, which resulted in the Plantation of North America by Englishmen, disclosing the Contest between England and Spain for the Possession of the Soil now occupied by the United States of America; set forth through a series of Historical Manuscripts now first printed, together with a Re-issue of Rare Contemporaneous Tracts, accompanied by Bibliographical Memoranda, Notes, and Brief Biographies. Collected, Arranged, and Edited by ALEXANDER BROWN, F.R.H.S. With 100 Portraits, Maps, and Plans. In two volumes. Royal 8vo, buckram, £3 13s. 6d.

IN THE TRACK OF THE SUN. Readings from the Diary of a Globe-Trotter. By FREDERICK DIODATI THOMPSON. With many Illustrations by Mr. HARRY FENN and from Photographs. In one volume, 4to, 25s.

Popular 6s. Novels.

THE EBB-TIDE. By Robert Louis Stevenson and Lloyd Osbourne. Crown 8vo, cloth, 6s.

THE MANXMAN. By Hall Caine. Crown 8vo, cloth, 6s.

THE HEAVENLY TWINS. By Sarah Grand, Author of "Ideala," &c. Fortieth Thousand. Crown 8vo, cloth, 6s.

IDEALA. By Sarah Grand, Author of "The Heavenly Twins." Tenth Thousand. Crown 8vo, cloth, 6s.

OUR MANIFOLD NATURE. By Sarah Grand. With a Portrait of the Author. Crown 8vo, cloth, 6s.

THE STORY OF A MODERN WOMAN. By Ella Hepworth Dixon. Crown 8vo, cloth, 6s.

A SUPERFLUOUS WOMAN. A New Edition. In One Volume. Crown 8vo, 6s.

A COMEDY OF MASKS. By Ernest Dowson and Arthur Moore. A New Edition in One Volume. Crown 8vo, cloth, 6s.

THE JUSTIFICATION OF ANDREW LEBRUN. By F. Barrett. Crown 8vo, 6s.

THE LAST SENTENCE. By Maxwell Gray, Author of "The Silence of Dean Maitland," &c. Crown 8vo, cloth, 6s.

APPASSIONATA: A Musician's Story. By Elsa D'Esterre-Keeling. Crown 8vo, cloth, 6s.

FROM THE FIVE RIVERS. By Flora Annie Steel, Author of "Miss Stuart's Legacy." Crown 8vo, cloth, 6s.

RELICS. Fragments of a Life. By Frances Macnab. Crown 8vo, cloth, 6s.

THE TOWER OF TADDEO. By Ouida, Author of "Two Little Wooden Shoes," &c. New Edition. Crown 8vo, cloth. Illustrated 6s.

CHILDREN OF THE GHETTO. By I. ZANGWILL, Author of "The Old Maids' Club," &c. New Edition, with Glossary. Crown 8vo, cloth, 6s.

THE PREMIER AND THE PAINTER. A Fantastic Romance. By I. ZANGWILL and LOUIS COWEN. Third Edition. Crown 8vo, cloth, 6s.

THE KING OF SCHNORRERS, GROTESQUES AND FANTASIES. By I. ZANGWILL. With over Ninety Illustrations. Crown 8vo, cloth, 6s.

THE RECIPE FOR DIAMONDS. By C. J. CUTCLIFFE HYNE. Crown 8vo, cloth, 6s.

THE COUNTESS RADNA. By W. E. NORRIS, Author of "Matrimony," &c. Crown 8vo, cloth, 6s.

THE NAULAHKA. A Tale of West and East. By RUDYARD KIPLING and WOLCOTT BALESTIER. Second Edition. Crown 8vo, cloth, 6s.

AVENGED ON SOCIETY. By H. F. WOOD, Author of "The Englishman of the Rue Cain," "The Passenger from Scotland Yard." Crown 8vo, cloth, 6s.

THE O'CONNORS OF BALLINAHINCH. By Mrs. HUNGERFORD, Author of "Molly Bawn," &c. Crown 8vo, cloth, 6s.

PASSION THE PLAYTHING. A Novel. By R. MURRAY GILCHRIST. Crown 8vo, cloth, 6s.

Five Shilling Volumes.

THE SECRET OF NARCISSE. By EDMUND GOSSE. Crown 8vo, buckram, 5s.

INCONSEQUENT LIVES. A Village Chronicle. By J. H. PEARCE, Author of "Esther Pentreath," &c. Crown 8vo, cloth, 5s.

VANITAS. By VERNON LEE, Author of "Hauntings," &c. Crown 8vo, cloth, 5s.

Two Shillings and Sixpence.

THE DOMINANT SEVENTH: A Musical Story. By KATE ELIZABETH CLARKE. Crown 8vo, cloth, 2s. 6d.

Heinemann's International Library.

EDITED BY EDMUND GOSSE.

New Review.—" If you have any pernicious remnants of literary chauvinism I hope it will not survive the series of foreign classics of which Mr. William Heinemann, aided by Mr. Edmund Gosse, is publishing translations to the great contentment of all lovers of literature."

Each Volume has an Introduction specially written by the Editor.
Price, in paper covers, 2s. 6d. each, or cloth, 3s. 6d.

IN GOD'S WAY. From the Norwegian of BJÖRNSTJERNE BJÖRNSON.

PIERRE AND JEAN. From the French of GUY DE MAUPASSANT.

THE CHIEF JUSTICE. From the German of KARL EMIL FRANZOS, Author of " For the Right," &c.

WORK WHILE YE HAVE THE LIGHT. From the Russian of Count LEO TOLSTOY.

FANTASY. From the Italian of MATILDE SERAO.

FROTH. From the Spanish of Don ARMANDO PALACIO-VALDÉS.

FOOTSTEPS OF FATE. From the Dutch of LOUIS COUPERUS.

PEPITA JIMÉNEZ. From the Spanish of JUAN VALERA.

THE COMMODORE'S DAUGHTERS. From the Norwegian of JONAS LIE.

THE HERITAGE OF THE KURTS. From the Norwegian of BJÖRNSTJERNE BJÖRNSON.

LOU. From the German of BARON ALEXANDER VON ROBERTS.

DOÑA LUZ. From the Spanish of JUAN VALERA.

THE JEW. From the Polish of JOSEPH IGNATIUS KRASZEWSKI.

UNDER THE YOKE. From the Bulgarian of IVAN VAZOFF.

FAREWELL LOVE! From the Italian of MATILDE SERAO.

THE GRANDEE. From the Spanish of Don ARMANDO PALACIO-VALDÉS.

A COMMON STORY. From the Russian of GONTCHAROFF.

In preparation.
NIOBE. From the Norwegian of JONAS LIE.

Popular 3s. 6d. Novels.

THE SCAPEGOAT. By HALL CAINE, Author of "The Bondman," &c. Nineteenth Thousand.

THE BONDMAN. A New Saga. By HALL CAINE. Twenty-fifth Thousand.

A MARKED MAN: Some Episodes in his Life. By ADA CAMBRIDGE, Author of "A Little Minx," "The Three Miss Kings," "Not All in Vain," &c.

THE THREE MISS KINGS. By ADA CAMBRIDGE.

A LITTLE MINX. By ADA CAMBRIDGE.

NOT ALL IN VAIN. By ADA CAMBRIDGE.

A KNIGHT OF THE WHITE FEATHER. By TASMA, Author of "The Penance of Portia James," "Uncle Piper of Piper's Hill," &c.

UNCLE PIPER OF PIPER'S HILL. By TASMA.

THE PENANCE OF PORTIA JAMES. By TASMA.

THE RETURN OF THE O'MAHONY. By HAROLD FREDERIC, Author of "In the Valley," &c. With Illustrations.

IN THE VALLEY. By HAROLD FREDERIC, Author of "The Lawton Girl," "Seth's Brother's Wife," &c. With Illustrations.

THE STORY OF A PENITENT SOUL. Being the Private Papers of Mr. Stephen Dart, late Minister at Lynnbridge, in the County of Lincoln. By ADELINE SERGEANT, Author of "No Saint," &c.

NOR WIFE, NOR MAID. By Mrs. HUNGERFORD, Author of "Molly Bawn," &c.

THE HOYDEN. By Mrs. HUNGERFORD.

MAMMON. A Novel. By Mrs. ALEXANDER, Author of "The Wooing O't," &c.

DAUGHTERS OF MEN. By HANNAH LYNCH, Author of "The Prince of the Glades," &c.

A ROMANCE OF THE CAPE FRONTIER. By BERTRAM MITFORD, Author of "Through the Zulu Country," &c.

'TWEEN SNOW AND FIRE. A Tale of the Kafir War of 1877. By BERTRAM MITFORD.

ORIOLE'S DAUGHTER. By JESSIE FOTHERGILL, Author of "The First Violin," &c.

THE MASTER OF THE MAGICIANS. By ELIZABETH STUART PHELPS and HERBERT D. WARD.

THE HEAD OF THE FIRM. By Mrs. RIDDELL, Author of " George Geith," " Maxwell Drewett," &c.

A CONSPIRACY OF SILENCE. By G. COLMORE, Author of " A Daughter of Music," &c.

A DAUGHTER OF MUSIC. By G. COLMORE, Author of " A Conspiracy of Silence."

ACCORDING TO ST. JOHN. By AMÉLIE RIVES, Author of " The Quick or the Dead."

KITTY'S FATHER. By FRANK BARRETT, Author of " The Admirable Lady Biddy Fane," &c.

MR. BAILEY-MARTIN. By PERCY WHITE.

A QUESTION OF TASTE. By MAARTEN MAARTENS, Author of " An Old Maid's Love," &c.

COME LIVE WITH ME AND BE MY LOVE. By ROBERT BUCHANAN, Author of " The Moment After," " The Coming Terror," &c.

DONALD MARCY. By ELIZABETH STUART PHELPS, Author of " The Gates Ajar," &c.

IN THE DWELLINGS OF SILENCE. A Romance of Russia. By WALKER KENNEDY.

LOS CERRITOS. A Romance of the Modern Time. By GERTRUDE FRANKLIN ATHERTON, Author of " Hermia Suydam," and " What Dreams may Come."

A MODERN MARRIAGE. By the Marquise CLARA LANZA.

Short Stories in One Volume.

Three Shillings and Sixpence each.

THE COPPERHEAD ; and other Stories of the North during the American War. By HAROLD FREDERIC, Author of " The Return of the O'Mahony," " In the Valley," &c.

CAPT'N DAVY'S HONEYMOON, The Blind Mother, and The Last Confession. By HALL CAINE, Author of " The Bondman," " The Scapegoat," &c. Sixth Thousand.

WRECKERS AND METHODISTS. Cornish Stories. By H. D. LOWRY.

WRECKAGE, and other Stories. By HUBERT CRACKAN-THORPE. Second Edition.

MADEMOISELLE MISS, and other Stories. By HENRY HARLAND, Author of "Mea Culpa," &c.

THE ATTACK ON THE MILL, and other Sketches of War. By EMILE ZOLA. With an Essay on the short stories of M. Zola by Edmund Gosse.

THE AVERAGE WOMAN. By WOLCOTT BALESTIER. With an Introduction by HENRY JAMES.

PERCHANCE TO DREAM, and other Stories. By MARGARET S. BRISCOE.

BLESSED ARE THE POOR. By FRANÇOIS COPPÉE. With an Introduction by T. P. O'CONNOR.

Popular Shilling Books.

PRETTY MISS SMITH. By FLORENCE WARDEN, Author of "The House on the Marsh," "A Witch of the Hills," &c.

MADAME VALERIE. By F. C. PHILIPS, Author of "As in a Looking-Glass," &c.

THE MOMENT AFTER: A Tale of the Unseen. By ROBERT BUCHANAN.

CLUES; or, Leaves from a Chief Constable's Note-Book. By WILLIAM HENDERSON, Chief Constable of Edinburgh.

Poetry.

TENNYSON'S GRAVE. By ST. CLAIR BADDELEY. 8vo, paper, 1s.

LOVE SONGS OF ENGLISH POETS, 1500–1800. With Notes by RALPH H. CAINE. Fcap. 8vo, rough edges, 3s. 6d.
⁎ *Large Paper Edition, limited to 100 Copies, 10s. 6d. net.*

IVY AND PASSION FLOWER: Poems. By GERARD BENDALL, Author of "Estelle," &c. &c. 12mo, cloth, 3s. 6d.

Scotsman.—"Will be read with pleasure."
Musical World.—"The poems are delicate specimens of art, graceful and polished."

VERSES. By GERTRUDE HALL. 12mo, cloth, 3s. 6d.

Manchester Guardian.—"Will be welcome to every lover of poetry who takes it up."

IDYLLS OF WOMANHOOD. By C. AMY DAWSON. Fcap. 8vo, gilt top, 5s.

Dramatic Literature.

THE MASTER BUILDER. A Play in Three Acts. By
HENRIK IBSEN. Translated from the Norwegian by EDMUND GOSSE
and WILLIAM ARCHER. Small 4to, with Portrait, 5*s.* Popular Edition,
paper, 1*s.* Also a Limited Large Paper Edition, 21*s.* net.

HEDDA GABLER: A Drama in Four Acts. By HENRIK
IBSEN. Translated from the Norwegian by EDMUND GOSSE. Small 4to,
cloth, with Portrait, 5*s.* Vaudeville Edition, paper, 1*s.* Also a Limited
Large Paper Edition, 21*s.* net.

BRAND: A Dramatic Poem in Five Acts. By HENRIK IBSEN.
Translated in the original metres, with an Introduction and Notes, by
C. H. HERFORD. Small 4to, cloth, 7*s.* 6*d.*

THE PRINCESSE MALEINE: A Drama in Five Acts
(Translated by Gerard Harry), and THE INTRUDER: A Drama in
One Act. By MAURICE MAETERLINCK. With an Introduction by HALL
CAINE, and a Portrait of the Author. Small 4to, cloth, 5*s.*

THE FRUITS OF ENLIGHTENMENT: A Comedy in
Four Acts. By Count LYOF TOLSTOY. Translated from the Russian by
E. J. DILLON. With Introduction by A. W. PINERO. Small 4to, with
Portrait, 5*s.*

KING ERIK. A Tragedy. By EDMUND GOSSE. A Re-issue,
with a Critical Introduction by Mr. THEODORE WATTS. Fcap. 8vo,
boards, 5*s.* net.

THE PIPER OF HAMELIN. A Fantastic Opera in Two
Acts. By ROBERT BUCHANAN. With Illustrations by HUGH THOMSON.
4to, cloth, 2*s.* 6*d.* net.

HYPATIA. A Play in Four Acts. Founded on CHARLES
KINGSLEY'S Novel. By G. STUART OGILVIE. With Frontispiece by
J. D. BATTEN. Crown 8vo, cloth, printed in Red and Black, 2*s.* 6*d.* net.

THE DRAMA : ADDRESSES. By HENRY IRVING. With
Portrait by J. McN. Whistler. Second Edition. Fcap. 8vo, 3*s.* 6*d.*

SOME INTERESTING FALLACIES OF THE
Modern Stage. An Address delivered to the Playgoers' Club at St.
James's Hall, on Sunday, 6th December 1891. By HERBERT BEERBOHM
TREE. Crown 8vo, sewed, 6*d.* net.

THE PLAYS OF ARTHUR W. PINERO. With Intro-
ductory Notes by MALCOLM C. SALAMAN. 16mo, paper covers, 1*s.* 6*d.*;
or cloth, 2*s.* 6*d.*

I. THE TIMES.	VI. THE MAGISTRATE.
II. THE PROFLIGATE.	VII. DANDY DICK.
III. THE CABINET	VIII. SWEET LAVENDER.
MINISTER.	IX. THE SCHOOL-
IV. THE HOBBY HORSE.	MISTRESS.
V. LADY BOUNTIFUL.	

To be followed by

The Weaker Sex, Lords and Commons, and The Squire.

Heinemann's Scientific Handbooks.

MANUAL OF BACTERIOLOGY. By A. B. GRIFFITHS, Ph.D., F.R.S. (Edin.), F.C.S. Crown 8vo, cloth, Illustrated. 7s. 6d.

Pharmaceutical Journal.—"The subject is treated more thoroughly and completely than in any similar work published in this country."

MANUAL OF ASSAYING GOLD, SILVER, COPPER, and Lead Ores. By WALTER LEE BROWN, B.Sc. Revised, Corrected, and considerably Enlarged, with a chapter on the Assaying of Fuel, &c. By A. B. GRIFFITHS, Ph.D., F.R.S. (Edin.), F.C.S. Crown 8vo, cloth, Illustrated, 7s. 6d.

Colliery Guardian.—"A delightful and fascinating book."

Financial World.—"The most complete and practical manual on everything which concerns assaying of all which have come before us."

GEODESY. By J. HOWARD GORE. Crown 8vo, cloth, Illustrated, 5s.

St. James's Gazette.—"The book may be safely recommended to those who desire to acquire an accurate knowledge of Geodesy."

Science Gossip.—"It is the best we could recommend to all geodetic students. It is full and clear, thoroughly accurate, and up to date in all matters of earth-measurements."

THE PHYSICAL PROPERTIES OF GASES. By ARTHUR L. KIMBALL, of the Johns Hopkins University. Crown 8vo, cloth, Illustrated, 5s.

Chemical News.—"The man of culture who wishes for a general and accurate acquaintance with the physical properties of gases, will find in Mr. Kimball's work just what he requires."

HEAT AS A FORM OF ENERGY. By Professor R. H. THURSTON, of Cornell University. Crown 8vo, cloth, Illustrated, 5s.

Manchester Examiner.—"Bears out the character of its predecessors for careful and correct statement and deduction under the light of the most recent discoveries."

THE NORTH AMERICAN REVIEW.

The London Office of this old-established Review has been removed to 21 Bedford Street, where copies can be obtained regularly on publication. Price 2s. 6d.

THE NEW REVIEW.

With January 1894 *The New Review* entered upon a New Series, and, whilst continuing to devote its space to the great problems of the day in a serious, competent, and popular fashion, it will give monthly a short Story, and Illustrations will be added to one or more papers in each issue. Price 1s.

LONDON:
WILLIAM HEINEMANN,
21 BEDFORD STREET, W.C.